Exodus

Also by Julie Bertagna

SOUNDTRACK

THE SPARK GAP

Julie Bertagna

Exodus

YOUNG PICADOR

Grateful acknowledgement is made to Corrina for permission to reproduce material from *External Moment* by Sandy Weores, Anvil Press Poetry, 1987, Ed. Miklos Vajda, Transl. Edwin Morgan, William Jay Smith
Illustrations © David Newton

First published in 2002 by Young Picador
An imprint of Pan Macmillan Ltd
Pan Macmillan, 20 New Wharf Road, London N1 9RR
Basingstoke and Oxford
Associated companies throughout the world
www.panmacmillan.com

ISBN 0 330 40096 7

1 3 5 7 9 8 6 4 2

A CIP catalogue record for this book is available from the British Library.

Phototypeset by Intype London Ltd
Printed and bound in Great Britain by Mackays of Chatham plc, Kent

Very special thanks to Tony Bradman, for a phenomenal wait for the Future Story that became this one; Graham Sim, for a forest of reading and inspired lanterns in the margins, so far beyond the great wizard hat; Elspeth King's The *Thenew Factor*; Keith Gray and his phone bill; my editor, Sarah Davies, for her act of faith; Caroline Walsh and to Riccardo and Natalie for their love.

SAVAGE EARTH

NETHERWORLD

NOOSPACE

Once upon a time there was a world . . .

. . . a world full of miracles. From the whirl of the tiniest particles to its spinning orbit in the unthinkable vastness of space, this world danced with miraculous life. Ur, the first people called their beautiful world, and the sound of that early name would carry down all the years, until aeons of time and tongues ripened Ur into Earth.

The people feasted upon their ripe world. Endlessly, they harvested its lands and seas. They grew greedy, ravaging the planet's bounty of miracles. Their waste and destruction spread like a plague until a day came when this plague struck at the very heart of the miraculous dance. And the people saw, too late, their savage desolation of the world.

The globe grew hot and fevered, battered by hurricanes and rain. Oceans and rivers rose to drown the cities and wasted lands. Earth raged with a century of storm. Then came a terrible calm. Imagine the vast, drowned ruin of a world washed clean. Imagine survivors scattered upon lonely peaks, clinging to the tips of skyscrapers, to bridges and treetops.

Now retrack to the dawn of the world's drowning. Stand at the fragile moment before the devastation begins, and wonder. Is this where we stand now, right here on the brink?

SAVAGE EARTH

No coward soul is mine

No trembler in the world's storm-troubled sphere

Emily Brontë

WING

Midwinter 2099

Earth spins. And Wing, the high island, is hurled into the sunless shadow of night.

It's just a minute past three.

The people of Wing are gathering in what's left of their village. Downhill, the salty, sea-lashed streets run straight into churning, cold-boiled ocean. The oldest islanders can remember a time when Wing's folding hills sheered away to sandstone cliffs that plunged on to a wide and rocky shore. The clifftops were still visible at ebb tide last summer, haunting the waves with their dark shadows.

Now it's all ocean.

The people turn their backs to the waves and head uphill through the field of windmills. The slow grind of the wind blades is only a hoarse whisper in this evening of rare midwinter calm. The Pole Star glitters overhead, a tiny torch that guides the islanders to a plateau high in the hills where eleven tall slabs of stone stand in an ancient circle. As the last of the sun's rays fade upon the ocean and night cloaks the island, the people banish all thought of the rising waves that surround them.

Just as their ancestors did, for time out of mind, they

stand in the middle of the standing stones to celebrate the midwinter solstice. Excitement fills the air as fireballs on ropes are set alight. Throwers grasp the long ropes and spin the flaming balls of straw round and round, then send each one hurtling high into the sky. Whoops and cheers echo all across Wing as the darkness is shredded with a cascade of falling stars to mark the death of the old year's sun.

Now a huge wheel, an ancient symbol of the fiery revolution of the stars, is set ablaze and sent whirling downhill. The islanders roar with delight as the fire-wheel flames a great track through the dark, all down the hillside and across the waves, burning itself out like a fading supernova upon the black ocean.

The darkness is absolute. People huddle closer together as it engulfs them, glancing up at the flickering stars for reassurance.

Old Tain feels his way to the centre of the standing stones. He has seen nearly eighty midwinter fires, more than anyone else on the island. He lifts out the ember that he has brought from his own fireside in a clay pot and lights the stack of dried peat and tindery driftwood at the centre of the standing stones. After a while the fire begins to spark and crackle. The people of Wing cheer as light breaks the dark, heralding the new sun that is about to be born.

Tain climbs upon the twelfth stone that lies fallen inside the circle. When he raises a hand the others fall quiet.

'Happy New Year!' he cries. 'Tomorrow we'll see the first sun of a whole new century!'

Tain eyes the happy crowd, knowing they are all anxious to eat and drink and party. He hesitates and the lines that plough his face deepen.

'Maybe the new century will bring us a miracle,' he declares. 'We'll need one to save us from that rising sea . . . But what if the miracle we all hope for doesn't happen? Listen to me. We must begin to plan for the future. We must look out to the world beyond these islands—'

'Oh, Tain, no!' cries Brenna, a small, apple-cheeked woman with a noisy brood of young children. She smiles at him to soften her rebuke. 'We don't want to think of such things on a night like this!'

'This is the very night we *should* think of the future,' Tain responds.

'The children are all here. I don't want them frightened,' argues Brenna, her smile fading.

'It's the children I'm thinking of. It's their future that's at stake if the sea keeps rising and we do nothing,' growls Tain.

An angry muttering starts in the crowd. Brenna's right, people agree, no one wants to think about the sea tonight. The anger swells and voices rise. A few islanders try to defend Tain but they are drowned out by the many who, like Brenna, just want to celebrate and forget. People begin to turn away for home. But a girl, cheeks blazing, dark eyes flashing, her long hair glistening like a midnight ocean, jumps up on to the toppled stone to stand beside the old man and pleads with the crowd to stay and listen to him.

There's a lull as the islanders halt for a moment, their attention caught by the fiery spirit of the girl, by her sheer energy as she stands upon her stone platform like an avenging angel, haloed by the flames of the sunfire behind her.

Tain takes advantage of the lull to try and calm everyone.

'Peace now!' he urges, in pacifying but resigned tones. He puts a steadying hand on the girl's shoulder. 'All right, Mara. Let's all calm down and be happy tonight. But before the celebrations begin, we'll join hands around the sunfire and ready ourselves for the future.'

The people regather and a moment of silence falls as they stand cocooned in the light and heat of their sunfire, snug together within a dark, cold world. A hundred hopes and wishes zip skywards with the sparks and smoke.

Now everyone warms up with steaming mugs of mulled beet-wine and fire-baked potatoes before the trek back down the hillside. The midwinter fires of the other islands scatter the ocean with a constellation of tiny lights that mirrors the fiery network of the skies. The procession ends back in the village as the island's church bell peals, finding its echo in others across the waves. Wing's narrow, huddled streets are soon full of firelight and feasting and rousing songs that drown out the noise of the ocean, long into the night, as the islanders celebrate the living power of the universe.

But Tain's words linger in the air. The new century will surely bring the miracle we need, the islanders tell each other. Earth may have abandoned others to its swallowing seas – people in far distant lands – but, they claim, that could never happen to *us*.

Yet tonight the ocean takes another hungry gulp, reaching further up the hillsides of Wing, ever closer to the village and the farms, towards the very doorsteps of the islanders' homes.

THE SWALLOWING SEA

April 2100

Mara Bell wakens full of restless flutterings, as if there's a tiny bird trapped in her heart.

The air is full of the noise of hammers and saws. Quickly, Mara unbolts her window and unlatches the storm shutters. Sunshine explodes into the room. She blinks, stunned and delighted, then leans out of the window and revels in the sensation of fresh air, in the panorama of sea and sky; an endless, electric blue.

Frantic activity fills the island as the people of Wing take their chance, during this rare lull in the weather, to repair the storm-battered barricades.

'Breakfast, Marabell!' her mother's clear, quick voice calls up, merging her two plain names into one beautiful sound, like water running over stones.

But first, before she does anything else, Mara reaches under her bed for her cyberwizz. The islanders have long abandoned such relics. No one has any use for the old technology now. No one except Mara.

She clicks open the small, solid globe of the cyberwizz, takes out two tiny solar rods that are almost out of power, and lays them on her windowsill to recharge in the sun.

Then Mara flings on her clothes and races downstairs to escape the house she has been trapped in for three interminably long months of storm.

'Hold on, hold on!' Rosemary, her mother, points to the kitchen table with one hand and holds up a hammer in the other. 'I said breakfast, Marabell. Then hammering. Lots of it.'

Mara ruffles her little brother's blond curls, steals a bit of his toast, then zips out of the door before anyone can stop her. At a safe distance down the hillside she turns to wave at her mother who stands at the door, hands on her slim hips, her short, dark hair ruffled by the wind as she shakes her head and brandishes the hammer. But the grin on her face matches her daughter's. Rosemary knows nothing will keep Mara indoors on such a morning. They also both know the storm clouds could easily be back before the sun sets, so every second outside is a gift.

Mara races down through the sloping field of windmills and solar panes. *Free at last!* It feels glorious. The world's wind sweeps across the ocean and wraps her in billows that swirl up her dark fall of hair. The morning sun on her skin is bliss. The neverending blue of sky and ocean is heaven to her eyes after months of dim lantern-light and staring at walls.

When she reaches the hump-backed road bridge where the old red telephone box sits alongside a storm-bent bus stop sign, she pauses. Once upon a time Wing had all sorts of vehicles – buses, cars, motorbikes, lorries and tractors. Mara has seen old photographs of them. But when the fuel ran out, over half a century ago, they were all recycled for other uses. Nowadays, the only vehicle Wing ever sees is the rusted shell of a car that's sometimes swept ashore and eagerly melted down for its metal. But the islanders could not bear to recycle the metal telephone box or the bus stop sign. They were part of the island's landscape, every bit as much as the church or the standing stones.

Mara feels a tremor of fear as she sees how much the ocean has risen over the winter. The hump-backed bridge runs straight into the waves. The sea can't come any closer, surely. The thought is too awful, so to put it out of her mind she runs to the edge of the waves to see what the storm has cast up.

A shoe! Mara rushes over to grab this precious bit of flotsam that the ocean has flung upon the grass. If she could just find *one* more. She looks down at her burst, heavily-patched terrainers, hand-me-downs from her mother and grandmother. She desperately needs new shoes and doesn't care how mismatched they are. She plans to rip each shoe apart and make herself a brand new pair. Meticulously, Mara searches until she finds a real bounty – a leather bag caught in a large branch at the sea's edge.

Leather *and* driftwood – a real find! She'll give the driftwood to old Tain; he'll understand that she and her family need the leather so badly. But Tain will be able to do plenty with a good lump of wood like this. Mara drags the hefty branch up the hillside to the old man's cottage, where the sound of hammering echoes, as it does from every other house on the island.

'Well!' he grins down from the ladder where he is securing a ripped storm shutter to an upstairs window. 'So you've found treasure!'

Tain descends the ladder slowly but with more agility, Mara judges, than you'd ever expect from a man of almost eighty. He hugs Mara and holds her by the shoulders to look at her.

'You've managed to bloom without sunlight,' he tells her. 'You've grown into a young woman over the winter.'

'Well, I've just turned fifteen.'

Tain nods, smiling. 'I didn't forget. Your present's inside.'

'That wasn't a hint,' laughs Mara.

Tain examines her finds with interest.

'The leather—' Mara begins, apologetically, but Tain cuts in.

'That young brother of yours will be bursting out of his shoes like nobody's business and yours look like they could do with a good bit of mending too. No, Mara, keep your treasure. I'm just fine.'

He stamps his extremely tatty but sturdy boots on the ground.

'I brought the wood for you though,' Mara insists. 'I dragged it all the way up here so don't tell me you won't take it. Look at my hands!'

She holds up her palms, raw from hauling the great branch.

'Ah well, I will then,' he concedes gruffly, but Mara sees deep pleasure soften the lines on his face as he picks up the branch.

'I'll finish off that shutter for you.' Mara picks the hammer from the grass and climbs the ladder.

'I'll boil us up some tea then,' says Tain and he looks suddenly weary. Fit or not, thinks Mara, he really is too old to be doing these repairs himself. But he won't let any of the other islanders help him – a mixture of pride and a selfless awareness of the struggle each household has to maintain a roof over its own head when the storm season hits.

Tain's stone cottage was built over two centuries ago.

The old man was born in it, as was his mother, and her mother before her. The rest of its long history is lost in time. Tain likes to slam a hand upon his home and declare that its rock-solid walls will last till the end of the Earth. Now he stares out at the enclosing sea with eyes that have watched the horizon for the best part of a century, as if he is no longer sure.

Mara loves this cottage as much as Tain does. It's her second home. When she was little, Tain took her under his wing and let her tag along with him as he stacked the peat and fed the goats and turned the cheeses, calling her his little helper, though really it was Tain who was helping Mara, making her glow inside, making her feel important and special when her father was so busy with the farm and her mother all tied up with baby Corey.

'People say it won't happen,' Mara bursts out. 'They say the ocean will settle again in the summer and we'll be safe.'

Now Tain's eyes brew up a look that's as wild as a turbulent sea. He juts out his great craggy chin and puts out a hand to touch the stone wall of his cottage. Silently, he seems to challenge the mighty ocean before he turns on Mara.

'But you can use your eyes, Mara, even if they can't!' he cries. 'You're not a child any more and I won't lie to you. We all have to open our eyes now and look beyond this godforsaken place at the edge of the Earth.'

Mara's heart sinks as she nails the shutter back in place. She has never heard Tain talk in such a way. His family, like hers, has lived on Wing for generations, longer than anyone can remember. Tain has never left the island; he only ever speaks of his heritage with pride. Until now.

A fat house spider scuttles on to the storm shutter. Mara

halts in mid-swing and lets the spider escape on to the window ledge before she smashes the hammer down. She has never left the island, either – at least, not in reality. Mara travels far in her own, secret way but she never tells anyone about these adventures. They belong to her.

Tain beckons Mara to come down off the ladder. When her feet touch the ground he takes her by the shoulders and gently but firmly pulls her round to confront the sea.

'Don't you do the same as the others. Don't look away and fool yourself. They're wrong. There's no great miracle going to save us. The only way we'll be saved is to face up to the truth.'

Mara's heart sinks even more as she looks across the field of whirling windmills and glinting solar panes to where there was once a long shoreline and road, a harbour and the island's school. Just a few years ago, Mara and her friends went to the school. Then the sea claimed it. Even at midwinter you could still see its flat roof. Now it is completely lost.

To the north is a network of small, craggy islands. Once, they were all joined as a single landmass but over the last century the plains and much of the hills have been swallowed by sea and now only the peaks remain. Scattered across the slow-churning ocean, they look like bits of storm-tossed litter. Over the last century many islanders have had to shift homes and farms and entire villages up out of reach of the rising ocean – some more than once. Wing, the largest and highest island, is now overcrowded with refugees from its northern neighbours, who have made makeshift homes in the ruins of its ancient stone cottages and farmyard outhouses.

'Oh, Tain!' wails Mara. 'What can we do?'

16

Mara feels the bird-like fluttering in her heart once again. This time it's not restlessness, but fear.

Tain sighs and juts out his chin. 'We should have done something long before now. It took *me* long enough to face the truth. But maybe there's still time, if we act now. '

Mara stares out at the ocean, lost in thought. When she turns back to Tain she catches the strange, wistful look he sometimes fixes upon her. Mara knows it's not really to do with her. It's because she looks so like her grandmother did, the girl he grew up with long ago.

'Tea?' she prompts, to bring him back to the present.

'Tea,' he nods, with a shy smile, and they go inside.

Mara munches gratefully on the large, warm, buttery oatcake that Tain hands her. The fresh air and a missed breakfast have made her ravenous. She eats it standing in a pool of sunlight by the open door, reluctant to miss a second of this glorious weather, while Tain stokes the stove and boils up the kettle. Mara finds his peaty brew too strong and bitter so he always makes her mint leaf tea with a spoonful of heather honey, which she loves.

'Tell me about you and Granny Mary,' she says, closing her eyes and lifting her face to the sun like a flower, preferring to fill her thoughts with stories of the old days rather than the threat of the future.

'I've told you all the stories,' he says briskly.

Mara debates whether she dare ask the next question – one that she has had plenty of time to wonder about through the long storm months. That wistful look of Tain's when he remembers Granny Mary has *made* her wonder.

'Did you love her?' she bursts out at last. 'You did, didn't you?'

Tain doesn't answer, just pours out the tea. They sit at

the table in silence, amid the bright sunbeams that spill through the open window.

'Ah, it's all far away in the past now, Mara,' he says at last.

'But—'

'All over and done with. What we need to think of now is the future.'

Mara's mind is spinning. It's just as she suspected. There *was* something between Tain and Granny Mary. That must be why he has always taken such a deep, fond interest in her. She knows she is her grandmother's image; all the old people tell her so and she has seen the striking resemblance in photographs of Granny Mary in her youth – the same intense expression and thick, dark sweep of hair; the same long, lean limbs; and even, says her mother, the same restless way of moving.

But no one has ever suggested that Granny Mary was anything other than happily married to Grandpa and they both died when they were old, so how is it possible that Tain—

'Listen to me, Mara.' Tain's voice breaks into her thoughts. 'Your future is not here on Wing. There might be no Wing left soon – or not enough for us all to live on. Your future lies somewhere else in the world.'

The puzzle of her grandmother's past is abandoned for the moment as Mara's mind fills with more urgent questions.

'What's the world beyond here like, Tain? No one ever talks about it.'

Mara thinks of the places she has seen on her secret travels. Amazing places, so strange and different to the familiar land and seascape that surround her. But her travels are not real, they're only electric visions.

'The outside world is a great mystery now,' says Tain. 'That's why we never talk about it.'

'But what do you *think*?' Mara persists.

Tain sighs heavily. 'I don't know. When the oceans first rose and swallowed the lands, we were all in shock. The supply ships from the mainland suddenly stopped and all our communication systems went down. We were petrified.' He leans forward and Mara sees a tremor of emotion, the reflection of that long ago terror, on his mouth. 'We had no way of knowing what was happening to the rest of the world. And there was so much to do. We had to change our whole way of life, move all our homes and farms far uphill, out of reach of the sea. We had to make ourselves completely self-sufficient in just a few years. All this in the midst of storms like you've never seen. We had barely any time to think of anything beyond ourselves and our own little patch of the world. It was a huge struggle just to survive. But at last, when the seas calmed enough, some of our fishermen set out to see what had happened on the mainland.' Tain pauses again, and the look in his eyes tells Mara he still finds it hard to believe. 'They found nothing but ocean. There were the rocky peaks of what had once been the highlands – solid rock that no one could live on – but no sign of any land. Once we heard that, we turned our thoughts away from the outside world. And that's how we stayed, never looking beyond these islands. Till now.'

Tain grasps Mara's hand in his.

'Mara, the seas are rising again. It happens in surges. Every few decades there's another great meltdown of the ice at the poles and then you get a sea surge. I know the pattern – I've seen it before. We've had long, scorching summers these last years and now we're getting the sea surge from the meltdown that the weather has caused. I think the last of the polar icecaps must be melting.'

Last summer the heat had burned the island almost barren. Mara remembers air so hot it shimmered like glass. Days so long and bright the relentless sun hardly slipped from the sky. The sea was a haven then – she lived on the rocks like a mermaid, her wet hair a long, cool cloak against the sun, endlessly plunging her burning skin into the soothing balm of the ocean.

'We need to move again,' Tain is saying. 'But not uphill this time – there's not enough land left for us.'

Mara feels panic lurch in her stomach. She grips Tain's hand.

'We need to find a new home in the world,' Tain declares. 'Soon, Mara, before it's too late.'

MAELSTROM

A new home in the world?

Mara stares at Tain with wide eyes. The thought is so terrifying she feels numb.

'But where?' she whispers.

'Do you remember when you were little I used to tell you about the giant cities built high above the rising seas?'

'That was just a fairy tale!' Mara exclaims.

Tain shakes his head. 'No, no. Remember I told you I saw a television newsreel about the very first of those cities when I was young. They were just beginning to build them. New World cities, they were called.'

Mara looks wistfully at the blank grey box that sits dead and useless in a corner of the room. Tain has told her all about television.

'So there really are giant cities?' she asks doubtfully.

'I don't know,' says Tain. 'I don't know if the ones they built survived the flood – but they were designed to. I don't know if they built more, as they said they would. In the time just before the flood all the news reports complained about an information blackout on the New World cities. Then the great flood came and there was no news

21

about anything. Like I said, we were struggling to survive here on Wing. Later, we tried to search for information on the Weave – that was the old worldwide computer network.'

Mara nods. She's well-acquainted with the Weave.

'We looked hard but we never found anything. The Weave was in ruins and searching for anything was like looking for a needle in a haystack. So we gave up wondering what might or might not lie out in the world beyond us and concentrated on the here and now. But I'm sure those cities were built! There was a plan to build lots of them.'

In frustration, Tain rakes his white hair with his hand. 'I always wondered if our fisherman didn't sail far enough south. They were brave men but they panicked when they saw the mainland was gone and turned back. If they had kept going though, maybe they would have found one of those cities. I don't know, but we need to find out now. Somehow we must. Those cities might be our only hope. Who knows what land is left in the world?'

He opens the old atlas that is lying on the table and studies it. 'I've searched and searched for other options,' he murmurs, 'but all the high lands are too far from here. We'd never reach them. Our fishing boats could never survive such a distance on the open ocean.'

But Mara is only half-listening, her mind filled with a picture of a beautiful city, towering safe and high above the ocean, far up into the sky. At the same time a shiver of dread runs through her at the thought of leaving Wing to live in such a place. It's unimaginable. She doesn't want to think of it. Dazed, she tries to collect her thoughts.

Tain puts a steadying hand on her shoulder. He knows her so well she doesn't have to explain what she is feeling.

'Your granny was a very special person,' he tells her now, as he has so often before. 'She was a real leader in this community when the world changed and we had to fight to survive. It was her vision and courage that helped these islands shape their own future in a world where people had lost heart and were ready to give up hope. I remember I almost did.' A smile deepens the lines on his face. 'But she wouldn't. She just would not let us all give up.' Now Tain's voice trembles and his eyes burn with emotion in a way that Mara has never seen before. 'She had a kind of greatness in her, Mary did. And you are her mirror image, girl. Her living image! You'll make a new future in the world, I know you will – because you've got that same strength and courage.'

'Why didn't you marry her?' Mara whispers. The words are out of her mouth before she can stop them.

Her grandpa, Granny Mary's husband, died before she was born, so it's hard to feel loyalty to someone she never knew; whereas Tain has always been close to her and has felt so much like a grandfather.

A sudden great gust hits the cottage. An almighty wind howls across the island. Doors shudder and shutters bang. Outside on the hills the blades of the windmills begin to thrash. Mara and Tain jump up and run outside to secure the shutters before they shatter the windows.

Storm clouds are already back on the horizon. Mara could cry with frustration. She can't believe her short burst of freedom is nearly gone. She hasn't even had time to visit her friends.

Tain has disappeared inside and returns quickly clasping a small, highly polished wooden box that is covered in exquisite engravings. He places it in Mara's hands.

'For me?' Mara exclaims. She fingers the beautiful

patterns of the box, then opens it to find a small mirror on the underside of the lid and tiny compartments in the base.

Tain nods. He is famed all over the island for his wood engravings, but nowadays there is rarely any spare wood. All the island's trees have long been cut down. 'I made it for your granny's sixteenth birthday. I was keeping it for yours but, well, you should have it now. A box for all your jewels.'

Mara laughs because he knows she doesn't have any. She hugs him tight. 'I've never owned anything so beautiful.'

And suddenly she wonders – does he mean he made it for Granny and never gave it to her? And if not, why not? Somehow, she cannot ask.

Instead she looks in the little mirror that is set in the box and blinks in surprise. The fresh air has whipped colour into her winter-pale cheeks and her eyes are brighter than she has seen them in months. Her hair is alive with sunshine. At her neck glints the iceberg quartz Tain made into a necklace for her last birthday.

The wind surges and there's a distant rumble of thunder. Mara looks at the approaching clouds in dismay and shuts the box.

'Go on home now,' warns Tain. 'I fear we're in for another hard blast. As soon as there's another break in the weather I'll call an island meeting and we'll make plans for the future.'

Mara runs down the hillside. Too late, she realizes that Tain never answered the question about Granny Mary.

Mara doesn't go straight home. She heads down to the village that lies in a fold of the hills and battles against the rising wind that is beginning to howl through the gaps between the houses. The hammers and saws have all stopped, the shutters secured, as Wing barricades itself up for more storms.

Mara thumps upon the shabby door of a cottage that sits near the edge of the village. There's a shout from inside, then a tall, lean, strong-looking boy with the reddish-blond hair and bright blue eyes of the Celtic inheritance that her father, young brother and many of the islanders share, opens the door. Mara's dark eyes and midnight hair is evidence of other ancestors – an ancient shipwreck of Spanish sailors – an inheritance that she shares with her mother, Granny Mary, and countless generations before.

The blond youth pulls her inside and quickly shoves the door shut against the wind. He's a mess, covered from top to toe in dust and dirt and cobwebs.

'Mara! What are you doing still out?' Rowan exclaims, but his lopsided smile says how glad he is to see her.

'I was just helping Tain and the storm came on so suddenly and I wanted—'

Mara stops because all she really wanted was to see her friends before the island blockades itself indoors again. But now she's here she finds she is desperate to tell them all about her conversation with Tain – yet she can feel the growing force of the storm. Is there enough time?

'You look like you've seen a ghost,' says Rowan as Mara falls silent. 'Are you OK – is your family all right?'

She nods mutely but she can feel her lips tremble. 'I can't stand any more of this, Rowan. I'll go mad if I'm stuck indoors any more. At least you two have each other to talk to.'

'*We* don't talk. *Gail* talks. All the time. My job is

to listen to her,' Rowan reminds her with a grin. 'But you've got Corey.'

'He's just a little kid.'

Mara knows she should go home. The slow boom of storm waves on the shore has begun. But she needs to talk. Her father will only argue against Tain's predictions for Wing's future. Her mother will say it's nonsense, then stay awake all night, worrying. Corey's too young to understand.

'Quick, come down to the den for a minute,' says Rowan. 'Gail was out looking for you. She'll want to see you.'

Mara hurries after Rowan, along the hallway and down a narrow flight of stone stairs. The stairs descend into the gloom of a musty cellar. One corner of the den is alight with candles and Gail sits there on a heap of sheepskin, bent over some sewing as Mara knew she would be, her blue eyes frowning behind a longer version of her brother's blond hair. Above her, in a billowing canopy, she has draped old curtains and adorned them with masses of shimmery, glinting things – silky scarves and ribbons and old necklaces. She looks as if she is sitting in a bedraggled but strangely exotic tent.

'Gail's winter project,' explains Rowan. 'Inspired by a picture in *The Arabian Nights*.'

Books and sewing materials – old bits of cotton, ribbon, nylon or silk – are like treasure on the island. Gail and Rowan beg and borrow the biggest hoard of each that they can find to occupy themselves through the storm season.

Gail looks up to see who Rowan is speaking to and bounds out of her Arabian canopy.

'Mara! Oh, I've missed you.'

Gail begins to talk nineteen to the dozen without a

26

pause for breath. 'I went up to your house to find you this morning and no one knew where you were and then I tried the shore and then I met some people and we talked and talked and by the time we'd finished the wind was starting up but I was just thinking I should have tried Tain's because maybe you'd gone there but then I thought surely you'd have come here first to see us because we haven't talked for *so-o* long.'

Gail grinds to a sudden halt, seeing the stricken expression on her friend's face.

'What is it?'

Mara flops down on a dusty cushion, then takes a deep breath and begins to tell Gail and Rowan about her conversation with Tain. Rowan listens raptly, shooshing Gail's many attempts to interrupt.

'Tain doesn't believe in miracles,' Mara finishes up. 'I don't think I do either. I wish I did. That sea is rising and rising and nothing's going to stop it. We can't just barricade ourselves up and hope that something will save us. We have to act.'

'But what can we do?' argues Gail. 'Even if it's true – and it's *not*,' she insists, 'we couldn't just launch out on to the ocean and hope we come across one of these New World cities. I don't believe they exist. It's too incredible. It'll be some film Tain watched on, um, tele-what's-it.'

'Television,' says Mara.

' . . . and now he's getting upset and confused,' Gail rattles on. 'He's an old man, after all.'

'He is *not* confused,' Mara interrupts hotly. 'He's the sharpest person I know.'

'Well, OK,' Gail backs down. 'But we would *know* if there were giant cities out there. Someone would have come and told us.'

'Like hell they would!' argues Rowan. 'They'd do exactly what we've done and just look after themselves. I bet no one in the outside world knows we exist. If there *is* any outside world left.'

'Do you think the rest of the world drowned?' Mara whispers. The thought is almost too terrible to voice.

'No!' cries Gail, horrified. 'Stop it, you two! I won't listen if you talk like that. Mum says God looked after us, so he must have looked after the rest of the world too. Of course he would.'

'God?' Rowan puzzles. 'What's God? Maybe that's just another old story. Then people convinced themselves the story was true. I love stories but how can they save us?'

He stares at the books that are piled in precarious towers all around the den. Then he shudders. 'When I read these old books and imagine all the amazing people and places that once existed, I wonder – well, is any of it still out there? What if we're the only people left in the world? And if we are, how can there be such a thing as God? Or else it's not the kind of God you mean,' he tells his sister, 'cuddly and caring. How can you decide you believe in God but not a giant city? You've no more proof of one than of the other.'

'Stop it!' Gail hisses, her cheeks hot. 'The stories about God are all up there in the church. They're carved into its walls so they must be true, or why would people have taken the trouble to do that?'

'Because people love stories,' says Rowan simply. He reaches out to gently touch one of the book stacks.

Mara stares at the books too, feeling cold inside.

'The problem is,' she whispers, '*I* haven't wondered at all. I've only really ever thought about here and now, about myself and my—'

My Weave adventures, she almost said. Not even Gail and Rowan, her closest friends, know about her secret travels. She would share any secret with them, except this.

'Maybe lots of people wonder,' says Rowan. 'We just don't talk about it. But Tain's right, we need to know what's out there.'

'I don't know what to think,' Mara confesses.

A great boom of sea hits the island.

'I must go!' Mara panics, gives Gail a frantic goodbye hug and runs upstairs where she bumps into Kate, Gail and Rowan's mother, who is bolting up the front door.

'Mara Bell! What on earth are you doing here? Get on home right now! Your mother will be frantic!' Kate talks at the same helter-skelter speed as Gail, only with considerably more volume. 'Rowan! Rowan! Come up here and see Mara halfway home! Hurry! Get a waterproof on! And watch how you go! Keep well away from that sea! I don't want either of you drowned, do you hear me?'

'The whole island hears you, Mother!' Rowan mutters as he and Mara escape Kate's onslaught and race out into the storm. As they run across the hillside an immense bolt of lightning turns the moment white and the skies explode with hailstones.

Side by side they battle through, shielding their faces with hands that are soon stinging from the pelt of the hailstones. The field of windmills is a maelstrom of ferociously whirling blades. Mara sees her father out on the hillside, watching anxiously for her. Guiltily, she turns to say goodbye to Rowan but he clutches her arm. The backs of his hands, like hers, are now raw.

'You think those cities really are out there?' he asks. His face is scrunched up against the storm; he has to shout to be heard.

'Mara!'

Mara peers up the hillside. Even at this distance and through billows of hail she can tell that Coll, her father, is furious with her for staying out in the storm.

She turns to go but Rowan still grips her arm.

'Do you believe in them?' he persists.

'I want to,' she shouts up at him, answering honestly. 'But I need more than Tain has told me. I need – I need evidence. All this talk of miracles and giant cities . . .' Mara tries to shield her face from a horizontal blast of hail. 'It sounds like something out of one of your books of fairy tales.'

There's a wet streak of blood on Rowan's brow where a hailstone has struck; it trickles down into his blue eyes. He puts his mouth close to her ear. 'Maybe – maybe people make up something to believe in when they *need* something to believe in,' he says.

Mara nods bleakly, then grabs him in a hard hug before she turns to run home.

'Take care!' she shouts over the roar of the wind.

In the second before she is hauled into the house, Mara sees Rowan – like a ghost in a crack of white lightning – running against a wall of black sea.

THE WEAVE

The storm roars day and night, as if the island is at the mercy of a battering giant.

'Fe fi fo fum! Huff and puff and blow your house down!' Mara's little brother, Corey, chants from downstairs, muddling up his fairy tales. 'But the storm won't get us, will it, Mum? Our house is made of stone.'

Mara leans her head against her bedroom window and feels the storm hurl itself against the thick wooden shutter, vibrating the glass pane. This trapped existence is torture. She feels like a wild bird in a cage. I *need* to be outside, she frets, pacing the room. She imagines herself smashing the window with her bare fist and tearing off the storm shutter to leap out into the immense fury of the wind.

She stops and stares at the imprisoning walls of her room. Restlessly, she toys with the apple-sized globe that lies on her windowsill alongside its tiny wand and crescent-shaped halo. The globe, wand and halo – her cyberwizz – is the only thing that stops her dying of boredom, she's quite sure. The cyberwizz is freedom, escape, release.

Mara scoops up the globe. Palm-snug yet weighty, it

has the feel of glass but a look of burnished metal. At her touch the globe begins to tingle, activated by the electric charge of her body. Colours start to swirl across its surface like clouds or shadows and a glow emanates from the core of the globe as its tiny solar rods power up.

With a thumb and forefinger, Mara presses on the hinges that are placed on opposite poles of the globe and in one smooth motion it breaks open to form two half spheres. The flat surface of one half is a compact keyboard, the other a blank screenpad.

Mara slips the crescent-shaped halo over her eyes to make a sleek visor. She picks up the little silver cyber-wand, taps a swift command upon the tiny keyboard, then scribbles a series of cryptic symbols upon the screenpad – the beautiful, complex language the cyberwizz has taught her, that merges alphabet, hieroglyph and number. The symbols gleam and fade, each one superseded almost instantly by another. Over the years, Mara has picked up cyberwizzdom with the greed and instinct of an animal on the scent of a hunt.

The cyberwizz powers into action. The halo glows and the swirling colours of the globe quicken and intensify. Mara stares into the halo, consumed by the vision she has called up. Excitement surges through her limbs as she exits realworld and plunges into cyberspace.

And the magic begins . . .

Mara zips and zooms.
Wizzing far beyond realworld.
Fast and free in the glittering strands of the Weave.
Joy-rush is amazing. Mara verves down a shimmering vertical strand to land on a wide electronic boulevard

that's lined with buzzing, sparking towerstacks – colossal Weavesites that reach ever upwards and onwards.

Up ahead on the boulevard, a gang of hazard spiders scuttle out, flashing red for danger. Alert for oncoming hazards, Mara sees none and spurns the red spiders with ease. Her path ahead seems clear. But in the Weave things are rarely as they seem. Every one of its glittering electronic strands splits into infinite possibility, an endless unfolding of choices.

In cyberspace there are no rules, no limits. Anything might happen.

Mara zooms onwards, ready and alert. She keeps a wary eye on the dark alleys between the towerstacks, on the lookout for the sleek, sly stalker that she sometimes senses. She never manages to catch more than a glimpse of whoever or whatever it is – just the glint of watchful eyes and a stealthy presence in the shadows that sends shivers down her spine.

Now the great boulevard breaks into sudden rubble. Here, mighty towerstacks have crumbled into giant junk-heaps. Mara scoots up one to see what she can find among the ruins. At the peak of the flickering junk mountain she sits down and sighs with pleasure.

It's beautiful, so beautiful.

The Weave glitters all around, as far as she can see. A vast datascape. The electronic knit of a billion computers. From here, on the top of the junk mountain, it looks stunning, but Mara knows that up close those glittering strands are bleak ruins and wasted boulevards. Their brilliance comes from the great spill of electronic litter that leaks from all the Weavesites. In the lonely back alleys behind the main strands and in the giant shadows of the tumbledown towerstacks, these rotting heaps of electronic rubbish have somehow sparked their own lifeforces to mutate into the strangest forms – weird Weave-creatures born of decay and chaos.

The Weave is wild and savage. Thrilling and scary. Here Mara owns a freedom that's impossible in realworld.

It's the best place ever.

Mara snaps to sudden attention. Something's happening. Something big. A raid? An attack? By whom, what? She feels the electric surge race across the network of communication strands. Whatever it is, it's coming straight for her. She scrambles from her exposed position on the data mountain but is only halfway down when it hits.

A pack of flying cyberdogs.

Fast and furious, short wings crackling, electronic jaws agape, and jagged teeth glinting, they spit their venomous froth of data-decay. They'll rip her to shreds. Mara grips her cyberwand, furiously dodging, desperately trying to keep her hands and head steady as the cyberdogs snarl and snap around her. She keys a frantic command into the cyberwizz . . .

. . . and zaps them all to bits. Shards of electronic dog scatter satisfyingly all across the Weave.

Venomous stuff! A truly elegant kill.

Her moment of glory lasts just long enough for her to zip on to a bridge that rises up out of the ruins. One instant she is zooming along the bridge path, zinging with joy, the next the bridge crumbles into nothing and she is hurtling off its broken end – down, down, down into a meltdown of electronic blue.

Backtrack – now!

But she can't. She's out of control and there's nothing she can do to stop. She crashes head over heels through

*the strands of the Weave. On and on she tumbles, falling
helplessly, until at last the glittering strands end.*

*Amazed, Mara hurtles into dark, unknown regions of
cyberspace. She has fallen right out of the Weave.*

FOX IN A FOREST

A giant, glistening coil looms up, surrounded by darkness. She must slow down – she's going to crash. But some vast magnetic force is pulling her onwards and with a great WHOOSH the coil sucks her in and now she's zooming helter-skelter down a spiralling silver vortex – or is it up?

Just when it seems the crazy helter-skelter will never end, Mara shoots out into a crackling haze of ice-blue static, so blinding it must have fire at its heart.

Wow.

Amazing.

She slows to a soft tumble. Something vast glints, then is lost again in the blaze of icefire. Mara stares as the vision glints and fades, glints and fades. She concentrates harder and the hazy vision forms into a thick trunk of unimaginably colossal towers, topped by a ferocious geometry of networks and connections. It looks like a gigantic crystal tree.

Mara stares wide-eyed, stunned by the vast, unearthly beauty of it. She tries to move forward but doesn't know how. How do you move through an ocean of static? The haze around the crystal tree-towers shimmers intensely, seems to rise up like a wall. Then Mara sees – it is a wall, a massive guard shield. Still, there must be a way through. There's always some tiny glitch that an ace wizzer like Mara can trick a way through.

But this is not the Weave. This is the unknown. The majestic towers look like something out of a fairy tale.

'Once upon a time,' Mara whispers, thrilling at the words that always began a story. 'Once upon a time, in a time out of mind . . .'

Her whisper radiates ripples in the ice-blue static. The most incredible thought strikes.

'Who are you?' a voice demands out of the blue, sending jagged shock waves through the cyberhaze.

Mara jumps in fright and looks all around. There's no one to be seen.

'Who are you?' the voice demands again; a husky, hungry voice. 'And what do you know about once upon a time?'

'I'm Mara,' she whispers nervously, searching frantically for the source of the voice. 'Who are you? Where are you?'

'I've been watching you for a while,' is the only reply.

Shivers run down Mara's spine as she senses the stealthy presence that must be the sly stalker, the one who's been tracking her, shadowing her movements on the Weave. But how on Earth did he – it sounds like a he – follow her here? Mara's heart thumps as something begins to form in the cyberhaze. A pair of disembodied, untamed eyes stare at her through the blue. Mara stares back in fright. Two sharp points appear above them. Ears? Now, below the eyes, a long white streak tipped in black forms into a dog-like muzzle. There's the sudden flash of a tawny tail . . .

A fox! Mara has a fleeting memory of the realworld fox that ravaged Wing's lambs and chickens before it was finally trapped and killed . . . but what on Earth is a fox doing way out here ?

The cyberfox is as still as a statue. Mara feels the fiercest concentration emanate from that intense stillness as the creature strains to sense all that it can of her.

'What do you know about once upon a time?' The cyberfox bares its teeth as Mara says nothing. She has no idea how to answer.

'Look, I've tumbled out of the Weave and I haven't a clue where I—'

She falters as the fox pads closer, its teeth still bared, a faint snarl on its breath.

'Where are you from?' it demands in a tone that prickles Mara's skin. 'I mean in realworld – where are you from?'

'Wing,' Mara answers automatically as the fox closes in.

'Wing?' The fox stops dead, turns still as stone, all senses on full alert. 'A new city?' the fox says at last, uncertainly. 'I've never heard of that one.'

Mara's eyes widen at this and she lifts her gaze from the fox up to the colossal towers.

'It's an – an island,' Mara stutters. 'But what do you know about new cities? Are there really such things?'

'An island?' the fox murmurs huskily, ignoring her questions. Its fur bristles. A glistening tongue trembles between its teeth. It licks its lips. 'There are still islands? Where? Where's this island?'

Mara drags her eyes from the gleaming towers and notes the fox-hunger, a desperate curiosity as intense as her own. She frowns. 'You asked where I'm from in realworld. How does a cyberfox know about realworld? Are you *real?' The frown lifts and her eyes widen. 'Do you exist in realworld too?'*

The fox looks at her warily, hesitates, then slowly nods.

Mara gasps. Never in all her cybertravels has she met another realworld being – only lumens and ghosts and all the other weird electronic creatures of the Weave.

'Who are you? Where are you in realworld?' breathes Mara. She looks up again at the crystal towers behind the fox and hopes with all her might that her hunch is right.

'I asked you first,' says the fox.

'I told you, I'm from an island. It's in the North Atlantic.'

'An island,' whispers the fox. Its eyes shine with wonder. 'You live on a real island? In the North Atlantic? Where's that?'

'It's the ocean,' says Mara, unsurprised by his ignorance because she knows so little of the world herself. Tain has told her that the lands once separated the oceans and they had different names, but the Atlantic is all she knows. 'But please tell me – I need to know – what are those great towers behind you?'

'The fox barely glances over its shoulder. 'It's the New World.'

'The New World!' cries Mara. She hugs herself with joy. 'Then it really does exist!'

And yet – she stops and her brow furrows in concentration. Those gigantic towers are only a cybervision. She needs to know if the real thing exists. She turns to the fox who is staring at her more fiercely than ever.

'Does the New World exist in realworld too?' Mara demands. 'Are there really giant cities that rise up above the oceans?'

'Of course,' shrugs the fox. 'It's all there is – at least I thought so. That's what we've been told. But you say you

live on an island. So there are islands in the world!'
The fox turns urgent. 'Tell me about your island. Tell me
about once upon a time. Tell me now!'

But Mara is filled with her own sense of urgency.
Beyond the fox, beyond the great towers, she seems to see
another crest rising faintly out of the cyberhaze. She looks
harder, deeper, further, and sees another, she is sure. Then
more and still more, only just visible. Endless crests, each
one more and more distant, stretching far deep into the
ocean of blue static like a forest of crystal trees . . .

'You've got to help me!' Mara cries. 'My island's
drowning. The sea is rising fast and we need to find a
new home or we'll drown. We need to get to the New
World. Please – tell me how to find it. Where are the
cities? How can I find them in realworld?'

The fox becomes stone-like again. The pupils of its eyes
become hard, black points of intensity. 'Are you real?' it
demands suspiciously. 'Or just a Weave ghost?'

'Of course I'm real!' exclaims Mara. 'Help me, please!
I'll tell you all about my island. I'll tell you everything I
know about once upon a time. I'll tell you whatever you
want if you'll help me find the New World.'

Fox eyes stare deep into her own and for a moment
Mara is sure she can see the real, human presence shining
through. She feels a tug inside – a deep, raw instinct that
urges her towards the fox. She is almost close enough to
reach out and touch that sleek, tawny fur – but in an
electronic universe there's no such thing as touch.

'Please,' Mara whispers.

'Mara!' calls a familiar little voice, from very far away.

Something wrenches her arm and she plunges,
sprawling, into the ocean of cyberhaze. Mara makes a
desperate, useless lunge at the fox's tail as an

overpowering electric surge swoops her backwards. A gulf of blue cyberhaze now separates her from the fox.

'Mara, Mara!' says the little voice, closer now.

'Help me!' she begs the fox, struggling with all her might against the grip of a huge reverse force. 'Tell me where you are!'

'New Mungo . . .' cries the fox, running after her, 'in Eurosea. Come back!'

The fox is vanishing in the haze, and the crystal towers fade as – feet first – Mara is sucked back through the spiralling coil and ripped across channels of electronic matter. 'Help me!' she screams over and over as she tumbles far away and out of reach of the cyberfox and the beautiful vision of the New World.

There's nothing she can do. Miserably, she hurtles back through the networks of the Weave.

'Mara!' gasps the little voice, scared now.

With a sickening wrench Mara crashes back into real-world. She pulls the glowing halo from her eyes and flings it away. She looks around her bedroom in a daze, a sob caught in her throat. Corey stands beside her, his big blue eyes wide with fright, clutching the wand he has pulled from her hand. The globe rolls across the floor.

'Mara! What's wrong?'

Mara stares blankly at her little brother. Her eyes nip with tears, her cheeks burn. She grabs the culprit.

'I could kill you!' she rages at him. 'Why did you do that? I lost the fox – I lost the New World, all because of you!'

Corey's face crumples, his eyes shut, his mouth forms a hard O and Mara braces herself for a huge wail. He musters a noise that could shatter rock. Mara tries to shush him before her mother hears.

'I thought something *ba-ad* was happening to you 'cos you were shouting, "Help me, help me!" ' Corey cries. 'And I was *sca-ared.* And I was *trying* to help you. And I was only wanting to show you my new wobbly *too-oof*!' He lets out a huge heartbroken howl, giving a wide display of his wobbly teeth.

'Mara, what's happening up there?' her mother calls.

Ashamed, Mara softens her furious grip to hug the rigid body of her small brother. She strokes his head until his howls calm and she feels his body soften. 'I'm sorry, Corey,' she mutters into his hair. 'It was just a game that went wrong and I got a bit upset. But I'm all right, really I am. It wasn't your fault. Scoot now and I'll come downstairs and we'll play, whatever you want.'

'Really?' Corey sniffs, scrubs away his tears, hiccups and recovers instantly. 'When?'

'Five minutes.'

'Promise?'

'Promise,' Mara lies.

Corey scoots and Mara flops on her bed. Outside, the sea surges around the island, something in the sound reminding her of the waves of electronic matter she was surfing through only minutes before.

It's unbearable. She could search cyberspace for years and never find the fox and the New World again. It was only by sheer accident that she found them at all. Mara springs to her feet and paces her room, thinking furiously. She turns, trips over a cushion on the floor and impatiently kicks it out of her way. The cushion bounces across the room and something hard that was lying under it clatters against the wall.

Oh no! Mara rushes over and sinks to her knees beside Tain's hand-carved box which she has unwittingly kicked, full-pelt, across her room. Earlier, she was lying on the floor, admiring it and scrutinizing her face in the little mirror. A small splinter has broken off the bottom of the box where it hit the wall but thankfully the wonderful carvings are unharmed.

Gingerly, Mara opens the box to check inside – and her heart sinks. The mirror on the lid has a horrible jagged crack right across one side. When she looks at herself her face is scarred by the crack, all across her left cheek. Mara groans and wants to kick *herself* now.

More than half a century ago Tain made this beautiful box for Granny Mary; it's only been hers for a few weeks and she's wrecked it.

Tain will never know, Mara vows. She'll make sure of that. But she *will* tell him of her amazing discovery – the evidence she has found that the New World really does exist.

And yet – Mara frowns. All her evidence really amounts to is that single stunning vision, a crystal forest of towering cities. And the word of a cyberfox. Mara runs a finger over the crack in the little mirror, something in its jagged shape reminding her of the beautiful, branching crests that stretched far into the ocean of cyberspace.

It's just not enough. It's not real, solid evidence. Not enough to convince anyone to launch out on to the ocean to find sanctuary in a New World. And now she's back in realworld, now she thinks hard about that unearthly vision, Mara is suddenly a lot less sure than she was. Her frown deepens, her eyes darken and she bites her lip. She sits and thinks with a hard-beating heart.

Could this really be our future? Might there be a safe refuge for us all in the New World?

She stirs herself. Time to work. If the New World really

does exist, she needs more than shimmering visions. She needs rock-solid evidence; something she can believe in. Something everyone can believe in.

Mara gathers up her cyberwizz. She scrapes her dark sweep of hair back from her face and slips the halo over her eyes. She picks up the tiny wand and repowers the globe. Then plunges straight back into the Weave.

DEAD EYE OF THE STORM

'Mara!'

Rosemary stands at Mara's bedroom door with a cremated loaf of bread in her hands. Mara stirs from the bed where she is huddled in an exhausted heap, sits up and rubs her eyes.

'What time's it?'

'Could you not *smell* the bread burning?' exclaims her mother. 'I asked you to keep an eye on it while I went out to the barn to feed the animals. This is a waste and you know we can't afford any waste.'

'You asked me to keep an eye on Corey too,' Mara yawns. 'Can't do everything, can I?'

'You don't do *anything* but play on that cyberwizz all night then sleep all day.'

'I wasn't playing, I was—' Mara stops, reminding herself that no one, not even her mother, knows what she really does on the cyberwizz. With a jolt of excitement she remembers what she found deep in the ruins of the Weave last night – something that might help save them all. But her mother is not in the mood for life-and-death discussions. Today's bread is a more pressing concern.

'Well, you can switch off now because you'll have to bake another loaf.' Rosemary takes the globe and wand from Mara's hands and replaces them with the blackened loaf. 'You can take that one out to the chickens first.'

Mara knows better than to argue. Her mother's normally good nature is balanced by a stubbornness equal to her own. It's simpler to punch a pillow and do as she's told.

But her mother stops her on the stairs with a soft hand and a twinkle in her eye. 'Didn't you hear what I said, sleepyhead?'

'You said—' Mara grumps then stops and catches the twinkle. '*Outside?* I can go outside? Can I?'

'Five minutes, that's all. It's just a break in the clouds.'

Mara doesn't care. She'll spin out every second. She thumps downstairs and when she opens the front door she walks straight into a fluttering red and yellow cloud. Mara blinks, then laughs as they tickle her face and hair. Butterflies! She watches them flutter off to dance among the windmill blades.

She is astonished at the warmth in the wind and the hot, plump raindrops. The thick stone walls of the cottage haven't let in a hint of summertime. But the sky is low and dark, an evening sky at midday that meets a sea of rainbows and frothy white horses. The northern islands are lost in steamy mist. Mara remembers what Tain said and feels a sudden dread at what the gathering heat must be doing to the great meltdown at the Earth's two poles.

When Tain was a boy, the Arctic meltdown turned the northern seas cold and Wing suffered biting ice-winds all year round, though the rest of the world was warming up. The polar ice sheets that once reflected the sun's rays back into space must have shrunk drastically, reasons Tain, and

Wing bakes in burning summers now that heat is trapped on Earth.

Mara forces herself to look and see how far the ocean has now risen. A lot, she concludes. The storm season has made a wreckage of the fields of windmills and solar panels. Twisted blades and shards of solar panels lie scattered all across the hills. But the old red phone box, that relic from another time, is still standing on the humpback road bridge. The bent bus stop sign is gone though. If the sea reaches the phone box, then we're in serious trouble, she decides. Surely it can't – yet she finds herself imagining the last cliffs of polar ice, frozen for aeons, cracking and sliding into a massive blue meltdown that will swell the ocean till the waves surge up and swallow the phone box.

Mara turns back to face the land and sees the fleet of boats that are harboured in a sheltered fold of hill above the windmills. She shivers at the sight, despite the muggy heat.

Her father struggles past with two steaming buckets of milk.

'Not another burnt loaf,' he cries, clattering the milk pails on the stone steps of the cottage. 'Don't tell me – you were plugged into that cyberwizz.'

'Sorry.' Mara smiles ruefully. Her father is well acquainted with her talent at bread-burning. 'Um, Dad,' she begins, then wonders how to break the news of her amazing discovery to him. Will he listen?

But Coll unwittingly helps her out. 'What's this New World fairy story Corey says you were telling him this morning?' he asks as he heads back to the barn. 'Giant cities above the sea – he's been talking of nothing else all morning.'

Mara bites her lip. Corey had crawled into bed beside her somewhere around dawn this morning, just as she had unplugged from a whole night spent searching the Weave ruins. She couldn't sleep, too excited by her incredible discovery, and ended up telling Corey what she had found.

'It's not a fairy story, Dad.'

Coll shakes his head as Mara follows him into the barn.

'I know the myths, Mara, but that's all they are. Don't upset your little brother any more than he already is.'

'He's upset by the storm, not by me,' counters Mara. 'And the New World's not a myth,' she ventures. 'Tain says it's real. He saw the cities on television when he was young – giant cities. He saw them being built.'

'I'm sure he did but they'd never have survived this.' Coll struggles to close the barn door against a punching fist of wind and Mara lends her weight. Then he stops to rub the sweat from his brow and stares around him in the gloom of the barn as if he's just woken from a dream. 'But the way things are going, I'm almost ready to believe in anything.'

'Dad,' Mara says cautiously, because it's unlikely her practical, down-to-earth father will listen. 'I need to talk to you about – about this New World.' Amazingly, he *is* listening, so Mara takes her chance. 'I used to think it was just a fairy story too but I've been searching for info on my cyberwizz for weeks and weeks now, and I think – I mean, I've found stuff that makes me *sure* that it exists. It's incredible. Really, Dad. I can show you. They built it so that it would survive all this.'

Her voice throbs with excitement. Her dark eyes plead with her father. He sighs.

'Oh, come on now,' he says, gently dismissive, tucking

wayward strands of her dark hair behind her ear. And yet he looks at her as if he wants to believe her.

'Dad, please. Just have a look at what I've found.'

Coll looks at his daughter long and hard. Then smiles wryly at the stubborn determination in her face.

'Well, we'll see. Show me tonight,' he says. 'Right now I've got the milking to finish, then I'll have to try and fix up the roof and the barn and that's just for starters. Don't go far and make sure you get safe back in the house as soon as the storm starts up again.'

Mara nods, amazed. She hasn't tried to tell her parents anything about the New World till now, until she had real evidence, because she was sure they'd never take her seriously. Dad never would have before. Things must be getting desperate, Mara decides. She studies the storm damage as she crumbles the burnt loaf for the chickens. The solar panel is almost completely detached from the cottage roof and there are places in the barn where the gale has ripped the wood from the thick nails that have held it for decades. It's always been like this. No one ever has time to make plans for the future when there's bread to bake and a roof to fix and a hundred other things to do.

And this storm season has been the longest, fiercest she has ever known.

Mara glances once again at the ominous fleet that sits above the field of windmills. All the island's boats are perched there, their hulls like the bodies of great birds, ready and waiting to fly.

Are we near the edge of summer yet, Mara wonders desperately, or just trapped in the dead eye of the storm?

A WORLD LOST

Mara groans as Rosemary ladles out yet another bowl of murky green soup. She is hungry all the time yet can barely stomach the food her mother serves up.

'I never want to eat another mouthful of cabbage as long as I live.'

'Smelly soup,' Corey agrees but he tucks in hungrily.

For the last month they have existed on a meagre ration of eggs, cabbage soup and potato bread. There's a small but dwindling supply of milk and cheese but the sheep and goats are reacting badly to such a long season spent in a dark barn with rations of mulch and hay instead of fresh pasture. Grain stores are frighteningly low and supplies of preserved fruit and vegetables are all eaten. If the storm lasts much longer they will have to start slaughtering precious livestock for food – but even that won't last long as they have so few animals.

Every night Mara tells her little brother a bedtime story. Corey always wants the *Three Little Pigs* or *Jack the Giant Killer*, and tonight as the story ends he touches the wall beside his bed.

'We've got a house of stone,' he declares. 'We're safe, aren't we?'

His bedtime story is the cocoon he builds for himself each night before he goes to sleep. He seems to have grown more babyish, younger than his six years, huddled inside himself to hide from the wolfish howl of the storm and its giant strength. While Mara feels she has, all of a sudden, grown up.

Once Corey is settled, Mara joins her parents. It's too warm to burn a fire, yet out of habit they sit around the dead grate and now they too cocoon themselves in stories to pass the evening. Sometimes Mara is hit by the strangest feeling that some part of her is already in the future, looking back on this lost scene with an aching heart. Tonight, Rosemary tells the flood legend of Noah and the ark, an ancient tale that is carved into the stone walls of Wing's church. Since their own great flood, few on the island have kept faith with the old religion and the church stands abandoned, but the richness of its stories has lived on among the people, passed down by the old ones and enjoyed as folklore on the long, stormy evenings.

Once the story is happily ended Rosemary looks at Mara hesitantly, then speaks her mind.

'I see we've got our own arks ready up on the hill,' she says to Coll. 'Are we supposed to be going somewhere in them?'

Now Coll looks at Mara. 'There's to be an island meeting about that in the church, just as soon as there's a decent break in the weather. Tain's organized it.'

'Tain wasn't out in the storm?' says Rosemary, concerned.

'He called round all the farms and the village during the lull in the weather.'

'What's going to happen?' Mara whispers, though she's not sure if she wants to hear.

Coll hesitates and doesn't answer directly. 'I spoke to Tain about what you told me, Mara. Maybe you can help. Tell me what you found.'

'How can Mara help with this?' says her mother. 'She's just a child.'

'I'm not,' Mara retorts, then begins to tell her story about the New World that lies way out in cyberspace, far beyond the Weave.

When she is finished her mother sighs and smiles.

'It's just a dream, Marabell. It's not real. I've heard Tain talk about the New World but it's just a myth, a story made from wishful thinking.' Rosemary stares at Mara with recognition in her eyes. 'Believe it or not, I do remember what it's like to be fifteen and full of dreams. Real life keeps getting in the way.'

Mara smiles. 'No more burnt bread,' she promises. 'But this dream is real, Mum. Wait. Wait till you see what I found.'

She runs upstairs and grabs her cyberwizz, then stands on a chair to lift a dusty, old screen laptop computer down from the top of her wardrobe. She hopes she can remember how to reassemble the homemade connection that she designed to pass the time during last winter's storm season.

'Where did you find *that* old thing?' laughs Coll, raising his eyebrows at the laptop, when she bursts back into the living room.

'What are you going to do?' murmurs Rosemary.

'The impossible,' grins Mara, as she struggles with wires and magnets.

Like the rest of the islanders, her parents have no use

52

for the old technology that used to be commonplace in the world. They look at each other and shake heads in bemusement as Mara connects the laptop to her cyberwizz. She picks up the globe of the cyberwizz and it tingles to life at her touch. She scribbles a series of commands upon its electropad. Grudgingly, the old laptop powers up. Mara finds it awkward to tap upon the big, flat keyboard and it is grindingly slow, but it's a reliable old machine. Frowning in deep concentration, she slips on her halo and enters the Weave. Then zips through site after site, following a mind-twistingly complex trail of links that eventually lead her to the hidden basement site in one of the tumbledown towerstacks that, after weeks of trawling and searching through the rot of the Weave ruins, she found at last, late last night.

It's the vital evidence she needs that the New World is real.

Coll and Rosemary watch as she scans newsreel from the beginning of the Century of Storms. Images of floods and tempests and global destruction fill the screen. Mara is shocked to the core, every bit as shaken as she was when she first viewed it last night. It all happened years ago, long before she was born, in far away places. But now the same thing is happening on her very doorstep. She cannot look away or dismiss it. She must pay attention.

While her parents murmur to each other, Mara draws a sharp breath as she reads the text that scrolls along the bottom of the screen – the final message on the Weavesite. Somehow, in her euphoric excitement last night, she never saw it. Now Mara is dumbfounded by what she reads.

Above the scrolling text, the on-screen simulation shows a cluster of towers, *colossal* trunks of towers, rising out of the flooded ruins of an old city. Now a vast, geometric construction – tiers and branching networks – begins to grow out of the central trunk, cresting higher and higher into the sky, mapping the air space between the towers with amazingly complex patterns, while massive roots bore down through the seabed, deep into the Earth.

Mara's parents gaze in astonishment at the vast structure that rises out of the ocean – a giant city in the sky.

'Impossible,' says Coll. 'It would blow down. How could it withstand a storm?'

Mara drags her eyes from the terrible message on the scrolling text and stares blankly at her father.

'The SOS,' she whispers. 'Did you see it?'

'That was all long ago, Mara,' murmurs her mother, uncomfortably. 'Never mind that now.'

'But—'

Her parents fix their attention firmly upon the image on the screen. Rosemary keys in Coll's question and the screen flashes up data about the sky city.

'Modelled on nature's genius to produce the toughest, most flexible of structures,' Rosemary reads. 'New World sky cities are designed to withstand the most brutal forces of nature. They are a feat of engineering, stabilized by immensely deep seabed anchor roots and ultra-powerful geomagnets that bond each city securely to the Earth's magnetic core. Constructed from intensely strong yet supple titanmera, a new non-corrosive material found deep within the ocean bed . . . Rosemary tails off in wonderment. 'People really *live* in that? I don't believe it.'

'Thousands live in it,' Mara answers. She turns her head to the window, distracted for a moment by what sounds like the distant peal of bells, though it's impossible to be sure with the noise of the storm. 'What's that?'

But her parents are still too enthralled by the vision of the sky city to answer.

'Where are these New World cities, Mara?' Coll asks at last. 'Are we near one?'

Mara calls up the world atlas that maps the sky cities as a glittering constellation scattered across the planet.

'I'm not exactly sure where we are in the world,' she confesses, ashamed at her own ignorance.

'The North Atlantic,' says Coll. 'That should be here.' He frowns. 'But this map seems to call it . . .' he peers closer then sits back, looking fazed, 'Eurosea.'

Eurosea! That was what the cyberfox said. New Mungo. In Eurosea. Mara watches as her father zooms in to a patch of Eurosea.

'We're about here, wouldn't you say?' He circles his forefinger on the screen map.

Rosemary nods. 'I think so.'

Wing and its surrounding network of islands are not even a speckle on the map but directly south of where they should be, a single star glows.

Rosemary reads the flashing label on the star. 'New Mungo.'

Mara lets out a cry. Her parents look up at her in surprise.

'That's it!' she bursts out. 'New Mungo. I – I've heard the name before.'

Somehow, she doesn't want to tell them about the fox. She will keep him to herself.

Rosemary slumps back in her chair. 'This is madness. What am I thinking of – falling for this New World myth. We'll see out these storms and then we'll move uphill.'

'Where to?' Coll demands. 'There's nowhere to go, no

houses up there. And this doesn't look like a myth to me. It's too detailed, too scientific.'

Rosemary shakes her head stubbornly. 'This is our home. We'll move this house stone by stone if we have to. We'll go as high as we can in the summer. The sea can't rise much further now.'

Outside, the ocean gives a defiant roar. The roar grows and they wait for the noise to ebb, for the rhythm of the waves to resettle. But the roar only rises, becomes a pounding blast that vibrates the thick stone walls of the cottage.

'Oh,' gasps Rosemary. She stands up and clasps her hands tight together till the knuckles turn white.

Mara gets up and links arms with her mother, while Coll stares at the storm-bolted door, daring a single wave to touch it. But there's nothing any of them can do except hope that the terrifying roar will subside.

After a long while, the roar dies. But a thunderous banging erupts on the cottage door. Storm-torn voices battle to be heard above the wind.

Coll rushes to unlatch the heavy planks of wood that secure the door. It bursts open and a clutch of terrified people spills through, sodden and shivering. It takes Mara a moment to recognize them as her neighbours from a cottage directly downhill. The children's eyes stare at her, wide with fear, through drenched locks of hair. The peal of bells is unmistakable now.

'Ruth!' cries Rosemary, grabbing the woman by the arms.

'It's gone,' the woman, Ruth, bursts out sobbing. 'Our home. The sea—'

'We were lucky to get out in time. There must be others

who didn't,' Quinn, her husband interrupts in a flat, dazed voice. 'A giant wave. Never seen such a wave, never.'

'Gail!' gasps Mara. 'Oh, and Rowan and Tain and – and everyone—' She clasps her hand over her mouth as if to stop the awful thoughts that might burst out.

'No, Coll!' Ruth catches Coll's arm to stop him rushing out into the storm to help. 'It's no use. They're either safe or gone. You'll risk yourself for nothing and your family needs you alive. Tain's high enough up. And a lot of the villagers have moved up into the church. Maybe Kate and Alex took the family there, Mara. I said we should do the same.'

The church sits on the hillside just above the village. It should be safe, thinks Mara, willing her friends to be there.

Ruth leans weakly against a chair, presses a hand to her mouth, and suppresses a sob. Quinn stares in a daze at his drenched, terrified children and his heavily pregnant wife.

'Sit down, Ruth,' says Rosemary anxiously, helping her into a seat. 'I'll see to the children. It'll be all right.'

Brisk and grim-faced, Rosemary takes charge, sending Mara to the kitchen to heat up soup while she finds dry clothes for them all. Mara hears her mother settling the two shocked children with the calm, soothing tones she uses with Corey but it's the even quieter conversation that is taking place between her father and the other two adults that she is tuned in to.

Once they are all dry and warmed with soup, the children settled in a makeshift bed on Corey's bedroom floor, the four adults gather round the computer where the star of New Mungo still glows on the screen map. Coll tells his neighbours of Mara's discovery and a glimmer of hope lights their stricken, desperate faces. They all sit by the old computer, staring at the star for a long time.

Rosemary shakes her head, biting her lip. 'I just can't believe in it,' she says, 'but I know it might be our only hope.'

Coll reaches out and squeezes Mara's hand.

'If it is, if this New World really is an option, then we need to figure out how to get to it – before we run out of time.'

Much later, when everyone else has fallen into exhausted sleep, Mara lies wide awake, bonded to her cyberwizz, racing at the speed of light through its electronic universe. She rips across the strands of the Weave, rampaging through its rotting ruins, its junk mountains and tumbledown towerstacks, frantically scrolling through the last messages on any news site she can find. It's almost dawn when she tears the halo from her eyes and flings the wand and globe on the floor, distraught.

She cannot believe it. How could she spend half her life in the Weave and never see the truth? How did she not see those awful cries for help that lie among the ruins and junk mountains of the Weave? She thought it was an adventure playground, that's all, and she's been so engrossed in her thrills and spills that she hasn't seen what should have stopped her in her tracks long, long ago.

The Weave is not a game or a picturesque ruin for her to play in. It's a lost world. A world of the dead. It hangs in cyberspace like an ancient cobweb, derelict, defunct – a ghost weave suspended between the old communication satellites that orbit a drowned Earth.

It's an electronic gravesite.

The news sites have been dead for more than half a

century. They all end in a horrifying SOS – the last, frantic cry for help of a drowning world – trapped for ever in the strands of the Weave.

How could I be so blind? Mara is appalled. It's the same blindness Tain accuses the islanders of when, surrounded by a swallowing sea, they still refuse to see the evidence that's right in front of their eyes.

And now she remembers Granny Mary trying to explain something to her, years ago, when Mara first found the cyberwizz, a forgotten relic tucked away at the back of a cupboard. But Mara hadn't listened, too excited by her find, too eager to learn the secret language that would bring the cyberwizz to life. Now she knows what Granny must have been trying to tell her – the Weave was dead.

But now she knows. Now she is looking at the world with eyes wide open. And she is almost sure that there is something out there. A New World, a haven above the seas. A future.

Mara picks up Tain's carved box, a box he made in the time the island still had trees, for a girl who had a kind of greatness in her; a girl who was Mara's living image. Mara opens the box and gazes into the mirror she has cracked and ruined. She can't see any signs of greatness in her own face – just the wide, scared eyes of a young girl who can hardly bear to think about what lies in front of her.

EARTH WINS

Summer 2100

Early next morning Mara is torn from sleep by the dull clang of Wing's church bell. She rips back her bedclothes and rushes downstairs. Outside, the world is calm at last, the sea and sky a misty blue. But Mara stops in shock and stares around her.

All that remains of Wing is its central peak. The higher farms and the upper reaches of the village are safe but beyond that, as far as she can see, there is only ocean. Nothing else. A few blades rotate above the waves – all that's left of the field of windmills.

Mara grips her father's hand as they face the impossible truth. All the islands in the north are gone. It's as if they'd never been there at all. Now it's too late for miracles. The entire network of islands has been swallowed by sea. Along with most of Wing.

'We're out of time, Mara,' says her father, heavily.

Furious, Mara runs down to the edge of the waves, crashes into the sea and struggles to reach the old red phone box that stands on the humpbacked bridge. Up to her waist in water, she reaches an arm through a window pane that's long emptied of glass and dials 999, the old emergency number on the dial. Why, she doesn't know. Who she is calling, she doesn't know either. Who on Earth does she think might answer? The line is blank, of course.

This can't happen, Mara sobs down the phoneline that's been dead for decades.

No one answers. They're all long gone.

Mara stands upon the stone altar of Wing's tiny church, her cheeks burning as she confronts the crowd of fellow-islanders that have gathered there.

'There *is* a New World,' she insists. 'There *are* real cities – beautiful cities that are built high above the oceans, just like I've told you. The evidence is there, I promise. It's our only hope. Where else can we go?'

'Maybe she's right,' someone calls out from the back of the crowd. 'Maybe there are cities out there. But even if there are, they won't take us all in – a whole island!'

'It's what they were built for – to house flood refugees,' Mara counters.

'The sea might calm down,' says Kate, Gail and Rowan's mother, uncertainly. 'It can't keep rising like this. I think we should stay put. What we know is safer than what we don't.'

'It's too late, Mum,' says Rowan. 'We have to face up to this, now.'

Mara glances over at Gail, who stands beside him. Gail sends her a trembly smile of support. Earlier, Mara had raced up to the church, sobbing breathlessly, terrified that her friends wouldn't be there. Their whole street was now sea; their home flooded to the top of the windows. Thankfully, they had found sanctuary at the top of the hill.

The toll of the bell had brought the islanders out of

61

their barricaded homes to gather in the old church. In stunned, broken voices, they told each other of the lives swept away and the homes lost in the great sea surge. Then, urged forward by her father, Mara suddenly found herself on the altar, telling everyone who was crammed into the tiny church of the evidence she had found of the existence of the New World. All the time she felt Gail and Rowan's blue eyes fixed upon her in amazement.

Now she has told her story, all that she knows of the New World; now it's up to the others to decide. Everyone is arguing, shouting their views and fears at each other across the church. It's so loud and chaotic that Mara can't tell whether the feeling is for or against her. Eventually, Tain strides over to the dust-caked organ that is centuries old – almost as old as the church itself. He lifts the lid and crashes a fist upon the keyboard. The most unearthly noise bursts in a cloud of dust from the organ pipes and stuns the crowd into silence.

'Remember who this young woman is!' Tain thunders. 'Remember who her grandmother was – Mary Bell, a woman whose vision and hard work helped this island survive at a time when we all thought that was impossible.'

A murmuring fills the church as the older people remember.

Mara blushes uncomfortably and shoots a glance at her mother. But the look on her face isn't what Mara expected at all. Suddenly Rosemary begins to push through the crowd and stands beside Mara on the stone altar.

'You all know that my mother was a woman of unusual courage and vision.' Rosemary sounds breathless, as if she has run up a huge flight of steps, but her quick voice rings clearly through the church. 'She worked endlessly for what was best for this island – so that we would all have a future.' Rosemary pauses, steadies herself, then gives Mara a look of deep pride. 'My daughter is made of the same stuff as my mother,' she declares. 'You should believe in her.'

Mara turns to her mother in surprise. 'You believe in the New World?'

'I believe in *you*,' says her mother.

Tain grasps Rosemary's hand.

'I think that swayed it,' he murmurs, keenly scanning the faces in the hushed church. 'We'll take a vote now.'

It is decided. In two days they will set out for the New World while the summer seas are calm and steady, before another storm or sea surge hits. But there's no way of forecasting the weather, no way of knowing if a storm will strike on the voyage, and no guarantee that they will find New Mungo or reach it safely.

People wonder fearfully if the island's fishermen have the skills to navigate the perils of a great ocean when they have only ever fished the seas close to Wing. The journey might take as long as a week, they reckon, but will there be enough room in the crammed fishing boats for all the water and food and provisions they will need? The talk is all about the sea journey but not about what lies beyond it, because no one can imagine what life in a New World city, high above the ocean, could possibly be like.

The last day on the island feels like a dream. Tomorrow they will set out on a perilous journey into the future, yet today everyone still tends to the animals and farm holdings as always – they stack the peat and prepare meals just as they always have. They don't know what else to do, thinks Mara, and neither does she, so she meets up with Gail and Rowan and they climb up to the standing stones to sit upon the ancient rock and look at the endless sea and sky. It's what they've always done on midsummer nights when their northern sky stays light all night long; a strange, forget-me-not sky that is the same intense blue as the wild flowers that once scattered the drowned field of windmills.

But now, the sight of all that empty ocean is too hard to bear.

As they walk home, Gail is talking up a huge, ridiculous fairy tale for their future but Mara and Rowan are quiet, looking all around, saying impossible goodbyes to every rock, every stone, every weed and wildflower that remains.

'What are you taking?' asks Gail. 'I've lost almost everything – all the beautiful clothes I made over the winter. Mara, can you give me something decent to wear in the New World?'

Rowan shakes his head, a comical look of disgust on his face. But Mara laughs, glad to have a bit of Gail's feather-brained chatter to lift the desperate mood. Only Gail could think about clothes at a time like this.

'Hmm,' Mara frowns. 'Something that travels well and won't crease too much in the crush of thirty people in a fishing boat.'

'It's important!' Gail declares. 'What if we land up in some great new city looking like gawky peasants?'

Suddenly Gail is in tears, choking on loud sobs. Mara hugs her friend tight, knowing Gail is not really a feather-brain at all: the frantic chatter is just her way of blocking out a nightmare.

'Let's go,' Rowan says heavily and he puts an arm round his twin. 'See you tomorrow, Mara.'

'Yes,' says Mara, but she can't imagine tomorrow. She

watches her two friends head towards their makeshift shelter in the church, then turns for home.

When she gets home her mother is weeding and watering their small vegetable field, clinging to every last scrap of her life here on the island for as long as she can.

'Find us some music, Mara!' Rosemary calls out, so Mara runs upstairs and powers up her cyberwizz to zoom into the Weave. Quickly, she locates the flickering tower-stack that's packed to the brim with all kinds of music, selects a soaring waltz from its electronic catalogue and zips back into realworld where she connects the sound-site up to an ancient speaker in her bedroom. She opens her window and lets the rousing music float out over Wing and the surrounding sea.

Downstairs, Mara grabs Corey by the hands and leads him round and round the garden in a dance until he is full of giggles. Rosemary sings along in her clear voice, smiling at the two of them – then, all of a sudden, her face crumples and she goes inside. Mara follows her into the kitchen and watches her mother plant herb cuttings in a tiny pot. The room is full of the green, mind-clearing aroma of her namesake, rosemary. She has tied it in bunches to dry over the fire. Mara knows why. Her grand-mother seeded that plant on the day Mara's mother was born. Rosemary won't leave without taking it with her to their new life. Mara plucks a small bunch of dried rose-mary and tucks it in the pocket of her jeans as she looks out of the kitchen window at her father, who is setting the sheep and the goats and their two horses running free on the hillside.

Later that evening, Mara downloads a movie she once found in the Weave – an adventure story of heroes and strange lands, with a comfortingly safe and happy ending.

She puts the glowing halo upon her little brother and lets him enjoy the story as he lies snug in his bed.

At sundown, despite the heat, the islanders light their fires. No one is sure why, but they do, and so, on the last evening, the people of Wing fill the air with the earthy peat smoke that has filled its winter nights, time before memories, time out of mind.

Mara knows she will remember this day, every detail of it, as long as she lives.

'Go now, Mara,' says Tain. 'Go. Find a new future.'

He pushes her towards the boats: every fishing boat and ferry, every sea-strong vessel the island owns. They knock together, rocking on strong wave surges.

Mara's family begins to board a boat that looks too full to take anyone else.

'Come on, Mara!' her father shouts urgently but she stands stubbornly beside Tain. The rest of the old folk stand on the hill beside the sea, dead-eyed but dignified.

'I won't go until Tain does!' she shouts back. 'There *must* be room for everyone. We'll have to *make* room.' All around her and in the boats people lower their gaze from her furious, accusing look. All except for her mother. Precariously, she stands up in her place in the boat and tries to push back through the crush of people on deck to get to Mara.

There are to be no old ones on the boats. It has all been decided but Mara can't believe it. She *won't* believe it. They cannot leave the old ones on the drowning island.

'We've had all the time in the world to prepare for this and we never made sure we had enough boats? We might at least have done that.' Mara clutches at Tain's sleeve as she did when she was his little helper. But she can't help Tain now. She feels useless.

Gail's father, Alex, the skipper of the last boat, is shame-faced and desperate. 'There's no room, Mara. Look for yourself. You tell me who to leave – the old ones or the children? The brown-eyed or the blue?' Alex lowers his voice. 'Listen to me. This is going to be a long and perilous journey. Those old ones won't make it. And what about once we get there? How would somebody like Tain manage in one of those cities? But they say they don't want to come anyway – they want to stay here.'

Mara glares at Alex with blazing eyes. Tain is furiously ordering her to go, right this second. Gail is pleading with Mara to jump on board with her family. Her mother is raging at Mara, raging at the crush of people around her who block her way.

'Tain is the last person who should be left!' cries Mara. 'He warned us all about this. He told us to prepare. We never listened and now he's been proved right, we're leaving him here to drown? It's not right! The ones who wouldn't listen, who said we didn't need to do anything, that this would never happen – they should be left behind before Tain!'

Mara hears a scream. Her mother's. She spins around and is drenched by sea spray. A large wave has hit the boats and they rock wildly, crashing each other. Some have already pulled away, a small exodus scattering the ocean. Mara can still hear her mother's cries and franti-cally she scans the few boats still at the edge of the waves.

No!

Her family's boat has pulled out on the wave surge. There is suddenly an expanse of sea between them – too far to jump. Already the boat is fogged in clouds of peat-smoke from the boat funnels.

'No, wait!' Mara cries. 'Please wait!'

She didn't mean this to happen. Mara tries to focus on her mother's face. She can't see her father or Corey at all, but she can hear her little brother's agonized wail.

'I'll see you in the city!' she sobs but the chug of the boats muffles her cry. In moments they are out of earshot, beyond reach.

The boat fades amid sea spray and smoke. Sobbing with shock, Mara turns to Tain, who looks stricken, blaming himself. Frail though he is, he lifts her bodily on to the last boat where Gail and her mother grab her and pull her on board beside them. Mara can't seem to let go of Tain's hand. In the moment before the boat pulls away she pushes her face into the sleeve of his oilskin jacket and breathes in the scents of the sea, the cheeses and the peat that are so much part of him, of her, of the island.

'I was born here and I'll die here,' says Tain gently, firmly. 'This is where I want to be.'

He juts out his craggy chin. And now Mara sees that Tain is speaking the truth. He doesn't want to come to the New World. The fear and hope that shine in his dark eyes are for Mara and all the others in the boats, not for himself.

The journey south will be treacherous. Maybe no one will survive it. Maybe they won't find the New World – the island's fishermen have tried to map out navigation charts using compasses and the pattern of the sun and the stars and Mara's screen map of New Mungo, but they can only hope that their calculations are accurate. And even if they do get there, who really knows what kind of life lies out there beyond the horizon? What kind of life could an eighty-year-old man make in a strange New World?

Tain will stay on the island he's never left, not once, since the day he was born. All his memories and stories and knowledge, all that he is, will disappear with the island when it is swallowed by the ocean.

The old ones begin to climb the hillside to the church that will now be their home, as the refugee boats struggle against an incoming tide, abandoning their island and the last of its people to the sea.

CITY IN THE SKY

Many times, in the long days and nights of the journey south, Mara is sure they will never make it. The ocean is a ferocious, swallowing beast. Somehow, Alex steers them up over huge, rolling walls of waves, across moving mountains of sea. Mara dreads each new wave; dreads the horrendous death-ride into a deep, dark valley, then the huge surge upwards into a white cliff-face of ocean. The wooden boat cracks and groans loudly, its timbers strained to their limit under the massive force of the waves. Mara grips the cold ship's rail until her fingers grow numb, her stomach churning with fear and sea sickness. She keeps her face turned to the seething black well of the ocean. Spray stings her face, crusts her eyes with salt, but she keeps looking out, cannot turn away. There's been no sign of the other boats in days. Mara's terror is so great she can hardly contain it. She knows that Jamie, the skipper of her family's boat, is much less experienced than Alex. The lives of her family lie in the hands of a novice skipper.

She longs to put her head down and sleep and not wake up until they find the New World – but that's impossible in a heaving boat, amid the crush of so many bodies. It becomes hard to believe that the journey will ever end, that the wails of the children will ever quieten, that the awful sea sickness will ever stop, that she will feel solid ground beneath her feet ever again.

The crush on board means that there wasn't room enough for sufficient provisions of food and water. They finished the last scraps of food yesterday and there's hardly any water rations left – just enough for the babies and the very youngest children. Everyone is praying that they reach the city today. They must. Months of meagre food rations during the storm months on the island have weakened them all more than they realized. No one has much strength left. And no one has ever experienced terrifying seas like these.

Trembling and fuzzy-headed from sickness, lack of sleep, hunger and dehydration, Mara begins to drift in a hazy trance. Gail is crammed beside her, their bodies so close and intertwined that the other girl's spasms of sickness, her listless fear, even her aching, restless limbs, feel like an extension of her own. Rowan, who began the journey full of tales and stories to pass the time, is crushed up next to his twin, his blue eyes glazed, his mouth too dry and sore to let him talk any more.

At dawn next morning Mara is suddenly shaken out of her daze.

'Look up ahead!' Alex shouts. He stares shock-eyed across the ocean.

All around her people are waking up and crying out in fright. Weakly, Mara struggles upright and looks out, but all she can see is ocean.

'There!' Gail cries in a parched voice. Trembling, she clutches Mara's arm and points.

The most colossal structure rises out of the ocean, swathed in mist.

Mara swallows. She can't seem to find her voice. Her throat feels full of stones.

Vast towers unwrap from the dawn mist. Towers so thick and high it's hard to believe they are real. As the boat draws closer the thinning mist reveals a stunning geometry of sky tunnels that connect the towers – branches and branches of gleaming connections. A molten sunrise spreads fire across the sky. When it hits the city like a silent explosion the brilliance is heart-stopping. The morning sun seems pale beside such radiance.

'That's it!' Mara croaks. 'That's New Mungo.'

People murmur in fear; some cry. But Mara feels blank as she looks at the stupendous vision. She doesn't know what she feels about that immense city in the sky. All she can think of is stepping out on to solid ground, stretching her cramped limbs – and finding her family.

As they draw closer and the last of the mist clears, Mara sees with a sinking heart what she always suspected would be there – an immense wall. It rises up out of the sea, encircling the city.

There is no land or harbour, only a blurred mass that heaves and bobs around the city. A huge, dull-coloured live thing. The vile, rotting stench of an open drain hits as the clustering thing sharpens into focus. Mara gasps as she sees it's a heaving mass of humanity. A chaos of refugee boats crams the sea around the city and clings like a fungus to the huge wall that seems to bar all entry to refugees.

Frantically, Mara begins to scan the still-distant mass of boats for her family. *Why* was she so stubborn? Why didn't she go with them?

'Where are they, Gail?' she panics. 'They'll have made it, won't they?'

She sees the look that passes between Gail and Rowan. She pictures her mother with Corey clutched close, her keen eyes searching, searching, searching for Mara; her father cursing her stubbornness, refusing to believe he has lost her.

Alex steers them towards the chaos of boats around the city. People huddle closer on the fishing boat that is now their home. The sense of loss is overwhelming.

'Heads down!' Alex suddenly yells.

A bulky, thuggish-looking, black speedboat roars out from behind the legs of an impossibly high sea bridge that stretches out into the ocean, then suddenly breaks off, unfinished. The speedboat, emblazoned with the words SEA POLICE and crammed with an armed, orange-uniformed police crew, cuts in front, its sirens blaring. A huge gun barrel glints above the bow windscreen. Now a fleet of orange waterbikes zips across the waves to encircle them. The speedboat fixes its large gun on Mara's boat, while the police waterbikers swivel their handlebar guns into position.

They are surrounded.

'Turn back! Turn back at once!' a harsh megaphone voice commands.

Alex looks petrified but stays on course – there's nowhere to turn back to. He even keeps his nerve as the waterbikers send thundercracking volleys of machine-gun fire overhead, in warning.

Then he cries out in horror and begins frantically wheeling the boat around.

'*Get down!*' he roars.

Mara can't see what's happening. But she hears something howl through the air, feels it hit the water close by, then is rocked by a terrifying force as a missile explodes in the sea.

The boat fills with screams. Mara struggles to prise herself from the crush, tries to jump overboard, desperate to escape. But there is no escape. She grips the rim of the boat and squeezes her eyes tight shut. *'Mum! Dad! Help me!'* she screams, but her voice is lost in the wave of panic.

There is the strangest lull. The boat lurches on a wave and Mara waits for the hit. The moment stretches – enormous, empty, dark and still. *I'm dead*, thinks Mara. *It's happened. It's over.* She opens her eyes. She is still in the boat. There's no screaming missile, no explosion, nothing. Then –

'They're going!' shouts Alex, his voice cracking with relief.

And it's true. The sea police have about-turned and are speeding off in another direction. Then Mara sees what has deflected them – a bigger target. A fleet of boats has appeared on the southern horizon and it's this that the police battalion is headed for. Alex takes his chance to steer hastily towards a mooring place on the edge of the boat camp that stretches far into the waters around the city.

'What were they going to do – kill us all?' Rowan whispers, his face grey, his eyes wide and unfocused with shock.

The shock deepens as they begin to enter the vast boat camp.

'I don't like this, don't like it,' Gail is muttering feverishly, like a small child. 'I want to go home, Mum. Oh, please, let's turn back and go home.'

Fishing boats, ferries, rusted military craft, once-luxurious cruisers, old and battered pleasure crafts and bashed yachts, all kinds of vessels, even ramshackle handmade rafts with patchwork sails; rich and poor, all ages, all kinds of people, are crushed here into a common pulp of human misery. The sea runs red with sunrise, the water steams, the noise and stench are terrible.

This is unreal, thinks Mara. It's hell on Earth.

'Where are they all from?' she whispers.

'Who knows?' says Rowan.

Alex nudges their boat into the crush.

'You'll have to move on – this is our space and it's too crowded already!' shouts a raucous voice. 'There's no room for anyone else.'

The owner of the voice is a furious woman who stands at the helm of what once must have been a sleek, luxurious yacht. Now it's dirty and battered, its deck overhung with a patchwork canopy of plastic bags and tatty tarpaulin. Grime has settled into the harsh, ungenerous lines of the woman's face.

'Where else can we go?' demands Brenna, one of Mara's mother's friends, staring back just as furiously. 'There's no room anywhere.'

'Should have got here earlier then, shouldn't you?' the woman snaps. 'It's your own fault.'

An ugly, unwelcoming grumble grows as the inhabitants of the surrounding boats stare resentfully from their ram-shackle floating homes. Some shout abuse, some even fling filthy waste at the new arrivals. Steely eyed, Alex continues to steer into the edges of the boat camp. There's nothing else he can do; there's nowhere else to go but the open ocean.

Mara puts her head upon her knees. She screws her eyes tight shut and puts her fists over her ears to block out the horror of the refugee camp. But she can't. The putrid, stomach-turning stench of sewage, sweat and sickness is overwhelming.

Although she's frail and shattered from the journey, and despite the surrounding hostility, Gail manages to strike up a conversation with a boy on the rickety boat next door. Gail could charm words out of a stone, if she wanted to. After a while, the familiar sound of her friend's chatter calms Mara just enough to let her lift her head from her knees and survey the noisy, frightening chaos she now belongs to. And she must look, she tells herself, she must look hard and keep looking till she finds her family.

'Ask about food and fresh water, Gail,' cries Brenna, struggling to cope with her brood of hungry and restless young children. 'Find out where we get them.'

After a few moments Gail turns round from the neighbouring boat, her face pale and scared.

'It's hopeless.' Gail slumps down on the deck. Everyone stares across the boats to the impenetrable wall of New Mungo.

'There must be some kind of aid from the city,' says Rowan. 'They can't keep us out here with no food and water.'

'Of course they can,' cries Brenna, nursing a limp and pale toddler. 'Why should they care? We should have stayed with the old folk on the island, all together, where we belonged. We'll die anyway in these rotten seas.'

I wish we had stayed on the island too, Mara silently cries, as an outburst of panic and anger explodes around her. *Anything but this*.

In the midsummer night that never quite grows dark, New Mungo cloaks itself in mist. Its shadows lengthen across the water and the people of the boats grow quiet as the city's brilliance turns sinister, menacing. While the other refugees huddle under mothy tarpaulins, plastic coverings and blankets, Mara jumps from boat to boat, calling desperately for her parents, peering through the dim twilight for the arrival of any new boats.

The city glints under the midsummer blue of a star-sprinkled sky. It's awesome, beautiful, an impossible thing. Mara gazes up, puzzling over the many strange, coiling mechanisms attached to the edges of the towers and the sky tunnels. They whirl in the wind, filling the air with ghostly moans and whispers. As she studies the vast geometry of the city, she feels a spark of her old curiosity. What kind of people could dream up such a thing?

Whoever they are, the cyberfox is one of them.

Where are you, Fox? she wonders. *Are you really up there? How can I get up there too? And if I did, would I ever be able to find you?*

In the middle of the night there's a clamour that sounds like the end of the world. Mara wakens with a start from her cocoon of blanket. A great swarm of police speedboats and waterbikes buzz around the city wall. Lights flash, sirens scream. Everyone is looking out to sea and as Mara looks too she sees the lights of a great white ship. As it draws close to the city the police send volleys of gunfire into the sky as a warning. Everyone keeps their heads down but as Mara peers upwards from the floor of the boat she sees a crack open in the city wall. The crack widens and Mara cannot help it – she stands up to look.

'Get down!' Rowan yells but Mara stays standing. She wants to see what's happening.

Great reels of sea crash them into the boat next door

and Mara has to hang on tight to the edge of hers. Chaos has broken out at the widening crack in the wall. In the few moments that the gate is open a number of refugee boats make a frantic surge forward as the ship, surrounded by swarms of machine-gunning sea police, enters the city. The refugee boats are either gunned into the great wall or into nearby craft. Some smash to pieces against the side of the ship.

'Why don't they just let us in?' Gail whimpers. 'I'm so hungry. Doesn't anyone care about us?'

'Maybe they don't even know we're here,' says Rowan grimly.

'How could they not know?' Mara despairs. 'All they have to do is look down and see. Why don't they do something?'

But she wonders if Rowan is right. Are the people of the sky city so bedazzled by their glittering New World that they can't see beyond it to the human catastrophe right outside their wall? Do they not know what is happening? But somebody knows, because somebody built that city wall.

'Look!' Mara cries as she sees something – the tiniest vessel, so tiny she almost missed it – slip through at the very last moment in the churning foam of the ship's wake.

Is it possible then? At the risk of being shot to pieces or smashed up by a supply ship, maybe there *is* a way in to the city.

ILL WIND BLOWS

Slow hours roll into stunned daylight, every second hot and breathless, drenched in steaming mist.

Gail groans weakly. 'Mum, I'm going to be sick again.'

It was the fish. Everyone is blaming themselves for not stopping her from eating the small, sun-roasted fish the boy on the neighbouring boat caught in the filthy water that's full of toxic algae. The smell of the fish turned Mara's stomach, but her insides groaned and ached so much for food that she wanted to do what Gail did: hold her nose and tear into the stinking fish, eating head, bones, eyes and all.

All through the night Gail was wracked with stomach pains, and violently sick. On the neighbouring boat, everyone who ate the catch of toxic fish was just as ill.

Around dawn, Gail began to chatter and they were all relieved, thinking she was beginning to recover. But her chatter has grown into an unstoppable, hot-fevered raving. Now, though she still mutters feverishly, her voice has become thin and shrill like a child's and her body has grown chilled and rigid. More than anything, Mara is scared by the distant look in her friend's eyes.

'Should have cut my hair before we left, shouldn't I?' Gail whimpers, pulling restlessly at a strand of her fringe. Kate strokes her daughter's hand, helplessly. 'And look at my nails, all dirty,' Gail frets. 'I'm such a mess.'

Mara turns away, unnerved by Gail's delirious state, to look back at the scatter of new arrivals in the boat camp. Since first light, her eyes have been fixed on the horizon or scanning the crush of boats, straining for a glimpse of her family's boat.

'I'm going to look for Mum and Dad and Corey,' Mara whispers to Rowan. 'And I'll try to find some safe food.'

'I'll come too,' says Rowan heavily. He can't bear seeing Gail so ill. All through the long night Mara could hear him telling Gail stories from the books he read on Wing. He wouldn't stop even when Gail fell asleep and, as she listened to his hoarse, parched voice from under her blanket, Mara knew Rowan was trying to believe that his storytelling would keep his twin alive.

Sometimes food and water are thrown haphazardly at the refugees from the supply ships, but it's never enough and people are forced to eat whatever fish and seaweed and shellfish they can find in the filthy, toxic seas that surround the boat camp. People get ill all the time because the sea is full of sewage. Those who try to fish farther out risk losing their place in the camp or being gunned down by the sea police, who strive to contain existing refugees within the confines of the camp, as well as barring entry to new arrivals. Some people make spears and arrows out of driftwood and manage to kill the odd seagull. Rain is gathered in anything that can be made to hold water. But there hasn't been rain for days now. Gail, who was so skinny people always joked she'd blow away in a strong gust, now looks as if the smallest whisper of wind would carry her off. But

80

there's no more wind than there is rain, just the heavy, damp, heat – the kind of heat that breeds disease.

'What's that?' Mara asks Rowan as a small, tightly bound bundle of blankets is passed through the boats, from hand to hand.

'It's a death,' says Rowan flatly. 'They burn them on the sea.'

Mara stares in horror at the child-sized bundle. She hadn't realized that's what the strange fires on the seas around the boat camp were.

'Find water, Rowan,' Kate pleads. 'Gail needs water. Your dad tried to find some earlier but he's exhausted.'

So Rowan and Mara begin a long, precarious journey around the boats, leaping from one to another, calling all the time for Mara's parents. They try to map out the boat camp in their heads but it's impossible – the human flotsam is too vast. Mara tells herself that her family will be searching just as hard for her. Sooner or later they must find one another.

Finally thirst and hunger get the better of them. Mara rummages in her backpack for something to trade for a bottle of water. Her cyberwizz is safely sealed in a watertight pocket, but she can't bear to part with that. Who would want it anyway? What good is it now? All anyone wants is food and water. Mara looks up at the city, watching the strange spirals that glint through the heat haze, whirling lazily in the soft breath of a breeze. Once again she wonders about the cyberfox and his whereabouts in that colossal city. She longs to be up there in the clear air, away up out of this hellish place.

The cyberwizz might yet be the key. It might be her only possible link to the one who could help her: the fox. So she must hold on to it. But a watch can only tell you how slowly time drags in the land of nightmare. Mara pulls her watch from her wrist and manages, after some pleading, to exchange it for a plastic flask of rainwater. She means to put the flask in her backpack and take it straight back to their boat, she really does. But her thirst is so savage that she tears off the top of the flask and gulps the water – great gulps that spill precious trickles down her chin and neck, and she has to force herself to stop and leave some for Gail and the others.

Rowan is trading his penknife for two containers of water. Shamed, Mara watches him take one single, controlled gulp from a bottle, then seal it again. The rest of the water he leaves for his sister and parents.

When they get back to their boat they are both hailed as heroes for bringing fresh water. Alex and some of the others are breaking off bits of wood from the boat to make harpoons, in the hope of catching seagulls, which must be safer, Alex reckons, than the fish. Gail struggles to swallow a few sips of water and again Mara feels ashamed of her desperate gulps, when she didn't care about anyone or anything other than her own thirst. And suddenly Mara is overwhelmed by the horror of it all. Mixed with that horror is a worse emotion – her own guilt. If she hadn't made everyone believe in the New World they wouldn't be here. The weight of guilt is so awful she can't bear it, so Mara huddles under her blanket and lets sleep, a huge wave of it, fall upon her.

When at last, hours later, she rouses and unbundles herself from the blanket she finds she is looking at the world with eyes and a head so sharp and clear it's as if she has crystallized into a shard of glass.

'Maybe it's hunger,' says Rowan. 'Hunger can sharpen you like nothing else.'

I must use this sharpness, Mara decides, and she takes the sprig of dried rosemary that's been tucked in her pocket and inhales its green, mind-clearing scent. With her new, clear senses she focuses on the curious splashings around the thick legs of the great bridge that reaches out east, and suddenly stops, unfinished, in mid-ocean.

'They're like water rats,' says Rowan, following Mara's gaze. 'Human water rats. I've been watching them since we got here.'

'Gail, look!' says Mara, gently urging her. Kate shakes her head and stops Mara. Gail doesn't stir. Mara bites her lip and whispers 'Sorry,' but Kate only glares at her.

Mara turns away, stricken by Kate's look. Her eye is caught by a mass of children who are playing around the legs of the sea bridge on metal bin lids, bathtubs, tyres, old doors – all sorts of odd junk rafts and vessels. At the sudden blare of a police siren the water rat children rush for the bridge legs like iron filings to a magnet, and disappear.

'Those bridge legs, are they hollow?' Mara puzzles.

'Must be,' says Rowan. 'Unless those kids are magicians.'

Mara almost smiles. It's the first real beat of life she's found in the world since she left her drowning island. What an impossible idea – a warren of water rat children living in the hollow legs of a sea bridge. *Who are they? Where are their parents?* Mara wonders, then realizes these wild urchins probably don't have any parents. They are the orphaned castaways of the drowned world.

Later, when one of the children skids skilfully across the waves on a tiny bin-lid raft, like a mucky cherub in a tin can, she does smile. She watches the child spin and flit across the waves, practising complicated manoeuvres.

When he crashes out of a spin and falls in the water laughing, Mara finds she is laughing too.

'They're not water rats,' she tells Rowan. 'Little sea urchins, that's what they are.'

Sun burns on the sky city and Mara's flicker of hope flames into a sudden bright image of a life up in New Mungo where there is no hunger or filth or disease. *I won't stay in this nightmare any longer,* she decides. *I must move, must act. I will find my family, then somehow I'll find the cyberfox and he'll help us get into the city and we'll make a life up in the New World.*

'We must get out of this, Rowan,' says Mara. 'We'll all die if we stay put.'

'Shoes,' Gail cries weakly from inside the woolly cocoon of blanket she has pulled up around her. 'I need some decent shoes. I can't go to the New World with these ratty things on.'

Kate looks down at her daughter with tears in her eyes. Rowan gives a sudden shuddery sob. Mara reaches over and feels Gail's forehead. It's burning hot. Gail's eyes are shut tight yet she chatters on. Mara looks around her and sees how they have all changed. Gail's mother looks twenty years older than she did on the island, her face grey and lined with despair; Alex has shrivelled to an old man, weary with defeat. Rowan is so begrimed he looks as if he has a deep tan. Mara runs her fingers through her own matted hair and feels the horrible sweaty filth on her skin. Can it really be just a week since they left the island?

'Come on, Gail. Wake up!' Mara shakes her. Gail is slipping away before her eyes and there's nothing she can do. But still she must try. 'Wake up now! We're going to get out of here.'

Gail only huddles deeper under her blanket, chattering

feverishly about all the things she'll do once they get back home.

'Leave her be. There's no way out,' mutters Kate. Mara hears the resentment in her voice. Kate hadn't wanted to leave the island and now they are trapped in a refugee camp with Gail desperately ill, all because of Mara's belief of sanctuary in the New World. Trembling, Mara tries to hold back tears.

The city gates open once again to let in a fleet of sea police. Mara scrubs away her tears to watch a mass of sea urchins make a reckless dash from their hideouts in the bridge legs. She holds her breath and keeps score. Umpteen crashes and near misses, at least five or six shot in the water. Only one, maybe two, get in. Lousy odds, yet it's still a better chance of survival than staying here in the boat camp.

When she turns back, a terrible stillness has fallen on the boat. Alex and Kate are crouched over Gail who has suddenly stopped chattering. Rowan is staring in horror at the blanket that contains his twin.

'What is it? What's wrong?' Mara grips Rowan's hand.

Alex stands up. His red-blond hair and beard seem to catch fire in the sunlight. In silence, as if words are beyond him or not enough, he raises his fists to the sky city.

The sun slips behind a cloud. Surrounding boats have fallen quiet and everyone seems to be holding their breath, waiting. A small wind blows.

Mara pushes forward and wraps her arms around Gail.

'Stay,' she begs the girl who has been her friend for as long as she can remember. She only just catches the words Gail struggles to whisper before the tiny gust of wind carries her friend away.

'Keep going and never stop.'

THE BIG BEAT

A new exodus appears on the western horizon at daybreak. As it draws closer a murmur grows among the refugees in the boat camp. *No room, no room*, says the murmur, once the size of the fleet becomes clear. The murmur grows until it sounds like a single, surly voice.

'Aren't they the ones who followed the supply ships?' someone cries. Now people stare even more hopelessly at the fleet heading towards them. If they have returned here that can only mean one thing: there's no sanctuary to be found in the place the supply ships come from.

A battalion of sea police rushes from the city gates, alerted by the scale of the fleet, and sends out volleys of gunfire. The procession is forced on past the city. As the boats pass, guilt settles on the camp like a pall of thick mist.

'Where will they go now?' people whisper. No one knows.

Mara strains to watch the line of boats until they disappear. Shaking with emotion she wants to scream out but they would never hear her. What if her family was on one of those boats? She clasps her hands together in a gesture that belongs to her mother and wills them to return. But they don't.

Later, a new hope sweeps round the boats like a fresh breeze. The Pickings have begun again. No one can tell Mara exactly what the Pickings are, but every few weeks the sea police circle the boat camp and select the young, fit and strong at gunpoint. Then they take them into the city. '*Me! Me! Take me!*' people plead, desperate to win entry to the New World. '*Take my son, my daughter, my baby . . .*'

But there are a few people who can't say why they feel in their bones that the Pickings might not be what they seem.

Mara can't say why either but she feels that same sinister chill in her bones when the Pickers approach, and hides under a blanket, pretending to be weak and sick. Once she has found her family, only then does she want entry to a new life in the city. Beside her, Kate's voice joins the clamour.

'Take my son!' she pleads. 'Look, he's young and fit and strong!'

But Rowan pulls his mother down and quietens her.

'I won't go,' he insists. And he huddles back under his blanket.

Once the Pickers are gone, Mara gets to her feet. She is determined to search the whole of the boat camp until she finds her family. She can't stay here. Kate can hardly bear to look at her, blaming Mara for the terrible thing that happened last night.

Mara keeps telling herself that it didn't happen at all.

It was such a small death. Light as a child, the bundle in the blanket that couldn't possibly be Gail was passed ever so gently, hand to hand, through the boats until it reached the sea. The bundle was placed upon a plank of driftwood, and set alight upon the waves, like so many others. And it became a beautiful thing, a sea star that blazed in the water. Mara saw it happen yet she cannot believe it was real – that the blazing bundle was Gail.

Wide awake all through the long night, she found herself repeating Gail's last words over and over like a mantra. *Keep going and never stop.* She will keep going and never stop, Mara vows, until she finds her family. There's nothing else she can think of to do. She seals up the few belongings she owns in her small backpack. Then turns to Rowan who is huddled, distraught, deep inside his blanket.

'Come with me,' she urges. 'Please, Rowan.'

Rowan barely opens his eyes. 'I can't leave them,' he says, meaning his parents.

'If you stay here, you'll *die*,' she says brutally, to make him see. Then in a whisper, 'Rowan, this is all my fault.'

'No. Don't think that.'

'Gail would still be alive if we hadn't come.'

'We had to leave. It isn't your fault.' Rowan reaches out, squeezes her hand then shuts his eyes.

'Please come with me,' Mara begs. 'I think I might have seen a way through to the city—'

'Haven't you done enough damage – you and your silly ideas!' Kate bursts out.

Mara gets to her feet quickly, unable to meet Kate's bitter glare.

'I won't forget you,' she whispers to Rowan. 'I'll come back for you. I promise I will.'

Mara leans to stroke his cheek, tucks the remains of her bottle of water inside his blanket and leaves.

After a whole day, she still hasn't completed a circuit

of the boat camp. She measures her progress against the position of the sun in the sky. Mara has shouted for her family until she is hoarse, scanning each boat, aching for the glimpse of a face, a hand, or a clump of hair that is as familiar as her own. Exhaustion eventually grinds her to a halt. She could spend the rest of her life in this useless, circling quest. Surely her family are searching for her too; surely they should have found each other by now. Mara tries to control the awful terror that is growing inside her.

'Mara!' shouts a voice. A voice she knows. She searches the boats for a familiar face.

'Here, over here!' It's Ruth, her island neighbour, almost unrecognizable now. Frantically, Mara clambers over the boats to get to her.

'My mum and dad – are they here?' cries Mara as Ruth hugs her, with difficulty – she is so heavily pregnant.

Ruth bites her lip and shakes her head. 'But you are,' she cries. 'That's good news.'

'But they'll be here somewhere, Ruth, won't they?'

Ruth looks away.

'We have to tell her, Ruth.' Quinn, her father's old friend, stands up. 'There's no use in her keeping up false hopes.'

'Tell me what?' gasps Mara, though all her instincts tell her that she doesn't want to hear the answer.

Ruth still can't meet Mara's eyes. 'I'm so sorry, Mara. It was on the second day of the journey here. We tried to turn back for survivors, really we did. But the waves were like mountains.' Mara stares at her, remembering those terrifying waves. 'Your mum and dad's boat overturned in one of those waves,' Ruth continues in a broken whisper.

'It sank. Oh, Mara! One moment it was there and then it was – it was gone.'

Jamie would have panicked. Inexperienced Jamie, the novice skipper. He wouldn't have had Alex's skill to steer through such seas.

'I don't believe you,' says Mara flatly. 'They're here. They must be here.'

'And do you think if they were here they wouldn't have ransacked every boat by now to find you?' says Quinn, softly. He puts his arm around Mara.

Now Mara has no way of controlling her terror and grief. Before they set out from Wing she had imagined all sorts of horrors; had even imagined them all lost at sea – but not this. This is far worse. Her family and best friend are dead; yet she is still here, alive in a world where they no longer exist.

'You're young and bright and strong, Mara,' whispers Ruth, holding her hand tight. 'You'll be all right, I just know it. You'll have a good chance in the Pickings. You'll make it into the city. But come and be with us for now. We're your own people. And the baby's almost here. It's due any day now. Stay with me. You're so good with little ones . . .'

Mara hardly hears her. She looks blankly at Ruth, then at the boatful of familiar faces. They are no comfort. Nothing can comfort her. Suddenly she is furious – with herself and the whole world. She has never felt such anger. It gets her to her feet.

'Kate and Alex and Rowan are round the north side of the camp,' she manages to tell Ruth. 'Gail died. Please help them.'

Mara pulls herself away from Ruth and clambers out of the boat. She begins to jump from boat to boat once again, until she reaches the outermost point of the refugee camp. Sea stretches in front and the immense city wall rises high behind. Mara crouches at the rim of the very last boat, tense and ready. The sound of a thousand voices moaning in sickness and despair carries round and round the boat camp on a breath of night air and merges with the ghostly whispers of the city's wind spirals.

Now all her fear and grief vanish because, suddenly, Mara is very clear-headed about how she is going to get out of this nightmare. It's easy. All she needs to do is jump. The sea will do the rest because, as she has discovered, the skin that separates life from death is a fragile thing, easily torn; a membrane as thin as a moth-wing.

And she will tear through it now.

A sudden burst of laughter makes her start – a high, rough, childish laugh. An urchin spins past on a round metal vessel. Masses of sea urchins are splashing around the bridge legs and just for a moment Mara can't help peering through the dimness to watch their antics. Behind their noise is another sound, one that she heard last night but couldn't begin to think what it was – a savage, tribal beat that, she now realizes, clanks and clangs from behind the city wall. The sound raises the hairs all over her body.

Mara stares up at the massive wall. What lies behind it?

A thunderous racket erupts close by. A colossal, rhythmic, metallic crashing, like a hundred dustbin lids bashing against a brick wall – a noise so loud the shock of it almost topples her into the sea. Yet Mara feels she has been longing to hear such a sound even though she has never known anything like it. It's the heart-stopping clang of something that defies the world and refuses to stop –

the answering crash of the sea urchins on the bridge legs to the mysterious beat behind the city wall.

Again, Mara peers through the midsummer dim and sees the urchins, their fists gripping the oddest assortment of metal junk, attacking the hollow legs of the sea bridge.

In the instant she jumps into the filthy ocean Mara doesn't know if she wants to live or die – but she jumps towards the noise of the beat.

NETHERWORLD

Through me the way to the grieving city . . .
Through me the way among the lost people . . .
Abandon every hope, you who enter.

Inferno, Dante Alighieri

SPIN TO THE CITY

Mara swims; she can't help it.

She tries to stop herself, to still her arms and legs by sheer willpower, but every time she slips beneath the waves some stronger impulse commands her limbs to move and she finds herself swimming across the dark sea.

It's not so easy to die, after all. So Mara gives in to the stronger impulse and begins to swim, hard, until she reaches the great legs of the bridge. All at once she is surrounded by a clattering, crashing wave of sea urchins. They spin around her on car tyres and bin lids, plastic bathtubs and old doors, splashing in her face, prodding and tormenting on and on and on, until at last exhaustion blunts their bullying. Mara feels her body grow numb, her eyes close and now it's easy to slip down beneath the waves.

There is a hard yank on her hair and the pain of it brings her back to her senses. She thrashes out, grabs at something solid, and finds she is face to face with a small urchin in a battered metal raft. Mara recognizes it as an upturned car bonnet.

The urchin sits in his strange craft like a muddy oyster

in an open shell, baby-faced, with dangerous eyes. The skin of his unclothed body is sleek with mud and sea slime. A small sparrow perches on his shoulder. The urchin paddles his car bonnet shell with an upended sign that says *STOP* in peeling red lettering. Again, he grabs Mara's hair and now she grabs her own handful of the urchin's hair and pulls, good and hard.

He lets out a loud wail and the sparrow flutters off in fright. The other urchins stop bashing and prodding her with their makeshift vessels and paddles. And now Mara has a chance to think.

This sea is full of disease. It's an open sewer for the boat camp. I have to get out of it quickly.

Urgency gives her an idea. She pulls off her iceberg pendant – the white quartz stone hung on a plaited strip of leather that Tain made for her. Mara dangles it tantalizingly in front of the child's nose. The urchin gives a yelp and tries to snatch the quartz, almost toppling from the car bonnet in his eagerness, but Mara has the leather plait wound tight around her fingers.

'Oh, no you don't. Not yet.' She raises the stone towards the city in the sky. The urchin stares, mesmerized by the tiny glowing iceberg.

'Do you want it?' Mara whispers urgently. 'Do you?'

The urchin squeals and stares at Mara with large, bright eyes. Mara takes her chance to clamber aboard his metal raft. She places the pendant around the child's neck and he chirps with pleasure.

'If you get me into the city . . .' Mara points to New Mungo, 'you can keep this pretty stone.'

The urchin follows the gestures she makes to accompany her words but he looks blank, as if he doesn't understand. He grunts and pats Mara once or twice as if she is a strange pet he has fished out of the water. Then he grunts again and begins to paddle them across to the bridge leg that is closest to the city gates. He lifts the iceberg quartz to catch the glow of the night sky, gabbling contentedly to himself in high, babyish sounds that don't seem to be words. Mara watches and listens, aching inside as she remembers Corey as a toddler.

In sudden tears, she turns away from the chirping child. He falls silent as her sobs grow. Mara is frightened by the violence of her grief. She never imagined it was possible to feel so afraid, so alone.

And yet, some instinct as strong and powerful as the one that made her swim against her will, says go. Keep going and never stop. It's the only way.

Mara grows calmer. When she scrubs the tears from her eyes she sees the urchin is trying to catch a solitary spider that is weaving a web in a small crack of the bridge leg. Weeds and wildflowers sprout there, and the toxic green algae that breed on the water reach up towards it too. And there's a single blue forget-me-not. It's a tiny miracle, all that life bursting out of such a barren little space. Mara remembers the junkheap she once stumbled across in a tumbledown towerstack of the Weave. In among the junk she had stopped to listen to the disembodied head of a Weave ghost describing a massive volcanic explosion that had devastated a whole island. Krakatoa, wasn't that the name? All life was extinct after the eruption – yet nine months later a spider was found quietly weaving its web on the barren island.

Deep in the night, the bridge leg begins to vibrate. The air fills with the engine noise of an approaching ship. Mara looks across the water and sees the ship's lights.

The urchin's eyes gleam and he fastens Mara's fingers tight to the rim of the raft and pushes her flat. When she protests he bites her, viciously.

I am in charge, the child's eyes and bite tell her.

Chaos breaks out as the ship slices a path through the boat camp. The urchin starts to paddle furiously. Giddily, the makeshift raft begins to spin towards the ship, faster and faster, until they are right alongside it. Wave upon wave drenches Mara and she is sure she will drown or die of sheer terror. Gunfire is close and relentless. But all at once the city wall looms up right in front, stretching high into the night sky. Mara closes her eyes tight just as the great gate begins to slide open – but they'll never make it, they're too close to the ship. The noise of its engines and the force of its movement are terrifying. If they don't crash the ship, they'll crash the wall. It's far too late to turn back now. They are caught in the churning foam of the ship's wake. Mara can only hold on tight and scream.

They surge and spin until Mara feels she must have whirled right out of the world. At long last the terrible spinning calms. Mara opens her eyes to see where they have ended up, but her head is reeling so violently she can still only grip the raft tight until the dizziness settles. Once it does, she gasps in shock.

The gentle dimness of the midsummer night is gone. The huge wall and some new, vast darkness overhead block out the sky and all light.

Disorientated, Mara looks up and sees a patch of still-blue midsummer sky and a single star twinkling through a gap in the great darkness above. Now she knows where she is – right underneath the thick network of New Mungo's sky tunnels. They made it through! She is inside the city wall!

100

'You're a genius,' Mara exclaims to the urchin, staring all around her.

The supply ship is already far beyond them. Mara peers across the great dark sea lake inside the city walls. The ship's lights allow Mara to follow its progress across the water. Judging by the distance it has travelled, the world inside the walls is much more expansive than she ever imagined from outside. She watches the ship slow down, then disappear into some harbour that's impossible to see in the darkness. But now, as her eyes adjust, she begins to pick out the vast trunks of New Mungo's central towers. The supply ships must harbour in them. And somewhere at the foot of those great towers there must also be the entrance to the sky city. Heavily guarded, no doubt. She's probably safe at this distance, but she feels overwhelmed by such vast, surrounding darkness.

Amazingly, the urchin's little bird friend has kept with them during their precarious spin through the city gate and now it hops nervously about the raft. With a shock Mara realizes that the child lies in a heap beside her, unconscious. What happened? She leans over him, struggling to see in the dark. A shadow stains his face. Mara touches it – blood. Now she sees the nasty gash on the side of his head. Don't let it be a bullet wound, she panics. Maybe some bit of junk was churned up in the waves and hit him – or perhaps he lost his balance and dashed his head on the metal raft. She feels for a pulse in the child's thin wrist. It's weak and shaky, but thankfully he's alive.

As she rips up a T-shirt from her backpack to stem the rush of blood from the child's head, Mara wonders what on Earth she is going to do now, in this dark and alien place. The one thing she knows she can't do is abandon a small child who risked his life to get her through the city wall.

WITHIN THE WALL

Desolate, Mara paddles through the dark waters of the netherworld that lies under New Mungo. She tries to think what to do. She never thought beyond her sudden impulse to get through the wall with the urchin, and now that she is here she is badly in need of a plan of action. Should she head for the great towers and attempt to make it up into New Mungo as soon as the urchin recovers? Mara remembers her filthy clothes and hair, feels the thick layer of grime on her skin. Looking like this, she wouldn't stand a chance.

Once again, she feels the urchin's pulse. He hasn't moved, but the pulse is stronger, she's sure. Mara reaches down and tickles his toes. The child's eyes snap open in surprise, though he still lies in a daze in his metal shell.

'You're alive then,' says Mara gently. 'Welcome back to the world.'

The urchin looks at her with limpid eyes. He touches his head and whimpers.

'It'll get better.' Mara pulls a strand of his long, matted hair from his face. Warily, wordlessly, he watches her every movement. Then, shakily, he sits up.

'What's your name? Say something,' Mara urges. 'You look about Corey's age. What age are you? Five? Six?'

He doesn't answer, just chirrups weakly to his sparrow. Mara peels off the blood-soaked T-shirt to have a look at his head but it's almost impossible to see in the dark. His injury can't be too serious or he wouldn't be sitting up, surely? Now the urchin grunts.

'Speak to me,' she pleads. 'Don't just grunt. Can't you speak at all?'

Has he had no one to teach him to speak? No one to look after him? How has he survived?

Now he chirrups, urgently, and stares out in front as if he sees something. Mara looks ahead but sees nothing. Yet as they move deeper and deeper into the netherworld her eyes adjust to the dark and she is able to pick out strange, unfathomable shapes.

'What's that?' she gasps. A huge black arm rises high out of the water. As they pass beneath she realizes it's a broken bridge that ends in mid-air – a bridge to nowhere. Mara catches her breath. It must be a ruin of the old, drowned world that lies beneath New Mungo. Could there be more? She leans over the side of the raft to peer into the black water and jumps back in terror.

Ghosts! There are ghosts under the water!

Mara steadies herself. *Now don't be silly, there are no such things. Keep calm and look again.*

Gingerly, she peers once more over the side of the raft. But they are still there – luminescent, ghostly things moving under the water. She takes a deep breath and forces herself to keep looking, her eyes straining to see in the dark, because there's more, much more. Beneath the silver darting things are all sorts of ghostly shapes and lines of luminescence that glow eerily beneath the waves. Something shifts in Mara's perception and all of a sudden she knows what she is seeing – rooftops and towers and crumbling walls. Right below her is an old, drowned city. It glimmers like a ghostly presence in the sea. And the darting ghosts are only fish, lit by that same, strange luminous light.

'*WHO?*' demands a sudden loud voice. Mara screams in fright. '*WHO YOU? WHO!*'

It's right behind her. Mara cowers in the raft, gripping the urchin, pulsating with fear. Again, she forces herself to look, searching the dark for the source of the voice.

'*WHO!*'

The voice is directly overhead now but still she cannot see anyone or anything. Then all of a sudden she does – it seems to swoop out of nowhere – a white, spectral face with wide, piercing eyes. It moves swiftly and silently through the darkness above her.

'*WHO!*'

'Mara! I'm Mara!' she cries in terror. 'Please – what – who are *you*?'

But there's no answer. The spectral creature vanishes as silently as it came, its ghoulish cry fading into ghostly echoes. Trembling, Mara stares out into the dark. What was it? Some strange creature that belongs to this world within the wall? Or was it – her heart stops at the thought – some phantom of the drowned city?

They paddle on for ages, passing all sorts of shadowy shapes that Mara can't identify. Suddenly the urchin bursts into excited chirps. Mara peers fearfully into the darkness but there's no sign of any more shrieking phantoms. The raft clangs against a pole that sticks out of the water and, as Mara steers away from it, she sees another shadow looming above the water right in front. She blinks, her eyes strained to their limit by the depth of the darkness, her imagination overwrought. What is it? Her heart thumps loudly – then, as before, her perception shifts and she sees that the shadow is nothing to fear. It's just a great hump of land, a solid mass of earth. An island in the drowned city? Does the urchin know something about this place? But he can't tell her, even if he does.

When the raft knocks against the land mass they climb out. Mara reaches down and touches grass. A large building sits on the island's hilltop. She can just make out a soft, flickering glow – this one as warm as the undersea glow was cold – that lights it from within. The urchin has erupted in another delighted, wordless babble.

'It's a church,' Mara tells him as they climb up the hill and she recognizes the solid, familiar outline. But as they draw closer she sees the size of the building and knows it is no ordinary church.

The child is tense, listening to something. Now Mara can hear it too. He twitters and yelps, pulling Mara towards the building's huge wooden doors. But she stops for a moment to read the name carved there.

Glasgow Cathedral

Wondering about the name, Mara follows the urchin through the heavy doors. Once inside, she gazes around at the huge stone interior. Its size reminds her of the Weave towerstacks – all those vast, abandoned halls littered with rotting mountains of electronic junk. But she has never known such a place in realworld. Now, as she stands in the great stone hall amid tall pillars and smashed stained glass windows and alcoves full of statues, Mara sees that a cathedral is a massive church. And Glasgow must be the name of the drowned city.

The cathedral is alight with small bonfires. Swarms of dirt-caked, naked urchins perch upon high window ledges, scramble across tombstones, and scamper among tall pillars. A cathedral full of sea urchins! Mara is laughing, yet her eyes fill with tears as she takes in the sight of all these lost little ones who have made a chaotic home here.

Her own urchin looks up and gives a sudden bright smile. Mara scrubs her eyes clear of tears and lifts a lock of his long, mud-packed hair to look at the head wound in the firelight.

'You'll live,' she tells him.

The light reveals that underneath the mud and slime his skin is tough for such a young child, his whole body covered with sleek hair – thick, seaworthy skin like a water rat or a seal. Mara shudders and takes a step back as, full of curiosity now, the child reaches up to touch her face. She is both drawn and repulsed by this strange little creature.

Don't be silly. He's just a child.

An abandoned little one in a drowned world. And somehow the urchin and his friends are surviving – somehow they've found enough food and this shelter and even learned to make fire.

'I'm Mara,' she tells him. 'My name is Mara.'

Now the urchin touches his own face and looks at Mara intently.

'You've no name? Never mind, I'll give you a name.' Mara wonders what she can call this strange little urchin. The name that springs to her mind is not a child's name but somehow it suits him with his quick, bird-like movements, chirping voice and spindly legs.

'Wing,' she announces. 'That's what I'll call you.'

Wing chirrups and runs off into the noisy mass of wild,

vagabond children. A sudden loud '*WHO!*' makes Mara freeze. She looks up at the vast, vaulted ceiling towards the source of the cry and sees what the white phantom is.

An owl. That's all. There are lots of them, perched high in nooks and ledges in the ancient stone – quite different in colour and marking to the barn owls on Wing. And quite different in voice too, with their loud and eerie hooting. Mara remembers the hissing shrieks of the owls that lived in her barn as they flew on silent wings past her window at night in search of prey.

She sighs with relief and tries to shake off her ghost-terrors. Now she leaves the noisy cathedral to walk across the grassy hill outside, finds a moss-furred slab of stone and sits down to rest and think. All around her the black sea glimmers and flickers with the ghost-light of the drowned city below and the dark reflections of New Mungo looming high above. Beyond the colossal geometry of the new city glows a forget-me-not sky. But Mara falls into an exhausted sleep with her mind upon what might still exist down here, in the drowned ruins.

When day breaks she is still out on the cathedral hilltop, fast asleep upon the thickly mossed stone. The scents and sounds of this strange netherworld under the sky city flow into her exhausted body and gently, unconsciously, she absorbs them. Her eyes are opened at last by a sharp shot of sun that breaks over the top of the city wall. For a while, as the sun climbs above the wall and before it is netted by the thick weave of the sky tunnels, the drowned city is filled with light.

Mara blinks, awake in a moment, and sees the massive trunks of New Mungo emerge from the steamy waters – then she sits up in amazement as the rest of the world within the wall unwraps itself from the early morning mist.

It's huge – even larger than she guessed in the dark. And Mara's heart leaps as she realizes that it's not all sea. Five, six, seven, eight islands are emerging! They lie in a scatter across the great walled circle of netherworld sea, around the vast trunk of New Mungo, as unguarded and forgotten as old secrets.

Some of the islands are tiny, just a few leaps across, but one or two are about the size of Wing's small village. Some are topped with ruins and – Mara gasps in delight – tall clumps of greenery surround the ruins. Trees! She has seen pictures of them in books but she has never seen a real tree before.

And now a mass of tall, dark shapes, like spiky wizard hats, materialize from the mist and float upon the sparkling waters.

Mara rubs her eyes. Then sees the wizard hats for what they really are – the steeples of drowned churches. She laughs and leans back to stretch upon the mossy slab. The bright green moss is soft against her face, the sun warm upon it. There is bee song in the air, or the lazy hum of a small wind. *Nice*, thinks Mara, stroking the soft moss. Beneath the moss there are grooves in the stone. She fingers them and recognizes the pattern of letters – and her heart jumps in horror. *No! Not a gravestone!* But it is. Now she can see the ranks of ancient slabs and tombstones, camouflaged with green moss, all down the grassy hillside.

I've been asleep in a graveyard!

But gnawing hunger and a desperate thirst override her fear. What's so scary about a peaceful graveyard anyway? The living world is far more terrifying. Mara recalls the silly things she used to worry about in her old, ordinary life; all the thrills of the Weave she used to enjoy scaring herself with. She stretches out her exhausted limbs and looks around, wondering where she might find water and food.

Suddenly a shadow falls. Mara turns her head and sees that New Mungo has eclipsed the rising sun. The graveyard takes on an unnerving aspect as gloom robs colour from the netherworld.

Now Mara hears something rush towards her and she can do nothing as it lands upon her with the force of a charging bull.

GORBALS

It's no bull. What has crash-landed upon Mara is a long, lean, boy with a moon-pale face, straw-like hair and wildly tattered clothing. He rolls in the grass beside her, clutching his foot in agony where he stubbed it on the slab of gravestone.

The tatty boy rubs his foot vigorously then puts it in his mouth to ease the pain. As he does so he catches sight of Mara and sits staring at her with the toes of one foot stuck in his mouth. Mara has to laugh.

The boy stares at Mara with wary astonishment. Swiftly, he looks her over, every part of her – hair, clothes, shoes, and finally her face. His eyes are huge, owlish, and their stare unnerves Mara. All she can do is stare back. They look at each other in silence for long moments. At last the boy takes his foot out of his mouth.

'Have you fallen from the sky?' He glances upwards.

Mara shakes her head. 'The sky?'

'The sky city,' the boy says edgily. 'Are you one of the sky people?'

'Oh, no,' says Mara.

His tatty clothing is made from plastic bags of all

colours, knotted and tied around him. Much of the plastic is torn, many of the knots worked loose, which gives him the appearance of a shredded plastic scarecrow.

He sighs with relief and relaxes.

'Who are you then?' he asks in a warm, curious voice.

'Mara,' says Mara.

'Where's that?' asks the youth.

'Where's what?' says Mara.

'Where's Mara?'

Mara stares at him, wondering if he is mad. He looks odd enough. She gets to her feet.

'I'm here,' says Mara. *And now I'm going*, she thinks.

'Wait,' calls the youth and he follows her. 'Don't be strange. I only wanted to know where you come from.'

'I'm not strange. I tell you my name, standing right here in front of you, and you ask where I am. *That's* strange where I come from.'

'Strange? I only asked you, where is Mara? Where is your name-place? Where is the place you are named after? Don't people ask that where you come from?' the youth persists. He steps forward, his plastic tatters rustling. 'My name is Gorbals. My name-place is over there.' Eagerly, he points across the waters of the drowned city. 'You can still see the tips of its towers at low tide. In the old city Gorbals was a place of tall towers – towers that were homes to many, many people. One of them is a foundation tower for the sky city.' His face hardens then he shrugs. 'Still, I'm proud to have its name.'

'I see,' says Mara. 'Well, I'm not named after a place. I was called after my grandmother, Mary, and my mother, Rosemary. I think Mara means bitterness,' she adds, remembering she has never liked that.

Gorbals wrinkles his nose. 'That's ugly,' he says.

111

'Well, it's my name,' says Mara, edging away again. She's not at all sure about this strange boy. Yet she hesitates. At least he can talk, unlike Wing.

'Where is your nest?' he asks wonderingly. His owl eyes grow even wider, as a thought seems to strike him.

He's mad, Mara decides, and turns to go. But as she turns and faces the huge, gloomy lake of the netherworld she remembers she is lost and all alone in this strange place. She hasn't a clue what she is going to do now or how she is going to live. Wing could be anywhere among the mass of urchins who have spilled out of the cathedral to romp among the gravestones. Suddenly Mara is in tears, a great flood of them.

The tattered boy rustles up to her and takes her arm, awkwardly but gently.

'Don't go,' he says. 'Come and meet my people.'

'I'm late again,' groans Gorbals.

They climb off the rickety log raft he has steered across the dim waters, through a cluster of spiky steeples and up to the bank of another island, the largest one that lies furthest from the city gates and the comings and goings of New Mungo. It is topped by a thick grove of tall trees.

'Late for what?' asks Mara, staring in awe at the huge trees that surround the curved ruin of a building that crests the hump of land.

'Sunup. I was supposed to be leading it.'

The boy begins to bound up the hillside, through a small orchard of stunted apple trees to the grove at the top of the island. Mara follows, but stops as she enters the tall, thick trunks and wide canopy of branches, wonderstruck by the magnificence of such ancient trees.

'They're so beautiful,' she whispers, breathing in the

fresh, green scents and reaching out to touch the cold, living pillar of a trunk.

Gorbals has disappeared within the grove and Mara is left to follow the noise of his plastic crackles. 'I'm sorry!' she hears him call. When she catches up with him he is in the middle of a group of about twenty people who have begun to rise from the circle they were sitting in around a smoky, fragrant ember fire in a small clearing under the trees. Like Gorbals, their clothing is made from odds and ends of plastic litter; all except for one very old woman, still sitting by the fire – her clothing seems to be woven from moss and leaves and grass.

'No, wait!' Gorbals calls after them as the people begin to disperse into the trees. 'I was working on my sun poem all night. I journeyed so far with the words that I lost track of the night and then I fell asleep on the grass and slept too late. Wait and hear it, please! And there's something else – look what I found!'

'Too much to do, Gorbals. Save it for sundown,' laughs a sweet-faced young woman with a sleepy baby strapped to her in a papoose made out of a plastic bag. As Mara emerges from the cluster of trees, the young woman stops dead in amazement then cries out in fear.

'But it's no use for sundown, it's a sun*up* poem,' wails Gorbals.

'I'll tell you what's no use, boy,' says the old woman in the earthen clothing. She is as gnarled as a tree with a face as pale as the moon. 'This latecoming is no good. We must have a poet we can depend on. You are always late, late, late.'

Now the old woman sees Mara and stares at her, wide-eyed and wary. 'Who is this?'

'I won't be late again,' flusters Gorbals. 'I promise. It's

just that sometimes I get so lost in the places the words take me to I forget where I am and—'

'*Who* is this person?' demands the old woman. Her wide, unblinking stare unnerves Mara. With a great crackle of plastic, the rest of the group gather round.

'Yes, I found a person!' exclaims Gorbals. 'That was the other thing that made me late.'

The crowd of crackling strangers encircles Mara. Like Gorbals, they all have huge, owlish eyes and moony faces. Standing so intent and still in the gloomy light of the netherworld they could almost be wraiths.

'This is Mara Bitterness,' says Gorbals, 'who is not a place. And she is not one of the sky people either. I don't know what she is.'

'Mara Bell,' Mara corrects him.

'Bell?' says the old woman wonderingly.

The young woman with the baby in the papoose comes close and studies the material of Mara's anorak. In the dim light her neatly plaited, earth-coloured hair and eyes, even her skin, have a greenish tinge, like a tint of grass and leaves.

Shyly, she reaches out and fingers the sleeve. 'It's as quiet and as soft as a feather and it gleams like a moon-beam.' She glances at Mara with a fierce curiosity in her huge pale eyes. 'What is it made of?' the girl murmurs.

'Nylon, I think,' says Mara. Her jacket, like all her clothes, is a much-mended, recycled cast-off, made before the world changed.

'Nylon?' frowns the girl.

Mara tries to remember what Tain has told her about the materials of the drowned world. 'It's something people used to make long ago, like your plastic clothes.'

The girl touches her knotted plastic outfit, which is neatly tailored to her body, unlike Gorbals's chaotic tatters.

'We find our clothes in the trees and the ruins and the water,' says the girl. 'They're good for the wetness but bad in the heat. Where did you find this?'

Mara smiles. 'In a wardrobe at home. It belonged to my grandmother. It's very old.'

'I've tried to explain all this to you, Broomielaw,' croaks the shrivelled, ancient woman, in the earthen clothing. 'I've told you about plastic and nylon and all those chemical evils but you don't listen, do you, because an old woman doesn't know anything about the world, eh? You should stick to the natural gifts of the Earth.'

The aged eyes gleam and the girl, Broomielaw, blushes deeply.

'But – but surely *everything* must come from the world,' the girl persists. She cannot take her eyes off Mara and her clothing. 'You can't make something out of thin air.'

The old woman laughs a stubborn 'Hah!' but her attention is fixed keenly on Mara. As Mara returns her gaze the old woman gives a sudden gasp.

'Enough, Broomielaw,' says Gorbals. 'Mara isn't like us. Mara is strange.'

'I'm not!' says Mara.

'You are to us,' smiles Gorbals. 'Very strange. We've never seen anything like you.' He touches her nose. 'A brown face with orange spots on the nose.'

'Spots?' Mara touches her nose and can't feel anything. 'You mean my freckles?'

The moon-faced crowd burst out laughing. *'Freckles, freckles,'* they murmur.

'What is freckles?' asks Gorbals. He is laughing too. 'Freckles, freckles, freckles. It sounds like a fire word.'

'Well, they're caused by the sun.' Mara looks around the dim netherworld and suddenly the wide owl-eyes and moony faces make sense. It must be the result of a lack of sunlight.

'Freckles are little sun spots,' she explains.

A murmur grows among the crowd and they crackle with excitement. The old woman stands up from her seat beside the ember fire.

'You are from outside,' she says sharply. 'From the sun world?'

Mara nods. 'From an island in the north.'

'An island in the world beyond the great wall?' says the old woman, trembling now.

'Yes,' says Mara. 'An island called Wing, in the Atlantic Ocean.'

There is a great gasp all around her.

Gorbals explains. 'We didn't think there were any places left in the world beyond this.' He glances over at the city wall. 'Long ago, our people would try to get out beyond the great wall to see. Most were taken by the sky people even before they got through, and the ones who did – none of them ever came back.'

'I don't think there are any places now except the sky cities,' says Mara. 'My island drowned.'

They all look at her with pity in their great owl-eyes.

'No one except the ratbashers has made it through in many, many years,' adds a woman with the longest hair Mara has ever seen. It hangs in a thick, dark plait to her feet.

'The ratbashers?' frowns Mara. 'You mean the urchins? The wild children?'

The old woman steps forward. Slowly, she extends a

gnarled hand and Mara takes it. The hand trembles in hers but its grasp is warm and strong.

'Welcome, Mara Bell from the island of Wing in the Atlantic Ocean. Welcome to the Hill of Doves, the island home of the Treenesters. I'm Candleriggs the Oldest. We have been waiting a long time for you.'

Mara takes a step back.

'For me? Sorry, but you've got the wrong person. It was sheer chance that I got here at all – I only managed it by the skin of my teeth.'

'How did you do that?' asks Gorbals, staring at her teeth.

Old Candleriggs motions to Gorbals to be quiet and looks at Mara, her eyes gleaming, and when she speaks her voice is full of emotion.

'The stone-telling promised you would come one day.' Turning to the others, she points to Mara's face. 'Look! What do you see? It's the Face in the Stone, the one we've been waiting for. Treenesters, our time has come. The stone-telling has begun.'

Every one of the Treenesters stares intently. Mara looks into Candleriggs's ancient owl eyes and shivers even before the old woman speaks her next words.

'The stone tells of you, Mara Bell. Now you are here the stone-telling shall be.'

THE STONE-TELLING

Mara turns to Gorbals to avoid the look of awe in the eyes of the crowd.

'What's the stone-telling?' she asks anxiously.

But Gorbals just stares, with the same awestruck look as the others in his huge eyes.

'This is a big mistake,' Mara tells them. 'I'm not whoever you think I am. I lost my home, my family, all the people I love and I ended up here because there wasn't anywhere else to go. There's nothing left in the world beyond the wall.'

'I'm sorry I tripped over you. I didn't know who you were,' says Gorbals in a hushed voice.

Mara shakes her head and backs away.

Old Candleriggs puts a gentle hand on her arm. 'We can't make you stay,' the old woman says. 'But if you come with me I'll show you the stone-telling and then you'll see who you are.'

I know who I am, thinks Mara. *I don't want to be whoever you think I am.*

And yet she is curious about the stone-telling. What can

there be in this strange, dim netherworld that is anything to do with her?

So Mara follows the old woman, just to see.

They pull out on to the steamy waters on rafts, a small exodus of them, paddling through a network of steeples and small islands, flitting in and out of the mosaic of sunlight and shadow made by the sky tunnels of New Mungo. They pass under the Bridge to Nowhere, which is packed with urchins climbing in and out of the rusted carcass of an ancient vehicle that Mara recognizes as a bus. They use the broken edge of the bridge as a giant diving board, jumping recklessly off it into the murky waters.

As the heat grows, the Treenesters untie much of their plastic clothing. There is no breath of wind and the great wall seems to act like a pressure pot with the metallic network of the sky city a huge grill, cooking the netherworld under slabs of midday heat. Only Candleriggs in her earthen clothing seems comfortable.

'Is it far?' Mara pants, as she throws off her jacket, dizzy from lack of food and water. 'This is unbearable.'

Candleriggs takes a leather pouch from a deep pocket in her cloak, takes a stopper out of it and offers it to Mara.

'Drink,' she says.

Mara takes a thirsty gulp. Flavour fills her parched mouth, a sensation so intense it seems to surge through her nerve channels to make the skin tingle on the back of her neck and her eyes prickle. The thick liquid fills her with a soothing glow. She drinks again, deeply. It's sharp yet sweet; thirst-quenching and soothing. It's delicious.

'What is it?' Mara gasps, forcing herself to stop before she guzzles the whole lot.

'Hupplesup,' says Candleriggs. 'Honey, herb and crab apple mead. A little will settle you, enough will make you happy and too much will put you to sleep.'

'Unless you're Pollock,' says Gorbals, 'then you'll drink so much it sets you on fire and you want to fight everyone, even the ducks.'

Everyone laughs except a lazy-eyed youth who Mara supposes must be Pollock. He glares thunderously at the back of Gorbals's head.

Gorbals points ahead now as a gigantic black wizard hat – a massive steeple – emerges from the steam. It sits upon the great central tower of a dark, castle-like building that must be on a hill because most of it rises clear out of the water. Across from it lies the half-drowned remains of a wide building that's topped with turrets and towers and honeycombed with windows and archways. The Treenesters's fleet of rafts steers right up to the turretted building.

'What are these places?' Mara asks. She cannot take her eyes off the great black wizard hat that seems to be made out of a spectacular latticework of stone and air.

'These are the places of the stone-telling. The old places where the drowned world left us signs and stories in the stone,' says Gorbals. 'Now, look up there – look at the statue of Thenew!'

He points up to an archway in one of the turrets. There, set in ancient stone, is the figure of a young woman. One hand grasps a hammer, in the other she holds a small boat and in her lap lies an open book. Her feet are entwined with the great stone-carved roots of a tree and her eyes seem to look out beyond the city walls. Mara looks up at the face and stops breathing.

The face in the stone is her own.

'It's a coincidence,' Mara protests. 'It just happens to look a bit like me.'

But despite the thick heat, the statue makes her shiver. Even though age has made an ugly crack all across one side of the face, Mara can see that Thenew looks a lot like her. The statue is a stone mirror of her own features. She wants to turn away from it yet she can't.

'This face that's yours isn't just here,' says Gorbals. 'It's set in stone all over the drowned city.'

The Treenesters stare and Mara can't escape the mass of owl eyes that peer at her through the dim and steamy light.

'How could it be me? It's impossible. This building is centuries old. I'm only fifteen.'

They continue to stare, as if they are awaiting some kind of pronouncement from her.

'What do you want me to say? What do you want from me?' Mara begins to feel panicky and helpless.

Old Candleriggs touches her arm gently. 'If you don't know what you are here for then we will do as we have always done.'

'What's that?' Mara asks.

'Wait,' says Candleriggs. 'The stone-telling will make sure that whatever is to be, will be. You are here now. What is set in stone will happen.'

But *what* is set in stone? Mara wonders as she looks back up at the stone girl who shares her face. 'It's just a statue,' she insists, yet she can't tear her eyes from the uncanny image of herself.

Candleriggs raises a bony hand and points to an engraving on another part of the building. 'Look at this story in the stone. It shows a fish with a ring, a bell, a bird and a tree. This story is all over the city, in so many places. This is the story we live by. We believe in the day when these things will come together. When that happens the stone-telling shall be, and we will be free from this deathly underworld. We will be free to find our true home in the world. Now that you are here it must begin, because Thenew is the key to the whole story. And you are the image of Thenew.'

'That's not the same as *being* her!' Mara protests, but quietens and feels another shiver run through her as the Treenesters begin a soft chant:

'The fish with the ring,
The bell and the bird and the tree.
When these all come together
Then the stone-telling shall be.'

'I still don't understand. What *exactly* is the stone-telling?' Mara asks. 'What's the fish with the ring and everything?'

'We don't know until it happens,' says Gorbals. 'We thought you would know and you would tell us.'

'But I don't,' says Mara helplessly.

'You're the Face in the Stone. You *should* know,' says Gorbals, a touch accusingly.

'Well, I *don't*,' Mara repeats. 'I'm sorry, but doesn't that prove I'm not who you think I am? If I was I'd know what this was all about.'

'Not necessarily,' says Candleriggs. 'We are all pilgrims in our own lives. Nobody knows what lies on the path of their journey until it happens. And our journey back to the trees should start now,' she tells the others, glancing up through the thick network of New Mungo to the sky beyond. 'There's a dangerous look to the sky and I feel the calm before a storm.'

The Treenesters obey Candleriggs instantly. Mara takes one last glance at her stone image as the rafts turn for home. Tain could always feel a storm coming, she remembers. It must be to do with having lived so long; you know the world by instinct. The air is intense and heavy. It could do with a good storm to clear it. Mara trails her hand in the water to feel some coolness on her skin. She no longer cares about the sewage that it might contain, she is too hot. The waters of the drowned city are less dirty than those outside and they don't smell like the open drain of the boat camp. Yet a nasty, sour odour hangs in the air.

Mara wrinkles her nose. It smells like bad breath.

'Listen and I'll tell Mara the legend of Thenew,' says Candleriggs. All across the small fleet of rafts the Treenesters settle themselves comfortably. 'Once upon a time there was a girl who lived on an island,' she begins, and Mara's skin prickles as she hears the tale of Thenew, the pregnant daughter of an ancient king who was wrongfully cast out of her homeland in a ramshackle raft. But the wind wafted her to a safe harbour on a new land and there she gave birth to a son who grew up to found a whole new city.

'His name was Mungo,' says Candleriggs, 'and the city he founded now lies drowned underneath us. But his name lives on in the city in the sky.'

She turns to Mara. 'Thenew was the name of Mungo's mother. She is the stone face that's to be found all over the old city, alongside the fish with the ring, the bell, the bird and the tree. She is the one who began the story. Without her the old city would never have been founded

123

here. And you are the face of Thenew, Mara – the one who will begin a new story for us. You are our saviour.'

'But she is something else too!' cries Gorbals. 'She is the bell – Mara Bell!'

'The bell that begins a new day,' Candleriggs nods thoughtfully.

Mara turns away from the keen expectation of the Treenesters. She leans over the side of the raft to drip cool water on her face. She doesn't know what to think. After everything that has happened it's all too strange, too mind-blowing, far too much. She spots something floating upon the water and focuses her attention on that instead. It's a book! The next paddle thrust should bring it within reach. Mara lunges out and makes a grab as the raft surges forward. But the paper is so sodden that the book falls apart in her fingers and she is left holding a bunch of loose pages.

'Look!' she cries to the others. 'A book!'

'There are lots,' says Broomielaw, shyly. She has hardly spoken to Mara since this morning. Ever since Candleriggs decided she was the Face in the Stone, the Treenesters have been treating Mara as if she is a special being, an angel fallen to Earth.

'The books spill out of the bad place,' Broomielaw points to the tall black tower topped with the great wizard hat, 'and litter the water. We dry them out to burn on our fire.'

'You burn them!' gasps Mara. 'But they're full of stories and all sorts of things – pictures and ideas.'

Imagine Rowan's horror if he knew that, thinks Mara; then a far worse horror strikes her as she remembers her last sight of him in the boat camp. Is he still alive? She wills him to stay alive until she can think of some way to help him. If only she could magic him through the city wall, right now.

'We don't need books,' Candleriggs tells her curtly, but Mara is grateful to have her awful thoughts interrupted. 'We have plenty of our own stories and good, strong minds to hold them in and we can make more if we want them. And we have Gorbals to make us poems.'

'Maybe Gorbals needs books,' laughs Pollock, the lazy eyed young Treenester who lolls beside Broomielaw, playing with her baby. 'Even his memory is clumsy!'

'I don't need books, I only need words!' Gorbals declares. 'He twists around to glare at Pollock but his sudden movement rocks the raft precariously. 'Don't you insult me – you spend all your time crawling in the bushes like a ratbasher!'

'I'm a hunter – but you're no poet,' snarls Pollock, anger colouring his face at the ratbasher insult. 'You're just a clumsy no-good who works with words because he can't do real man's work, like hunting.'

'It takes a lifetime to become a poet. I could learn to hunt in a day. You might be a hunter but you're a thief too!' Gorbals explodes.

'What I've got's all mine,' sneers Pollock.

'Pollock, stop it!' whispers Broomielaw. Her head is bowed but Mara can see the distress on her face and wonders.

'Pollock Halfgood, try to live up to your name,' orders Candleriggs. 'Or I will change it to Nogood At All. Stop your nasty tongue. Do you want your fighting to land us all in the water – your baby too? She turns to Gorbals. 'And you, calm down and sit still. A poet should put all his energy into words, not pride-fighting. Are you planning to be with us in time for sundown or do we do it all ourselves like we had to this morning?'

Gorbals sits down, shamefaced, and Pollock manages to stop his tongue, but they throw each other thunderous looks until the raft bumps up against the Treenesters's island.

'Would you like to look at this book once I dry it out?' Mara asks Gorbals, gently shaking the water from it as they walk up through the stunted apple orchard to the large trees near the top of the Hill of Doves.

Gorbals doesn't even glance at the wet pages, just stares furiously after Pollock. 'Necrotty rat!' he spits out.

'Gorbals!' Broomielaw is horrified. 'The Face in the Stone was speaking to you.' But she looks at the book as if a venomous snake might slither from its sodden pages.

'Please don't call me that.' Mara smiles uneasily at the girl. 'I'm not the Face in the Stone. Believe me. Just call me Mara.'

Broomielaw bites her lip. 'Mara, then. We're about to prepare a meal – will you stay?' They have reached the grove of trees at the top of the Hill of Doves. She kneels and pulls out a handful of carrots and potatoes and herbs from a clay pot that sits in the nook of the oak tree. 'It feels like a big storm is coming,' says Broomielaw. 'Candleriggs says please would you nest with us tonight? You'll be safe here.'

Mara looks up at the trees. *Nest?* What does she mean? She remembers Gorbals asking where her nest was . . . and then she sees them – huge, human-sized nests in the branches of the trees. She stares up at them in aston-ishment.

Her attention is brought back to earth by the smell of cooking. Mara's stomach aches and groans at the sight of Broomielaw and the others preparing their meal. When was the last time she ate? The hupplesup is the nearest thing to nourishment she's had in days. She's weak and trembling with exhaustion and hunger. The leaves in the trees tremble too with the change in the air and the water is restless. Mara listens to the doves calling nervously to each other. There's definitely a storm coming; she can feel the vibration in the air, smell the oddly metallic scent of it in the wind.

Again, she thinks of Rowan and the others in the boat camp. Will they be safe in a storm? Now she is safe, how can she help them? Tomorrow she must think hard about that. But tonight there's someone here in the netherworld that she must look out for – Wing, the little bird-like urchin.

'I need to find the child who brought me here,' she tells Broomielaw. 'He was hurt – I need to see if he's all right.'

Mara has been so caught up with the Treenesters that she hasn't seen Wing all day.

'A little one from your island?' asks Broomielaw, concerned.

'No, one of the abandoned children. There's a horde of them up in the cathedral.'

'A ratbasher?' Broomielaw's face wrinkles in disgust. 'Keep away from those wild, dirty creatures. They're dangerous little animals, full of sicknesses they catch from the waters and the rats they play with in the ruins. They breed when they're little more than children but thankfully they die before they're much out of childhood, or else they're taken. I won't have any of them near my baby!' Broomielaw seems to remember that she is talking to the legendary Face in the Stone and falls silent, her cheeks on fire.

Mara frowns. 'Wing isn't a rat-whatever, he's just a child with no one to look after him. And I won't let him die – I'm going to look after him. I know they're strange children but you're *all* strange to me. You're not like my own people.'

'They're horrible little things,' Broomielaw insists. 'But please tell us about your people,' she says eagerly, as she chops the vegetables roughly with a slate knife. 'We've got things to do now but please tell us your story at sundown.'

'There might be no sundown tonight if there's a bad storm coming,' warns Gorbals, sniffing the air and peering tentatively through New Mungo to the distant sky. 'It might be straight to nest.'

'Then I *must* find Wing,' cries Mara. 'If there's a bad storm coming I want to know he's safe.' A thought suddenly strikes her. 'Broomielaw, if the Face in the Stone asks the Treenesters to give shelter to the child who brought me here to you, you would do that, surely?'

Broomielaw lowers her eyes. Still she hesitates. 'Of course,' she says at last. 'Oh, but be careful!' she protests as Mara races down the Hill of Doves to the rafts.

The world turns electric. The sky flashes and booms. The ferocity of it makes New Mungo shudder. And now the thought of the ancient stone face that mirrors her own no longer makes Mara shiver; now the idea of it sends a wild-powered current surging through her.

It's just the storm in me, she tells herself, then has a fleeting moment of wonder. *What if it were all true and I really am what they say?*

Whatever it is, for the first time since leaving the island, she feels alive again.

THE BASH

In the gloomy daylight of the netherworld the cathedral is full of dim colour and shadows. Mara peers through the tints cast by the shattered stained glass windows that reach up to the vast, vaulted ceiling. A million sparkling motes of dust drift like minuscule floating lanterns. Even amid the noisy games and quarrels of the urchins there's a sense of peace, pure and deep, distilled by centuries of stone.

Now she sees Wing. He's perched close to the feet of one of the statues that shelter in alcoves all around the cathedral. The man's gentle stone face smiles down at him from under a crown of thorns, beatifically oblivious to the pain of the thorns and to the rabble of hundreds of naked, dirt-caked urchins. Wing has strewn gifts of coloured glass chips all around the feet of the statue and smiles up as if he believes the stone man is real.

Mara thinks back to the stories that belonged to the old religion on Wing. This man, with his crown of thorns, was supposed to be the son of God, yet somehow he could not, or did not, save himself from a torturous death on a cross. Mara could never understand that story – why would anyone who was able to save themselves choose not to?

'Wing!' she calls over to the mesmerized urchin. 'Are you OK? I'm so sorry I left you. See, I met some people here, they live in the trees on another island . . . '

Mara stops. What's the use? He can't understand a word. She looks around the cathedral, at the mess of junk and debris the urchins have littered everywhere.

'Are you hungry? Have you eaten?' She gestures to her mouth and rubs her stomach to show what she means.

Wing holds out a dead pigeon that he has torn apart. In disgust, Mara sees the tiny head the child grasps in his other hand, the blood and juices that run down his chin and chest. He's eating the bird raw. But an even worse horror is her own hunger, so strong and vicious it over-powers her revulsion at Wing's barbarity. Mara turns away before she rips the bird from his hands and begins to tear into its raw flesh herself.

Screams erupt behind her and Mara spins round to see a girl of about ten attacking a younger child, trying to pull a green plastic bottle out of her hands. Bright litter is the urchins's playstuff; it's gathered in little piles all over the cathedral, sorted into colours. Groups of children play and fight and squabble over it. But this girl's attack is ferocious.

'Hey!' yells Mara.

She pulls the girl off the younger child and now finds herself fending off an assault of bites, punches, kicks and vicious, tearing fingernails. Mara's own temper gets the better of her and she fights back, inflicting her own stinging wounds. A crowd of urchins gathers to watch, Wing among them, curious and excited but unperturbed at what is happening to Mara. And it's the shock of his carelessness, along with the sudden fear of the savagery of these wild children, that chills Mara's fury and sends her running to the door of the cathedral. She wrenches it open and bursts out into the storm then races down to the water's edge to find Gorbals waiting for her. He is holding a flickering lantern high so that she will see him in the gathering gloom.

Mara runs up to him, shocked and shaken. Gorbals takes her hand and helps her on to the raft. His sullen mood is all gone and he eyes her with deep concern.

'What happened?'

Mara's mouth trembles in her effort not to cry. She can't answer.

'I came to row you back because the storm is making the water wild,' he says, then sighs. 'Mara, those ratbashers are wild and dangerous!'

Mara nods, shaking. He is tactful and doesn't ask about the ragged, burning wound the wild girl has torn across her face. But he picks a large dock leaf from the grass and gently places its healing coolness on her bleeding cheek. Mara murmurs her thanks. Shock has replaced the bright surge of hope and energy she felt such a little while ago; now the netherworld feels dark and alien once more.

'I hate that place. It's full of necrotty,' Gorbals mutters darkly as he places the lantern on Mara's knees and begins to steer the raft out from the gravestones and the cathedral, back through storm-chopped waters. He steers it expertly through a succession of poles that stick up out of the water. The flickering lantern light just picks out the shapes of a fish, bird, bell and tree attached to each pole. 'You should stay away from there. So should I,' he adds.

'What do you mean? What's necrotty?' says Mara, staring at the strange twig-woven lantern that Gorbals has set upon her lap. It's full of huge moths. They glow like moonbeams and cast a gentle, fluttery light.

'Dead stuff is necrotty – all the drowned, rotten things. The cathedral hill and the waters are full of it – look, you can see it at night.'

Mara looks down into the water and once again sees the luminous glow of the drowned city.

'That's the Foss.'

'Foss?' says Mara wonderingly.

'It's the ghost light that comes from all the necrotten things. Never touch it,' Gorbals warns her. 'It's full of death.'

A high-pitched, blood-chilling noise pierces the air behind her. A fat black creature swoops down and flaps in her face. Mara screams and tries to beat it off, then sees the vicious little face, with such nasty, tiny, ravenous teeth, trying to poke through the gaps in the twig lantern to get at the moths.

'Get off, you rodent!' Gorbals whacks the creature with his paddle and it surges high into the air. Mara hears a satisfying plop in the gloom as it hits the water.

'Bats,' says Gorbals crossly. 'They're always after the moonmoths.'

'That was a bat? I've never seen a bat so huge and so vicious,' gasps Mara. There were bats on Wing but they were tiny, harmless creatures that lived quietly in the church and the farm buildings. That one was as big as a winged cat.

Gorbals is frowning at the storm-fretted trees as they approach the Hill of Doves. 'No sundown tonight. The storm will kill our fire – but we'll still have stories. You must tell us yours. We're always hungry for stories.'

'My story?' says Mara as they disembark. She doesn't think she can bear to tell her story.

She helps Gorbals drag the raft safe out of the water's

132

reach. Three sheep are running nervously through the stunted apple trees on the hillside. Large wet drops splatter her face and Mara looks up in surprise at the sudden clangour above her head: the percussion of the rain on the sky city.

Gorbals grunts as he hauls rocks on to the raft as an anchor against the wind.

'You must have stories,' says Gorbals. 'Stories are the world's heartbeat. That's what keeps us all alive. But Mara, about the ratbashers – Broomielaw is right. They live like animals. They have short, wild lives and they breed too fast, too young. They have no language and yet they move together as one, in flocks like animals. They're not human like us.'

'But they're more like us than not. And they *are* human beings, children – wild children, maybe – but they've been abandoned by the world and they deserve kindness, not hate.'

Gorbals looks at her thoughtfully. 'I never thought of it like that. But . . .' in the glow of the moonmoths she sees him smile, 'do you really feel kindness for the savage creature who ripped your face like that?'

Mara smiles back ruefully. 'Not right at this minute.'

She follows the glow of his flickering moth lantern up the Hill of Doves into the thicket of trees. There's no sign of the Treenesters. The clearing is empty.

'Where have they all gone?' Mara wonders, as a single metallic beat rings out somewhere in the netherworld. That strange, lonely sound amid the gusts of wind makes her uneasy.

'They're already nesting,' says Gorbals. He nudges past a goat and springs up a ladder that hangs down the side of a chestnut tree, then disappears inside one of the human-sized nests that Mara spotted earlier. A host of owl eyes stare down at her from the storm-tossed branches of surrounding trees. The Treenesters are all snug inside their enormous nests, each one dimly lit by the fluttery glow of a moth lantern.

'Come on up,' Gorbals calls down softly. 'There's room in here.'

There's a smothered burst of laughter from the other nests. 'I'm fine down here,' says Mara, awkwardly. She huddles into the wrinkled base of the chestnut tree. Two roots stretch out on either side of her like an armchair. A couple of chickens nestle in a nook of the tree next to her.

'She doesn't want to share a nest with *you*,' she hears Candleriggs rebuke Gorbals. 'Mara!' the old woman calls down through the rising moan of the wind. 'Please come up here and share the greatnest with me.'

So Mara climbs a ladder made of tough grasses that hangs down the side of the huge oak and pulls herself up into Candleriggs's roomy nest. By mothlight she can see that it's woven securely into the branches and thickly lined with moss. Overhead, twigs and branches are meshed into a roof.

Candleriggs hands her something warm wrapped in a leaf package. Mara sniffs it then ravenously unwraps the leaves and bites into a thick potato pancake filled with herby vegetable stew. It tastes like the most delicious food in the world. When she's full, she lays her head down and ever so gently a moss quilt is tucked around her. She curls up in bliss. Then jolts back into guilty wakefulness. The wind has increased to a ghoulish howl that echoes through the netherworld. A huge gust hits the trees and Mara thinks of Rowan and all the others, starved, sick and dying in the misery of the boat camp, in such a wind. She tries to block out a mind-picture of the storm smashing the boats up against the great wall. The image shifts to another: that of a single, mountainous wave about to swallow up a small fishing boat. The wave looms over the helpless boat, then crashes down with the weight of a falling cliff. All that remains is the heaving blackness of the ocean.

Mara cries out for her lost family. The wind takes her cry and hurls it across the netherworld.

The eager rustlings of the Treenesters, anxious to hear her story, stop. Candleriggs leans over to grasp Mara's hand and, tucking the quilt around her, insists that her story will keep, that she should sleep now.

Yet exhausted though she is, Mara fights off sleep, afraid that the nightmare of what has happened to her family will come back to haunt her dreams. To keep herself awake, more than anything, she begins to tell the story of her island home swallowed by the ocean. She tells them all about Tain, her lost friends, and of the nightmare of the boat camp that clings to the other side of the great wall. She tells them how she got in to their world and how she could never have done it without Wing, the wild urchin.

She doesn't tell them what happened to her parents; she can't, not yet. And she senses the gentle Treenesters will hear what she doesn't say and know why.

When Mara finishes all she can hear is the storm. The Treenesters say nothing and she wonders if they have fallen asleep during her long story – or perhaps they couldn't hear her through the noise of the wind. Beside her, old Candleriggs has her eyes shut tight, her mouth set in a grim line. Then Mara looks out of the greatnest and sees all the eyes gleaming among the mothlit branches of the trees, brimful of the unspeakable hurt the Treenesters feel for her.

'Gorbals,' says Candleriggs, opening her eyes at last. Her gnarled voice shakes with emotion. 'Spin Mara a good, strong story to hold on to on such a stormy night in this harsh world.'

'Won't we get blown away?' Mara asks, as another great fist of wind grabs the trees and shakes the nests with a fury.

'Of course not,' says Candleriggs gently. 'We're as safe as birds' nests. And on nights like this the spirits of the drowned ones rise up from the waters to guard us and keep us safe. Can't you hear them sing loud and strong among the branches?'

Mara hears only the wind and the hoot of an owl. But as she listens the ghoulish sound of the wind seems to change until it does sound like a strong, invisible choir among the trees, and she feels comforted as she imagines the guardian spirits of her family here among the branches, watching over her and singing her to sleep.

'Once upon a time,' Gorbals begins, 'there lived a girl.' And he tells the tale of the girl who is whisked out of her world by a great wind and flung into a strange new land where she wanders lost until she spies a rainbow. Not knowing what else to do, she follows the rainbow to its end; she doesn't know why, only that she must.

'And when at last she reached the end, there she found a crock of gold,' Gorbals says.

'*Crock of gold, crock of gold,*' the Treenesters murmur contentedly and at last Mara falls asleep, cradled by the sound of the words and the wind and the rocking of the nest.

Deep in the night it's not the storm or a nightmare that wakens Mara but a silent presence near the foot of her tree. Instinct tells her it's there. She wakens with a start and, looking down out of the nest, finds herself locked in the amber gaze of a fox. The fox doesn't blink or move, just sits as still as a statue and stares up at her. Mara stares back, goosebumps prickling her skin as she remembers the cyberfox and the magnetic pull of its eyes. *I'll find you again – somehow I will*, Mara vows, as her eyelids drop and she falls back into sleep.

In the morning it's all the sun can do to graze a white patch in the clouds; but the storm has passed and the netherworld lies in a pot of soupy grey mist. Dove calls and birdsong waken Mara and she wonders how they manage such carefree joy after last night's vicious blast. She stretches out her limbs, feeling rested and new. Today, she will scrub herself from top to toe, wash her clothes and plait her long hair to help keep cool in this heat. Then she will explore the netherworld and try to think what she will do next.

'Candleriggs.'
'Clyde.'
'Molendinar.'
'Springburn.'
'Firhill.'
'Parkhead.'
'Ibrox.'

What on earth are they doing? Mara peers over the side of the nest. The Treenesters sit in a circle on the ground below. One by one each stands up, shouts out their own name and points towards a part of the drowned city.

'Gorbals.'

'Cowcaddens.'

'Trongate.'

'Gallowgate.'

'Possil.'

'Pollock.'

'Partick.'

The ceremony continues until it reaches Broomielaw who holds up her baby.

'And my precious little Clayslaps.'

The others laugh as baby Clayslaps waggles his arms and legs. Then they burst into song. Mara flops back in the greatnest and laughs too. It's ridiculous. The Treenesters are a bunch of walking place names, the living limbs of the lost city.

Gorbals brings Mara's breakfast up to the greatnest. A woven grass mat is her plate, a bird beak her spoon and a bird claw her fork. Mara decides she'd rather use her fingers. She tastes a morsel of what looks like a mushroom omelette. The mushrooms taste and smell of the netherworld – of earth and trees, darkness and salt.

Now Gorbals offers her a clay cup of some steaming, aromatic drink. 'This is rosehip tea but you can have nettle or dandelion or mint. I put some honey in it.'

'No, this is good,' Mara tells him. 'What were you all doing just then?'

'At sunup and sundown we remember our lost name places,' Gorbals explains. 'Each year we lose more of the old city to the waters and each year our island shrinks until one day soon there will be nothing.'

'Just like my island!' Mara exclaims.

Gorbals nods. 'Yes,' he says heavily. 'This year the water rose more than ever. If that happens next year we'll have no land left. Just like you.' He looks at her intently.

'We believe that's why you are here now. The stone-telling must happen soon or we will drown. But now we know the signs will all come together and we'll be saved. You'll make it happen.' Mara shakes her head helplessly at him but his large eyes are full of faith. Shyly, he touches her face. 'Molendinar will heal this wound with a tree sap cure. Oh, and Candleriggs asks if you had a dream last night.'

'A dream?' Mara fingers the sore rip on her face and tries to remember. 'I'm not sure. Why?'

'Dreams are full of signs. Candleriggs says if a dream visited you it might tell you something useful.'

Mara sighs. Then she remembers.

'There was a fox,' she exclaims. 'But I don't know whether I dreamed it or not.'

'A fox!' Gorbals relays down to the others who, Mara now sees, have gathered underneath the greatnest in expectation. 'She might have dreamed a fox but she's not sure.'

He waits patiently as Mara tries to remember more.

'Well, it – it just stared at me. That's all. No, now I'm sure it was real, a real fox.'

Once again she remembers the cyberfox and wishes she could reach him. But maybe she still can. Mara looks around the greatnest, finds her backpack and checks that her cyberwizz is safely sealed inside.

'I once knew a fox,' she tells Gorbals. 'Not a real one but he felt like my friend. He had the eyes of a friend.'

Gorbals settles himself upon a branch beside her and waits expectantly, as if for a story.

'On your island in the great ocean?' he prompts.

'Not exactly.' Mara tries to think of a way to explain about cyberspace to a plastic-clothed boy who lives in a nest in the trees. She can't.

'I suppose it was like a dream, or a game. Real but not real. The fox was in another world.'

'You have been to another world?' Gorbals stares at her in astonishment.

'Sort of,' says Mara. 'But my body was still in this one. Only my mind was in the other one. It's done with a machine called a computer. A cyberwizz.'

'A magic machine!' Gorbals cries.

'No,' says Mara, and she leaves the cyberwizz tucked away in her backpack for now because if she shows it to him and tells him about the Weave and how she got there using her globe and halo and wand then it does sound like magic. And it *was* a kind of magic, she realizes now, as she climbs down from the greatnest. A magic that was so much part of her ordinary life she took it for granted.

'Maybe the fox is a sign,' Gorbals says, later, once Mara has scrubbed herself clean in a bath full of rainwater in the tumbledown ruin at the top of the hill.

'A sign of what?' Mara asks. Her skin glows and tingles from the cold water. She feels fresh and clear-headed again.

'I don't know,' he says. 'Wait and see.'

'I don't want to wait and see. My mother used to say patience was not one of my virtues.' Mara smiles tearfully at the memory. 'Is that all you people do around here,' she teases Gorbals, 'wait for something to happen?'

'Yes,' Gorbals says simply. 'We live our lives and watch for the signs of whatever will happen. It's all we can do.'

'Haven't you ever tried to break out of here? Did nobody ever want to see what's beyond the city walls? Or try to get up into the city? Or take a boat and just sail out

140

into the ocean? Didn't you ever wonder about the outside world?'

Even as she says the words Mara feels shame because she sees there's no great difference, really, between the Treenesters and the islanders of Wing.

'In the beginning, yes,' Gorbals says darkly. 'Then we learned not to. Too many of us died, or disappeared. We saw that the only way was to live quietly and try to keep safe and believe that one day we would be saved. We have put our faith in the stone-telling,' he says simply. 'And it's happening. Now you are here and the signs are gathering something must happen soon.'

'Oh, Gorbals, there are no signs – please don't believe in me. I never helped my own people, I only made things worse, so much worse, and I can't think of a way to help them now,' Mara despairs.

'I believe in the stone-telling,' Gorbals insists. 'I believe in the signs – and the signs *are* coming together. Like the wound on your face.'

Mara touches her cheek. Molendinar's sap ointment has soothed it. With a jolt Mara remembers the ugly crack upon the stone girl's face. The wound the wild girl ripped across her face now mirrors that crack in the Face in the Stone. And Mara turns cold inside as she remembers something else – the crack she made in Granny Mary's mirror, inside the little carved box made by Tain that she keeps tucked away inside her backpack. That crack rips a scar across her face too when she looks in the glass. Like her wound and the crack on the face of the statue, it too is on the left side.

Much as she wants to, Mara cannot explain away such uncanny coincidences. But a few cracks and scars don't mean she's the one who is going to save the Treenesters.

'How did you manage on your island if you didn't know how to read the signs of the world?' Gorbals suddenly asks.

Mara doesn't answer because not reading the signs was the reason she is here, now, having lost everything.

Mara spends the day getting her bearings. She explores the Treenesters's island and sees why they have chosen it as their home. As well as being the largest and most tree-covered, it lies farthest from the central towers of New Mungo and the ever-present threat of the sea police. The occasional wail of a siren and the reels of tide made by the supply ships are a constant reminder of the workings of the New World that overshadows this dank, gloomy one.

Mara rafts over to the cathedral island, and then to the wrecked bus on the Bridge to Nowhere to look for Wing. At last she finds him up on the curving ruin of the building that tops the Treenesters' island. She spies his grubby face peeking out through a large red and yellow plastic sign that's lopsidedly propped upon the building's crumbling balcony; a bright yellow *M*, like a twin golden archway. Was this once the sign of some special, sacred place?

Wing sits among the flocks of urchins that perch upon the rooftops to throw rocks at the birds. The curve of the ruin forms a kind of amphitheatre that resounds with the chirruping, whistling racket of the birds and the urchins. The urchins are vicious with birds, for ever attacking and tormenting them, mimicking their voices, tearing them apart when they stone them down, eating them raw, dead or alive. Mara is sure they punish the birds in envy of their winged freedom. Only Wing's own little sparrow, guarded fiercely by him, escapes such cruelty.

Mara climbs through the rubble of bones and bottles and weeds that lie inside the ruined building. In the middle of a room with no walls or roof sits a smashed television set, its innards overgrown with chickenweed and dandelions. A kitten cries like a lost child in a wasteland, but as Mara clambers through to get up to Wing she sees it's not really a wasteland at all. The place is teeming with wildlife – birds, bluebottles, beetles, cats, goats, a wild dog, chickens, wasps, worms, slugs, spiders and ants. Nature has reclaimed the ruins of the human world.

Tentatively, Mara climbs the remains of a staircase, stumbles and plunges into a mass of stinging nettles. She looks around for a dock leaf to rub on her stings and as she reaches out for one she almost thrusts her hand through a huge spider's web. The crumbling building is full of gaps and holes, its doors and windows are wide open to the elements, yet the web survived last night's ferocious storm.

How can so much life survive in such a ruined place? Mara wonders, then she spies Wing.

'I searched and searched for you,' she tells him when at last he scrambles down, 'but you've been here all the time.'

He stares at her mouth, hopping about on his spindly legs, trying to drink in the meaning of her words with his eyes while his bird-friend flaps around his shoulder.

'I want you to bring me your friends.' Mara gestures up at all the urchins on the rooftop then points to herself. 'I've had an idea. But,' she adds, pointing to the rip-wound on her face and shaking her head sternly, 'I don't want any more of this.'

Wing stares at her in concentration. He reaches up and puts a finger to her lips. Mara repeats her request and

143

pantomime of gestures. The child blinks once and runs off.

In a moment he's back, trailing a flock of urchins. So he understood after all. Mara leads the way down to the ground and they gather around, tense and curious. She flinches as a hundred eye beams fix upon her. She knows it's a risk meeting these children alone here; they are truly wild, they might do anything to her.

'Do any of you have names?' she asks nervously. 'Do any of you understand me?'

The eyes burn upon her.

'I – I can give you names, if you like,' says Mara. 'All the names of the lost islands in the ocean beyond the wall. Would you like names?'

They don't understand a word, of course, but it seems only right to ask.

Mara points to herself. 'Mara.'

She points to Wing. 'And you're Wing, remember? Wing. Now say it,' she tells him. 'It's no use having a name if you can't say it. *Wing*.'

Mara puts her finger to his mouth. The child watches hers intently and attempts to mirror the shape of the word on her lips.

'Wuh,' he grunts at last, trying out the sound. He bashes his head with his hand and tries again. 'Wuh-eeng. Wu-ing!'

Mara claps her hands. 'Good! That's it, that's who you are: Wing.' She turns to another child, a noisy girl of around eight. 'You're obviously meant to be Yell. That's where my father was born.'

She comes face to face with the girl who attacked her in the cathedral. Mara and the girl stare each other out for a moment.

144

'Scarwell,' Mara laughs. 'That's the name for you.'

Mara works her way round the urchins, dishing out names at random. She repeats each name until the child can say it. Jura, Skye, Iona, Barra, Benbecula, Tiree, Orkney, Harris, Foula, Hoy, Unst, Copinsay, Stroma, Lewis, Fetlar, Muckle Roe and so many more; all the drowned islands. She moves on to lost villages and hamlets when she runs out of islands, until each child has a name. Then all of a sudden she sits down in the midst of them as a great wave of emotion hits her. It's as if until this moment, when she gave away the legacy of their names, she never truly believed that the islands were lost to the world.

Something clear and harsh rings out in the netherworld. Wing jumps up and the urchins scatter, yelling excitedly as they run off down the hillside to the water. Mara listens to the sound and remembers the same lone, harsh beat that struck through the heart of the storm last night and the night before when she first met Wing at the sea bridge. More urchins rush out from the ruins and from other secret places all over the drowned city. They hurtle off the Bridge to Nowhere and flock upon water that the falling sun has turned red. Mara peers through a bolt of sun to watch in astonishment as the urchins seem to speed across the surface of the sea.

A hundred children zip across the water's sheet of fire.

Mara runs down to the water's edge. A silver network has emerged from beneath the waves. At first she can't fathom what it is, this glistening trail that maps the water – and then she knows. It's the rooftops of the drowned city, the ones she saw glowing like ghosts in the dark the other night. The very tips of them have been revealed by the low tide and it's these tracks that the sure-footed urchins race upon, zipping and zooming in all directions across the secret silver maze on the red sea, rushing chaotically through a forest of chimney stacks.

But the chaos has a pattern only the urchins know. They flock into clusters around all the churches, then climb up the church steeples into the bell chambers. As the red sun moves behind the towering steeple of the giant wizard hat and sets fire to its network of stone and air, the urchins begin to bash the bells of the drowned churches with sticks and stones. Mara feels the beat echo in her bones and turns dizzy as the netherworld reels in a chaotic red haze.

'They must hear it in New Mungo,' thinks Mara. As if in answer to that thought, the howl of sirens rises across the netherworld. Far across the water Mara sees the lights of a supply ship. The sirens grow closer, louder.

Gorbals and Broomielaw race out of the grove of trees, grab her and drag her up the hillside.

'Get up into the greatnest! It's not safe! If the sky people see you they will take you away!' cries Broomielaw, climbing up into her nest where Molendinar is hushing baby Clayslaps.

And now Mara sees how they keep themselves safe. To outside eyes, there isn't a sign of any living soul. The sundown fire has been stamped out and scattered with branches, the moths set free from their twig lanterns. If Mara didn't know better she'd think those glimpses of plastic were bits of litter blown into the trees. The Treenesters have made themselves invisible to the prying eyes of New Mungo and its police.

But Wing and his friends are out in the open. And at the outburst of the sirens, the Bash stops.

Once the sirens recede, the Treenesters climb down

from their nests. Swiftly, they hunt for moonmoths to relight their lanterns, they clear and restoke the sundown fire, then sit in their circle around it. Mara wants to look for Wing but they insist she will not be safe and make her sit down among them. Now Gorbals begins to build his own gentle beat with words. Mara slips into the comforting rhythm of his poem and feels her heart settle and her body relax. When his poem has ended, the other Treenesters stand up, and one by one each shouts out a name that remembers the lost places of the drowned city.

The red ball of sun slips suddenly below the city wall. The light dies and for a moment the whole world seems to fall away. But the Treenesters's sundown fills the air with a stubborn shout of life.

INSIDE THE WIZARD HAT

Earth turns. Days pass. And Mara is stuck in the netherworld.

Rain quells the steamy heat. Water pours day and night as if there's some giant celestial tap in the sky. The ting of a million drops upon New Mungo fills the air with a heavenly sound that's undermined by the ghostly moans and whispers of the city's windspires.

Birds fly south. Mara watches them through the sky tunnels, remembering the winged arrows that flocked in ever-changing patterns across the island skies this time every year. Each glimpse of the birds' freedom intensifies her frustration. Somehow she must break out of this deathly netherworld and find a safe home in the world, one that is beyond the reach of the ocean. But where is there to go, and how could she get there?

Time binds into a pattern. Nest-building, food-gathering and meal-making fill the gloomy daytime. While Mara tries to find an answer to the urgent question of the future, she busies herself with the here and now. She learns which roots and mushrooms are safe to eat and which never to touch, which pungent leaves and herbs must be rubbed on the skin to repel the disease-bearing mosquitoes and malaria flies. She builds her own treenest, helps Broomielaw search for the soft, scented moss she uses as nappies for little Clayslaps and the sweet nuts she grinds into butter that he loves to suck from his fingers. Molendinar shows her tree sap medicines and herbal cures and she gathers and dries driftwood with Ibrox the firekeeper. Evenings, she helps hunt for moonmoths to put in the twig lanterns that hang in the nests and fill the trees with a dim, fluttery glow.

Nights are deep and dark. The Treenesters fill them with music and song and poems and many, many stories. Mara sits by the fire listening as she tries to patch together a pair of new shoes to replace her leaky terrainers from the piles upon piles of old, sodden ones that the tide dredges up from the drowned city on to the Hill of Doves. Or she snuggles in her treenest and watches the ghosts of the old city glimmer in the sea as the tales unfold. Clyde tells of his incredible birth in a tree during a vicious spring storm. Broomielaw describes the sudden disappearance of her father and brother one long-ago night – grief at the loss led to her mother's death soon after. Gorbals tells of the crop of necrotten mushrooms that poisoned the soil in the vegetable patch, killing many Treenesters and leaving him orphaned. The lives of the Treenesters have been harsh and tragic. They show Mara a strength and compassion that helps her grow strong enough to bear her own terrible loss.

Near the end of each day there's a space of time when the sun breaks through the gap between the high city wall and the umbrella of the sky tunnels. Suntime, the Treenesters call it. Mara joins them as they gather on the mossy slope of the Hill of Doves to catch the low amber rays. Their faces lose a little of their pallor in the evening sunshine and their owl eyes crinkle against the brightness as they loll about the hillside, happy on hupplesup, relishing every second of suntime in this strange netherworld.

Their only freedom, thinks Mara, is the light that breaks through another world.

She spends any spare time collecting book litter, drying out and flattening the pages under stones, then reading them in her nest by the flickering light of the moonmoths. All the time she is thinking, thinking, furiously turning ideas over in her head, trying to devise a rescue plan that might salvage a future in this drowned world.

The most surprising thing is that she *wants* a future. Her grief over her lost family is so terrible that she has quickly learned to make her thoughts circle around that reality. It's a wound so achingly raw she cannot bear to touch it. And she endures continual, horrible waves of guilt over her part in bringing everyone here to New Mungo – but somehow, incredibly, she no longer wants to die.

The fate of Rowan and the others in the boat camp deeply scares her, but she knows that even if she managed to make it out through the wall again, the chance of getting herself back and the others safely through to the netherworld is near-impossible. And the netherworld is not an answer to their future. The Treenesters are anxious to escape the rising waters of their island, but they do nothing. They wait for her to act, claiming she is the one who will save them; a presumption which annoys and overwhelms Mara, yet also increases her growing sense of purpose. Desperately, she hopes that her friends in the boat camp can cling to life until she can think of some way to help them. She hopes with all her heart that they're not already dead.

Somehow, for everyone's sake, she must come up with a plan – and fast.

Ibrox is sparking the morning fire, scattering fresh pine needles on last night's embers when Mara climbs down from her nest just after dawn. She has lain awake for most of the night, thoughts racing through her mind. An amazing idea in the fragment of a book she rescued from the waters has set her imagination ablaze. Could this be the key to their future? But as yet, she can't see how it would be possible.

As the air fills with the mind-sharpening scent of roasted pine needles, Mara longs for the lost pages of the book. Maybe they would answer some of her questions. She needs more information, much more. She could search the Weave, of course, but looking for anything in there is like looking for a needle in a million haystacks. It takes for ever and time is what Mara does not have. Could there be quicker answers lying in the realworld ruins?

'It's enough to make a tree angry!' Ibrox explodes as an urchin crashes through the trees and pulls out a length of half-flamed log, upsetting his expertly stacked fire.

The small girl escapes with the precious fire and runs with it up to the ruin at the top of the island.

Mara chuckles. The urchins scavenge anything, even fire.

'Never mind, Ibrox. Can I help anyone?' she yawns, jangling a wind chime made of coloured glass fragments to keep Clayslaps happy, while Broomielaw fastens his swinging nest securely with a tough knit of sticky moss.

151

'You can help me collect the rainwater from the bathtubs at the top of the hill,' Partick shouts over his shoulder. 'Grab a bucket. Possil and Pollock are out on an all-night hunt and this old man has to do it on his own.'

'Then you can boil up the water and make tea,' grins Molendinar, handing her a bunch of tea herbs.

'And milk the goats,' shouts Springburn, as she rounds up the herd.

'The eggs need collecting before Gorbals gets up and stamps all over them with his clumsy big feet,' giggles cheeky young Clyde.

'Then you need to scramble the eggs,' adds Trongate.

'I want eggflap,' argues Gallowgate, hanging freshly washed plastic upon a prickly gorse bush to dry.

'Boiled,' Gorbals grunts sleepily, shaking his moss quilt out of his nest.

'What would you like, Candleriggs?' asks Trongate. 'You decide for us. Scrambled, boiled, eggflap . . . '

'Peace!' calls Old Candleriggs as she climbs down from her nest. 'That's what I want first thing in the morning. What a racket you all make!'

'Mara will stay right there and rock the baby,' smiles Broomielaw. 'She's still half in dreamland.'

The Treenesters no longer treat Mara like an angel who has fallen to Earth.

'He likes the rock-a-bye-baby song,' says Mara. 'My mum sang it to me and my brother.'

Mara sings it to the baby as she rocks his swinging nest. Up above them, the wind rocks New Mungo.

'Please don't sing that any more!' Broomielaw exclaims. 'It's a horrible song.'

Mara starts in surprise, the brutality of the words

striking her for the first time. There couldn't be a worse lullabye for a baby Treenester.

'The ratkin is here,' says Broomielaw. For Mara's sake she tries to hide her disgust and has stopped calling Wing a ratbasher, gentling it to ratkin, though Mara argues he's much more like a little bird; but Broomielaw still won't have him anywhere near her baby.

Mara sneaks Wing a fire-baked potato. She's also got a little pile of the bright litter he treasures – shiny bottle tops and bits of coloured glass – to use as a bribe to entice him to raft over with her to the place the Treenesters have warned her never to go near. She could go alone but she'd far prefer to have some company in that daunting place. And since the Treenesters won't go, there's only Wing.

She has grown used to the urchin's comings and goings, sometimes not seeing him for days as he roams the netherworld with his own kind. Try as she might she can't tame him into a replacement little brother. Wing is wild. He does as he wants. No matter how tender she tries to be or how hard she tries to teach him words and language, he makes it clear he's having none of it. But he answers to the name Mara gave him and seems fond of her; at least, he's fond of the treats she sneaks him.

This morning, unexpectedly, he has brought her a present – an armful of cockles and mussels and whelks. Mara takes them hungrily; she loves shellfish and they'll be good fire-roasted.

'No!' Broomielaw smashes the hoard of shellfish from Mara's hands. 'Don't touch it. It's necrotten stuff.'

Mara looks at the scattered shellfish longingly.

'I won't let you eat it,' Broomielaw insists, and when Mara sees the fear on the girl's face she obeys.

'Wing eats it and he's all right.'

'He's a dirty ratbasher,' says Broomielaw. 'It might kill you.'

There's no arguing with Broomielaw on the subject of the urchins. Mara watches Wing tear into the potato then feed morsels of it to his sparrow. When he's finished every bite and licked his mucky fingers, she calls him over.

'You can have these.' She points to the pile of bright litter. Wing chirrups in delight and makes a grab at a gold bottle top. Mara holds him back and wags a finger at him. 'Not yet. But you can have them all if you come with me over there.'

She points across to the great wizard hat that rises majestically out of the foggy waters.

'No, Mara!'

'Oh, Broomielaw, please stop telling me "no" all the time,' Mara sighs in frustration. 'I'm not Clayslaps.'

'But Candleriggs has always told us it's a dangerous place, full of bad, necrotten things.'

'Maybe. But it's also full of books. That's where they spill out of, you said, and I need books. I've found something in this one . . .' Mara holds up the tatty pages, 'that's given me an incredible idea. Something that might help us. But I need more information than there is in these few pages. And anyway . . .' she hides a mischievous smile, 'doesn't Thenew, the Face in the Stone, have a book on her lap? Maybe this is part of the stone-telling.'

Mara doesn't believe that, but it'll do no harm if Broomielaw thinks so. The girl falls silent and looks from Mara to the great black steeple with huge eyes.

'Be careful,' she whispers fearfully.

Up close, the building makes her dizzy.

There's something ferocious about it, as if it's been built

in a rage of obsession by a hand and mind that could not keep still. Mara gazes in awe at the vast patterns of stone, the latticed windows, the towers and turrets tipped by spinning gold weathervanes that seem to be an army of tiny spears thrust at the caged sky.

Low cloud rushes past, blanking out all sight of New Mungo. The cloud speed gives a sudden illusion of movement and Mara feels as if the great black steeple has broken loose of the Earth; that it – not the speeding clouds – is surging forwards, with her on board. But now the cloud clears, the sky city reappears, its windspires whirling and whooping in the high wind; and she is still caged within the netherworld.

Mara steers the raft through an archway that leads into the large central tower topped by the huge steeple. She sails into a dark forest of stone. Here in the undercroft the sea glugs and gulps, thick with the pulp of books. Echoes of water music run through a honeycomb of caverns and pillars, vaulted chambers and archways. Mara has to lie flat to steer through without hitting her head on the roof caverns. Wing helps paddle. He stops and makes a lunge into the murky water, then brandishes a cold blue lamp that Mara sees with a shudder is a dead fish, luminous with necrotty. But once they are deep in the dim caverns Mara grows thankful for its deathly light.

What was this place? she wonders, peering down through sludgy water to the stone floor that so many people must have walked upon once. But what did they do here?

When they reach a wall, Wing clangs his metal paddle against the stone until there's a crunch. He starts bashing and Mara sees that what he is trying to smash through is the tip of a wooden door.

'We'll never get in,' says Mara. 'It's too solid.'

But she's wrong. The soft, rotten wood is disintegrating. Mara wrenches out a great splinter with her bare hands, kicks and struggles alongside Wing until they have broken right through. The raft will never fit so she ties it to a stone pillar with a rope made from lengths of knotted plastic, slips off and swims through the splintered gash in the door. She is barely inside when she encounters hard stone and finds herself sprawled upon the broad step of a huge, sweeping staircase. Mara struggles to her feet and, with Wing close on her heels, makes her way up the sweeping staircase, along a grand hallway until she comes to a giant doorway.

'Wing!' She grabs his hand, suddenly afraid of what might lie behind such a colossal door. Mara takes a deep breath and, the rusted hinges groaning, she pushes through.

The hall is vast and utterly wrecked.

Were they giants, the people who built this? Mara wonders.

It's only one of many vast halls. The next one is full of golden names set in stone pillars with a symbol beside each one. A musical symbol for Beethoven, Wagner and Mozart. *Musicians*, thinks Mara. There's a paintbrush for Michelangelo, Cezanne, Van Gogh and many others; pens and paper scrolls beside the names of writers and poets; crowns for kings and queens; and many more golden names with ancient dates, their greatness lost in time, all cast in everlasting stone.

High on the walls there are portraits of the faces belonging to the golden names. Mara walks past, studying each one.

There are more stone carvings on the walls – a loaf of

bread with a golden plaque to remember the bakers, hats for the bonnetmakers, wool for weavers, cloth for tailors, plants for gardeners, bricks for builders. All the unnamed, ordinary craftsmen and women.

Now Mara walks into a hall full of glass boxes. Inside each one is a vast assortment of objects, every kind of human invention. And suddenly she understands. These halls hold the golden names of long-gone people who dreamed up the visions that took humankind from wooden clubs to space telescopes, from bone daggers to metal guns, from bread-making to the building of cathedrals, from baked-clay vases to violins and oil painting, from brittle twig combs to the delicate mechanisms of compasses and thermometers, then to computers and cyberspace. And finally to cities in the sky.

Mara is walking through a history of dreams.

Suddenly she sees that the nature technology of the Treenesters must spill from the same well of ingenuity as that which made the New World. It's the same human impulse that drives the urchins to create junk vessels, that made the islanders of Wing find fuel in the peaty land and knit clothes from the sheep they farmed and build homes from island rocks and stones; the same spark that fuelled Mara's adventures through a universe of cyber-dreams on the wings of sunpower.

The shatter of glass wakes her from her daze.

'Wing!'

He appears with a bleeding hand, carrying a dagger and a doll. Then he spies something else he wants, smashes its glass case with his dagger, reaches in and pulls out a fishing net. He pops the wooden doll in the net and looks around for more objects to loot.

'Don't!' Mara rebukes him. But what does it matter?

There's nobody left to see any of these forgotten dreams. All of human history lies on the seabed, all except this, and one day soon the waters might rise further and this will be lost too. Wing may as well take what he wants.

A small object in a case of its own catches her eye. Mara reads its metal plaque then smashes the glass with Wing's paddle, reaches inside and lifts out something that is older than Earth – a tiny meteorite made of the raw material of the universe.

Wing runs up to see what she has looted but grunts in disinterest when he sees the small black rock. He is much more excited by a life-size model of an apeman. At the end of the great halls Mara finds herself in a corridor of many doors.

Which way? Somewhere in this maze of halls and doors there are books, she is sure, but where?

Each door opens into another room and yet more doors. When she comes face to face with a dwarf-sized door set in a curving section of wall, Mara remembers the motto she always followed in the Weave.

When in doubt, always take the most curious route.

It's curious all right. When she squeezes inside she trips on the first step of a tight-winding staircase. Mara follows the steep spiral up and up and up. It feels never-ending.

After a thousand dizzying stairs she spills out through the last door, gasping for breath, her legs like water. And finds herself in a storm-blasted room full of towering book stacks. Book avalanches have made paper mountains of the floor. There are so many books she can't believe her eyes.

If only Rowan could see this!

Beyond this room there are others. Mara walks through room after room – square tower rooms and round turret rooms – all interlinked by doors, all crammed to bursting with a vast clutter of books. At each door she is met by a silence that's immense. Sometimes she thinks she hears a yawn or a cough, a footfall or the whisper of a page turning. But there's no sign of any human presence – it's just the noise of the birds who nest here among the books. Their feathers and droppings are everywhere.

Mara finally flings herself down upon a paper mountain. The wind batters books around the room, flinging loose pages up against stone walls. Her head is reeling. She never guessed there were so many books in the world. The e-texts of every book ever written were stored in just one of the Weave's tall towerstacks. It was filled with tiny, moving scrolls that she could download to read on her cyberwizz. Except Mara never bothered. They looked so flat and boring. She hardly gave the Weavesite a second glance before zooming off elsewhere.

All this – all these books full of ideas and stories – were shrunk to virtually nothing in cyberspace.

And how much more once existed in the rest of the drowned world? So many lost visions and dreams, Mara imagines she'd need a thousand lives to explore them – and even then she'd never discover them all.

Mara picks up a book at random and sits in a window seat. How will she ever find the information she needs in these mountains of books? She leans back in the seat, suddenly struck by what she holds in her hand. It's heavy and the pages are edged in gold, hinting at treasure inside. It smells of dust and wood and leather. She fingers the beautiful patterns on its bound cover. Mara opens the book and the words are settled and calm on the creamy paper. Yet out of their stillness emerges a story. Mara starts to fall into it.

Everything before us and nothing before us . . .

The words build into pictures – but there's no time to read now. She must begin her search. Reluctantly, Mara puts the book down and unfastens a plastic bag she has tied around her waist. Inside, in a second layer of plastic, a double protection to stop the fragile paper getting wet, are the precious fragments of the book that has fired her idea.

The Athapaskans, she reads, *are a mobile people who inhabit the huge, mountainous boreal forests of the Arctic Circle, one of the emptiest, most forgotten places on Earth. They have not devastated the natural world around them as so-called civilized societies have, but have co-existed in fine balance with the land and its animals for thousands of*

And that's almost all there is. The rest of the paper fragment is torn and water-smudged. Mara can only make out the odd sentence about potlatch gifts and a great flood which occurred way back in distant time. But those few lines about the Athapaskans have fired her imagination because they sound as if they are natural relations to the Treenesters. Could there still be mountainous forests at the far north of the world? Tain had searched his old atlas for habitable, mountainous lands but they had all been too far away, he said, unreachable in Wing's old fishing boats. But Tain had always looked south – why didn't he or anyone else think to look north to the Arctic lands?

Now, guiltily, Mara remembers that in the meeting at the church Jamie, the young fisherman who skippered her family's boat, had tried to raise the idea but he had been shouted down by the older fishermen who said the Arctic was a meltdown of ice; you couldn't make a life in a place like that. Then Mara had told them of the New World and all thoughts of going north had been forgotten.

Mara puts her head in her hands. What if Jamie had been right all along? What if the only land within reach was at the very top of the world?

Well, she must find out. And surely an answer lies here, somewhere, among these paper mountains.

NECROTTEN DREAMS AND
JEWEL HEARTS

'*City Songs* by James MacFarlan,' whispers Gorbals, eyeing the fine gold lettering on the book cover with awe. 'A gift for me? Thank you, Mara.' But he doesn't take the book.

'Why are you all scared of books?' Mara flings herself and the book on the grass under the trees, tired and downcast after a long and fruitless search.

'They're full of poisonous necrotty,' Broomielaw reminds her, looking worriedly from the book to baby Clayslaps who is crawling on a patch of grass nearby. 'Candleriggs says so.'

'This isn't – it hasn't been near the water. I found it in a room high up in the great black steeple.'

'Broomielaw told us you went there,' whispers Gorbals. 'Don't let Candleriggs find out.'

'But I will,' Mara insists, 'because I want to know why she fears that building and its books. Gorbals . . .' she sits up now, her face alight, 'you must come with me tomorrow. It's an amazing place full of so many books and things of the old world you won't believe it. Please,

Gorbals. I need someone to help me – it's important. If you want a future you *must* come.' Mara picks up the book again and holds it out towards him, insistently. 'This could have been written for you – read it!' she urges him. Tentatively, Gorbals takes the book. He holds it in his hands as if it's a bomb. 'My mother loved words,' he murmurs. 'She taught me to read from pages she saved from the water – like you do. She wouldn't listen to Candleriggs either.'

Gorbals gingerly turns the pages, and Mara takes her place for sundown beside the others as the Bash begins. Ibrox the firekeeper has scattered the flames with soothing lavender and the scent calms her body and mind, even amid the racket of the Bash.

Gorbals cries out in sudden amazement, his eyes drinking in the words of the book.

'Mara, you are right! Treenesters, listen to this. '*Again upon my senses beat the city's wave-like din*,' he reads. 'This poet has written about the Bash and he hates it too.'

Mara wrinkles her brow. 'It was published over two hundred years ago. There wasn't a Bash then.'

'There must have been,' says Gorbals. 'How else could he write that? Listen, his words are like treasure: he speaks of *Brave hearts, like jewels*. And what does this mean?

But does no lingering tome survive
To prove their presence more than dreams?

'What's a "tome"? Is it like a tomb? A necrotten place?'

'A tome is a very large book,' says Candleriggs quietly. She is frowning fiercely at the book in Gorbals's hands. Now she turns to Mara; but Mara has steeled herself for the old woman's displeasure. 'You were in the library of the university? What were you doing there?'

'Universe city?' asks Gorbals, wonderingly.

'University,' snaps Candleriggs. 'The old place of learning.'

'So that's what it is,' Mara murmurs.

'Then why have you always warned us never to go near it, Candleriggs?' cries Gorbals. 'You've always told us that it's a necrotten place, a place that brings sorrow and heartache. That its books are full of poison. Why?'

'Because it's true,' says the old woman. 'You will not go back there, Mara.'

'I have to,' says Mara. 'Because I think it might hold the answer to the future – yours and mine. Isn't that what you want?'

Old Candleriggs stares at her furiously, then her owl eyes mist with sadness.

'But where's the heartache in learning, Candleriggs? There's no sorrow in that,' says Molendinar. 'If there's learning in those books they might help me with my cures and medicines. There's so much I don't know, so much we need to know.'

Candleriggs shakes her head miserably.

'Mara says that the books of the university might be part of the stone-telling because the statue of Thenew has a book on her knee,' ventures Broomielaw. 'It's true, she does.'

The old woman stands trembling and points up to the sky city. '*That* is the sorrow and heartache that learning ends in. A place that lives only for itself in its own world of dreams and forgets the rest of the world. Now don't ask me any more. It's a story I can't bear to tell.' Candleriggs composes herself. 'But if Mara feels that it's a necessary

164

part of the stone-telling then I must put my faith in her, whether I like it or not. '

Candleriggs sits down again weakly. Broomielaw and Molendinar try to comfort her but the old woman shrugs them off.

Gorbals clears his throat. 'This James MacFarlan has written about our world. His poems are far better than any of mine. So if – if Candleriggs will allow it I'll use his words, not my own, for tonight's sundown.'

Candleriggs mutters as she stares into the sundown fire but she doesn't object.

Pollock sniggers. 'No words of your own left, Gorbals? Got to steal someone else's?'

'I don't steal,' Gorbals says coldly. 'I have what I need and I don't steal what doesn't belong to me.'

The two young men match each other sneer for sneer.

'Stop this,' says Broomielaw breathlessly. 'I hate it. Why is everyone unhappy tonight?'

'The sun is almost gone and you two are bickering yet again,' growls Candleriggs. 'Well, read this poet from long ago, Gorbals. Let's hear if his words are treasure – or poison.'

As the sun drops and light dies in the sky, the din of the Bash recedes. Gorbals flicks through the pages, stops suddenly and peers close at the book.

'*The Ruined City*,' he announces. 'I'll read from this.'

The Treenesters fall still and quiet and settle themselves within the ember glow of the fire. Gorbals begins to read.

'And still this city of the dead
Gives echo to no human tread.'

Mara is covered in goosebumps as the words form pictures.

'And when the sun is red and low,
And glaring in the molten skies,
A shadow huge these columns throw,
That like some dark, colossal hand . . .'

How could he know? wonders Mara. What uncanny future dream did that poet have so long ago?

'Day rises with an angry glance,
As if to blight the stagnant air,
And hurls his fierce and fiery lance,
On that doomed city's forehead bare.
The sunset's wild and wandering hair
Streams backward like a comet's mane,
And from the deep and sullen glare
The shuddering columns crouch in vain,
While through the wreck of wrathful years
The grim hyena stalks and sneers.'

'He knows our city,' nods Broomielaw in the silence that follows. 'But what's a hyena?'

'It's a creature that makes a horrible noise like screaming laughter,' says Candleriggs.

'Well, we know them, don't we?' Ibrox says to Mara. 'We hear the grim hyena screaming every time the door in the wall opens and the white ships come through. They're the orange sky people that invade our world and take away the ratbashers.'

The sea police, thinks Mara, with their orange uniforms and hyena-like sirens. 'They take the urchins away? Where to?'

'Up to the city in the sky,' says Gorbals.

'What for?' asks Mara.

'They use them for work because the ratbashers can swim in the deep water. And they can climb fast and high like rats,' says Possil. 'Pollock and I sometimes see them when we go on our travels to the dangerous parts of the islands on the other side of the water, near the sky towers or the door in the great wall.'

'But they're pests, those ratbashers,' adds Pollock, curling his lip. 'It's good that the sky people take them away and make some use of them. I might have to start culling them myself if they didn't.'

Mara is outraged at Pollock's brutality but she controls her anger because she needs to know more.

'What work are they used for?'

Possil and Pollock look at each other vaguely.

'Tunnels,' yawns Pollock.

'Bridges,' shrugs Possil.

Mara thinks back to the Pickings in the boat camp and feels sick. If the people in the sky city use urchins like Wing as slave labour then is that also why they pick out the young and strong from the boat camp? To be slaves? Mara remembers the spine-chilling feeling she had when the Pickers came round the boat camp and feels sure she is right.

Above them, the city gleams. A maze of starlight glistens far beyond. Stars like diamonds.

'And souls flash out, like stars of God,' murmurs Gorbals.

'From the midnight of the mire.
No palace is theirs, no castle great,
No princely, pillared hall.'

Mara thinks of the wealth of dreams that lie abandoned among the pillared halls of the university. If the New World uses the refugees of the lost, drowned world as slaves to build its empire, then it's a vile and necrotten place and she wants no part of it, ever. She wants to rip that city out of the sky.

Tomorrow she will search again for information on the mountainous lands of the Arctic where the Athapaskans live. She will search and search until she finds the answer she needs. She is struck by an image of Rowan huddled inside his blanket in the boat camp and hopes harder than ever that he's still alive.

She'd better find that answer fast.

Mara watches Broomielaw feed her baby from her own body. The girl looks blissful, in a state of grace that Mara doesn't understand, yet envies. Now Broomielaw puts the baby down to sleep and smiles at Mara.

'Clayslaps will see his two hundredth sunup tomorrow,' she announces proudly as she rocks his swinging nest to the sway of the wild and windy music some of the others are playing on the weird instruments they fashion out of twigs, bones and feathers, bits of metal and plastic and glass.

'We'll celebrate him,' announces Candleriggs. The old woman has recovered from her earlier upset. She holds up the round object she is moulding out of intricately woven grasses. 'See, Broomielaw, I'm making him a soft play ball.'

Broomielaw smiles and lifts up a clay cup that Mara has watched her shape and dry and stain red with berry juice. 'I've made him his first cup.' She turns to Mara. 'How many sunups have you seen, Mara? Maybe a thousand less than me, I think.'

'How many since I came here?' Mara looks blank.

'No, I mean how many have you lived?' smiles Broomielaw.

'How could I know that?' laughs Mara.

'You don't know?' says Broomielaw. 'I've seen six thousand six hundred and thirty-four sunups.'

'I've seen six thousand two hundred and seventy-eight,' says Gorbals. 'Candleriggs has seen over *thirty thousand*.'

'Where I come from we count in years,' says Mara. 'I'm fifteen years old.'

'Years?' says Gorbals frowning. 'My mother told me about years when I was little – a year is something to do with the sun.'

'A year is from one winter to the next,' says Mara, trying to remember whether Earth circled the sun, or if it was the other way round. The more books she reads, the more frustrated she is about how little she knows of the world.

Gorbals shakes his head. 'A year is too long to hold in mind but you can hold a day easily enough.'

'But it's too hard to remember days,' says Mara.

'It's easy,' says Gorbals. 'You just add one on after another. And at the end of each day you can look at how you lived it. You could never do that with a year, it's too big.'

'The Earth works in years. So do we,' Mara explains.

'People live by sunups and sundowns,' insists Gorbals. 'Now, a hedgehog or a squirrel might count its life in years because they sleep in winter and wake in summer but we sleep at sundown and wake at sunup. So we are part of the story of days.'

Pollock is stretched on the ground tearing into a roasted rabbit. He gives Broomielaw a dismissive wave with a rabbit leg. There is something in those eyes of his, huge eyes as lazy as stagnant water, that Mara dislikes. She can't understand why Broomielaw has anything to do with him. Though Clayslaps is his baby too, and he'll swing his little nest from time to time, jingling his wind chime, all care of the baby is done by Broomielaw. He prefers to go on night hunts with Possil, the nervy, fidgety one, then sleep all day. Mara's not sure if she likes Possil either, but she will need their hunting skills if the plan that's taking shape in her mind is to work.

'I wanted to ask Pollock something,' says Mara.

'Pollock?' says Gorbals, sending him a filthy look. 'He's good for nothing unless it's bad.'

Pollock hurls his ravished rabbit leg in return for the look and it bounces off Gorbals' head, to Pollock's loud delight. Gorbals grabs a branch and looks ready to thwack Pollock with it until Ibrox intervenes and threatens to roast them both on the fire if they don't behave.

'What's between Gorbals and Pollock?' Mara whispers to Broomielaw. 'They seem to hate each other.'

Broomielaw's gentle face stiffens. She leans over to prod the fire. 'Me,' she answers, indistinctly. 'I'm between them.'

'You?' says Mara, astonished. 'But how?'

Broomielaw leans closer to Mara so that their conversation is private.

'Once Gorbals loved me but I turned his love to ash,' Broomielaw says sadly. 'There's nothing I can do now. He hates Pollock, though he's kind enough to me and Clayslaps, I suppose. I can't blame him.'

'What happened?'

Broomielaw glances nervously at Gorbals and Pollock but they are both now safely occupied.

'One night,' she whispers, 'instead of nesting I went off with Pollock. I was restless and the night was too warm. The skies were like blue glass. It was high summer when they never darken and it seemed a shame to waste

170

such a night. Gorbals was busy as usual with a head full of poems and I – I was lonely and fed up. Pollock began telling me about a tiny island way over by the golden pod that flies up to the sky, a place we never go near because it's too dangerous. The sky people kill anyone they find there who's not from their world.

'Pollock told me he knew a hidden route to the island, over the path of an old bridge that only appears at low tide. He said we could go there and watch the ship that comes in through the great door in the wall – the door you came through. He told me the island was full of secrets and magic, the kind of magic you want on a night like that. He described a strange plant which only grows on that island, a special herb, and he made me want to try it. So I went with him to the island. I was curious and it sounded exciting.

'But the herb was strong and dangerous. It magicked me out of myself and into a dream where Pollock seemed much more than he really is. In the morning I felt dull-headed and sick and Pollock was just Pollock again. I wanted to run away from him and forget everything that had happened. I didn't want Gorbals to know, and I made Pollock promise not to tell him. But I couldn't keep it a secret because little Clayslaps came from the magic of that strange night. And so that's what is between them.'

'He's ruined your life,' says Mara flatly. 'He stole it. Gorbals is right, he *is* a thief.'

'It's not ruined,' says Broomielaw. 'Clayslaps is the most wonderful thing that has ever happened to me. It was my own fault that I lost myself in a false enchantment.'

'But you still love Gorbals?' Mara asks.

'It doesn't matter if I do,' says Broomielaw bitterly. 'He

has built a great wall around his heart to keep me out! A wall made of words.'

Molendinar shakes her head and sighs over the pot of herbs she is grinding. Mara puts a gentle hand on Broomielaw's shoulder. She doesn't know what to say.

'What did you want to ask Pollock?' says Broomielaw. Her gentle face is flushed with distress yet she manages a small smile.

'I want him to do some hunting for me,' answers Mara.

'Well, he's eaten a whole rabbit, so he's happy,' notes Molendinar dryly, 'and he's had plenty of hupplesup too. He's more of a pest than ever when he's been guzzling hupplesup but you're the Face in the Stone, after all, so he might watch his tongue.'

Mara looks at Pollock keenly. He feels her gaze on him and shoots a sly glance at her, frowning and fidgeting. 'It wasn't me, it was Possil!' he bursts out. 'He looked at it while you were away today.'

'I did not!' yelps Possil. 'It was you, Pollock. You said, let's—'

Possil flinches as Pollock shoots him a venomous glare.

'You looked at my magic machine?' Mara guesses. 'It has your fingerprints all over it, Pollock.'

Pollock wriggles as if he's caught in a trap.

'You mean you sneaked into my bag and looked at my belongings while I was away?'

'Pollock!' gasps Broomielaw, outraged.

'Well, I need you to help me with something,' Mara tells Pollock. 'If you agree to do what I want we'll forget about it.'

'You will do as Mara asks, Pollock Halfgood,' Candleriggs declares, 'to make up for your prying. I'll give you

172

one last chance to live up to your name before I change it to Nogood. Do you hear me?'

Pollock nods sullenly.

'I want you to catch me a sky person,' says Mara.

The others gasp. Pollock sits up.

'Dead or alive?' he whispers. He looks at Mara, his pale, sullen eyes now wide and gleaming.

'Alive,' says Mara. 'I just need their clothes. Then you'll let them go.'

'Difficult,' says Pollock, looking at Possil.

'Very difficult,' echoes fidgety Possil. 'You see, to catch something it must be within your grasp. That's the trick. To get it in your grasp you have to sneak up on it. But there's nobody can sneak better than Possil,' says Possil.

'Or you get it to fall into your trap.' Pollock's sly smile spreads across his face and he makes a snapping sound with his fingers. 'It's all about knowing what kind of trap is best for the one you want to catch. The right kind of trap, that's the trick. And there's nobody sets a better trap than Pollock,' says Pollock.

Mara hears a sharp gasp from Broomielaw.

'Think like a spider,' he continues. 'A spider has the best ambush tricks I've ever seen, the most beautiful traps in the world. They never run after anyone. They get their catch to walk right into their pretty trap every time.'

Broomielaw stifles a sob, gets to her feet and disappears into the trees. Mara can't help herself – she bounds over and kicks Pollock. He yells in shock. Then Mara grabs a mothlight and runs after Broomielaw, following the sound of her sobs. At the top of the hill behind the ruined building Mara catches up with her.

'I hate him,' Broomielaw cries. 'I have his baby but I

was just a bit of hunting practice. I fell right into his pretty trap.'

'He's a bigger rat than any ratkin,' says Mara. 'I kicked him – hard. Do you think that's part of the stone-telling, Broomielaw? The Face in the Stone kicks Pollock the rat?'

Broomielaw giggles through her tears. Then she beckons to Mara. 'Come and see this. It's secret.'

The netherworld is full of the slow moans and whispers of New Mungo's windspires. Broomielaw's owlish vision takes her quickly and easily through the dark. Mara hurries after her through the trees, beating moth-hungry bats off the twig lantern with a stick. Owls sit among the branches like white phantoms, hooting softly, dropping from the trees like dead weights when they spy a mouse. Glow-worms and fireflies are the only points of light beyond the fluttery lantern and Mara yearns to be back at the bonfire preparing to nest. Where is Broomielaw taking her?

At last they stop at a thick spread of bramble bushes. Broomielaw reaches under the thorns and berries and tugs out a large, flat, plastic-wrapped board. She unfastens the plastic and reveals a huge broken mirror. Mara looks closer and sees that it's a mosaic of tiny glass and mirror fragments that have been painstakingly jigsawed together. The light of the moonmoths makes a flickery magic upon its crazy patterns.

'Did you do this?'

'Yes,' says Broomielaw. 'You see, my life is not all ruined. I have my baby and I've still held on to the dream of who I am. I just don't have much time for it these days. Clayslaps takes up all my time and energy but maybe he can help me once he's grown a bit.'

174

'What is it?' says Mara, fingering the massive mosaic in awe.

'Sunpower. For a long time I've been dreaming of ways to hold the sun in our world, to use its power. This mirror is my idea to catch the sun each morning and beam it straight on to our fire and light it. I don't have the settings right yet and it's not strong enough in winter and the sun changes its place a little each morning. But one day I'll get it right. I have another dream – to forge metal panels to catch the sun's heat.' Broomielaw pulls out a plastic bag, heavy with flat-hammered metal odds and ends. 'That's not even begun yet. But one day we could have fire and hot water ready for us when we waken each morning. There are other things I've thought of . . . '

As Broomielaw trails off into thought, Mara remembers what bothered her as she walked through the vast halls of the university, looking at the portraits of the golden names. There were no dreamswomen. Apart from the odd mythical figure or queen, not one of the golden names had belonged to a woman. All the great dreamers had been men.

Now Mara sees how it could have happened. The women might have dreamed just as hard – as hard as Broomielaw does now – but their dreams had become all tangled up with the knit of ordinary life, with meal-making and babycare and nest-building. Yet wasn't precious little Clayslaps more wonderful than anything dreamed up by those golden names?

'You must keep working on this,' Mara urges. 'It's really good.'

Broomielaw looks at Mara with hope glimmering in her eyes. And Mara sees the power the girl takes from her words because she thinks it's the wish of the Face in the Stone.

'Don't give up on it.'

'I won't,' murmurs Broomielaw, fingering her mirror mosaic. 'I won't ever, now. Me and Clayslaps, we'll do it together.'

As they return to the grove to nest, Mara wonders how many of those golden names in the great halls had dreamswomen as mothers – women who helped them find and follow a dream. Maybe one day, long into the future, Clayslaps would be famous for the dream of sunpower begun by his mother. But would Broomielaw be remembered too?

If I have anything to do with it, she will, Mara vows.

And what about her own dream? The plan that she is trying to dream up is beginning to take shape, bit by bit, like a great mosaic. A plan that just might save them all and find them a future. But there are still crucial missing pieces that she cannot find, that she *must* find. Mara sits for a moment at the foot of the beech tree she nests in and tries to believe that there really is a future on this drowned Earth. Beneath her, the grass is ribbed with great tree roots. She lies flat on her back and looks at the skyward-reaching branches of the tree, mirrored by the roots that reach deep into the Earth. Each tree is an explosion of life. The planet is alive! She must hold on to that belief.

She still can't believe in the stone-telling or that she is the Face in the Stone, but it's odd – this plan of hers, if she can really bring it all together, will save the Treenesters, just as they believe she is meant to. Just as if she really is the Face in the Stone.

Mara sighs wearily. The stone-telling prophecy is like a pebble in her shoe that she cannot shake out.

But her plan is completely practical and it's got nothing to do with visions or superstition or birds or fishes with rings or any of the other signs and statues that the Treenesters claim is the stone-telling. If she can just find a map and more information about the high lands of the Arctic among the paper mountains in the university, and get hold of the clothes she needs to make her look like a New World citizen – then all she has to do is find a way to access the ships which dock in the great towers. And that's the bit of the plan she hasn't worked out yet.

If only she could find the cyberfox and get him to help her . . .

Mara climbs into her nest and takes out her cyberwizz, recharged on snatches of netherworld sunbeams. *Later*, she tells herself. And she feels a shiver of the old excitement at the thought of plunging back into the familiar cyberworld of the Weave. Maybe, just maybe, she will find the fox. But right now she must begin to prepare the Treenesters. She must start to tell them something of her audacious plan and get them ready.

'Treenesters!' she announces to the surrounding nests. 'Listen! I have a story I want to tell you. It's the story of a people called the Athapaskans that live in a forgotten highland forest at the top of the world. People that sound a lot like you.'

THE LAND OF THE PEOPLE

Next morning Mara is awake even before Ibrox the fire-keeper – ready and eager for a full day's hunt in the book rooms of the university. She calls up to Gorbals, hoping to persuade him to come with her, then begins to gather fallen twigs to stoke the sunup fire. Pollock's small hunting axe is lying on the ground. Mara picks it up, shivering beside the paltry fire. Only the gloomiest dawn light filters through the sky city, and the netherworld is a dank and bitter place. As she raises her arms to axe a low branch of a birch tree, someone grabs her wrist, painfully. She spins round and it's Gorbals.

'What are you doing?' he demands, amazed.

'We need some more wood.' Mara tells him. 'The fire's too low and I'm cold. Why, what's wrong?'

Gorbals wrenches the axe from her fingers. He stares as if she'd suggested fire-roasting baby Clayslaps.

'We do not kill trees,' he says sternly then looks at Mara searchingly. 'Maybe you're right. Maybe you can't be the Face in the Stone. Tree-killing is a terrible crime.' Now he looks worried, wary. 'You haven't killed a tree before, have you?'

'There weren't any trees on my island,' responds Mara. 'So I didn't have the chance. Anyway, I wasn't killing it, I was only chopping a branch or two.'

'That is killing,' Gorbals insists. 'What if I chopped one of your limbs off? Tree killing is part of the story of the world's drowning. When Candleriggs was young she lived in the age of tree crime. The Earth needs its trees.' He frowns. 'There were no trees on your island? Not even one?'

'I never saw a tree till I came here,' Mara confesses.

Gorbals shakes his head, stunned.

'Maybe that's why your island drowned. A place without trees is a dead place. We treat our trees with respect. We knock on them politely before we go to nest – yes, I've seen you smile – we leave them food offerings too and they eat them. We—'

'The birds eat them, stupid,' Mara retorts, but gently. Then she remembers something Tain told her. 'Wing did have trees once. Lots. The roots of them made peat in the Earth and we used the peat for our fires. Long ago, Wing was all forest.'

'And what happened to the trees?' Gorbals asks. 'If they were killed and their dead roots were left in the Earth then your island was a necrotten place.'

Anger takes Mara by surprise. How dare he say such horrible things about her island? It all happened hundreds of years ago. It was nothing to do with her. The ancient forest was burned down to free the land for farming.

She begins to gather up the small pile of twigs at her feet and throws them furiously on the fire. The words stick like thorns inside her.

'Mara, I'm sorry,' says Gorbals. 'I said cruel words.'

Mara bites her lip and nods tearfully. 'But you think

179

we lost our island because of what the people long before us did?'

Gorbals sighs. 'We lost *our* city because of that too. Candleriggs says human beings burned up the power of the Earth, not just the trees but so much of the goodness of the planet that the world grew hot and the great ice mountains melted and flooded the lands. She lived through it all.'

'Our ancestors stole our future.'

'Yes, and the sky people have only built themselves a safe island up above the ocean. It's not up to them to find an island for us.' Gorbals shrugs and glances up at the city he is trapped beneath. Mara's dark eyes follow his gaze and she frowns, no longer sure what she thinks about anything.

'Come to the university with me,' pleads Mara. 'Please, Gorbals, I need your help – you know words and it's words I'm looking for. Words that will tell me what I need to know if we are to escape from here and find a safe home in the world.'

Gorbals looks over to the university steeple with the same fearful, yet eager expression Mara saw in his face when he took the book from her.

'I found the book I gave you,' Mara tells him, 'in a great round room piled high with books. Thousands of books, full of poems. Imagine, Gorbals, a room filled with *mountains* of poetry.'

'I'll come,' he nods. 'Your story last night about the people at the top of the world decided me. I will come with you and give you whatever help I can.'

Gorbals walks with Mara through the vast hall of dreams, gazing up at its colossal windows. The glimmer cast by the night lights of New Mungo is just enough to let them read the names in the coloured glass. Mara begins a roll-call of the world's great dreamers.

'Galileo. Newton. Einstein. Fleming. Virgil. Plato. Shakespeare. Milton. Dante. Byron. Burns. Tolstoy. Rousseau. Marx.'

Gorbals stares into the depths of the far halls. 'Who were they?'

'Creators,' says Mara. 'And all men, it seems.' She points up at the portraits of all the great names and she tells her theory of dreams, of the missing women in the mosaic of creation.

'But women grow the living dreams, the human ones,' Gorbals argues. 'A human being is the greatest creation of all. Each of us is a new living dream.'

'Except we've become a living nightmare,' says Mara. 'The human dream's all gone wrong. I can't believe there were no great dreamswomen in the whole history of the world. I bet there were loads. So why are none of them remembered here?'

They walk slowly through the vast halls. 'There must have been many unknown men whose names and dreams are lost too,' says Gorbals after a while.

With a stab of pain, Mara thinks of her father; then Tain and Alex, and all the unknown, ordinary men who farmed the land.

'True,' she says softly. 'But still, there are no women at all.'

'Courage, perseverance, fortitude,' Gorbals reads from a stained glass window that tells a picture story of an ancient battle.

Mara leads them down the last of the vast halls, through the dwarf door set in the turret, and they begin the climb up the dizzying spiral of a thousand stairs, until they reach the book rooms that fill the huge tower beneath the great wizard hat steeple.

'Mara!' Gorbals clutches her hand fearfully as they walk through the tumbledown stacks and mountainous heaps of books. 'So much – so many – I can't believe it.'

Mara stops in the doorway of the seventh room.

'This is the room full of poetry,' she whispers.

Wonderstruck and trembling, Gorbals stares around him.

'I'll leave you here for a while and I'll begin searching,' says Mara.

'Don't leave me alone!' gasps Gorbals.

'They're only books, Gorbals. They can't hurt you.'

'That's not what Candleriggs says.' But already Gorbals is on the floor, rustling through the treasure of pages.

Mara walks through to the next room. Where to begin? How will she find information on the Arctic among all this. *History*, she reads, noticing the sign above the door. Of course! The book rooms must be divided into different subjects. Mara walks back through the rooms, reading the sign above each door. Philosophy? What could that be? Art, literature, anthropology, history – and so many books for each. Archaeology, geography . . .

Mara stops. Geography. Isn't that the one? Geography is to do with atlases and the Earth. She dives into the room and begins hunting. There are books about every land on Earth – every land there once was. China and the Far East, the Americas, Russia, the Middle East, Africa, Asia, Scandinavia, Europe, Australia . . .

'Found anything?' Gorbals stands in the doorway, looking more of a plastic scarecrow than ever. Books stick out everywhere, from all the ragged pockets in his plastic tatters. 'I don't care what Candleriggs says,' he cries. 'I must have these, I must! But now I'll help you,' he says, seeing the weary look on Mara's face.

Hours pass as they search the book stacks and shelves and the piles of blown and toppled volumes on the floor. At last Mara slumps back against a heap of books.

'It's useless!' she cries and bursts into tears. 'I'm useless. But I *have* to find an answer, or else Mum and Dad and Corey and Gail all died for nothing!'

Gorbals rushes over to her. 'Mara, Mara, don't cry, we'll – *ow!*'

He stubs his big toe on a fallen bookcase and hops about in pain, then crashes backwards into the tottering bookstack next to him. Books flutter and tumble from the shelves and dust and cobwebs fill the air with a thick haze as ancient pages disintegrate all around them.

Mara covers her head, coughing and spluttering, as books thump and flutter upon her.

'Oh, Gorbals!' she sobs, but she can't help laughing too. 'You clumsy big – *ow!*'

A final volume falls with a *thwack* on her head.

Gorbals rakes away the pile of books that have landed in her lap, sneezing and blinking in the dust clouds.

'*Greenland,*' he reads wistfully, catching sight of the silvery title of one. He opens it wonderingly. 'What a beautiful name. Maybe it's a land of trees. I wonder where it is.'

'I don't know,' sighs Mara, 'but it's sure to be drowned like the other lands. It's the Arctic we're looking for.'

Mara rubs tears and dust from her eyes, and forces herself to begin searching once again.

'Mara,' says Gorbals, after a while.

'Mm,' she says distractedly as she scans title after title.

Then she registers the excitement in his voice and turns around. 'What?'

Gorbals is still engrossed in the silvery-titled book.

'Greenland *is* in the Arctic. It's a land of mountains that's been trapped under ice for millions of years. But the people who live there don't call it Greenland because strangely it's not green at all – it is white with snow and ice. They call it Kal-aall-it Nun-aat,' he sounds out the strange word carefully. 'Kalaallit Nunaat. The land of the people.'

When he looks up at Mara her eyes are almost as wide as his own. 'But it will be flooded too,' she says.

'No, listen. *Greenland is a vast, empty land of mountains locked in ice,*' reads Gorbals. '*The interior has been sunk beneath the weight of colossal ice sheets. If ever that weight of ice was to melt it would engulf and drown the lands of the Earth with a billion litres of water for each person on the planet. Yet once freed from her immense burden of ice, Greenland would bob up like a cork, her highlands revealed for the first time since they were locked in the deep freeze of the Ice Age.*'

Mara listens in amazed silence.

'Where – where exactly is this land?' she asks at last, wishing that she knew more of the world, ashamed once again at her own ignorance. Gorbals takes the book to her and shows her the map. And Mara cries out in dismay because Greenland is the massive island that divides the North Atlantic from the Arctic Ocean, north of Wing. It's far north, much further than the distance New Mungo was to the south; but maybe just within reach. *Oh, we should have gone north! We might have done if everyone hadn't listened to me.*

But we didn't know, Mara reminds herself. We thought

it was in meltdown, that the land would be sunk too. We never knew it would bob up like a cork once the ice was gone. How could we?

Mara flicks through the book, her eyes gulping in information.

'Oh, Gorbals!' Elated, she clasps the book to her chest. Then she jumps up to hug him, gleefully. 'This is it! This is what we need!'

Gorbals looks amazed and delighted. 'Then there *is* a place in the world for the Treenesters? In Greenland? The land of the people.'

Mara nods, her eyes shining. 'I think so.'

'But how will we get there? So far across the ocean!'

Now Mara shakes her head and her dark hair falls across her face. 'I don't know yet.'

'Last night you said you wanted the clothes of a sky person, then you ran off after Broomielaw and you never said why.'

'Well, the only way I can get near the ships is if I look like a sky person. A scruffy refugee like me doesn't stand a chance. The problem is, even if I can get into the city I don't know what to do then – we need to overpower the city guards and police to steal a ship – more than one ship because we must help the people in the boat camp too. But there aren't enough of us – they'll shoot us all. Oh, Gorbals, I just can't see a way to do it! But now we've found this . . .' she clasps the book on Greenland, 'I can't give up. I must keep trying to think of a way.'

'You will,' says Gorbals warmly. 'Because you are the Face in the Stone.'

'I'm not, Gorbals, really I'm not. I'm just a girl called Mara and somehow I've ended up in such a strange place.'

'Mara, then. Ma-ra, Ma-ra . . . it's the sound of a wave rolling in to shore.'

Mara smiles. 'I like that.'

Gorbals smiles back. 'We should get going now,' he says, but neither of them moves. Silence falls, as dark and deep as the book stacks, ghosting through the vast halls and up through the staircases and book rooms of the steeple tower.

Gorbals reaches inside one of the ragged pockets in his plastic tatters and takes out a book. Mara nestles down beside him as he begins to read a poem he has found called *By the North Sea*, about a land lonelier than ruin and a sea stranger than death.

'Is that what the sea is like?' he asks fearfully, once the poem is finished. 'Stranger than death?'

Mara is puzzling over something else. 'Gorbals, what if the sky people have taken Greenland for themselves?'

Gorbals frowns then shakes his head. 'Candleriggs once told me they don't want to live in the world any more, only the sky – and even beyond.'

'Beyond? What's beyond the sky?'

'The stars. Candleriggs said that's where their eyes are fixed – on a journey out into the stars. They want to make New Worlds out there too,' says Gorbals.

Amazed, Mara tries to imagine a New World city on some distant planet in space.

'How does Candleriggs know all this?'

'She lived through many things she won't talk about,' shrugs Gorbals. 'Terrible things in the time when the world drowned.'

His stomach rumbles loudly. Mara reaches over for her backpack and takes out the plastic-wrapped package of food they have brought, along with flasks of rainwater and hupplesup. They munch ravenously on thick rolls of herby potato pancake. Full stomachs and hupplesup set them yawning after their early rise and expedition across the water, followed by their long hunt in the book rooms.

Mara nestles sleepily into a hillock of books.

'The littlest of naps.' Gorbals yawns loudly. 'We must get back well before the Bash starts and the ships come in. We're much nearer the sky people here.' He snuggles down too, just for a while.

All too soon, Mara wakens with a jolt. A fox has wakened her – a dream fox this time, whose eyes and flashing tail torment her amid the ruins and junk heaps of the Weave. Each time she thinks she's close the fox slips out of reach and disappears. Then, just as she finds it and reaches out a hand to touch that tawny fur, the fox turns on her, snarling and vicious.

'Bats?' Gorbals murmurs, feeling her jump, his voice full of dust and sleep. 'Ratbashers?'

Mara shivers. 'No, just me. It's all right.'

Now she's wide awake, feeling desolate. Gloom has descended upon the netherworld and she wonders what time of day it is. She looks out through the smashed window but the clouds are too thick to let the sun through so it's difficult to judge. It can't be too late, surely. They were up so very early.

'Garlic and sapphires in a puddle,' Gorbals babbles in his sleep.

Mara feels around the pockets of her backpack and takes out her cyberwizz globe. It tingles in response to her touch. Her heart is beating fast as she grips the wand then slips the halo over her eyes for the first time since she left the island. She powers up the cyberwizz and verves into the world of the Weave. When she drops down a shimmering strand right into the heart of it she is suddenly panic-stricken. It all feels strange and alien. The noisy electronic buzz and flicker of the once-familiar towerstacks and junk mountains fill her with fear. She tries to zip and zoom as she used to but the speed unnerves her. What's wrong with her? She feels as if she has been gone a hundred years, as if she is a stranger. And then suddenly she knows what's wrong.

Before, fear was a game. Now it's far too real. Mara tries to make herself venture into the ruined back alleys where a fox would stalk and roam, but she can't. To her left, something shifts in a pile of electronic litter that has tumbled off a junk mountain. A long, electronic feeler reaches out towards her. Mara stifles a scream and tries to leap, but she's forgotten how – forgotten the cryptic symbols that used to give her such effortless speed and power. The feeler hovers above her head, sparking venomous decay.

Mara rips off the halo and crashes back into realworld. She stuffs the cyberwizz in her backpack and sits, sobbing silently.

Now the Weave is lost to her too. Now she hates it. Everything that she has lived through has left her a nervous wreck. She'll never be able to find the fox again now.

Mara gets up and wanders among the dim forest of bookstacks, more lonely and desolate than ever. She really should waken Gorbals – but wait. At the end of a long run of shelves she spies a doorknob sticking out of a gap between the books. A blackened brass door knob, but no door.

Strange, thinks Mara. Well, there's only one thing to do.

And she tugs with both hands on the doorknob until at last something gives. The bookcase moves – or at least part of it does. Mara cowers, waiting for books to clatter upon her head, but they don't. The books seem to be stuck fast upon this bit of shelf. Is it a false bookcase?

It's a secret door.

Mara tugs it full open and steps inside. And is deflated. It's just a walk-in cupboard. Why bother with a secret door to an empty cupboard? But no, set in the back wall of the cupboard is another door, smaller still. Mara tugs that too, half-expecting to find another cupboard within that, a door to yet another door. But this door won't budge. There are rusted bolts at the top and bottom and a key stuck fast in a lock. Mara looks along the book stacks and, selecting the sturdiest hardback she can find, bashes open the stuck bolts. Then, wrapping her fingers in her jacket sleeve for protection, she breaks the ancient tryst of key and lock, and at last the door bursts open.

Mara steps up out into the open spire that sits at the top of the great steeple. Wind blasts her and she gazes upwards in amazement. She is standing at the centre of a huge cone, an immense network of stone and air.

I'm right inside the great wizard hat!

Just above her head hangs the most colossal bell. Facing her is yet another spiralling staircase. But this one is only for the most brave – or the most foolhardy. It's an impossibly sheer and narrow, wide-open staircase that winds up through thin air. It spirals all the way up, past the giant bell, to the utmost tip of the steeple. Beyond which is nowhere. Why risk life and limb to climb to the top of the steeple when there is nowhere else to go except oblivion or straight back down again? Mara puts her foot testingly on the first step of the staircase. On the other hand, why not?

Just a few steps, just to see if I can, just to prove I haven't lost all my nerve and courage . . .

She begins to climb. Storms have long since smashed the wooden handrail to useless stumps. The wind throws punches, making her climb even more precarious. The entire staircase is a danger zone. One careless step, a loose stone, even an instant of dizziness could prove fatal.

'Mara!'

Shock-white as a ghost, Gorbals peers round the door frame.

'What are you doing? Get back down here!'

'Come and get me,' grins Mara, shakily, from her perch high above him.

'Down, Mara,' pleads Gorbals. 'Now!'

Mara is almost at the top. What a waste to get so far and no more. Ignoring Gorbals, she climbs the final coil of the spiral, then looks out beyond the steeple. It's a big mistake. The drowned world spins and sways beneath her, the sky city lurches above. Mara grips tight, unable to move. She can just hear Gorbals's voice over the thundering beat of her own blood.

'I can't come any higher, Mara. The stairs are too unsteady and both our weights might be too much. Just step back one foot at a time.'

Mara closes her eyes tight shut and begins to climb slowly backwards, step by trembling step, the gap between each a timeless moment of terror, until at last Gorbals grabs her and pulls her safely to the ground.

He is furious. 'Mara, are you mad? What were you doing?'

She needs to cry but can only laugh. Fear has turned

her body into a rubbery, useless thing. She sits huddled beside Gorbals, trying to calm herself. What *did* she think she was doing?

A crack of low afternoon sun finds a patch in the cloud and breaks over the city wall. Suddenly the dark world is aglow. Gorbals stares out at the golden panorama of the netherworld. Then he gasps and stands up, pointing over to the city wall.

'Look! I can see over the wall and the world is alive! It's all glitter and sparkle!'

Mara stands up to see. 'It's the ocean,' she tells him.

'The ocean!' breathes Gorbals, his owl-eyes wide with astonishment. 'But I thought it would be a dark and deathly thing, like it said in the poem. I never imagined it would be beautiful.'

'Oh, it's beautiful,' says Mara wistfully. 'And the wide-open sky – Gorbals, wait till you see that on starlit nights or full of sunset or stacked with gigantic clouds.'

'But *will* I ever see it?' says Gorbals. 'Or will I be trapped in here all my days?'

Mara sees the hunger in her friend's eyes for the outside world he has never seen. She grips his hand. 'Just you wait,' she tells him.

From inside the steeple there's a clear view of New Mungo's central towers where the supply ships harbour. How, Mara puzzles again, can they get a ship out of there and through the city gate? And even if they could, how could they navigate it all the way to Greenland?

It's useless, Mara decides. Then she looks over to the city wall, so high there's no sign of the boat camp that lies on the other side of it. But it's there so she must keep trying to think of a way.

The rooftops of the drowned city have risen from the

low tide like the sunken hulls of ships. Below, a tall flagpole with its ancient flag now a faded, tattered rag creaks like the great mast of a sailing boat, trapped within the netherworld.

'We must go now, Mara,' says Gorbals anxiously. 'It's getting late and the Bash will begin soon.'

They make their way back to the glugging, water-filled caverns of the undercroft where they have anchored their raft. Urgently, Gorbals begins to paddle across the shadowed and sun-streaked waters.

'We'll be all right,' Mara tells Gorbals. 'The urchins are more interested in their bashing than in us.'

'It's not just the ratbashers,' he begins, 'it's—'

A sudden grim howl fills the netherworld. Mara jumps with fear. Over at the great towers of New Mungo, lights crash upon the waters. The noise and glare are horrendous.

'The sky people!' yells Gorbals. 'We must find somewhere to hide!'

He digs his oar into the water and they surge up on a wave, right on to the roadway of the Bridge to Nowhere that rises like an arm from the sea and ends in mid-air.

'The bus!' cries Mara, and they race for cover into the battered rust shell of the bus that was abandoned there so long ago. Through a window frame they watch a fleet of police waterbikes and speedboats scream across the netherworld. The blaring battalion roars past, sirens and searchlights full-on.

'They're headed for the cathedral,' says Gorbals.

'The urchins!' Mara gasps. 'Oh, no!'

'*Wondrous hive!*' Gorbals rages at the sky city. '*Where dark reptiles congregate. Oh cold and careless barren blast!* No, Mara!' he yells as, before he can stop her, she begins to race back down the Bridge to Nowhere and jumps on the raft they abandoned on its crumbling arm.

Horrified, Gorbals runs after her and jumps on alongside as she oars out into the churning wake of the sea police.

WIPEOUT

Crouching deep among thick reeds at the water's edge, round behind the cathedral, they are safe – at least for the moment. Gorbals grips Mara hard by the arms to make sure she doesn't dash out of the cover of the reeds and run up through the gravestones towards the front door of the cathedral, where the sea police have gathered in a blare of lights and sirens.

'Mara, we can't go any closer. It's too dangerous. We need to get away from here, now, before they find us. The ratkin might not even be here – he could be anywhere. But even if he is here, there's nothing we can do.'

'I can't let them get Wing! I can't.'

'There are lots of them and only two of us. What can we do? They'll only take us or kill us!'

'My family died, Gorbals – my little brother was only six – he was like Wing,' sobs Mara. 'Then my best friend died. My other friend, Rowan, might be dead too. I couldn't help any of them and it was my fault because I brought them here. So I can't do nothing now and let Wing and the other children die too!'

194

'You didn't let anyone die, Mara. It's what happened. There was nothing you could do.'

Children's screams and gunfire erupt from the cathedral. 'I can't bear it!'

Mara tears free fom Gorbals and fights her way through the reeds. There is a curse and then a splash behind her as he follows. Mara darts between the gravestones on the hillside and manages to make it safely to the rear of the cathedral. She grabs a broken-off chunk of gravestone and hurls it through a window set low in the wall of the cathedral. Gorbals helps her kick in the last shards of coloured glass and she drops down through the window frame into darkness.

Above her head, in the main hall of the cathedral, is the most sickening noise; terrible screams and wails, crashings and gunfire. Now she's here she knows it's useless. There's nothing she can do.

Mara sobs. 'Gorbals, they're killing them.'

But Gorbals doesn't answer. Mara peers into the darkness. Gorbals is not there.

The horror seems never-ending. At last the screams and gunfire end. Mara sits in the dark, too shocked and terrified to move. All of a sudden she knows she is not alone.

'Gorbals?' she whispers.

There's no answer. She jumps as she sees the two liquid points of light that are fixed upon her. Two eye beams. Mara holds her breath and peers into the dark. Then she sees the shape of pointed ears, hears the flick of a tail on the dusty floor. With a shock, Mara realizes she is staring into the eyes of a fox.

Its presence somehow brings her back to life. Keeping her movements smooth and unhurried, Mara manages to build a precarious ladder out of the chapel's broken pews to reach the high window she smashed through. Shaking, she clambers up and emerges out into the thick gloom of the empty hilltop. The sirens of the sea police are just a faint echo upon the water.

Mara walks round to the front of the cathedral. She takes a deep breath and forces herself to push open the heavy oak door. Nausea hits her as she steps inside. It's empty; a terrible ringing emptiness that seems to reverberate from the vast stone. Then she sees that it's not entirely empty.

'Wing!' she sobs as she sees the shadow of a small, crumpled body on the floor. She rushes over – but it's not Wing, it's another little one. Mara begins to shake violently, seeing the broken, bloodied bodies that lie here and there among the pillars. She makes herself check each and every one. Just as she thinks she's finished her awful task she sees a shoe sticking out from behind one of the ancient tombs. Tentatively, Mara walks round the tomb – urchins don't wear shoes.

The shoe belongs to one of the sea police. Mara checks the pulse in his wrist. Dead. Good! She is about to turn away when something makes her bend to ease the awkward angle of one of the lifeless arms. And as she leans over the body she sees with a shock that it is a young woman. She can't be more than eighteen or twenty, not much older than herself. Mara stands up, shaken by a confusion of emotions.

Then she slams back out through the oak door and stands blankly among the gravestones, feeling sick to her soul.

Somehow she makes herself move. Somehow she finds the raft stuck among the reed bed. Somehow she gets herself across the water to the Treenesters' island and stumbles up the Hill of Doves.

There is complete silence within the grove of trees. Mara cries out in panic.

'We're here, Mara!' Broomielaw calls from the branches. Mara hears the rustle and thump as the Treenesters jump down from the safety of their nests.

'We were so worried about you!' Molendinar hugs her tight.

'But where is Gorbals?' cries Broomielaw.

Mara stares at her. 'But he came back here, didn't he? He must have.' Though how could he, without the raft?

No one answers. Through the dimness, the owl eyes of the Treenesters stare at her and Mara stares back with equal horror.

Broomielaw bursts out sobbing, and Mara turns away. She sinks to the ground and covers her face with her hands. *It can't be true! The sky people can't have taken Gorbals!*

Mara cannot face the others. Once again her actions have led someone she cares for into disaster. She climbs the beech tree and burrows deep within her nest, so shamed and guilt-stricken and terrified for Gorbals she can hardly bear it.

After a while someone climbs up into the nest beside her. She hears Clayslaps's soft, baby breath at her ear and looks round.

'Cuddle him. It'll help,' whispers Broomielaw, settling little Clayslaps's soft, sleepy body next to her. Mara hugs the baby tight and close and after a while his live warmth soothes her a little.

'Gorbals might be scared and hiding, or hurt, somewhere on the cathedral island. Some of the others have armed themselves and gone to check,' Broomielaw tells her quietly.

'I can hear them now!' Candleriggs calls up. 'They're back.'

Mara jumps out of the nest and runs down the hill but there is no Gorbals, only the grim-faced Treenesters. Ibrox shakes his head. 'We checked all the bodies, looked everywhere,' he says. 'He's been taken, not killed.'

Mara looks up at the sky city. Taken to be a slave worker for the New World? Wing too? She slumps upon the ground.

'It's not your fault, Mara,' says Molendinar.

But Mara knows that she made Gorbals go to the cathedral island instead of taking cover as he begged her to.

Night falls like a coffin lid. The sea moves in the slowest of shudders; the only light in its blackness is the cold, reflected gleam of New Mungo. The Treenesters sit in silence around the sun fire.

'Eat, Mara,' urges Broomielaw, but the girl herself has not eaten and is trembling violently.

'She's too full of nettles and thorns,' says Ibrox, pushing his food away. 'Me too.'

'Tell us a story, Candleriggs,' pleads Broomielaw. 'We need one so badly tonight.'

'*Yes,*' murmur the others. '*A story, Candleriggs, a story.*'

'I've no heart for stories tonight,' sighs the old woman. 'I'm too sickened by a New World which builds its empire out of such cruelty and decides its citizens are the only true human beings in the world – that the rest of us are no better than vermin.' Candleriggs stares from eyes that are sunk in folds of time. 'There are some stories that should never be told.'

The old woman falls silent and brooding.

Mara rouses herself. She finds her voice. 'But maybe now is the time,' she ventures.

Candleriggs looks up at her and Mara flinches at the bitterness in the old woman's face.

'Maybe you're right, Mara. Maybe now it's time for this story,' she cries out at last. Her voice is harsh and strong. 'Treenesters, I'll tell you a cruel story for the cruellest of nights.'

The Treenesters gather closer, nervously.

'Once upon a time,' Candleriggs begins, 'I gave my heart to a young man who was full of dreams. We had so many grand dreams for the future in the old place of learning, the university on the hill. The place you find your books,' she tells Mara. 'But the Century of Storms came with a fury that blew our future away.'

Candleriggs sighs deeply.

'We were students of natural engineering – the science of the future, it was called back then. Caledon, my love, was the most brilliant student of us all, always dreaming up the most incredible structures that were inspired by the patterns of nature. Cal was snapped up by the World Task Force that had been set up to tackle the floods. He had sent them his ideas for sky cities that would withstand the floods – I remember I almost laughed at those first designs of his; they looked so impossible. But it *was* possible, as you can see.'

Everyone glances upwards at the vast structure that looms overhead. Candleriggs continues.

'Cal believed we should leave Earth and our problems behind, that we could be reborn as creatures of the sky.

199

Human angels, that's what he said we'd be. It seemed such a brilliant dream at first but it soon turned into a nightmare. When I saw the edge of that nightmare I told him to stop, or I tried to – but it was useless. We were both young and stubborn and angry and his dream had filled him with a ruthlessness that turned his heart to stone.'

Mara is seared by the pain she recognizes in the old woman's face.

'Learning was the fuel that made his dream possible. Learning took him too far beyond the real world, far beyond his true self.' Candleriggs looks blankly into the dark. 'The university was the place of his learning. If it wasn't for the ideas that he found in its books there would be no bars between our world and the sky, no wall to trap us inside and the others outside, no police to steal slaves to build that empire in the sky. So do you see now why I hate the university and all that's in it?' Her head droops and her voice shakes. 'That necrotten place turned the boy I once loved with all my heart into the man who dreamed up the cruel sky cities of the New World!'

The Treenesters sit like statues, in stunned silence. But Mara ventures to ask something that is desperately bothering her.

'Candleriggs, he did save lots of people – those cities hold thousands and they built lots more sky cities all across the world, didn't they? So his idea saved thousands upon thousands who would have drowned. He couldn't save the whole world. But, Candleriggs, why didn't he save you? Why are you out here when you should be in the New World, with him?

'In the beginning,' says Candleriggs, 'the New World was meant to be for everyone – yes, I'm sure that was what Cal wanted. He wanted to save as many people as he could. But in the scorching hot summers of the '30s and '40s the oceans rose faster than anyone ever expected. All the predictions had been wrong. And all the political agreements that were supposed to prevent global warming had long fallen through. The world's governments couldn't seem to agree on anything – or stick to any treaties that they did manage to agree on. Suddenly it was all too late. Great floods struck, all over the world. At first, Europe escaped the worst. But when the floods devastated New York and Tokyo, two of the world's most powerful cities, there was mass panic. Governments began to collapse everywhere. Economies crashed and everything that held society together started to fall apart. The people lost control. It was as if the world was a great ship, suddenly wrecked and sinking fast. I couldn't begin to describe the terror and chaos of that time.

'The first of the New World sky cities were just built. New Mungo was the prototype – Cal insisted the very first was to be built upon his home city. People were now living as far inland as they could, or up on the highest parts of the old city, crammed together in the tower blocks and hills, on rooftops, anywhere they could find refuge from the rising sea. We had watched in amazement as the huge towers and all the sky tunnels were built at impossible speed, high above our heads. They were so strange, terrifying . . . and wonderful. Everyone felt full of hope then – we were all going to be saved. By now, Cal was no longer *my* Cal. He had become a very powerful young man – the one who owned the idea of the New World. His idea had spread as quickly as the oceans had risen. All over the planet, governments tried to reclaim the confidence of the people by building their own sky cities as quickly as possible. Then . . .'

Candleriggs's voice falters but she pulls herself together and continues. 'Then everything changed – Cal too. I was already in New Mungo with him. Our families and friends were due to move up any day when the one thing that everyone said could never happen, did. A massive sea surge hit Europe. The whole continent was wiped out.'

There is a long pause. Candleriggs stares into the fire.

'I always knew in my heart that the New World cities couldn't house all the Earth's refugees, but instead of trying to rescue everyone we could and cramming in every last person we could manage, instead of speeding up the building programme to make more cities as quickly as possible and providing some form of shelter and protection for the ones we couldn't house – boats and food and water supplies at the very *least* for the mass of poor souls who had made rafts and floating shelters out of whatever they could salvage from the floods – instead of that, the New World barred its doors. The great wall that I thought was built to protect the city from the sea became a fortress to keep refugees out.

'Now the New World was to be only for what it judged to be the best of human beings: the most brilliant minds, the most technically skilled. An intelligence test was set for entry and only those who scored highly were allowed in. Everyone else was regarded as an alien, an outcast – even family and friends. Cal said we couldn't make different rules for ourselves, but I was sure he had his parents and young sister hidden away somewhere in the city. He would never have abandoned them,' Candleriggs declares bitterly.

'Now, instead of reaching a hand outwards to help the survivors of the floods, all the imagination and energy of the citizens of the New World turned inward. I couldn't believe what was happening. I challenged Cal and we argued furiously about it. I could see he knew I was right, but he was too caught up in his New World dream to surrender it. He pleaded with me to forget those we couldn't help – there were far too many to even attempt to help, he said, and if we tried to take them in, the New World wouldn't cope. The new cities would be over-whelmed, the system would collapse and we would all perish. It was best to put the rest of the world out of our minds, be thankful for what we had salvaged for ourselves and live for the future – a future that was to be lived high in the sky in a world peopled by the most brilliant of human beings.'

The old woman wrings her hands in misery.

'But I couldn't share that dream. So I became a rebel. There were others like me – not many but some, who couldn't forget the rest of the world either. We formed a revolutionary group and tried to speak out for the rest of the world, for the abandoned ones. But most people refused to listen. They were too grateful to be saved from the drowning and too scared to join us in case they were thrown out, back into the nightmare of the world outside. I thought they were evil then, but now . . . now I think there were many people who were good at heart, who cared about the refugees, but it was fear for their own future that made them selfish and cruel. Maybe if we had had more time to argue our cause, if we had been less hot-headed and rash and had spoken calmly to people about their fears, maybe we could have convinced them that reaching out to help others needn't devastate their own future . . . maybe then more people would have joined us and we would have spoken as the voice of the people.

Then Caledon and the other City Fathers would have *had* to act. But so few spoke out, it was easy to destroy us.'

Candleriggs pauses for a long moment, trembling with great emotion.

'What happened?' Mara whispers.

'They rounded us up. Cal came to me in my prison cell and begged me to break with the rebels. He still loved me, he said. We could still live happily ever after in his empire in the sky. All I had to do was forget the outside world. And I almost did,' Candleriggs whispers, 'because I loved him so much. I wanted to be with him. And I was so frightened. But then I saw that what I loved was what he once was, not what he had become. He tried to say that it was all out of his hands, that he didn't have the kind of power I thought he had, that others were in control of the New World, not him. He had *convinced* himself that there was nothing he could do. But the truth was that his dream of the New World consumed him – he couldn't see beyond it, didn't want to.'

Candleriggs holds her head in her hands, as if the memory of what happened is too awful to contain.

'I told him I hated him. He looked as if I had stabbed him in the heart. But my hate was all mixed up with love. I felt there was a savage war raging inside me. I was thrown out of New Mungo with the rest of the rebels. Cal saved us from being shot, at least. Instead we were flung outside to drown, but we survived and made our world here among the trees and ruins of the lost world.'

She stares blankly into the darkness.

'At first I thought I would die of a broken heart. I wanted to die. There was nothing to live for. My family and friends were all gone and there was no one and nothing on Earth that meant anything to me any more.

But when we settled ourselves among the trees and found a way to survive, we looked around at what was left of the world and began to see the signs set in the stone of the old city. They were everywhere. They gave us a story to live by and believe in. We took the names of the old city so that it wouldn't be forgotten, and the stone-telling became our faith and hope. It was all we had.'

Tears are streaming down Mara's face. Many of the Treenesters are quietly sobbing. Broomielaw reaches out to hug Candleriggs but the old woman shrugs her off, as if there's nothing in the world that can take away the pain of what she has lived through.

'Cal, my wonderful dreamer – what happened to you?' murmurs Candleriggs. Her head droops and her eyes are suddenly leaden and lost.

'Time to nest now,' Molendinar tells her gently.

The old woman murmurs Cal's name again as Ibrox and Molendinar help her to her feet. Then she turns and there's something in her face now that lets Mara see the fiery young girl this old woman must once have been.

'I broke his heart though! When I refused to stay in his selfish New World his stone heart broke in pieces!' Candleriggs declares. 'I know it did because when he said goodbye a splinter flew from his heart and pierced my own. And it's still there. I still feel it.'

As she goes away to nest, her hand clutches at the place where the stony splinter is stuck in her still-sore heart.

LONGHOPE

Deep in the still centre of the night, when even the bats and owls fall quiet, Mara shakes Broomielaw awake in her nest.

'What is it?' Broomielaw panics.

'Come with me to the cathedral,' Mara pleads urgently.

'Now? In the dark? Be calm now, Mara, it's nest time.'

'It's important, Broomielaw. I have to.'

Broomielaw sighs but she rises and climbs down from her nest. 'Wait,' she says. 'I must get Molendinar to nest with Clayslaps till I come back.'

While she does so, Mara takes a moth lantern from under its bat-proof covering in the nook of a tree trunk. Then they take a raft and set off across the water to the cathedral island.

'What are we doing?' asks Broomielaw.

'There's something I need to do if I'm to get Gorbals and Wing back,' Mara replies.

'Oh, Mara,' wails Broomielaw, and she bursts out crying again. 'We'll never get Gorbals back, or Wing. No one ever returns once they are taken. They're lost for ever. For ever!'

Mara hushes her. Then, to calm Broomielaw, she begins to tell her how the crack in Thenew's stone face matches her own scar and is also uncannily repeated in the crack in her grandmother's mirror, which reflects as a scar upon her face. All three scars occur on the same side, the left cheek.

'It's strange, Broomielaw. It's a small thing but it's so odd,' she finishes. 'I really don't know what to think. I can't believe I'm the Face in the Stone because I'm just me – Mara. Yet I'm determined to find a way to save us all. It's got nothing to do with the signs in the stone, though, it's just what I feel I must do. It's the only way I can live with myself. And part of what I must do is try to find Gorbals and Wing, because I owe it to them. There are other things I'll explain later, to all of you.'

Broomielaw jumps off the raft to bring them into shore.

'The scars are to do with the stone-telling,' she says simply. 'I'm sure of it. And you think there's something in the cathedral that will help you?'

'Yes,' says Mara.

They enter the dark, empty cathedral. The mothlight shows the dark shadow of blood spilled in many places among the ash on the stone floor.

'What should we look for?' asks Broomielaw nervously.

'A girl,' says Mara. 'One of the sky people. She's been left behind. The other sea police can't have seen her – she's behind one of the tombs.'

Broomielaw looks terrified.

'She's dead,' Mara reassures her. 'It's her clothes I need.'

They step carefully around the small, crumpled bodies that lie among the vast stone pillars. Broomielaw lets out a hard, dry sob and Mara watches her bend over a tiny urchin and close the child's eyes.

'You're right, Mara. They're only children and what's been done to them is a horror beyond words.' Broomielaw turns away, stricken. Then she stoops to pick up something from the ground. She holds up the mothlight to let Mara see. 'Look! Isn't this Wing's?'

Mara cries out in surprise. It's the bone-handled dagger that Wing looted from the museum halls of the university. Gratefully, she takes the weapon. The ancient bone handle feels sound and sure in her grip. Its stone blade is cold and crude. Yet it could still, after thousands of years, rupture human flesh. It could still kill.

'This way,' says Mara, moving carefully through the bodies to the back of the cathedral.

'It's a sign,' says Broomielaw, 'a good sign, finding that.'

'I hope so,' whispers Mara. But there's no sign of Wing. Yet somehow, with his dagger in her hand, she feels stronger, more certain of what she is about to do.

'She's here,' says Mara quietly, reaching the body of the girl who has fallen so awkwardly behind a tomb.

'She's been shot?' puzzles Broomielaw. The mothlight reveals a small, dark bullet hole in the girl's forehead. A pool of blood makes an angry red halo around her head.

'They shot one of their own by mistake,' Mara nods, but she can't take any pleasure from that fact.

'You want her clothes?' says Broomielaw.

Mara nods again and together, gently and silently, they undress the body from its waterproof orange uniform, taking the soft, sleek clothing beneath that and the light, tough shoes. When they've finished, Mara covers the young woman in a moss quilt she has brought with her.

'We must bury her,' says Broomielaw. 'We must bury

all of them. But we can't do it ourselves. We'll come back with the others and do it at first light.'

Mara turns away from the girl's body, overcome by the sweet, thick smell of death all around her. She feels sick to her soul, wants out of this awful place, needs fresh air, *now*. Mara grabs the policewoman's bundle of clothes and runs for the door – but in her hurry to escape, she trips over the leg of a dead urchin. Horrified, she steadies herself against the thick trunk of a pillar. The cold stone calms and soothes her body. She leans her hot cheek against it for a second. And finds herself face to face with the word *Remember*, cut thick and deep into the stone.

Behind her, Broomielaw's moth lantern flutters just enough light to illuminate the rest of the inscription on the pillar.

Read the story of the past
Ponder its lessons –
And think not to leave
Without lifting up your heart.

Though Mara does not believe in signs set in stone, she can't help but shiver at the uncanny aptness of ancient words that seem to know what she has already decided to do.

Mara is packing her world into her small backpack.

The book on Greenland and *A Tale of Two Cities* by Charles Dickens, Wing's bone-handled dagger, the tiny black meteorite and the young policewoman's wallet inside which she found several small, shimmering, wafer-thin disks; all go into her bag.

In the bathtub up in the ruins at the top of the Hill of Doves, she has scrubbed herself clean of netherworld grime, brushed her teeth with applemint leaves, smoothed the tangles from her hair with a brittle twig brush until it gleams like dark water. Now, back down among the trees, she checks her reflection in the cracked mirror of Tain's little carved box before putting that back in her bag. She can't help staring at the crack in the glass that runs parallel to the fading scar across her face.

Last of all, she checks out her cyberwizz.

The Treenesters whisper nervously and huddle together when they see it. Pollock has told the others all about the magic machine that he spied in Mara's bag. Mara takes out the globe, the silver halo and her tiny cyberwand. She holds the globe snug in her palm and feels it come alive at her touch. The Treenesters gasp as colours swirl and shadow across the globe's surface and Mara feels a rush of emotion for that old, safe existence when the most difficult thing she had to face was a close shave with a Weave demon.

She has re-charged the cyberwizz with whatever rays of netherworld sun she could catch, but she'd better double check. A sudden, wicked idea strikes her. She bends her head over the globe to hide her grin and scribbles a quick cyberspell upon its electronic pad. Then she slips the silver halo over Pollock's eyes.

'Hunt that,' she tells him.

He looks at Mara in puzzled wonder for a moment, then his eyes focus on some vision that only he can see and his expression changes to horror. He screams, loud and long, rips off the halo and hurls it at Mara.

'Monsters!' he yells and runs off into the bushes.

'Monsters?' Gingerly, Broomielaw puts on the silver halo and immediately yelps with terror and turns to run for safety. Mara catches her and pulls off the halo.

'M-monsters,' the girl repeats dazedly.

'Not real ones,' says Mara apologetically. 'It's a kind of picture story.'

Pollock's eyes stare out in horror from the bushes. The other Treenesters have all backed off.

'A m-monster nearly ate me,' they can hear him sob.

'It's gone now, Pollock,' Mara tells him drily. 'Broomielaw scared it away.'

She picks up the young policewoman's clothes and shoes and goes behind a tree to change. Broomielaw has meticulously scrubbed the blood from the orange uniform where the girl's head wound stained it. Mara pulls off her own clothes and her leaky, sodden terrainers. The uniform fits well but the girl's shoes are too tight. Still, they'll have to do. Her old terrainers would give her away instantly. But her nylon backpack, well-scrubbed, should pass. Its material is not dissimilar to the policewoman's uniform.

'Candleriggs wants to know what you are doing, Mara,' says Molendinar, from the other side of the tree.

'What I have to do,' Mara replies.

'No, Mara, no,' Broomielaw cries. 'This is not the stone-telling.'

'How do you know?' says Mara as she emerges, all neat and clean, dressed in the luminous orange uniform of New Mungo's sea police. The Treenesters stare.

'You look so strange,' Broomielaw shakes her head ominously, her huge eyes brimming with dread. 'Not our Mara. Like one of *them*.'

'Good,' says Mara. 'That's exactly how I need to look because I'm going up to the New World.' The Treenesters erupt in horror. Mara holds up her hand to quieten them.

'I've made up my mind. Listen! I'm going to try to get Gorbals and Wing back. And we need ships. Remember I told you about the Athapaskans – well, just before he was taken Gorbals found a book in the university that convinced me there *is* land in the north, in a place called Greenland – a huge land that was covered in ice until the meltdown which flooded the oceans. It has lots of high land and it must be free from ice now. It's the kind of place we could build a new life, but to get there we need a ship – more than one, because we must rescue the people from the boat camp outside the walls. So I need to go up to the sky city to find a way to get access to those ships. We can't do it from down here.'

'It's too dangerous!' Broomielaw protests.

'And look,' pleads Molendinar, 'we've put wish gifts all over your nest tree so that Gorbals and Wing will come back safe and sound. So you don't need to go up after them. And a new little bird has come – I think it might be the ratkin's, so you must stay and look after it for him.'

Mara looks up at the branches of her beech tree that are strewn with bright rags and plastic ribbons and food and scraps of paper scribbled with wishes. Glass wind chimes make a gentle, happy music to put the tree in a wish-granting mood.

'Thank you,' she says. 'You've been real friends to me. Wish *me* luck now because I *must* go.' Mara gives in to the huge wave of emotion that is rising in her and grabs Broomielaw in a tearful hug, then Molendinar, then all of the Treenesters, even Pollock and Possil. 'You want Gorbals back, don't you, and I want Wing back too. This is the only way. Broomielaw, cuddle little Clayslaps every day for me. And look after the sparrow, just in case it's Wing's.'

Broomielaw nods, unable to speak.

'Take this,' says Molendinar. She hands Mara a sprig of dried herb. 'Thyme. For courage.'

Mara breathes in its scent and remembers something. She unseals a small inner compartment of her rucksack, takes out her mother's sprig of rosemary and binds it with the thyme.

'Clear head and courage,' she tells Molendinar.

Broomielaw grips Mara's hand. Tears stand in her large, green eyes. 'You were wrong when you told us Mara means bitterness. I think Mara must mean a strong, long hope that doesn't give up.'

'Longhope.' Mara finds herself smiling in surprise as that was the name of their farm hamlet on Wing. She clasps Broomielaw's hand. 'I'll find him, Broomielaw. I won't come back till I do.'

Broomielaw nods tearfully. 'I've believed in you from the first day. But wait now.' She springs up into her nest and returns with a bundle of water-warped pages, covered in clumsy writing, that have been sewn along one edge with tough grasses to make a book. 'Take these with you. They're Gorbals's poems.'

'I can't take them,' Mara protests. 'He meant you to have them.'

But Broomielaw pushes the lumpy pages into her hands. 'Gorbals always says a poem belongs to whoever wants it or needs it. Don't you want it? You might need it . . .' she nods fearfully, 'up there.'

Mara bites her lip and takes Gorbals's handmade book of poems. Carefully, she seals it away in an inside pocket of her backpack.

'Be ready,' Ibrox warns her. 'For whatever is to happen.'

And now she really must leave or she'll break down and won't be able to go. But there is still Candleriggs to say goodbye to. Mara walks over to the oak tree. The ancient owl eyes peer down from the greatnest.

'You might lose your life, Mara Bell,' Candleriggs says quietly.

Mara gazes up at her. 'I know. But, Candleriggs, I wanted to die in the boat camp after I lost my family and my best friend, just like you did when you were thrown out of the New World. I tried to die but somehow I couldn't – though if Wing hadn't got me out of the boat camp I could well be dead by now. It's my fault Gorbals was taken so I have to try to get him back. Also, it's a risk I have to take if we want to find a safe home in the world. But Candleriggs, it's more than that. See, I've found something to live for again. Strangely enough, it's worth risking my life to have that. And most of all . . . '

Mara pauses and swallows hard. 'I need to do it for my family – so that their lives weren't lost for nothing.'

Candleriggs nods slowly.

'Well, all I can say is what I know,' says Candleriggs. 'It's this – you can betray someone with a word or an action. You can betray them with silence or inaction too. And in betraying that one person you can betray a whole world. I've seen almost thirty thousand sunups – that's more than eighty years in old time – and that's the most important thing I've learned. Except that the opposite might also be true. So yes, I think it's worth risking everything to save another person's life. And I know this too: the future will not depend upon the human mind; it *belongs* to the human heart. But Mara – don't you believe any of this is part of the stone-telling?'

'Um, possibly – I mean – well, not really. Oh, I don't *know*!' cries Mara in confusion.

'Don't twitter like a sparrow,' says Candleriggs. There's

a spark of amusement in her voice. 'Tell me what you really think.'

'Well,' Mara debates, 'maybe I'm meant to do it – who knows? I just can't believe that the future is set in stone. Surely things only happen because of what you choose to do. And I choose to do this because I'm the only one who *can*. And because I feel I should, not because of those signs in the stone. They don't mean anything to me.'

But Mara has remembered something else. Now she tells Candleriggs about the water-smudged sentence she read in the fragments of pages about the Athapaskans. It told of a gift called a potlatch, the gift which must be returned. This is her potlatch for what Wing and the Treenesters have done for her.

'And maybe,' her dark eyes flash and she grins up at Candleriggs, 'maybe I want to get up there and just *see*.'

Candleriggs laughs and the owl eyes disappear as she settles back in the greatnest.

'Goodbye then, Mara Bell,' the old woman calls softly. 'Try to do what I never could – keep a cool head above that fiery heart.'

Mara lifts up her entwined sprig of rosemary and thyme and crushes them lightly in her palm to release their scents. 'Clear head and courage,' she declares shakily. 'Candleriggs,' she hesitates now. There's something she has wondered about and never asked. 'What was your real name?'

The old woman's answer is the faintest of whispers among the rustle of the leaves.

'Lily.'

Mara remembers the white lilies of the valley that scattered Wing's shoreline each spring.

'That's beautiful.'

'Once upon a time, so was I,' says the whisper.

'Goodbye, Lily,' Mara whispers back.

Down the dark hillside she runs, down the Hill of Doves and through the crab-apple trees that are aglow with moonmoths. Then she jumps on a raft and oars out into the branches of the night.

NOOSPACE

**What you don't trust in stone
and decay, shape out of air.**

Eternal Moment, Sandor Weores

Noos: mind, intellect (Greek)

FOX TRAIL ONE

Night is Fox time.

A time for creeping to the very edge of things. A time for sneaking and snooping to the old, abandoned networks of the primitive cyberworld once known as the Weave, where the people of the New World never go. A time for prowling ancient nooks and crannies where once in a blue moon a fox can get lucky and dig up a precious nugget of a past that lies forgotten, undestroyed. There are some places only a fox can sniff out. Places full of lost and dead things. These are the night places where Fox goes.

He is the rarest of creatures, a dreamer who gets things done. By day he zips through cyberspace, a Noosrunner for the New World's Stellarka Project, snooping out new, glinting chips of scientific research and ideas that might one day take the New World into space, to a city in the stars. But that's just his job. What Fox really lives for is the night. That's when he seeks what he knows is the real treasure, the lost gold that is the past.

Fox wants too much. Sometimes in the rush of hyper-speed he dreams impossible dreams, things that cannot be. The difficult thing, he has discovered, is not just knowing how to dream but knowing what to dream. And the most difficult thing of all is when you find the answer to both. Then you start to believe in your dreams – the impossible dreams that can't come true.

He is a child of New Mungo, the only child of two top cybergineers who are rarely at home. His family is at the heart of the great global power that governs all the cities of the New World. Bored, brilliant and lonely, Fox knew at the age of ten that most people use only a tiny kernel of the brainpower they own, and that somehow everything in the world had gone wrong. Now he only believes in what he finds among the crumbling ruins of the old Weave.

Fox is a rebel. He wants to raise the past from the dead, the real past that lies abandoned in the trash-heaps where the Grand Fathers of All have flung it. The past has become a carnival, a pantomime of what it really was. The New World roams and plunders a synthetic Theme Park of the past – caring nothing for truth, only for fun.

Fox knows about the past. He knows the only parts of the real, authentic past the Grand Fathers of All have not remade or banished are those guaranteed not to shock. What Fox thinks he has found shocks him to the core.

At night, Fox joyrides at hyperspeed. He lives on his wits, too-curious, with too-little fear. Fox-instinct tells him when to stop and hide, when to escape from the half-lit highways where weird cybercreatures and Weave-ghosts roam. He prefers to steal among the lonely lanes that lie in shadow, searching, searching, for whatever truth he can find.

Once, only once, there was someone else. A zip-zooming wizzer who verved through the Weave with daredevil skill. For a long time Fox stalked her, until one day she crash-landed into Nowhere, the vast chasm of cyberhaze that lies like an ocean between the Weave and the Noos. She held a key to the past, he was sure. Only that one time, when he saw her lost and floundering, did he let himself be seen. But he was too suspicious, too fox-wary, and all at once she slipped out of reach, vanished with a cry of despair that he will never forget. She never came again.

Always alone now, Fox sifts the back alley dustbins, searching forgotten nooks and crannies for morsels of the past. What he finds, he hoards away in secret pockets of cybermemory. He remembers each morsel, each hiding place, for one day he might use it. Fox tries to believe in the day when these true nuggets of the past will mean something once more. He feels lost in a world that lurches blindly into the future with no sense of its own past. Day by day now, his heart hardens against his world, and the only place he feels at home is among the shadows of the past.

Night is Fox time. And somewhere in the eternity of cyberspace there is always night.

CURIOUSER AND
CURIOUSER

At the very last moment Mara almost loses heart.

The door of the lift capsule to the sky city is wide open. Workers from the early morning supply ship are surging through, sweaty and dirty and tired, along with a squad of sea police. Wearing the orange uniform, it's easy to merge in. As she approaches the lift capsule she almost stops. A single step more will take her across the threshold that separates the two worlds. It feels like an impossible chasm. In the end it's the crush of those behind rather than her own will that pushes her through the doorway into the large golden capsule.

Mara is sure she is falling, not rising, when her heart plummets into her stomach as the lift moves upwards in a smooth surge of speed; but it's the world below that is tumbling away and the Earth-pull is strong. For a supercharged moment Mara feels, sees, hears and smells everything that is the netherworld. Then it all dims and is gone.

*

The first difference is the light. It's too harsh and strong for eyes used to netherworld gloom. The next thing Mara sees when she steps out of the lift capsule is a line of city guards. Heart pounding, she avoids eye contact and walks past. Despite the beautiful white, flower-like logos across their chests and backs, the grey uniforms of the guards are still threatening. Mara's stomach lurches, and not just from nerves. She feels as if she is on a ship at sea – gently but unnervingly the city sways to the rhythm of the world's wind, as it is built to do.

'Hey, you! Over here!' a guard shouts and Mara forces herself not to turn around, to keep moving with the rest. Her instinct is right. It's someone else they want. Mara follows the crowd from the supply ship down a short corridor and waits her turn in the queue, trying to look at ease but concentrating fiercely on everything around her.

'To enter, please insert your identi-disk here,' announces a voice, over and over, at the head of the queue.

The voice is smooth, bright and completely artificial. Its owner is a blankly smiling young woman who stands at the head of the corridor at what must be the official doorway to New Mungo. The material of the girl's short dress flickers restlessly through each colour of the rainbow and loops back again. With relief, Mara sees that she's only a lumenbeing, crafted from light. She has met the girl's broken-down ancestors in the Weave, wandering aimlessly and stuttering reams of data nonsense to anyone they meet. Mara used to bully and bother those defunct cyberbeings, just for fun. The lumen girl points at the slit in the wall where Mara should insert an identi-disk. The long, noisy queue has given her time to think and she has ready the two shimmery, coin-sized disks that were in the young policewoman's wallet.

'To enter, please insert your identi-disk here,' the lumen girl instructs. Mara guesses and inserts one of the disks. The young woman flickers for less than a second – the lumenbeing equivalent of an irritated frown. 'Incorrect disk.'

The slot in the wall ejects the first disk. Behind her, the queue mutters impatiently. Mara doesn't dare look at the line of city guards and frantically, her fingers shaking, inserts the second disk, willing it to be the correct one.

The sliding door opens. Mara slips through, her heart beating painfully.

And is in! Amazed, she stands inside a long silver tunnel.

Mara struggles to control her fear as she walks down the gleaming walkway, trying to get used to the shifting world below her feet. She feels utterly lost.

A clear, cool head and courage. One step at a time.

The first step is to get out of her orange police uniform; it's far too noticeable. Mara slows so that the crowd from the supply ship surges ahead of her round the bend of the tunnel. Then, with a quick check over her shoulder, she wriggles out of the orange uniform and crams it in her backpack. Underneath, she is wearing the soft, sleek, everyday clothing of the young policewoman. She runs to catch up with the rest of the new arrivals who stand waiting on a platform inside an adjoining tunnel. Mara stands with them, since they seem to be waiting for a purpose – and realizes that the crowd has shrunk con-siderably.

Where have all the others gone? She hears a loud spar-king and the echo of diminishing voices. Quickly, Mara follows the echoes to an adjacent tunnel and, as she peers into it, just glimpses the last of the crowd as it speeds round a bend in a single, flowing movement, leaving a smoky trail of sparks.

Mara walks back to the smaller group of waiting people, feeling dejected. What gave the sparking crowd such speed? She must find out. She envies that speed, wants that power and freedom.

In a few moments a red and silver train zooms almost noiselessly into the tunnel. Mara boards with everyone else and the train moves fast and deep into the maze of sky tunnels, stopping at stations every few minutes. Mara hasn't a clue where to get off and listens carefully to the voice that announces each station. The other passengers are either elderly or young children with parents, she notices.

They pass through Nursery Bough, Senior Citz Care-farm, Great Western Harmony Block, Arcadia, then come to a halt at City Centre, the final stop. Mara disembarks along with the remaining passengers.

She follows the others as they exit the station platform and walk down a short tunnel that opens up into a vast airy hall. Straight ahead, she sees a pulsating sign above a tall, wide door that slides open and shut every few seconds, busy with people. *Cybercath*, pulses the sign. Nervously, Mara approaches the door. It seems to be a hub of activity, so she may as well start exploring here.

She stops for a moment to study the picture story that is etched in the huge metal door. At the foot of the door is an ark struggling through storms on a heaving ocean. Above that, numerous people are shown engrossed in industrious tasks – all kinds of building, creating, inventing. The figures work under a shower of mathematical-looking symbols, tools and instruments. At the very pinnacle of the picture story, perched on top of all this

227

human endeavour, are two angelic beings, a winged man and woman.

The huge door slides open.

A lumenbeing in a luridly flowered shirt beckons Mara to come inside. 'Come on in and grab a free cupule,' he urges. 'Have an interesting day!'

Mara walks through the great door with a composure that is as fake as the doorboy and his welcome. She walks in as if she knows exactly where she is going and what she is doing. Which, ultimately, she does. All she needs to figure out is how.

Mara stands awestruck inside the colossal hall that is New Mungo's cybercath. *Cybercath.* She mulls over the word. It must be short for cybercathedral because a cathedral is exactly what this place reminds her of, only it's much bigger than the one in the netherworld. You could fit ten of those in here. And instead of stone this cathedral-like place seems to be created out of light and air, glass and crystal and mirror – and yet more light. And wide open space. And soaring walls and ceilings that make you look ever upwards.

But never down or out.

Several thousand quietly industrious voices fill the air with a hum of discordant mutterings. The sound is oddly musical, almost choral. Is the fox here? Mara wonders, staring at rows upon rows of bent heads. He could be anywhere among the thousands who sit in the vast honeycomb of work cubicles that fill the cybercath. A city guard catches Mara's eye and she jumps in fright. She must be careful to look normal and purposeful.

Quickly, she finds a free workstation among the vast honeycomb. She sits down and the chair moulds itself around her like a cosy hug. *How do you get out of it?* She tries to stand and the hug chair releases her with a gentle sigh. Mara smothers a nervous giggle and sits down again, enjoying the hug this time.

Now she thinks she sees what it is they all hum into – the tiniest boxes are clipped like brooches at chest level onto every person. She sees too the coloured crystals that are stuck upon each forehead. There is a single instruction engraved upon the gleaming table of her cubicle.

Do not remove godbox or headgem from this cupule.

Godbox. Mara picks up the tiny box attached to a pin. Must be this. *Headgem.* That must be the coloured crystal. She clips the godbox to her chest as the others do. Then she puts the headgem on her forehead. It sticks as if by magic. Body magnetism? Mara can only wonder.

Her priority is to locate Gorbals and Wing, and then figure out a way to access the boats, so she needs information about how the city works. If only she could find the cyberfox and get him to help her. But the only way to do any of that is to get to grips with the New World technology. That is her first, urgent step. Going by the tuneful murmurings all around her, voice seems to be part of the key.

Mara tries asking the godbox for information on how to work the system. It doesn't respond. She tries asking it in different voice tones. Again, nothing happens. She can't understand the function of all this melodic humming but Mara suspects the New World cybersystem is a universe ahead of any technology she has ever known. The industrious hum of the voices and the concentration on every face makes it clear that the thousands in the cybercath are here to work, not play – but what kind of work? She can't ask anyone; her ignorance would instantly give her away.

229

High above her head is an enormous, revolving lumen globe. Mara gazes up at it and sees the great empire of New World cities that have been built all over the planet. It's a breathtaking sight. A crystal tree represents each sky city. How many are there? Fifty? Eighty? Mara gazes at the forest of crystal that glitters around the globe.

She looks around her. The gleaming walls of the cyber-cath are electronic noticeboards that flash up a constant volley of information under the heading *New World Trade Index*. The cyberworkers watch the noticeboards closely and the communal hum greets each newsflash with an excited rise in volume or a low mutter of dismay.

Mara reads the Trade Index and tries to make sense of it.

Globus geomagna up 5.2, Texan Cleanoil down 8.6, Eurosea Oceanores – supertitanium up 28.4! Megalumen phosfission down 2.4, Greenex limestone stable, New Season Afrikelp – global auction imminent! Indisea silica stable – hornblende and feldspar to clear, Chinorock silicon
– SELLING NOW!

Each name has a logo attached. Some words, like kelp and oil are familiar, but what does it all mean? Mara frowns up at the flashing noticeboard, recalling the primitive trade network that used to exist among Wing and the nearby islands and wonders if this is some vast, complex version of that – an electronic marketplace of New World commodities that operates between the sky cities.

A leap of time vanishes as Mara listens to the workers around her and tries again and again to find the words and tone that will gain her entry to the system. Hunger finally grinds her to a halt. It's mid-afternoon and she can no longer ignore the pangs that tell her she has hardly eaten a bite since yesterday – not since lunchtime, with

Gorbals in the university. It feels a world away. There's a potato pancake and plastic bottle of hupplesup in her bag but she can hardly consume them here. Maybe she could find some toilets and gulp them down . . .

Mara pulls the magnetic headgem from her forehead and unclips the godbox. She holds them in the palms of her hands and frowns. Her tummy grumbles loudly and she gives in. Right now she needs to organize herself – she needs food and somewhere to sleep.

She is pulsing with nerves but switches on a smile as bland as a lumenbeing's as she stands up to exit the cybercath.

All she needs to do is look as if she has lived in a sky city all her life – not easy when at every step there are such wonders that all she wants to do is stop and stare. Mara explores the city centre, trying to get her bearings. The cybercath seems to sit right at the heart of New Mungo, at the central intersection of all the sky tunnels. The tunnels lead off into Arcadia – vast, surrounding arcades full of bright shops and strange entertainments.

Zoominlum, says a sign above one large window. Mara peers through and sees what looks like a deep pool, but instead of water, people wheel and tumble through cascades of colour. Further along, in the middle of a linking arcade, on a stage constructed out of golden rods of light, a group of lumens perform impossible acrobatics for the crowd. After the dim netherworld, Mara feels overwhelmed by so much glare, noise and movement, and by so many people.

But New Mungo is beautiful. Its long silver tunnels gleam and its arcades are vast airy places that look as if they, like the population of lumens, are crafted purely

231

from light. The citizens are beautiful too. Mara realizes with a shock how painfully thin she has become as she watches these well-nourished, healthy beings. The sleek material of her New World clothes – light, clingy top and trousers – reveals her drastic weight loss.

Candleriggs said Cal wanted to create a world full of brilliant beings, human angels – well, he has, thinks Mara. That's exactly what these people look like to someone who has only ever known weather-toughened islanders, the sick and malnourished masses in the boat camp, and the pale, sun-starved Treenesters.

Is that what the cyberfox looks like in real life? Mara wonders. A human angel?

A happy crowd of boys and girls near her own age zip past on skates. So that's the secret of their speed and power! Mara stares enviously at their strong bodies, bright smiles and smooth skins. She stops at a humpbacked bridge that sits under a crystal sky and leans upon the bridge wall to look into the still mirror of a pond. And sees the new, thin sharpness of a face that used to be round and soft. She runs her fingers through her hair, relieved that it at least still feels thick and healthy. Months of indoor life during Wing's storm season, followed by the trauma of the sea journey and the boat camp, then weeks in the gloomy netherworld, have paled her once bright complexion to a paler skin tone, not unlike the New World citizens.

'Rest upon the Leaning Bridge,' oozes a disembodied voice. 'Gaze into the magic of the Looking Pond. Whisper a secret wish in the magic Wishing Well.'

Mara relaxes into the gentle wind-sway of the city as she watches the fish swimming round the Looking Pond and listens to the birdsong in the tree beside the bridge.

Now the pond fills with glimmering rainbow lights that ease seamlessly into blue skies full of soaring birds. A radiant sunset spreads across the screen of water, deepening and darkening until the pond is midnight black and full of star fire.

It would be so easy to forget the rest of the world, so tempting to slip inside this magic spell and ignore what lies outside.

Mara yawns, then blinks as a bell clangs and breaks the hypnotic trance of the Looking Pond. The bell – not the solid, ringing clangour of the netherworld Bash but a harsh alarm with a shrill electronic edge – brings forth a mass of workers from the cybercath. They surge out, most of them skating off into the tunnels. Now Mara thinks of that other mass of workers – the city's slaves. Where are they? What's happening to Gorbals and Wing? A wave of anxiety and loneliness sweeps over her and Mara wishes she was back in the netherworld. She imagines the Treenesters gathered round their fire, trying to keep warm as the sun falls behind the city wall. Now the horror of the boat camp on the other side of the wall rushes upon her, along with the memory of her lost family.

She looks at the pond with clear eyes. The fish are fake and swim in endless electronic circles. The tree and its bird, the crystal sky and sunset, are all fake too. Even the bridge is made of mock-stone. It's a false enchantment. Now Mara is bitter, right to the brim. It gives her the burst of energy she needs. A cool, clear head and courage. One step at a time. The next step is to find food and somewhere to stay. She can't wander the city all night.

A single star shimmers in the violet depths of the Wishing Well.

'Wish upon a star,' gurgles the voice of the Wishing Well, 'and make your dreams come true.'

'I wish myself luck,' Mara tells the star. 'All the luck in the world.'

'Your wish is granted,' trills the trembling star. 'There! Isn't that nice?'

The city's attractions and facilities are advertised by lumenbeings on every corner and though the twisting central tunnels are sign-posted as pedestrian areas, they are hazardous, crammed with power skaters who hurl themselves in sparking loops round the cylindrical walls at reckless speed. It's nerve-shattering after the slow-moving life of the netherworld. Now Mara sees why the sky trains were full of older people and families with young children: the city's youth have taken over the tunnels as a perilous skateway.

At last Mara finds a food canteen – a vast, cavernous room. The canteen is almost as scarily confusing as the tunnels but she walks up to the door, nervously, trying to figure out the system.

A lumen flickers in front of her, barring her entrance.

'You forgot to check in with your ration disk!' the lumen cheerfully but firmly scolds.

'Sorry,' Mara mutters and digs about in her backpack for the wallet that contains the policewoman's disks. Which one did she use for entry to the city? The shimmery gold one, wasn't it? So the ration disk must be this other icy blue one . . .

'Have you forgotten your ration disk?' The lumen scolds in that annoyingly cheerful voice.

'Got it,' Mara mutters. She inserts it in the slit in the wall beside the lumen.

'Thank you!' beams the lumen. 'Have a delicious meal!'

Mara escapes the lumen and glances around for an empty seat. A girl with wispy blonde hair and a dull, empty expression on her face sits alone at the end of a table. There's a spare seat next to her. That'll do, thinks Mara. And so will the wispy, dull girl. Dull is perfect. The duller, the more empty-headed, the better.

'Hi.' Mara tries to smile casually.

'Hi,' says the girl, without a flicker of interest. She's stroking a creature that's all purple hair, a ridiculous purple puffball. It's emitting annoying whining noises.

'Mind if I sit here?' asks Mara. The girl stares into space, munching on a plateful of brightly coloured food. 'I'm a visitor so I don't know many people round here.'

'Go ahead.'

Mara looks around. Does she just go up and pick something to eat?

'What's your name?' she asks the girl, stalling for time. Something dull no doubt.

'Dolores,' says the girl unexpectedly. The puffball yaps.

Far too exotic for you, thinks Mara. She doesn't ask the name of the puffball thing, just glances hungrily at the girl's bright food.

'Dol for short.'

Mara hides a smile. That's as near *dull* as you can get.

She watches people come into the canteen, insert their ration disks, collect a tray and choose a meal and sit down. So that's all you do. Mara braves the food counter and, as she chooses from a vast array of exotic-looking dishes, she is willing Dol to be as vacant and dull-minded as she looks. Because that is what she needs – someone to give her answers, lots of answers and ask as few awkward questions as possible.

235

'Don't you have zapeedos?' Dol asks in mild surprise, as they exit the bustling canteen into a chaotic, noise-filled tunnel.

Mara has told the girl she's newly arrived from another city and is feeling lost. Dol has unenthusiastically agreed to show her to the visitor accommodation area.

'You need zapeedos to get around the nexus.' Dol nods towards the tunnels. 'Surely you zap in your city?'

'Uh-huh,' says Mara. 'I just forgot to pack my, um, zapeedos.'

'You'll get mown down if you go about on foot, and you don't want to be stuck on the sky trains like a sloped.'

'Definitely not,' agrees Mara.

'Oh, well. Better switch off my power if you're walking, otherwise you'll never keep up.'

Dol flicks a switch on the heel of her power skates. Zapeedos, Mara notes, memorizing the term. And she called the tunnels the nexus. Now the girl taps the purple puffball on its head and, to Mara's relief, not only does that switch off the thing's stupid whining but makes it collapse as if it's been stamped on – something Mara has been itching to do. Dol stuffs the now flat animatronic pet in her trouser pocket.

Mara jogs to keep up with Dol's unpowered skating as they enter tunnels that are full of swirling, surging waves of electronic music. Mara remembers the similar-sounding music she used to find on the Weave – the music her mother liked because, she said, it both calmed and lifted your spirit. *Waltzes*, that's what they were called. It was waltz music she danced to, round and round the garden with little Corey, that last-ever day on the island. Now she watches zappers swarm through the silver tunnels, doing crazy zigzag antics up the sides, zooming round and round in floor-to-ceiling loops at incredible speeds, in time to the waltzes.

'Do you work in the cybercath?' Mara asks, worming for information.

Dol nods.

'What are you working on?'

Now Dol comes alive. She is a Noosrunner, she says proudly, and as she chatters excitedly Mara gathers that her guess about the trade network was right. New ideas and inventions, alongside more mundane, essential products are the currency that the New World trades in. Dol prattles on about the teams of Ideators in each city who try to outdo each other in ingenuity, dreaming up ideas that will create yet further wonders for the New World – new forms of energy and communication and overseas travel, new bondings of sea chemicals, new metals and materials, foodstuffs, entertainment, and all sorts of gadgets and gimmicks – even some ideas that might, in time, take the New World far beyond Earth, out into space. Just as Candleriggs predicted, Mara remembers.

Noosrunners like Dol are specialized cybertraders. They search cyberspace for the best of these new ideas to buy and sell among the cities of the New World.

'I spotted a brand new alloy in one of the Chinasea markets,' Dol declares. 'Hardly anyone else is on to it so I'm not telling you what it is, but if it takes off I could win a top bonus. Here we are.'

Dol skates out of the head of the tunnel into another wide, squat one. 'These are the visitor sleep pods – there's bound to be a free one.'

Mara only just manages to keep up. The heels of Dol's

237

zapeedos click together as she comes to a neat halt beside what looks like an empty pink pod.

The pod is part of a long honeycomb that crams the walls all the way down the squat tunnel. Some pods are sealed and gently glowing, others open, dim and empty.

'Sleep pods?' Mara's heart sinks. It will be like sleeping in a pink coffin.

Dol nods. For the first time a flicker of doubt disturbs her face. That was careless, Mara chastises herself. A visiting New World citizen would know these are sleep pods.

'Oh, we have much the same in my city,' Mara gabbles. 'Just a different shape and colour and we call them coffins.' It doesn't sound right. She improvises. 'Cosy coffins.' That's worse.

Dol nods again. She seems to swallow each lie with a stunning lack of interest. Mara remembers the hungry welcome for any visitors that came to Wing, even though they were only ever from the other islands. The Treenesters were intensely curious about her, longing for stories of the outside world. And though the netherworld is now far below and out of reach it still feels far more real and alive to Mara than this bright, bland, beautiful place.

Mara laughs to herself as she recalls Pollock and the cyberwizz. By now, that will be set in memory as a Treenester legend – the night the Face in the Stone magicked up a monster that chased boastful Pollock Halfgood into the bushes. Dol glances at her sharply now and Mara realizes she has laughed out loud.

'Cyberlag,' mumbles Mara. 'I come from a different world zone. Thanks a lot, Dol. Um . . .' she hesitates, 'you – you wouldn't have a spare pair of zapeedos, would you? Just till I sort myself out.'

'Sure,' Dol shrugs.

'See you tomorrow at the cybercath?' Mara calls after her but Dol has zapped off.

Mara climbs up the ladder into an empty pink pod. Inside it's warm and soft, like a spongy nest. Once the sliding door of the pod is shut Mara is enveloped in a comforting pink glow.

From Dol's chatter she has figured out that the New World pays its workers by disks which buy generous rations of food, clothes and a vast range of entertainments. Bonus disks are won by the workers for good performance. The very best Noosrunners and Ideators are rewarded with superior accommodation, and Dol talks enviously of these stylish apartments at the very top of the towers. Dol lives in much more basic accommodation, on a lower level of the central towers, but she's clearly ambitious to move right to the top.

I'll find out more tomorrow, Mara tells herself, and snuggles down inside her pink pod to read some more of *A Tale of Two Cities*. She groans with relief as she kicks off the young policewoman's shoes from her aching feet. They are far too tight and are giving her blisters. The sway of the city is more insistent now. She feels as if she is in a ship's cabin, far out upon the ocean. It must be windy tonight in the outside world. The Treenesters will be rocked hard in their nests, the boat people smashed about like so much flotsam and jetsam.

Mara sighs and the book falls from her hands.

'Time to settle down and sleep now,' a gentle, cajoling voice urges.

Mara jumps. She swivels around and yells in fright.

A large, motherly lumenbeing face glows like a soft nightlight on the shelf above her bed.

'Goodnight,' Mara snaps, hoping that's the code to get rid of it.

The face fades and the pink pod darkens. But the lumen eyes of the motherlight remain, glimmering and unblinking in the dark.

'Great,' groans Mara.

Now she is stuck in the dark, alone and unsleepy with a pair of creepy lumen eyes watching her. As she lies restlessly in the bed and pulls the spongy quilt around her, the eyes begin to haunt her with the memory of other eyes. Mara aches for those real mother eyes that would soothe her each night as a child when she was tucked up in bed. Mara would wriggle and giggle under the covers, fighting off sleep because she wanted yet another story, another song, another cuddle, another smile.

Those real mother-eyes were always the last thing she saw at night before she closed her own. Mara tries to switch off their image but they burn on in her mind, far stronger than any lumen.

FOX TRAIL TWO

Mara dreams.

Secret, sly dreams that she can never quite track. All night they prowl through her sleep and she wakens sweaty and sticky in her pink pod. It's as if something is trying to sneak through a locked door in her mind, a door from another world. One that opens just a crack, only when she is asleep.

All night, Mara dreams. Then wakens to yet another strange day.

ENTRANCED

Next morning it takes Mara ages to search through the thousands of people in the cybercath, but at last she spots Dol muttering in tuneful, excited tones in a cupule near the back. She finds a free cupule nearby and settles down to pretend to work but really she's listening hard to Dol and the others around her. Halfway through the morning a bell rings and the cyberworkers stop for a break.

Mara sips the warm, frothy, bitter-sweet brew that has popped out of a hidden compartment in her cupule. She's not sure if she likes it but it seems to give her a much-needed buzz of energy. Dol is gesturing upwards and Mara glances above her head at the *Thought for Now* slogan that beams above the heads of the workers in the cyber-cath. The huge *No enemy in New Mungo* slogan has started to scramble.

'Hackers,' grins Dol. 'Watch.'

The letters scramble at top speed. The hum of the cybercath falls quiet as everyone holds their breath. A great cheer erupts as the letters settle and the workers break up in laughter at the *Thought For Now* which proclaims there's *No meeny in New Mungo*.

Mara laughs too and settles in her hug chair till Dol is ready. She has agreed to give Mara a short training session. It turns out that Dol is not as dull as she looks. Quite the opposite. The dullness is a veil of boredom, behind which lives an ace wizzer. Real life bores Dol, Mara now knows, after watching her come alive on the dive into cyberspace. With a pang she recognizes the fierce, feral excitement on the girl's face. It's what she used to feel in the Weave.

Perhaps Dol feels trapped inside the walls of New Mungo, just as Mara did inside the walls of her home in the storm season on Wing. Perhaps luxury means little when there's no real freedom in the world.

She has told Dol that she is a trainee cyberworker on an apprenticeship from New Wing, a northern city still under construction; that she has been sent here to update on the New World technology – she claims to have been stuck on an out-of-date system. Dol has questioned none of this story; she seems to have no interest in anything much beyond the cyberworld she works in. And Mara is anxious to learn about that as fast as she can. It's clear that the cybercath is the nerve centre of New Mungo, so gaining access to the system is surely her best means of locating the slave workers and finding a way to rescue Gorbals and Wing.

'Put on your godgem and I'll help you link in,' Dol instructs.

Mara picks up the tiny box and the green gem. 'I thought it was a godbox and headgem,' she says, eyeing the notice in her cupule.

Dol points with extreme patience to the little godbox. 'This is your power, it gets you whatever you ask for.' Then to the crystal headgem. 'This is your mind's eye, it gives you cybervision. Godbox, headgem – godgem for short. You must know *that*?' says Dol a touch crossly. 'Don't they give even basic training to newcomers?'

'Sorry,' says Mara humbly, as she puts on the godgem. 'I couldn't get to grips with it at all the other day. My teacher in my own city sent me here because she said the best way to learn was from a top Noosrunner,' she flatters, 'like you.'

Dol brightens at the compliment. 'Really? Well, OK, I'll log you in on my password. Now just say *"be"* to your godgem . . .' Dol's voice hits a melodic note as she says the word, 'then jump in and voice-steer to whatever or wherever you seek. See, you get a deeper level of control if you use your voice tonally to steer. If you're stuck, hop on a help platform, they're all over the Noos, and send out a search ball if you know what you're looking for.' Dol glances at Mara. 'But you haven't a clue, have you? Well, just freefall till you get a feel for it. You can be as you are or you can call up a help wizard and be anything you want – any creature, any form. Ready?'

'No,' Mara sighs to herself. Dol will find her out, she is sure, but she has to risk that. Even more than unquestioning dullness, Mara needs a wizzer like this who can teach her what she needs.

Dol sighs too and Mara feels spectacularly small-brained.

'Well, I'll knit you into the system,' she says with weary patience. 'But I can't hang around, I'm on the track of that new stuff I told you about – I want to try and get in ultraquick in case there's a world trade rush.'

'But if you could just – oh, never mind,' says Mara, catching Dol's impatient expression.

'I'll start you off then you're on your own,' says Dol,

clearly itching to lose such a tedious ignoramus. 'Now jump!'

'Jump where?' Mara panics. 'Be!' she instructs the godgem, then cries out in fright as she freefalls into the strangest experience she's ever had. In realworld she stops breathing as she spins out of her cupule in the cybercath, far away into another dimension, into a world of utter beauty, grace and chaos. Mara feels a rush of cyberjoy zip through her like electricity, as she drops into the wonders of this stunning, strange, new, live universe.

All around, above and below, as far as she can see, the godgems of the New World have merged to create an organic frenzy of colour and pattern. Fractals and feathers, frosts and ferns and flowers, crystals and corals, constellations and cloudbursts and galaxies, shells, stars, strata, streamers and spirals, bird flocks and bubble clusters and butterfly wings, roses and acorns, loops and spheres, lichen, rainbows and honeycombs, fungus, snowflakes, spheres, pyramids and prisms, webs and jungle weaves, knits and knots and so much, much more. Everything imaginable and beyond. All of it linked by an endless pattern of connections. A living world of info and data within each pattern. All of it endlessly changing and mutating and repatterning. All dying and recreating every microsecond.

It's like looking into the mind of the universe.

Mara's eyes fill with tears at the wild and savage beauty of it all. It's miraculous. And a whole world had to end before she could see it.

It is Noospace, the stunning new universe. The Noos, they call it; the amazing creation of the global Supermind that has sprung into being among the cities of the New World.

Like a genie let loose from a bottle, the beautiful Noos has wrapped itself invisibly, powerfully, around the Earth. And holds its world spellbound.

In time to the music, but out of time with everyone else, Mara waltzes through swarms of zappers. Sparks fly from their feet as they race at frightening speeds through the gleaming maze of the nexus. The combination of too-tight shoes that nip her feet and the pair of zapeedos she has borrowed from Dol being several sizes too big, so that they keep slipping, doesn't help. She'd like to buy a pair of shoes and zapeedos that fit properly but she has no idea what rations she can buy with the stolen disks. And she must be careful – the young policewoman's absence will surely be noted by now. Will her ration disks be cancelled? Maybe not immediately, but Mara decides she can't risk any extra purchases that might lead to her discovery. She'll have to make do with ill-fitting shoes and zapeedos and only use the ration disk for essential food. And hope for the best.

For now, Mara tries to keep up with the fleet feet of Dol and her friends, but it's almost impossible. She's had a few nasty smashes but at last she seems to be finding her own feet.

Well, I seem to have found my balance at least, Mara congratulates herself. *Now all I need to do is get the hang of speed and steering.*

The bright lights and speed of New Mungo make her eyes ache and her head spin after weeks in the dim netherworld and fifteen years on tranquil Wing. She yearns for natural light and for Wing's long, still horizons. At the very least she could do with one of the coloured vizzers the zappers wear to protect their eyes from each others' sparks as they surf the sides and loop the loop, zipping hazardous circles around the walls. All Mara can see as she looks through the nexus are bodies – upright, sideways and upside down, and every angle in between. The silver tunnels smoke, spark and crackle with friction.

Suddenly Mara's own zapeedos flash with sparks and she lets out a scream as she takes a bend far too fast and wide. But wait – amazingly, she's done it! She grins in triumph as she rounds the bend and manages to stay on her feet.

'Hey, Dol, look! I've really got the hang of this.'

'Mara! Stop!'

Dol is just a blur as Mara zooms past. She does the worst thing possible, tries to turn in the middle of a tunnel and makes a spectacular crash against the metal wall, smashing through a cluster of nearby zappers. Mara screams again as the tunnel fills with sprawling bodies and erupts with an outburst of zapeedo rage. Dol speeds over, but before she gets there Mara is pulled to her feet and steered out of the way of the chaos she has created.

'Lethal, you are,' says her rescuer, a tousle-headed boy. He rubs a reddening lump on his forehead.

'Sorry,' Mara gasps.

'She's a learner,' says Dol, apologetically. She puts her hand on the boy's head and gazes into his eyes. 'You OK, David?'

Apart from the concussion,' he replies drily.

Mara tries to stammer an apology but Dol pushes her towards a door marked

Entrance

The word pulsates. The door zips open and shut every

247

couple of seconds as throngs of brightly clothed people rush in and out.

'Entrance to where?' asks Mara dazedly.

Dol gives her the deadpan look that Mara gets from her quite a lot. The look that says: *how thick are you?*

'Not entrance, En*trance*,' says Dol as she shoves Mara through the door. 'The best sensawave club in New Mungo.'

'Oh,' says Mara, feeling every bit as thick as Dol must find her.

Once inside, Mara feels she has entered a mirror world of the wild, electronic chaos of Noospace. She grabs on to Dol, reeling as if she's in freefall.

'En*tranced*?' Dol laughs as she kicks off her zapeedos. Then she speeds off into the swarm of dancers.

Mara edges to a wall and looks around. Sound engulfs her. Colour swamps her. Living patterns swirl all around and above. Scents and sensations sweep through her. Wave after wave in the mix of colour, sound and patterns cause pounding surges of excitement. The dancers seem to be constantly on the verge of some great event. Mara waits to see what – but nothing ever happens. It just goes on and on.

Mara leans against the wall, feels nothing – and falls flat on her back.

Stunned, she scrambles to her feet. The wall's a lumen. Its surface patterns are gently mutating as if it's alive. Mara looks around but luckily everyone seems so entranced by the scene that surrounds them they haven't noticed. Except one – the boy who rescued her from her tunnel crash. He is standing alongside her, the chaotic lights dancing in his eyes. As Mara struggles to her feet the boy looks away, laughter making his lips twitch. She burns with embarrassment. He must think she's a blundering clown.

Gail's voice echoes from what feels like a far distant time and place. *What if we land up in some great new city looking like gawky peasants?* Well, I've done it, Gail, thinks Mara. Gawky peasant just about sums me up – yet on Wing I felt so smart; I thought I was a world ahead of everyone else.

Mara looks through a doorway in the lumen wall and sees an open mountain top – a lumen illusion that makes the floor and walls fall away into a fake worldscape, roofed by an endless, glittering sky. Cool air breezes all around and dancers whirl coloured lumen sticks above their heads, creating fronded waves of brightness. The mix of light and sound and illusion are softer here, the electronic spell broken by ghostly scraps of human voice. It's simple and infinite. Multi-sensory, out of your mind, moment-to-moment being, no beginning or end, going nowhere.

'Beautiful night,' says a voice close behind.

Mara jumps then recovers herself to shoot her very best lumeny smile at the owner of the voice – a tanned, smooth-skinned boy, older than herself. But ages are confusing in New Mungo. Mara is sure, though she can't exactly tell why, that many of the youthful-looking people are much older than they seem. It's something in their voice, in their movements and most of all in their eyes; something they have lost and something else gained that is different in nature to true youth. Noosrunners all appear to be roughly the same age – not too young and not too old. This boy, for instance – really more man than boy, now that she looks closely – he looks eighteen, twenty at most, but some deep instinct tells Mara he is much older – thirty, maybe even forty.

'You're not one of us, are you?' he says.

Again, Mara jumps in fright. What can he tell? She has tried hard to look like everyone else here.

'I'm on a training visit,' Mara answers, a trifle too sharply.

'Ah,' says the man-boy. 'Where's your own city?'

'In the north,' says Mara. 'It's very new, still under construction.'

'What's it called?'

'New Wing.' she answers flawlessly.

'Don't know that one. Anyway, the more the merrier,' says the man-boy. He waves an arm around him. 'So, how do we compare with New Wing?'

'It's all one world,' says Mara, mouthing one of the New World slogans that she's seen flash above the heads of the workers in the cybercath.

He smiles and nods. 'By the way, I'm Tony. Tony Rex.'

He leans closer and his hair shimmers. Beautiful, longish black hair that Mara is suddenly sure is not real; the sheen is too liquid and bright. His clothes are made of the sleekest material Mara has ever seen; like the oiled pelt of an animal. And yet it ripples like silk. He bares his teeth in a lascivious smile.

'You haven't told me your name.'

Mara hadn't. She wants rid of him, but she can't risk saying or doing anything that will mark her out as different. Reluctantly, she answers him.

He stares at her and Mara's heart beats nervously. He looks her up and down, slowly, sleazily, grins and leans even closer.

'You should do an audition for Noostars.'

Mara doesn't ask what he means, just shakes her head and turns away. It doesn't faze him.

'You should give it a try,' he persists. 'They're short on this year's quota. Imagine – you get to be famous right across the New World for a whole night! Can you sing? It's no problem if you can't. It's the look that counts – they'll give you a makeover and fix you up a voice in no time.'

Mercifully, someone tugs him into the dancers. Mara heaves a sigh of relief and moves to the door. She's really not in the mood for the *Entrance* scene. As she leaves she catches sight of Tony Rex once again, eyeing her through the crowd, and for a split second Mara sees something flicker across his bland, cheerful face – something that disturbs her.

Suspicion?

Mara skates back through the nexus. As she climbs into her sleep pod, her head is ringing with dance noise and from the tunnel waltzes, reeling too from the city sway, but she is thinking hard. She must watch her step. Something about Tony Rex has made her uncomfortable; something that shines out of his sharp, watchful eyes and defies his pleasant, young – but somehow not-so-young – face. Something dangerous, she's sure.

ONCE UPON A TIME

Mara looks at her plateful of bright and beautiful noofood.
Yuk.

All around her in the cafe, people are happily tucking
in to exotic-looking platefuls of the stuff, but it turns
Mara's stomach. The aroma and flavour of real food haunts
her. She lies in bed at night longing for a plateful of
the Treenesters's herby mushroom stew and some heart-
warming hupplesup.

There's something wrong with noofood. It looks tempt-
ingly beautiful, comes in every colour of the rainbow, yet
it all leaves a salty aftertaste on the tongue. It turns to
pulp in the mouth and even a small plateful is strangely
filling – yet somehow unsatisfying, as if it swells like an
empty balloon in the stomach. And though the New World
citizens obviously don't agree, Mara feels there's something unappetizing about blue beans and pink potatoes.

Noofood is made from a mulch of seafood, fish, kelp
and plankton; the last two, she has learned, are grown and
harvested in vast sea farms. Each city has its own noofood
factory, where the mulch is pumped with bloating, fibrous
texture, with added nutrients, flavourings and colour, then

manufactured into this array of bright, bland fodder that parodies the real food of the old world.

The city gives a lurch. Mara feels a wave of nausea and pushes her plate away. It's not just the food – the constant movement of the city makes her queasy. Tonight, it feels as if they are all on board a ship in a tempest. And her feet are sore with blisters from her too-tight shoes.

To take her mind off sky sickness and sore feet, Mara runs through everything she has discovered about the workings of the city over the last few days.

The New World cities are built on almost identical designs, all based on that feat of natural engineering that Cal, Candleriggs's lost love, pioneered in the years when the Earth first began to drown. Each city is powered by a mighty mix of sun and wind and sea. The city nets all possible energy that comes its way. Solar power is soaked up, sponge-like, through microscopic pores in the city's titanmera fabric and channelled into great sunmills that turn it into lumenergy. Wavepower is churned through vast watermills in the support towers. Windpower is flumed through the spiregyres – the hundreds of strange, twisting coils on the edges of the nexus of sky tunnels that Mara puzzled over in the boat camp. Immense spiregyres helter-skelter all down the sides of the great towers and pump out the city's used air straight down into the netherworld.

Mara's stomach turns again. So that explains the sour, bad-breath odour of the netherworld air.

She already knew that the massive central towers harbour the supply ships. The higher levels of the towers house the citizens and lower down are storehouses and production factories for noofood and all sorts of other goods. Everything else is shipped in from supply cities which manufacture whatever the New World needs or wants.

In the cybercath, Mara has studied gleaming lumens that display 3D plans to develop sea bridges out east to link up with the nearest of the Eurosea sky cities – dangerous, precarious work in the stormy thrust of the oceans that will surely require yet more slave labour. But there's no hint of storms or slaves in the gleaming lumen plan; all danger and cruelty is made invisible for the citizens of the New World.

Mara can't bear to think that while she lives in comfort and luxury, Gorbals and Wing and so many others are forced to endure such an existence. She can only hope that they have not been shipped off to another project across the ocean. Or worse – Mara's heart almost stops dead at the thought – how far have the Ideators of the New World developed their schemes to colonize space?

I must get my plan together, quickly, and act.

Mara rouses from her thoughts. Scattered around her in the cafe are Dol and her gang. They sit at tables bickering over all the things they might do tonight, chatting to friends on the voice-controlled knuckle phones with ear stud connectors that make them all look as if they are muttering into their fists or listening to invisible presences. The cyberfox could never be one of them, she is sure. They're all too shallow and self-obsessed, not interested in anything beyond here and now and having fun. Mara swallows her bitterness. It's not their fault. They know nothing of what she has seen and lived through. If she had been born into this life she'd probably be just like them – frittering away her leisure time in the shopping malls or scenic chat cafes in the Noos – Dol regularly visits one that meets in the beams of a rainbow. Then there are cybervizits and safaris, realsports and feel-movies, blisspools, solhols, zoominlums, colourjetting, sensawave clubbing, fear circuses and a hundred other entertainments.

The only problem anyone ever has in New Mungo is deciding what they want to do. And yet Mara feels a grudging awe. The New World and all its wonders were created while the rest of the world drowned and the people of Wing and the islands only just managed to survive.

'She's not a *total* slo-ped. She's turned out quite zippy – after a truly lousy start-up. These newcomers really do need the expertise of top Noosrunners like us to get them up to scratch,' she hears Dol boast. Mara glances over and sees Dol winding a strand of her wispy blonde hair round and round her finger, her face flushed with triumph as she chatters breathlessly to David, the boy Mara crashed outside *Entrance*. David must be an ace Noosrunner, she supposes, from the way girls always hang around him, treating him like a young god, each subtly trying to elbow her way into his affections. Yet he is distant and cool with them all; off-puttingly so, in Mara's opinion. But she pricks up her ears now, all too aware that the slo-ped Dol is mocking in a superior tone is very probably herself.

'We really must be the nux of the New World, when you see what slo-peds the other cities' runners are,' Dol murmurs. She leans closer to David, gazing into his eyes. If she leans any closer she'll go cross-eyed, thinks Mara.

'Who is she?' asks David, seeming to prefer the frothy orange dregs of his glass of Noobru to Dol's rapturous gaze.

His voice is husky and attractive. A night-time voice, good for fire-stories, thinks Mara wistfully, wondering at the unexpected tingle that runs down her spine. She leans her chin on her hand and lets her hair fall casually across her face to hide the fact that she's listening hard. Anyhow, he's better to listen to than look at, as he's very ordinary-looking: pale and intense, with a scrunchy mess of light brown hair. She can't help wondering why he's such a hit with the other girls. Although, beneath the messy hair – Mara casts a quick glance at him from behind the smooth, dark sweep of her own hair – he does have dreamy eyes.

Dol nods abruptly in her direction without taking her eyes from David's face. 'Mara,' she replies.

David turns and looks straight at Mara. He gives her a long, pensive look but there's a distance in his eyes that suggests he's half-thinking of something else. Just as Mara begins to feel uncomfortable he briskly shifts his gaze back to his drink and Mara is left watching his fingers, drumming restlessly on the cafe table. His quick, sharp movements seem at odds with the faraway eyes.

'Where's she from?' he murmurs to Dol, and Mara feels her body stiffen, immediately on the alert. He's not quite as distant as he appears.

'Um, New Wing – I think that's where she said,' says Dol, looking as if she's itching to find a way to turn the conversation round to herself.

'New Wing?' His restless fingers fall still and he stares hard into his frothy drink. He glances at her once again, for barely a second this time, but Mara feels the faraway eyes focus and narrow to shoot her a hot bolt of a look. Her heart beats painfully. What is it? Has she been caught out? Does this ace Noosrunner know there's no such city? But already he has turned away, the sharp expression switching to instant boredom. Beneath her relief, Mara feels stung by his lack of interest.

What a terrible island mentality they all have – anyone from outside New Mungo is a second-class citizen. And anyone who isn't a New World citizen is worthless, their most basic human rights sacrificed to the needs of the New World.

Mara rages silently as she sneaks away from the cafe crowd, puts on her zapeedos and zooms out into the silver nexus. Now she's got the hang of it, zapping is sheer release. Dead air is wind in her face and speed is freedom. She even enjoys the occasional drama of tunnel rage; it's all exhilarating stuff. Yet tonight not even skaterush can kill the black mood inside her. Fuelled by adrenalin, she tries to fix her mind upon her rescue plan. She's got all of the pieces in her head, she just can't find a way to fix them together.

After a long skate, Mara winds up in the cybercath. This late, with its lights dimmed and only the low, melodic hum of a few night workers, it's as peaceful as a church. Mara slips off her zapeedos and chooses a work cupule far away from anyone else. Then slumps in the hug chair in despair.

Fox, where are you? I need you.

She must find him. If only she could figure out how. One trip into the Noos devastated her hopes of finding him there. She could search through Noospace for the rest of her life and never find him, it's so vast and complex – and ever-expanding. But she really needs an ally, someone she can trust. She can't see how she will manage a rescue plan all on her own. It could take ages to get her head around the detail of everything she needs to know. And time is what she doesn't have. Gorbals and Wing are suffering now, this minute; as are all the refugees in the boat camp. She can only hope that Rowan and the people from Wing are still alive.

Every time she thinks of Rowan and the others in the boat camp she feels a rising panic at the length of time that has passed since she left them there. Panic makes her helpless, unable to focus and plan and act. The only way, she decides, is to try not to think about the camp, to push it to the edges of her mind until it seems unreal and remote. Only then can she concentrate on the task in hand.

What she lacks is someone who really understands the city, who can work its system expertly, who could find a way to reach the slaves, access the boats and disarm New Mungo's security for long enough to let them all escape. Who better than a sly cyberfox? But even if she could find him, could she trust him? *Would* he help her? She remembers that single moment of connection she had with him out in the cyberhaze between the Weave and the New World. The magnetic tug that pulled her towards him, as if by instinct. She remembers the human presence behind the cyberfox eyes and tries to have faith. You wouldn't feel that kind of pull towards an enemy, would you? For someone who meant you harm?

There are thousands of people in this city. He could be anywhere. The scale of her isolation hits Mara, hard.

She looks around the vast, almost-empty cybercath, at the honeycomb of cupules that are filled during the day, wondering which one Fox might sit in – and jumps nervously as her eyes meet a pair of sly ones. The eyes of Tony Rex. As soon as she spots him the slyness slips from his features and he assumes a pleasant, cheerful expression. The change is so swift and subtle that Mara is left unsure whether it's just her own nervousness that made her imagine the disturbing glint in his eyes. What she does know for sure is that she can't seem to shake him off. He always seems to be on her tail – in the tunnels or peering at her through the ranks of faces in the cybercath, watching her in the cafe or the canteen. It's beginning to feel as if he is stalking her.

Mara's heart thuds as a sudden, awful thought strikes. What if the cyberfox is not her natural ally? What if her impression of him is all wrong? She only met him for the briefest of moments. It would be easy, amid all that blinding cyberhaze, to misread the look in anyone's eyes. Now Mara begins to doubt her own instincts because the only solid evidence she has of the character of the cyberfox is his sly, predatory ways when he stalked her for so long on the Weave. The very same sleek, sly manner in which Tony Rex seems to be stalking her now.

Trust no one, Mara warns herself. For all I know, Tony Rex could be the fox. Forget the fox. I'll just have to work things out on my own – somehow.

She smiles blandly at Tony Rex and murmurs tonefully, pretending to be thoroughly engrossed in some long, complex bit of cyberwork. When at last he leaves the cybercath she lets out a huge breath of relief. Then she puts her head in her hands, aching to cry.

She has lived with the idea of the cyberfox for so long that to cut him out of her mind feels like chopping off a limb, severing a lifeline.

It's no good. I can't do this on my own. I may as well go back down to the netherworld – but I can't. I promised the Treenesters I'd bring Gorbals and Wing back with me, that I wouldn't come back until I'd found them. But they'd understand, surely, if I said I tried and failed. Or would they? Did they only take me in and be my friend because they thought I was their saviour? Maybe they won't want me back once they see that I'm not. And anyway, I haven't tried, have I? I've hardly tried at all. But how can I ever find Gorbals and Wing? And even if I do, how could I ever rescue a mass of slaves and refugees and escape in a ship? I must have been mad to even think I could do it.

But if she doesn't try, who will? Gorbals and Wing will be condemned to life as slaves. All the others too – all the stolen urchins and refugees. Soon the ocean will rise again and the Treenesters will lose their tiny island and drown. And she will be trapped here in New Mungo for the rest of her days – or until she is discovered, and cast out. So she must try. What does she have to lose?

My life. Just one small life among so many that have been lost.

But it's her life and to Mara it doesn't feel small. It feels like everything. Yet she *will* try, even if it means losing her life – because she won't be able to live with herself if she doesn't. And nothing is impossible – she should know that by now. A world can drown. People can cling to life in boat camps and nests in trees. A new world can rise out of the oceans. Its citizens can live amid wonders and luxury and know nothing of the human catastrophe that exists all around them.

Anything can happen. That means anything is possible. So I will find a way.

But right now she must find a way to get herself through the night. Mara needs more than a hug chair. She wants real arms to hold her, not this synthetic embrace. But there's no one. Mara thinks of the next best thing.

A story. I want a story.

Somewhere in Noospace there must be a story to settle her, to burrow into and let her forget her worries and fears. Mara longs for Gorbals and his night-time fire tales. A memory runs through her and she sees the wide eyes of the Treenesters gazing through the firelight as Gorbals's story spins a comfort nest around them all. Mara dashes away tears and the memory too. She puts on a godgem and jumps deep into the chaotic patterns of the Noos.

She's just beginning to get the hang of the tonal voice-steering that by day fills the cybercath with its choral hum. Falteringly, Mara uses her voice to get to a Noos-station, one of the floating help platforms.

'I want a story,' she instructs the small glitter-ball of electronic energy that immediately bounces towards her.

The glittering search-ball bounces high into Noospace and explodes in a million fragments – electronic questers – that scatter across the mutating patterns. Moments later, like a reverse explosion, the fragments zoom back into a ball, having searched the Noos to find what Mara wants.

Storey as in floor, level in building? the glitter-ball reports back.

'No, S-T-O-R-Y,' says Mara. 'As in once upon a time.'

The search-ball explodes again.

Falsehood, lie, it suggests, when it's back in one piece.

Mara sighs. 'No. Try books.'

Boots?

'Books!'

The search-ball scatters yet again and takes a moment longer than usual to gather back the questers. Mara's hopes rise as she watches the glittering fragments gather back into a globe.

Defunct word, it claims uselessly.

'I just want a *story*!' Mara bursts out.

She catches the eye of a guard at the door and quickly lowers her voice. 'Story,' she mutters stubbornly. 'I don't

261

believe there isn't a single story in the whole of the Noos. Any kind of story will do – fairy tale, ghost story, adventure story, love story. You choose. I'll sit here all night and ask if I have to. Just find me a story.'

Store, bounces back the search-ball, just as stubbornly. *Try stockpile, save, stash.*

A useless heap of words that are nothing to do with a story. Mara feels blank. She doesn't know what to do. *Hoard, treasure,* the search-ball chatters on. *Would you like to try any of these?*

Oh, shut up, thinks Mara, but something odd is happening. The heap of words reshuffle, sorting themselves into a pattern that becomes a flickering picture in her mind. A familiar, moving picture. A story.

Hoard, treasure. Goosebumps prickle all over her body and the words seem to grow hot inside, flaming into a story she knows, the one Gorbals told on the night of the storm about the lost girl who followed a rainbow and found a hoard of treasure at the rainbow's end. The crock of gold.

'All right, I'll tell *you* a story,' Mara whispers to the little search ball, as she wriggles deeper into her hug chair. 'Once upon a time,' she begins, but she has hardly breathed the words when there is a deep electronic shudder in the godgem that ripples out, disturbing the patterns of the Noos. The glitter-ball bounces off in fright.

'Hey, come back,' Mara calls after it. 'Oh, all right, I don't care. Well, once upon a time . . . '

She falters. The familiar words sound so alien and empty in the vast loneliness of Noospace.

There's another electronic shudder. Then a voice that does not belong to the godgem or the search-ball.

'Once upon a time,' echoes the voice.

Mara sits bolt upright in her seat. The words tingle inside her and she shivers as if she's caught a cold. The low, wary voice has taken her back to a time and place that feels worlds away now. Mara is so shocked she can barely speak.

'Where – where are you?' she gasps at last. Then jumps in surprise as she finds herself alone on the Noos-station platform, staring into the eyes of the cyberfox.

The fox is as still as a statue. All senses alert.

'Once upon a time,' says the fox. 'I followed you. We met out in Nowhere, out beyond the Weave. You screamed for help then vanished. I've been searching for you ever since.'

Mara looks at the fox and the fox looks back. A tangle of Noos patterns reflect in its liquid, untamed eyes.

'You have?' breathes Mara.

The fox pads closer. And through her joy and disbelief cuts a sudden flash of panic, because Mara doesn't know if this cyberfox is friend or foe. She doesn't want her New World cover blown because then she's sunk. She wants to run and hide. But curiosity, and the pull of that other, deeper instinct is too strong. So Mara stays her ground, her eyes never leaving the fierce, vivid gaze of the fox.

FOX DEN

Mara is thinking faster than she has ever thought before.

'I still need help,' she whispers. 'But can I trust you?'

Who are you? she wonders frantically. *Who?* She glances around the near-empty cybercath and reassures herself that Tony Rex has not returned. And the voice is not his. But if you can take on a new form in the Noos then surely you could assume a new voice? And there are mobile godgems, so he could be working from anywhere in New Mungo.

'Can I trust *you*?' says the fox, unexpectedly.

'Me?' exclaims Mara in surprise. Then lowers her voice as she senses someone stir in a work cupule several seats behind her. She steals a quick, fearful glance, but the Noosrunner's head is bent, engrossed in whatever he or she is working on.

'OK, here's a story for you, a story from the old world,' Mara blurts out, because if it is Tony Rex she's already caught. If it's not, she has to take a leap of faith. It's her only chance.

'Once upon a time there was a Weave-wizzer, an ace wizzer. For years she played in the old network called the

Weave. This girl – I mean, the wizzer – had no idea that what she thought was everything was really just the ruin of a dead old world and that a whole new electronic universe had sprung into life out beyond the patch of cyberspace she knew. One day she fell out of the Weave and saw what lay beyond it. And she met a cyberfox. But her whole world was about to fall apart. Her island in realworld was drowning . . .'

Mara pauses, swallowing hard. When she is able to speak, her voice cracks with emotion.

'She lost everything, her family and friends, everyone. But somehow she survived. And all the time, all through the nightmare that followed, she held on to the hope that she would find the cyberfox again – that he might help her.'

It's hard to go on. The fox says nothing, just stares at her. If a fox could cry, this one looks close to it.

'Do you understand?' Mara asks.

The fox nods. Mara is sure tears stand in its eyes.

She lets out an enormous breath she didn't know she has been holding. A sob shakes her. She glances around quickly but the Noosrunner behind her is still too deep in concentration to notice.

'It's a long story, too long to tell it all now, but amazingly I ended up here in your world,' Mara whispers to the fox. 'I asked you for help once. I still need your help. Desperately. I need someone I can trust in realworld. I don't know if I trust you but . . .' Mara grinds to a stop. She must trust him. She has no choice. She looks into the unblinking fox eyes and takes a deep breath.

'Where exactly are you? Where can I find you?'

There's a long pause. Then the fox speaks.

'Turn around,' he says huskily. 'I'm right behind you.'

Behind her? But he's here, in front of her, on the Noos-station platform. What does he mean? And then it dawns on her. The shock of it rushes like a hot wave through her body. He means in realworld. The fox is here, right behind her, in the cybercath.

Mara turns around. The Noosrunner in the cupule several rows behind is looking straight at her. Mara stops breathing.

It's David, the ace Noosrunner. The boy she crashed into in the tunnel, who was so cold to her in the cafe tonight.

Or appeared to be.

Mara doesn't know what to do, so she turns back to her godgem, back to the cyberfox in the Noos. They stand staring at each other, a girl and a fox on a deserted platform with the chaos of the Noos swirling all around.

'How did you know?' she gasps.

'When I heard your name and the name of your island.' The fox looks electric; its hair stands on end. 'You told me and I never forgot.'

'I thought I'd never find you. I couldn't think how I ever would.' Mara is trembling. 'What do we do now?' she whispers into the godgem.

'Leave the cybercath,' says the fox and suddenly Mara feels scared. 'Go straight to the Leaning Bridge and I'll meet you there.'

Her heart pounds as she takes off the godgem. It feels unreal. After all this time, after all that has happened to her, she is going to meet the human being who is her old Weave-stalker, the fox. She stands up and tries to make her face as bland as a lumenbeing's. Fear and excitement are racing through her but she must be careful not to show it. In his work cupule, David seems deep in his work.

266

At the Leaning Bridge Mara pretends to gaze into the shimmering water of the Looking Pond. A noisy mob of zappers pass by, then silence falls and the tunnel is empty. Out of the corner of her eye she sees David leave the cybercath and head towards her. Mara leans upon the mock-stone wall of the Leaning Bridge, so full of suspense she can hardly keep still. Her senses are so heightened she can hear the soft pad of the boy's feet as he nears the bridge.

The pad-pad of his feet stops. Mara waits. David has paused right behind her – she can hear his breath, light and fast. Her heart thuds painfully.

'Hello,' breathes the husky voiced boy at her side. The fox, who is just a boy called David, leans over the edge of the bridge.

Mara turns and meets the untamed eyes of a dreamer. They gaze into hers through his mess of tawny hair. David gives her a wobbly smile.

'Hello,' Mara whispers back.

Neither seems to know what to do or say. Mara craves the safety of a cyberworld – some synthetic moment where she can cloak herself. Reality is far too raw, too naked.

'I want to know the rest of your story,' David-Fox says at last.

'But can I trust you?' pleads Mara.

'Can I trust *you*?' he repeats, and again Mara wonders what he means. Some zappers zip past and he pauses, watching her closely till they are gone. Then he seems to decide and nods with a sharp, foxy movement that is so at odds with his dreamy eyes.

'OK,' he decides, but wary still. 'Let's go to my place.'

*

Fox's place is one of the superior tower apartments that Dol talked of so enviously. He has a spacious round living room with walls that look strangely soft, as if they're melting in the gentle waves of colour which ripple across them.

'Take a seat.'

Mara sits on an armchair so plush it feels as if she is perched precariously upon nothing – a sumptuous, enfolding nothingness that moulds with amazing gentleness to every curve and fold of her body.

'Ooh, this is gorgeous. Would you, um, mind if I take off my shoes – they're too tight and my feet are killing me.'

'Make yourself at home,' he says, amused. Yet he sits tensely on the edge of his own seat.

She floats in the moment, in the blissful sensation of being held in invisible arms. But the moment shatters as she recalls Fox's riddle of words just a moment ago, as they zapped through the nexus to his apartment. She sits up.

'What did you mean just now when you said the New World has no past?'

'Just that. The past is banished. It's been deleted. All anyone ever thinks of is here and now. '*There is only the power of now,*' he chants. 'That's what we all believe,' he adds, drily.

'But now is only now when it's now. Then it's past. And right bang in front is the future,' says Mara. 'It all knits together.'

'Well, no one sees it that way here,' says Fox.

'How come you live like this?' Mara demands, gazing around his luxurious apartment. 'You must be a really ace Noosrunner to get promoted so highly so young!'

A quick, wry grin breaks upon his face.

'I'm a pretty hot Noosrunner,' he responds. 'But the truth is, I live like this because I'm the grandson of a Grand Father of All. *The* Grand Father of All, as it happens. Caledon, the Supreme Ideator, the creator of the New World – that's my grandpa.'

'Oh, so that's why all the girls—' Mara begins with a knowing smile, then stops in astonishment.

Caledon, creator of the New World. The Grand Father of All. Cal. The one who dreamed up the idea of a city in the sky. Cal, who threw Candleriggs out of the New World when she rebelled against the cruel empire it had become. Fox is his grandson?

Mara is dumbfounded.

'Fox, there are things I have to tell you,' she gasps, once she finds her tongue. 'So many things.'

He lifts his head sharply, but gazes at her with the gentle, yet untamed eyes of a dreamer. But Cal was a dreamer too, Mara remembers. Can she trust the grandson of such a man? She has no idea. She can only hope that what she thinks she sees in his eyes is true.

Mara takes a deep breath and begins her incredible story.

THE TUG INSIDE

'Slaves? People who nest in trees? And a boat camp?' Fox paces round and round the room, then suddenly slumps down on the floor beside her chair. He is trembling. 'I've wondered about the outside world for so long but I never knew there was a wall around the city. I never knew there were refugees . . .'

'What exactly *do* you know?' Mara asks gently.

Fox takes a deep, tremulous breath.

'I knew something of the true story of the world's drowning from all the SOS messages on the dead Weave-sites and from listening to Weave ghosts. That's why I was amazed when we first met in Nowhere,' he continues, 'and you said you were from an island. I'd thought there was no land left in the world. We're taught at school that the world is all ocean. But I knew from what I'd found on the Weave that they'd hidden the truth of the past from us. That's what I've been searching for, the truth.'

He laughs huskily, sourly. 'Nobody has any interest in the past or the truth or the outside world. No one talks or thinks about any of that. The old people must know what happened but most of them are dead or in carefarms now. Officially, we all believe that everyone was housed in the New World during the Meta, so everything's fine.'

'What's the Meta?' Mara interrupts.

'The world change. But this boat camp – and slaves? *Child* slaves?' Liquid eyes plead with her. 'I can't believe my own grandfather would allow that. He's not a bad man.' Now his brown eyes grow hard. 'Maybe there's another side to the story. I can't believe he would allow the New World to use refugees and children as slaves. If it's really true, I can't believe he knows about them.'

'Then why was that great wall built? To keep out refugees!' cries Mara. 'Where does he get all the labour for his New World expansion projects from? Slave labour. Maybe he started out meaning well, maybe he's a nice old grandpa to you, but it's all gone wrong somewhere. It's turned bad, and so has he. My best friend died out in that boat camp and my other friend, her brother, might well be dead by now. My family drowned before they even got here, on the way to that stinking camp. My six-year-old brother!'

Suddenly she is choking on tears. Fox looks at her, shocked and silent.

'What could my grandfather have done?' His voice breaks. 'How could he save everyone in the world? Maybe the people of the New World did what they could!'

Mara rubs away her tears and tries to steady herself. Now she tells Fox the story of Candleriggs and her rebellion over the New World's refusal to take in anyone that didn't pass its stringent intelligence test, of the abandonment of the flood refugees, and of how his grandfather had thrown the girl he once loved out of the New World with the other rebels, in order to save his dream.

'Candleriggs was sure that there must have been people in the New World who felt as she did,' Mara remembers, 'but they were too fearful for their own safety to speak out. She wishes now that she had been less hot-headed and had spoken out with more understanding about their fears. Then the rebels might have had many more people with them, they might have changed public opinion and Caledon would have had to listen to his citizens – he couldn't throw them all out of the New World, could he? He would have *had* to make the kind of world that they wanted to live in. But nobody else spoke out so it was easy to get rid of the rebels. Fox, there might be plenty of good-hearted people here who would be horrified if they knew the truth about the outside world. Surely they would want to help.'

Mara thinks of Dol and her friends. She has judged them all so harshly. Perhaps, if they knew about the slaves and the refugees, they would be appalled. But would they be willing to stand up against it?

Fox is trembling violently, shocked to the core by what she has just told him. Suddenly Mara is full of fear too. What if he's so upset that he confronts his grandfather? Then she will be found out. Or he'll decide he doesn't believe her after all and then what will he do?

She must calm him down.

'Look,' she says softly, and slips off the armchair on to the floor beside him.

Mara takes off her small backpack. It goes everywhere with her, to keep its contents safe.

On the floor she lays out her treasures: the black lump of meteorite, Wing's bone dagger, Gorbals's book of

272

poems, *A Tale of Two Cities*, the dried herbs, her old-fashioned cyberwizz. And the book on Greenland.

'This dagger,' she tells him, 'is thousands of years old. It's from a museum in the old place of learning that sits high on a hill in the drowned world – the university your grandfather went to. It's the place he began his dream of the new cities. An urchin found it, a small child who risked his life to get me out of the boat camp and inside the wall. He has nothing, no parents, not even a name, so I called him Wing, after my island. Now he's a slave.'

Fox stares.

'This lump of meteorite is even older than the dagger,' she continues, holding it in the palm of her hand. 'It's older than anything on Earth – as old as the universe.'

Mara points to her globe and halo and wand. 'Here's my cyberwizz that I used on my island, when you stalked me on the Weave. It's ancient technology compared to yours.' She touches the leather-bound books. 'These are from the book rooms of the university. This one is an amazing story of the old world. The other – well, I'll tell you about it later. These . . .' she picks up Gorbals's notebook, 'are the poems of a Treenester. My friend. He rescued book litter from the sea, pulped it into new paper and wrote his poems on it with charcoal embers from the sundown fire. But like the little urchin, he's been stolen from his world to be a slave for yours.'

Now Mara opens the book to the pages where she has pressed the sprig of rosemary entwined with wild thyme. 'Herbs,' she tells Fox, 'one from my island, the other grown in the netherworld. All these things are from the past or from the drowned world.'

Now Mara opens a page of Gorbals's lumpy paper and begins to read the clumsy scribbles.

THE STARS ARE NIGHT DAISIES

TRAPPED IN HIGH BRANCHES   I CAN NEVER REACH

BUT I CAN SAIL ON MY RAFT

PLAY PEEKABOO MOON

CATCH BRIGHT SEA FLOWERS

NIGHT DAISIES

THAT FLOAT UPON THE ROOFTOPS OF THE SUNK WORLD

SO FRAGILE

THEY   SCATTER AND   BREAK   IN MY

HANDS

Fox stares at Mara's treasures. Gingerly, he reaches out and picks up the sprigs of rosemary and thyme, sniffs them and blinks in surprise at their sharp scents that are so unlike the synthetic aroma of noofood. One by one he picks up each object and examines it closely. Last of all he picks up the bone dagger and turns it over in his hands, testing the blade. His eyes are faraway and full of thoughts Mara can't read. But he's calm now.

'I didn't just come here to find you,' she says quietly. 'I came here to find my friends, Gorbals and Wing – the Treenester poet and the little child who were taken to be slaves. I came to rescue them. The Treenesters are surviving on a tiny island in the ruins of the drowned world but if the ocean rises again, and it's sure to soon, they won't even have that and they'll drown too. Then there are all the people in the boat camp . . .' Mara sighs in despair. 'Fox, I need you to help me. Maybe I can't rescue them all but I want to give as many people as possible the chance to escape, to get them in boats and—'

She stops.

'And?' Fox demands. 'What will you do then? Set them free upon the ocean to drown there?'

'No,' says Mara, picking up the book on Greenland and hugging it tight to her chest. 'There's land in the north of the world. I'm sure of it. This book convinced me. It's called the land of the people. I'm going to get there – I'm going to take the slaves and the Treenesters and the boat people – as many as I can rescue. But Fox, the New World should be doing all this! It could. Even if it won't take in refugees it could at least seek out whatever high, safe places there are left on Earth and provide ships and give us a chance to have some kind of future. Why can't you do that? You don't need those places. You're all stuck up here, safe in your own world, and you just don't care!'

There is a long, awkward pause. Fox doesn't look at her. He stares at the floor, his face mostly hidden by his hair.

'Why do you care so much?' he asks quietly, at last.

'Look at me,' Mara commands.

He flinches at her tone and looks up. Then flinches again at her fierce gaze. But her eyes hold his.

'I care . . .' Mara's voice shakes with anger, 'because I'm one of them. *I'm* a refugee.'

His lips part. He gives a soft gasp and his pale face flushes.

'And because of my family and all the people I've lost,' she says bitterly.

'Of course,' he murmurs.

Fox blinks, and she feels him, in one long, encapsulating glance, register her skinny body, her skin tone, the sharp bones of her face and the fading scar on her cheek. Her body burns with humiliation; she can feel him judging, gauging, evaluating her in an uncomfortably different way from before. When he meets her blazing eyes, he drops his gaze in confusion.

'I suppose I was imagining a refugee would be, well, different. You *are* different – different from anyone I've ever met – but you're not so unlike me . . . I mean you're not – not . . .' he trails off, embarrassed, unwilling to voice what he thought.

'Not what? Not stupid? Not dirty? Not quite human? Just some kind of – of outcast?' Mara's anger becomes confusion as she remembers gentle Broomielaw's contempt for the urchins for exactly these reasons. And also, she's scared. Scared that Fox won't want to have anything to do with her now that he knows what she is – someone his world considers to be less than human, undeserving of care or compassion or even the right to a life.

'I'm sorry,' says Fox. His face flushes even deeper. 'You're obviously not any of those things. You're quite, um, amazing, I think.'

'Amazing, am I?' Mara lets out a breath of relief. Then she gives a brittle laugh. 'I was filthy enough in the boat camp and the netherworld. And I've certainly been stupid.' Her voice shakes and she swallows.

Hesitantly, Fox reaches out and touches her hand. The touch zips up her arm like electricity.

'Listen,' she says, his touch unsettling and steadying her, all at once.

Now she tells him the final part of her story – all about the legend of the Face in the Stone and the statue of

276

Thenew that is her own image, even down to the scar on her face that is also strangely repeated in the crack in the mirror of Granny Mary's little box. Last of all, she describes the signs in the old city that the Treenesters believe is the stone-telling.

'And they say that when the signs come together then the stone-telling will happen and they will be free. The one who is the Face in the Stone will lead them to their true home in the world. That's what they believe. They believe it's me,' Mara finishes quietly. Her face crinkles in a frown. 'I don't believe it's me but somehow I seem to be trying to live out their expectations because – because . . .' she casts around for the reason and finds it, 'I don't have anything else to live for.'

Fox stares at her, mesmerized.

'Will you help me?' Mara pleads.

Fox puts his head in his hands. The tawny tangle of hair spills over his eyes again, but this time his eyes stay fixed on hers. Mara feels the tug inside that pulled her towards him even in a distant electronic universe. Nervously, hesitantly, she reaches out and touches his hair.

'Help me,' she urges, 'and maybe I can help you.'

His face tightens. 'I'll help you, Mara,' he tells her. 'But how can you help me? And why would you want to?'

Mara can't answer; she only knows that she does want to.

They talk deep into the night. At some point, in the gap between words, they both fall asleep, sprawled in exhaustion beside each other on the floor with the scatter of old world treasures all around them. In the middle of the night Mara wakens in fright. The world sways and lurches and she can't remember where on earth she is. On a boat out on the ocean? In a nest in a tree?

'Mum?' she whimpers. 'Broomielaw?'

Someone reaches out and pulls her close. Mara hears the gallop of heartbeats – her own and another. She feels her own fear and the still intensity of the other one. And something else, something raw and primitive, thrilling and scary.

'Fox?'

'Here.'

His touch becomes the whole world. His mouth, hands, hair, every limb and muscle, every cell of his body, becomes part of her own. All thoughts of the past and the future scatter. The outside world and the sky city all round them, everything beyond this moment and this room, seem distant, fragile, unreal. All that exists, all that Mara feels, is the power of now.

MEENIES IN NEW MUNGO

Mara wakens as darkness is lifting. Drowsily, she watches light ooze into the room from some unknown source, like a gently breaking sunrise. Yet there are no windows in the room, just the undulating walls. Fox is still wrapped around her, his face soft with sleep.

She still can't believe she has found him. As she gazes at the face that, until last night, she had never seen, studying his features, learning him by heart, he yawns and opens his eyes, wide awake in an instant. For a second he looks bewildered to see her there, right beside him. And all of a sudden Mara feels shy and strange to be so close in the bright morning light to someone who is, in so many ways, unknown. His face mirrors her own clash of emotions. Then he closes his eyes again and, slowly, kisses her. The kiss rushes through her like a live current. Her body knows with an astonishing certainty what her mind still struggles to comprehend – that she has never felt such a strong connection with anyone or anything in the world.

They lie together, close and silent, for a while.

'I'm *starving*,' he suddenly grins.

He jumps out of bed and grabs a jug of juice and a bowl of the large, soft bread rolls that seem to be full of air. But Mara tucks in ravenously. Fox gulps juice, watching her, as if he hasn't a clue what to do about this girl who has fallen out of the Weave and crashed into his life.

'What about your parents?' she asks, to break the tense silence. 'Where are they?'

He mentioned them only briefly last night, Mara noticed, though they talked for hours.

'They head the start-up team for new cities so they're always away on business – but we meet up almost every day in the Noos.' Fox frowns, swallows a mouthful of bread. 'My other relatives are over in New Texaco. Apart from Caledon, my grandparents are dead.' He sighs. 'I've always felt different, hankering after the past instead of living for now, like everyone else does. Maybe it's because that old Treenester woman should have been my grand-mother. Maybe I really belong to the old world. No, no, that doesn't make sense either,' he bursts out. 'I loved my own grandma. She was the only one who was always here for me. Always. I can't believe *she* knew about all this brutality, I just can't . . . '

He breaks off, chucks his bread roll on the bed and sinks his head in his hands. His devastation tears at Mara's heart.

'But it's not your fault,' she tells him. '*You* didn't know.'

'But now I do and if I don't stand against it, then I'm part of it,' Fox counters. 'Caledon's cruelty becomes mine. From this point on, for the rest of my life, I'll be guilty too.'

'Not if you help me rescue everyone that we can.'

'I'll do that. I'll do whatever I can to help you. But

even if we rescue every slave and every refugee and set them free, that doesn't change the fact that this world of mine is rotten at the core. How can I live in a world that, day by day, I'll hate more and more? I'll begin to hate myself too, if I live in a place that's built out of other people's misery.'

Mara's heart leaps. She has hardly dared to hope for this. The future – that black, terrifying thing – is suddenly shot through with light, as if the sun just broke through the heaviest storm.

'Don't stay here – come with me!'

He doesn't answer.

Mara fumbles on the floor to find the book on Greenland. She picks it up and hurriedly flicks through the pages till she comes to a map. 'Look! There's land here, I'm almost sure of it – high lands that have been freed from mountains of ice in the arctic meltdown. They should be within reach if we have good, solid ships – like the supply ships.'

Fox studies the page, sighs, and lays the book back down.

'You must come with me,' Mara murmurs. 'Now that we've found each other. You *must*.'

Fox turns his head away. 'I can't.'

He sounds broken. Mara stares at him in bewilderment.

'Why can't you? You can't stay here. You hate this world now, you said so. If you come with me, we could try to build a world that's better than this one, the kind of place you'll be proud to live in, not full of hate and shame. That's the kind of future you want, isn't it?'

Fox still doesn't answer, just looks wretched beyond words.

'Is it because of your family – you can't leave them? I

281

understand that, of course I do, but you said you hardly see them.' Mara feels desperate. Her self-control breaks. 'What will you do? Fox, what is there in this world for you now? If Caledon could throw Candleriggs out of his world then he's ruthless, he's capaple of anything. He might be just as ruthless with you, if he knew you were his enemy.'

Fox gets up. Restlessly, he paces round his room.

'What are you thinking?' Mara pleads when she can stand his silent pacing no more.

He stops and faces her.

'I'm thinking that for good or for bad, this *is* my world. I can't abandon it – or I'll be just like him. He abandoned his world for this one, didn't he? And that's what we're blaming him for. I need to understand the past, Mara. I need to understand exactly what happened and why. Then, maybe, I can begin to change the future.'

'You'll change the future *now* by helping people escape. You don't need to do any more,' urges Mara.

'Yes I do,' Fox responds. 'Because I won't have changed the way this city *is*. It'll still be rotten at core. And what about the other New World cities? What about the corruption in them? Won't they use slaves too? Won't they have walls to keep out refugees?'

'But what can you do about any of that?' cries Mara. 'They're so far away.'

Fox sits down beside her. 'You told me that Candleriggs believed there were lots of good-hearted people in the New World and that they probably only acted as they did out of fear. I want to believe that she's right. I want to . . .'

He reaches out and takes her hand.

'I want to be with you. But I'm the only one who can restart the battle that Candleriggs never got a chance to

282

fight. See, this is *your* battle, Mara. Mine is to come and it might be even worse than yours because I'll be fighting my own people, my own family. Can you imagine that?' Mara can't. 'I *want* to come with you but if I do . . .' Fox gives a huge, shaky sigh, 'well, I think this world will haunt me for ever. What I might have done will haunt me till the end of my days.'

He's on the verge of tears. Miserably, Mara wraps her arms around him and holds him because she knows he is right about the haunting; the ghosts of her own lost world will always haunt her.

'But how can you start a revolution all on your own?' she demands tearfully. 'Once Caledon finds out he'll lock you up – or worse. It's not possible.'

'It *is* possible.' Fox frowns, thinking hard. 'Caledon won't be able to do anything to me because I'll already be gone. When you escape, I'll go down to the ruins of the old world and I'll take my mobile godgem with me. It's all I need. They're satellite-powered so I can make my own connection from the ground. I don't need to go to any other city. I don't need to go anywhere. The whole of the New World meets in the Noos every day – I can reach people there, plant seeds of dissent and gather support. I won't be caught. I've got endless tricks. I'll be as careful and clever as a fox.'

He gives her a shaky grin. 'I'll hide away in the ruins, and there are plenty of places for a fox to hide in the Noos – you know I can run faster than anyone. They'll never catch me. And then one day . . .' his face grows still and serious, 'one day, when I'm ready, I'll come back and I'll begin the revolution – the one Candleriggs wanted, and fight to make this world a fairer place.'

Mara bites her lip till it hurts to stop herself from

crying. She can't bear to think of him alone in the nether-world when he could be with her. She can't bear to lose him when she has only just found him. She can't bear any more loss or pain. She will tell him that. She'll sob her heart out, then he'll see that they cannot be parted, not for anything in the world.

Mara takes a deep breath, and swallows hard.

'If only you could meet Candleriggs,' she says softly, her voice barely under control. 'She could help you. It's so strange, as if – as if you really are her grandson, more than you are Caledon's.'

He nods. His eyes look hot, his fingers grip hers. He is just as tormented and torn apart as she is. She hears him take a deep breath, hears him swallow hard too, feels him rein his emotions, just as she has.

'Right,' he announces. 'You need to find your friends. You need ships. That's the first thing. So let's get to it.'

Mara nods bleakly. She remembers the slogan that the cybercath hackers scrambled.

'All right,' she says bitterly. 'Let's do it. Let's be meenies in New Mungo.'

The first thing they must do, says Fox, is find a way to disable the city. If they don't, the whole plan is a non-starter.

'Security is so tight that once you'd found the slaves you'd never get them out of the city. You wouldn't stand a chance of escaping.'

'I know. But how can we disable the whole city?' Mara despairs. 'I've thought and thought and I can't see a way.'

Fox shoots her a red-hot glance from beneath the scare-crow mess of his hair.

'You know a way?' Mara's face lightens.

He just grins as he clips on his godgem.

The rooks are their main threat. Rooks, says Fox, are secret police who live like normal Noosrunners among the citizens of the New World, but are on constant lookout for any deviants or criminals that might undermine the smooth running of the system. Occasionally, someone disappears and everyone assumes they've had to leave in a hurry for a work placement in another city, but often they've been taken by the rooks. And even if anyone did suspect that the rooks were involved, says Fox, they would probably just tell themselves that that person had it coming. They must have been up to something that was a threat to the rest of the New World.

You never know who the rooks are, says Fox, but they're everywhere, trained to look and act just like any one else.

Dol could be one, thinks Mara. Tony Rex could easily be one.

'You could be one.' Fox shoots her another of his lightning-bolt glances. 'You could be an elaborate trap to root out the meeny in New Mungo that is Caledon's grandson.'

'Or you could be a rook out to catch me,' Mara returns.

He laughs. Excitement lights his face; his eyes are beautiful with it, as he gears up for a cyberleap. She hasn't a clue what he's doing. But he grabs her hand, squeezes it tight and his husky voice is breathless with excitement:

'I feel like I've been waiting to do this all my life.'

TWENTIETH-CENTURY
GHOST PARADE

'Who are they all?' Mara gasps.

They come in cyberwaves, one after the other, on and on and on – life-size lumenbeings that move, talk, sing and shout right in the middle of Fox's room. He has the lights down low to let them see the figures more clearly, and each glows with a ghostly aura. They are so real that Mara can see sweat gleam on one face, emotion in the eyes of another.

'They're twentieth-century icons,' says Fox. 'A ghost parade from the last century. For years I've collected them from derelict sites and dustbins in the back alleys of the Weave and hidden them away. And now I'm bringing them all back from the dead.'

Mara sinks back in her chair and lets the twentieth century wave wash over her. The tide of faces and voices is hypnotic. Shakily, she reminds herself that they're not real, only lumens.

'Wow, who's she? Can you slow this thing down?'

Fox reverses the images, stopping on a blonde woman. 'This one?'

Mara nods, entranced by the woman, who is so beautiful she seems to be made from the stuff of dreams. She captivates the watcher with a seductive charisma of eyes and mouth and movement.

Fox calls up a biography and it scrolls at the woman's feet. *'Marilyn Monroe, film star. Death by suspected suicide at the height of her fame.'*

They reel through more. Tens of faces reel into hundreds. Mara begins to feel dizzy.

'I think I've had enough – no, wait a minute. Who's that?'

But Fox has already stopped on the solitary figure of a young man in a spotlight. A guitar is slung over his shoulder and a slick quiff of black hair falls across a shy, sullen face. A beautiful face. He looks uncertain, endearing. Silently, he raises his arm with the intensity of a coiled spring. Now he's dangerous, utterly magnetic. What is it that's so compelling about him? Mara wonders, as she stares open-mouthed at the life-sized lumen just a step in front of her. Then she knows what it is.

Electricity; he's full of it – he could explode.

And then he does. Mara jumps in her seat as his hand hits the guitar and he lets rip in a song. A ghostly frenzy of screaming teenagers fills the room, almost drowning out the raw, hungry voice. Now he's like a tiger; lean, savage and graceful, prowling an invisible cage.

'What was *that*?' Mara gasps as the explosion of human energy ends.

Fox grins. 'That was rock 'n' roll.'

'*Who* was that?'

'That was Elvis.' Fox doesn't need to read the biography on this one; he knows it off by heart. 'Elvis Presley, the king of rock 'n' roll, singing *Hound Dog*, the song that shook up the world.'

'Shook *me* up,' Mara grins back. Her heart is racing. 'He self-destructed too,' she notes, scanning the biography text.

'Watch this one.' Fox is calling up something else from his lumen ghost bank. 'He led the world into an abyss before he self-destructed.'

Mara finds herself staring into the most terrifying eyes she has ever seen. They lock with her own and seem to bore through her skull with a mesmeric, overpowering presence.

'Stop it!' she tells Fox. 'I don't like this one.'

'It's only a lumen.' Fox puts his arm around her. 'You must see this.'

The man stands alone in a spotlight. His hair is black and the fierce, ugly white face is slashed by a slab of black moustache. Somehow Mara knows that he is utterly dangerous.

He raises his arm in silence – then explodes into frenzy. He barks out words with a ferocity that makes him foam at the mouth like a rabid dog. He's a ridiculous spectacle, repulsive and undignified ... and yet Mara cannot look away. The noise of a vast, invisible crowd rises like a tidal wave around him.

It's uncanny. Mara is spellbound by words she cannot even understand, hypnotized by the wild-dog eyes. The man's passion infects her – it's a savage possession of spirit; a chaotic sensation disturbingly close to the way she felt watching Elvis.

Except the essence of one is joy, the other hate. One is fuelled by the energy of life, the other by death. Somehow, she is sure of that.

'Who is he?'

'Hitler,' says Fox. 'Leader of the German Nazi Party. Responsible for the deaths and suffering of millions in the Second World War.'

'One man did all that?' Mara's heart is pounding. She feels nauseous and upset.

'Well, one man sparked all that. He couldn't have done it if lots of others hadn't followed his dream, could he?' Fox looks at Mara meaningfully. 'You can't change the fate of the world all on your own.'

'I don't see the point of all this, Fox.'

But he's not listening. He stops on the echo of a voice and backtracks.

'*I have a dream*!' shouts a voice.

A young black man appears.

'*I have a dream!*' he shouts again. The emotion in his voice is so intense there's an unsettling, almost musical tremor to his words. Mara yearns to know the dream that consumes him. It excites her even though she doesn't know what it is. Then he tells his dream.

'*To be free at last! Free at last! Free at last!*'

It sounds like a shout of the future – yet it's an echo from the past.

'This is the one!' cries Fox. 'Martin Luther King.'

He reads out the short biography. 'Human rights activist who fought for a fair and equal world. Won the Nobel Peace Prize. Assassinated at the height of his influence.'

A better world – so that was his dream, thinks Mara. And he died for that dream.

'*And if a man has nothing to die for,*' cries the strong, tremulous voice, '*then his life is worth nothing.*'

Mara is magnetized. The words cut to her core.

The image judders, fades, and Martin Luther King is

replaced by a huge and vicious lump of metal – a lumen missile that looks terrifyingly solid and real. Mara screams and dives for cover behind her chair as it cruises towards her, slowly, with deadly precision. A handspan from her face it switches direction. There's the deep, rising moan of a siren, a sound so petrifying it stuns the moment. Mara grips the chair as she seems to fall sharply out of the present to land with a jolt in some alien, bomb-blasted street. In the heart of the devastated street appear the figures of four mop-headed youths. *'Help!'* they sing urgently, over and over, as the missile weaves menace around their heads and the siren-moan dies and rises, dies and rises. There's a loud *crump* and the street fills with smoke and dust.

Mara watches open-mouthed as two more figures briefly materialize. A pigtailed girl in glittering red shoes and a bespectacled boy with a lightning zigzag on his brow race across the street. *'Which way – which way to the wizard?'* the girl in red shoes cries, as they fade into ghosts.

'Something wrong here,' mutters Fox. He bangs his godgem with his fist. 'Sometimes images get jumbled and they overlap.'

Mara is struggling to read the muddled text reel.

BEATLES HELP! cruise missile attack

Fox ducks as the missile zips towards his head then stands up, embarrassed, and mutters into his godbox. The images collapse and vanish and the room feels strange, as if reality has gone flat. Mara stares at the emptiness, then turns to Fox.

'*Well*? What on Earth was that all about?'

'It's about the past,' Fox declares. 'It's about infecting the present with the past and – with luck – changing the future.'

Fox jumps up and prowls the room, his eyes fixed on some vivid vision that Mara can't see.

'I'm going to create a virus,' he announces. 'A ghost virus so powerful it will crash New Mungo out of the Noos, disable all the functions of the city – doors, lights, electrics, security, the lot. Then you can escape.'

THE NUX

A window of time, that's all she'll have. And when that window slams shut, her chance to escape will be gone. But the virus will hit like a tidal wave, Fox promises.

For the last few days they have burrowed away in Fox's apartment, working out their plan, grabbing snatches of sleep whenever exhaustion grounds them to a halt. Now he explains how it will work, using a handful of coloured glass pebbles from some kind of board game that sits on the floor. He scatters the pebbles all over the floor.

'Imagine these pebbles are godgems all over the Noos, all over the Earth. I pick any old godgem, a random selection from all around the world.' He grabs one at random, then another and another. 'Then I put a germ in the machine, a ghost germ. Now that godgem becomes a zombie – it contains one of my living-dead lumens. The godgem still works as normal but it's a carrier for my ghost virus. The rooks are always on anti-virus Noos raids but the beauty of this one is it's almost impossible to spot– because it takes the form of a ghost. I program all the zombie godgems to pass on the virus every time they connect with another godgem. The ghost virus spreads fast, but nobody knows it's there. Not yet. I'll give it time to spread far and wide, into godgems all around the Noos. In just hours it'll infect thousands, in a day it could have infected a million. Then . . . '

Fox grins. 'Then I turn the ghosts live and call them all back home. In they'll come, crashing downline – and hit the city in a colossal tidal wave!'

They stare into each other's eyes. Mara really hasn't a clue what he's on about but she believes in him now; she trusts him with her life. If anyone can tackle the incredible technology of the New World, it's Fox.

'Cyberflood,' he whispers. 'Total systems wipeout. Once the system is crashed, the security systems are all down too. That breakdown is your chance to find the slaves and get them out of the city and on to the ships. Harbour security and the city gates will be disabled too.'

Mara nods, frowning in concentration. 'But the slaves – *how* do I find them? I need to find out where Gorbals and Wing are so that I can make sure I get them on a ship. And what about the ships? Fox, how on Earth do I navigate a ship?'

Once again Mara feels overwhelmed by the sheer scale of what they are trying to do.

'The ships are pre-programmed,' says Fox. 'We can work out something there. But the slaves – that's stumped me so far.' His brow wrinkles in thought. 'The slaves aren't on the central identi-disk system, I'm sure. We've searched and searched and there's nothing. But I expected the whole slave labour situation would be top secret. We could try and hack into the rooks' system – I'm sure they operate in a hidden pocket of cyberspace, some black hole outside of the Noos – but it'll all be encrypted and it could take ages to break through. That's if we could. And they're

293

sure to be able to track intruders into their system. No, our best bet is . . .' he grins, 'to use my connections. We need to go up to the Nux.'

'The Nux?'

'That's where the City Fathers have their private chambers. And it's where the Grand Father of All – my grandpa – lives and works. There might be something there that will tell us where the slaves are. If not – well, I'll just have to find some way to break into the rooks' system . . . '

Fear grips Mara's heart.

'Fox,' she asks breathlessly. 'Can I – can I meet Caledon?'

'Do you want to?' he asks curiously.

And despite her fear, Mara knows that she does. Just to *see*.

The Nux is hidden away in the very heart of the city.

Fox takes her hand and leads her past a phalanx of city guards – they stand aside at a mere nod from him – up to the very top of a coil of stairs that wind up through a vertical tunnel shaft. When at last they reach the top, Mara's head is spinning. She looks around at the cavernous chambers and is disorientated.

And suddenly doubts that it's all real. She has an instinct that the grandeur of the Nux is an illusion, that she might actually be standing in an ordinary-sized hall and the apparent vastness is one big trick, a magic of mirror and light. The Nux is right above the cybercath's lofty dome – a ceiling which could itself be a mirror-trick designed to hide the existence of these secret chambers.

Before she can voice these thoughts to Fox, he puts out an arm and presses a red crystal button on a wall.

Mara has walked right past it. 'It's David,' he announces to the red button. 'I'd like to see my grandfather.'

'Why are there no City Mothers or Grand Mothers of All?' Mara suddenly wonders.

'Well, there are a few. My grandmother was one. It's just – they're just called fathers because . . .' Fox trails off. 'Well, I'm not sure why. I never thought about it before.'

Suddenly the wall parts like a metal curtain and a figure passes through the gap. He walks slowly towards them with a stiff, aged step. Mara's body tenses as the Grand Father of All stands in front of her.

She can't breathe, can't seem to raise her eyes to his face. A jumble of emotions rush through her – fear, anger, but also undeniable curiosity and awe for someone who could dream up a whole New World, and make that dream come true.

Caledon puts a kindly hand on his grandson's shoulder. The skin of his hand is like the pulped, lumpy paper Gorbals rescues from the netherworld waters.

'Grandpa, I'd like you to meet Mara,' says Fox.

The Grand Father of All turns to her.

Caledon says nothing and with his silence he forces Mara to look at him. She feels dizzy with fright. And she shivers, unnerved, as if the chambers of the Nux have suddenly filled with ghosts. *Remember*, the ghosts seem to say. *Remember what happened to the world. Remember what this man did. Remember Candleriggs . . .*

Mara remembers as she looks into the eyes of the Grand Father of All. And something in him flinches. He looks away.

'Mara's an ace runner,' Fox is proudly telling his grandfather. 'A real wizzer. One of the best.'

Caledon smiles graciously and they follow him through into his private chamber. As she snatches glances at the old man, Mara is struck by how Candleriggs is so much more gnarled and ancient-looking than he is. But of course Caledon hasn't lived the last sixty years or so clinging to a storm-tossed tree in a drowned world.

Mara is suffused with rage at this gracious old man. But she must keep a clear, cool head and hide her feelings. Now, as she watches Caledon smile and chat with his grandson, she sees something tragic in the map of fine lines that etch his face and the ruins of dreams in his watery eyes. She sees the tremble in his papery hands and the slow, defeated movements of an old man who knows he's running out of time in the world.

He is so much less than Mara expected. And he seems much more fragile than tough old Candleriggs.

With a jolt, Mara sees the logo that is embroidered over the breast of his silver-grey clothing, right next to his heart. It's the same one that the city guards wear yet, for the first time, she realizes exactly what it is.

Suddenly she wants to get out of here, now, away from this old man and the torment of his past. But it's Caledon who gets to his feet first.

'You'll have to excuse me, Mara. I have a meeting with the City Fathers,' he smiles, as he pulls a grey cloak around him.

They walk with Caledon back through the chambers of the Nux and part from him at the top of the vertical tunnel of spiralling stairs. As Mara watches him retreat deep inside the Nux, she sees the same graceful logo embroidered on the back of his cloak.

'What's the flower logo for?' she asks Fox, though she's almost sure she knows.

'The lily?' Fox climbs back up the coil of stairs he has just pretended to descend, in case his grandfather looked back. 'It's the logo he gave to the New World. He wants to project the image of a white lily on to the moon – it'll be the first step in the New World's colonization of space.'

The flutter of Caledon's cloak disappears within the great chambers and the Grand Father of All is gone. She should hate him, but at this moment Mara feels unutterably sad as she thinks of Caledon and Candleriggs – the lily he threw away, yet still keeps close to his heart; whose namesake he wants to shine from the moon.

EARTH'S GREATEST
ENGINEER

Back outside his grandfather's chamber, Fox stops beside
the red crystal button and requests entry again.

'Won't security be suspicious that we're back?' asks
Mara nervously.

'It's just an electronic door guard,' he smiles. 'Voice-
activated. I can always say I left something behind.'

The wall parts and they enter. Fox walks through his
grandfather's chamber and double-checks an adjoining
room. He nods.

'Right, we've got a couple of hours at the max.' He sits
down at an ancient screen computer and switches it on.
'This is where he hoards all his work ideas and files.
Maybe we'll find some kind of a clue here that'll tell us
where your friends are. Now let's see.'

Mara is astonished. 'The great brain behind the New
World uses one of those old things? Caledon's a
screenager?'

'I know,' Fox laughs. 'It's embarrassing.'

While Fox works his way at primitive speed through
the computer files, looking for information on building

298

projects and slave labour, Mara wanders around the room. It has the same kind of clinical luxury as Fox's apartment, but with nothing personal or out of place to give her any clues about Caledon, the man.

'Check his bedroom,' Fox suggests. 'He often works in there too.'

Mara goes through to the adjoining room – and gasps. She seems to be standing in a room from another world. An old, lost, drowned world.

So there's no past in the New World? Well, this room is straight out of the past. It might have been transplanted from the old university in the netherworld. It couldn't be more at odds with the rest of New Mungo. A hefty, stained oak table is strewn with books and papers. Bookcases line the walls, crammed with ancient books on nature and the animal world; a world that's all but vanished. Their dusty scent fills the air. Mara picks up a book lying on the table and reads its title – *Nature, Earth's Greatest Engineer.*

A cracked leather armchair sits facing two maps that hang on the wall. One shows Earth as it must have been a hundred years ago, before the drowning. Mara stares at it. The top of the world is ice, crusting a great basin of sea. But encircling the Arctic basin is land – vast stretches of ice lands and small, scattered islands. Most will be drowned now, like her own. But maybe not all. Mara peers closer – yes, there's the vast expanse of white with long ranges of snowy peaks that is Greenland, and the mountainous boreal forests of Alaska and Northern Canada where, she hopes, the Athapaskans have survived. Mara's heart lifts. There *is* land. The question is, can they reach it?

The other map shows the world as it is now – at least, how a Grand Father of All sees it: as an empire of sky cities scattered all across the Earth. The New World has divided the planet into seven oceans: Eurosea, Indisea, Chinasea, Afrisea, Hispanasea, Amerisea and Austrasea. There is no evidence on this map of Greenland or the Arctic. Am I wrong? Mara wonders. Do they no longer exist or is it just that the New World sees nothing beyond its own empire? She suspects the latter because, looking at the old map of the World, there must be other high lands still left on Earth. Mara compares the maps. The mountain ranges are clearly marked on the old one – the Himalayas, the European Alps, the Andes, the Rocky Mountains and more. None of them are shown on the New World map. No, she decides, the New World has no eyes for anything outside itself.

Papers are scattered untidily across Caledon's table and she has to brush them clear of little pink fragments before she can study them. The whole table is covered in these spongy crumbs. Mara picks up a thin wooden stick with a dark point and a squashy pink blob on the other end. She scribbles on the paper with the dark end then rubs the pink bit on the scribble it makes. The scribble disappears, like magic.

Excellent.

Now she spots a pile of blueprints and sketches. Mara flicks through them, pattern upon pattern inspired and adapted from nature – worm tunnels, a termite ventilation system, lots of web, honeycomb, hive and ant-like structural designs. They seem to be ideas for a huge variety of work projects. She pauses at a schedule for the Eastern sea bridge extension plan. The date of the project launch catches her eye. Date of commencement: late August 2100. Right now. Exactly when Gorbals and Wing were taken.

Quickly, Mara checks through all the other bits of paper but those designs are still in the planning stages.

'Fox!' she cries, her heart in her mouth. 'I think I've got something.'

It's the simplest thing. All she has to do is fold the paper map of the Eastern sea bridge plan into a tiny square and put it in the toe of her shoe. No gadgets or machinery necessary when you want to view it later. And Mara couldn't resist sneaking out some sheets of paper and one of the pink-tipped scribblers. It's stuck down the side of her shoe.

'That's a rare antique you've got in your shoe,' Fox comments as they leave. He doesn't miss a thing. 'And half a tree stuffed inside your top.'

'What is?' Mara pretends innocence, though she's clasping sheets of paper tight against her stomach in case they fall out. 'Well, I couldn't help it. What are those little wand things? They're brilliant. Why did people stop using them?'

'Pencils? I think they ran out of trees to make pencils and paper in the years just before the Meta,' says Fox. 'Even the rubber erasers on the ends are made from trees. From the bits of info I've stumbled across on the Weave I've gathered that the worldwide extinction of the trees was one of the things that contributed to the floods.'

'That's what the Treenesters say,' nods Mara, remembering Gorbals's horror of tree crime. 'Yet Caledon has his own private supply of all this extinct stuff.'

'He's the Grand Father of All. He can have anything he likes. Someone, somehow, gets him whatever he wants.'

'Well, he can't have my friends for his slaves,' snaps Mara. She's exhausted and scared. It's just beginning to dawn on her that the rescue plan is, for the first time, looking as if it really might be possible. More than possible. Fox is such a hot Noosrunner, he understands the detail of the New World system so well and has access to all kinds of secret information. She would never have managed on her own but now, with Fox's help, the plan is coming together, thick and fast.

Almost too fast, thinks Mara, as she tries to gather her courage for what lies ahead.

'Now for the ships,' says Fox. 'We'll try to work out a navigation chart from your book on Greenland and I'll put it on disk. Then the ship will more or less sail itself – at least it should.'

'What about the other ships?' says Mara. 'We'll need more than one. I don't know how many slaves I'll find and there are all the refugees in the boat camp. That's a lot of people. We might need a whole fleet of ships.'

Fox groans. 'All I can do is make a batch of disks and somehow you'll have to issue instructions to someone on each ship.'

Mara frowns. Once the city is in breakdown there will be chaos. There won't be time for her to stand around issuing detailed instructions; everyone will have to run for their lives. And how will refugees and slaves in that kind of panic manage to work out how to make a shimmery disk navigate a great ship? The plan won't work unless people know what to do once they reach the ships.

Back in Fox's apartment, Mara flings herself down on the floor and kicks off her tight shoes. She brings out the bundle of paper and the pencil she has stolen from Caledon's private chambers then digs in her bag for the bone-handled dagger and the small black lump of meteorite.

With a frown of deep concentration she begins sharpening the stone blade against the hard surface of the oldest material on Earth.

After a while she throws down the dagger and grins brightly at Fox.

'I've got it!' she exclaims. 'I'll use the pencil and paper to write out instructions for each disk with all the details of the plan included – then people will know exactly what to do!'

THIS IS IT

Almost time.

Mara watches the seconds flash by on the cybercath clock. Each second feels like a minute; these final minutes are endless. When at long last the hour flashes she lets go of the breath she's been holding and is dizzy with the sudden surge of oxygen and adrenalin.

This is it.

Now there's nothing she can do to stop it even if she wanted to. All she can do is be ready. At this very moment Fox is starting to scatter the ghost virus all over the Noos. Soon New Mungo will crash right out of Noospace.

'Mara!'

She jumps as Dol taps her on the shoulder. Jumps again when she sees Tony Rex right beside her.

'Hey, we never get together these days. You're always with David, aren't you?' Dol grins at Tony and hugs her whining purple puffball pet. 'You two must be in a romance situation – don't deny it.'

'David? Oh, you mean Fo – I mean, David, yes, I mean, no, I mean . . . '

Mara has got herself in knots. She can't seem to function in the real world tonight; she's too full of what is happening out in the Noos. But Dol takes her confusion as a yes and grins again at Tony. He beams a wide smile but his eyes still have an unsettling gleam.

'So, are you going to be mooching around with David tonight or will you manage to tear yourselves from each other's arms and come out with the gang?' Dol asks. Mara can't help noticing that her popularity has suddenly shot up now she's with Fox. 'You must come – Tony's organized a Noos War Game. He's promised *sensational* injuries and *real, extreme* fear. It'll be nux.'

Tony is still smiling that fixed, broad grin yet the indefinable edge in his eyes sends vibrations of fear through Mara's already shattered nerves.

'How on Earth do you manage *extreme* fear, Tony?' she blurts out. 'Is it *real* pain, *real* death? If not, well, it's just not sensational enough for me.'

She should have kept her mouth shut but she wants so badly to wipe the smile clear off his face for just a second to see what lies underneath. And she does – for an instant. As Tony's smile slips a fraction, Mara sees something as nasty as necrotty beneath his smarmy exterior and wishes she had left well alone.

You don't know who they are. They're trained to look just like any one of us.

That's what Fox said about the rooks, the secret police.

Now Tony leans close towards her till she can feel his breath on her cheek. 'My kind of girl,' he murmurs. 'You know I've got my eye on you, Mara.'

Dol giggles but Mara gets up unsteadily, mumbles good night, and quickly exits the cybercath. With trembling fingers she snaps on her zapeedos and begins to head for the Leaning Bridge where she is to meet Fox for the last

305

time. As she zips along the silver tunnel Mara wishes it could all stop and never happen at all. She wants to snuggle down with Fox amid the softly undulating walls of his room, rest her aching head against him, and try to blank out all thought of Tony Rex and rooks and the cyberflood and everything else that lies before her.

She wants the world to stop.

But that's not going to happen. The virus will already be live and loose. Cyberflood is on its way and she can't stop it.

Fox is already there, leaning over the humpbacked bridge, more tousle-headed than ever, gazing into the Looking Pond as if he hadn't a care in the world. Mara feels full of thorns. She is full of pain; she can't believe she will never see him again. They have been together less than a week, but this kind of love cuts quick and deep and keen as a blade.

Mara skates up and bumps to a halt beside him. When he turns towards her, she embeds his face, the way he looks at her now, deep in her mind. She will keep it there for ever. For the rest of her days.

'It's begun,' he whispers.

His forehead is damp with sweat. He slips a hot hand into hers. Mara lets out a great sigh and squeezes his hand. They stand together in silence, trying to grasp the enormity of what they have taken on.

'Mara,' he says after a while, and his husky voice shakes with more than just nerves. 'I'll never forget you. Never, as long as I live. You've changed everything for me.'

'Fox, I – I . . .'

She can't find the words she needs. Now the moment is here she cannot endure it, cannot bear to leave him.

The future *must* include him or it will always feel empty. But there's too much to say and so little time. And what could she say now that would change anything?

So she doesn't say a word.

Fox leans heavily upon the bridge.

'Stay. Stay with me,' he whispers, just when she thinks he is never going to speak again. 'We could get everyone on the ships, then you could stay and fight with me. I don't want you to go. I've never met anyone like you in my world and I don't believe I ever will.'

He grips her hand so tight it hurts. The powerful tug inside that pulled her towards him from the very first now becomes a tearing, red-hot pain.

Mara tries to say yes. It's what she wants to say. But somehow she can't. The wrong words seem to be drawn from her against her will, like knives from raw wounds.

'I'm scared the Treenesters wouldn't make it without me. They've never seen the outside world, never seen the sky and the ocean – except Candleriggs, and that was long ago. She'll be just as frightened as the others. They might panic and not know what to do. I can't let them down. And the refugees and urchins – this is their only chance for a future. For the rest of my life I'd wonder what happened to them, if they survived. I'd feel so guilty that I abandoned them all – and I just can't live with the guilt of any more deaths. But I can't bear losing you. I don't want to go – I want to be with you.'

They can't look at each other, can't speak, can't do anything except hold on to each other so tightly it's impossible to believe that either will ever let go.

Finally, Fox speaks.

'I'll meet you in the Weave. At night, every night. I'll wait for you by the broken bridge.'

307

The Bridge to Nowhere. Mara sobs silently.

It won't be the same. It'll never be the same as his true presence. A cyberfox will never be enough now that she knows the real, live Fox. Yet it will be something. He won't be lost to her completely.

'I wish you all the luck in the world, Mara,' he says. 'And happiness.'

I don't know if there's any happiness left in the world, thinks Mara. *But there's love. Maybe it's strong enough to bridge an ocean.*

To have found this love amid so much pain and horror feels miraculous – even if, just as she finds it, she must lose it.

'I'll be there,' she promises. 'Every night, on the bridge. Always.'

His lips crush hers in a last kiss, unlike any other – a burning, bruising, fast and brutal kiss, full of pain.

And then suddenly, shockingly, he's gone.

Mara leans over the Looking Pond and wants to scream. She feels as if someone just wrenched a limb from her body.

'Is the big romance off?' says a familiar voice. 'Well, plenty more fish in the sea.'

It's the very last person she wants to deal with right now – Tony Rex.

'I've been looking for you,' he says, grabbing hold of her arm so that Mara can't skate away. 'Lost anything?'

Horrified, Mara suddenly realizes that she has.

My backpack!

Tony flips something from over his shoulder and Mara sees that he's got her precious backpack. Has he looked in it and seen her treasures? If he has and he's a rook, she's finished. As well as her treasures from the old world and her cyberwizz, there are all the disks that Fox has made for the ships, each one wrapped in her carefully pencilled instructions for the mass escape from the city, sealed inside waterproof wallets.

'Thanks. That was nice of you,' says Mara coldly, but her shaking voice betrays her emotion.

'My pleasure.'

Tony smiles as if in sympathy with Mara's distress, but she is sure he's enjoying every second of her discomfort.

Fingers clumsy with nerves, she takes the backpack from him, wondering what is going to happen now.

'Goodnight then,' she mutters.

'Goodnight, Mara. Don't feel too lonely and sad,' he leans close and murmurs in her ear, just as she's about to skate off. 'You know I'm never far away.'

His words are not meant as comfort, she is sure. They feel like a threat.

Less than two hours till midnight. Then the virus goes live and it's cyberflood wipeout.

Mara lies in a sleep pod and feels each passing second beat within her. She can't sleep. She's too deeply frightened by Tony Rex and by the enormity of the rescue plan she is about to undertake. She must ready herself for what is to happen. This is what she has come to New Mungo for. But Mara doesn't feel ready, not at all. She will never be ready. She wants to snuggle down in the pink glow of her sleep pod and forget it all. But even here she can't feel at peace, with the lumen eyes of the motherlight watching her.

Maybe I could get out of this. Maybe I could persuade Fox to forget it all. We could let the cyberflood come and do nothing. We could live together and have a nice, snug life here in the New World. Why do I have to be the big heroine? Why me? I don't want it to be me. I'm too scared. I'm just an ordinary girl and all I want is an ordinary life. It's not up to me to save the world. And I want to be with Fox. I can't bear to leave him. I just can't.

Misery engulfs her. Mara huddles down inside the spongy quilt, closes her eyes and tries to find oblivion in sleep.

I believe in you.

The voice jolts her back into wakefulness. Mara stares at the motherlight. But she knows it was no lumen's voice. That was the voice of her own mother, echoing out of the past.

My daughter is made of the same stuff as my mother.

Mara turns over on to her back and begins to think. She thinks of Granny Mary, who fought so hard in her youth to build a future when it seemed there was none – the future that she, Mara, inherited. She thinks of Candleriggs, then of Thenew, the Face in the Stone; all of them salvaged a future out of the wreckage of their young lives. And each one had some deep inner wound to bear. Thenew was thrown out of her own land and set adrift, pregnant and all alone on the ocean. And Granny Mary – did she have some deeply hidden wound too?

Mara digs into her backpack and takes out the little carved wooden box. She opens the lid and looks in the mirror – looks beyond the scar in the cracked glass, deep into her own eyes, and confronts the thought that she has kept tucked away at the back of her mind for so long. Suddenly she is sure of what she sees: eyes that are as dark and determined as Tain's.

She closes the little box. Deep within her something is

settled. She will never know the answer to that puzzle of the past but she no longer questions it.

Now Mara knows why she must act, and it has nothing to do with the stone-telling. Her own eyes tell her why. All the signs she ever needed lie within herself. She must fight to save what she can of the future that her parents, and her grandparents, Granny Mary and Tain, struggled to give her. The future that Gail and her little brother, Corey, lost.

The only way she can give any meaning to their lost lives is to keep fighting for her own future, and the futures of the urchins, the Treenesters and the refugees. Then the deaths of the people she loved won't have been for nothing at all.

And Fox must fight for a future he can be proud of in the world his grandfather built.

In just a few hours the fight will begin.

FOX TIME IS NOW

Fox feels them coming, a tidal wave advancing.

The shock waves rip across the Noos, thrilling all its patterns. His twentieth-century ghost wave, a massed army of history's lost and dead, is about to engulf New Mungo. In they come, using every godgem channel they can find – in their hundreds, thousands, millions.

An oceanic feeling sweeps Fox as wipeout hits. Pure joy. Too good to be true.

Chaos and panic erupt all around. Fox waits. He knows how to still it. Using the only virus-free godgem in the whole city he keys in the code that will shake New Mungo to its roots. And sits back to watch.

Martin Luther King appears as a colossal lumenbeing above ten thousand heads. A giant with a giant's voice.

'I have a dream!' he booms, and Fox feels that the strength of will in that immense voice could shatter the city in pieces. 'I have a dream – to be free at last! Free at last! Free at last!'

The cybercath freezes in shock. Martin Luther King pauses. Fox sees open-mouthed amazement reflected ten thousand times over upon the faces of the New World citizens. He tingles all over, his hair stands on end. The atmosphere turns electric, volatile.

This is it, his own voice roars in his head; this is what you were born to do.

But now comes the dangerous bit, the test that Fox has created for his city, a test of its heart and soul. The cybercath is silent, breathlessly still, as Martin Luther King begins to tell the people of New Mungo the story of the old, drowned world. He tells them the truth. And the people of the New World don't turn away. They listen. Now, for the first and only time in his life, Fox feels part of his own city. He feels the past link with the present and begin to knit the fabric of the future as he stands among his fellow-citizens and hears the truth from the mouth of a giant lumen ghost.

Simultaneously, in every cybercath in every city of the New World, Fox has programmed a lumenbeing of Martin Luther King to do the same.

Fox turns to go and sees his grandpa, the Grand Father of All, surrounded by Nux guards and a posse of City Fathers. He looks unutterably alone. In that moment Fox feels for him in a way he never has before – deep anger, and a pity that's deeper still. But not love, because for the first time in his life Fox knows what love feels like.

The lights begin to flicker as Fox's ghost virus hits. As the city's systems begin to crash Caledon breaks free of his grandson's lumenspell and his eyes scan the vast cybercath. Fox knows his grandfather is looking for him. He should be at his side at a moment like this. But a worse moment is soon to come and Fox will not be at his side then either. For Caledon is about to see his New World dream wrecked, at least for a day, and when he

313

*searches for Fox and does not find him, then he'll know
who did this.*

*Fox moves swiftly to the edges of the mesmerized crowd.
He stops at the grille of a large air vent set low in a wall.
Late last night, as the city guards dozed and chatted, he
loosened the screws. All it needs now is a sharp yank.*

*Unseen and unheard, as the city plunges into chaos,
Fox rips the ventilator from the wall. Feet first, he jumps
into the coiling chute of a spiregyre. And now he zooms
helter-skelter down its winding tunnel, down through the
cushioning blast of waste air, down and down in a terrifying, interminable spin – and finally shoots out at the
foot of one of New Mungo's great towers to crash into
the black water of a netherworld he has never known.*

*Cold sea swallows him whole. The necrotten glow of
the old city ghosts all around him, like a vast lumen
landscape. Fox struggles desperately, but he can't find the
surface. He's lost in the ruins, drowning among the past,
and his heart cries out for Mara and the power of now.*

NO TIME TO KILL

Mara zips and zooms through the silver tunnels of the nexus, her zapeedos sparking on the bends. Already she's far beyond the crowded waltz tunnels, veering way out east to the empty edges of the city. The pattern of these outer tunnels is imprinted on her mind's eye – she has spent days memorizing them. In the toe of her left zapeedo is Caledon's pencil sketch of the Eastern sea bridge plan, the building project she thinks Gorbals and Wing are working on. She can only hope that's where they are, because if not, Mara doesn't know what she will do.

The robo-dogs that guard the outer limits of the nexus are a menace. Mara zips up the curve of a wall and loops round the roof of the tunnel to avoid the snap of a metal jaw on her ankle – and only just escapes the bite of its nasty little friend as she zooms back out of the loop. She kicks out hard and hears a satisfying electronic whine as the blade of her skate slices off the robo's tail. She laughs, looks back in triumph – and her heart thumps with fear.

Someone's on *her* tail. Ordinary zappers don't come this far out – there's nothing here and you could easily lose a leg to one of those dogs. She glances back once again and this time her heart almost stops because she's sure it's Tony Rex. In that split second of shock the pattern of the nexus tangles in her mind's eye. Mara panics as she zooms up to a fork in the tunnel.

Which way? Oh, which way?

As soon as she chooses she knows it's the wrong one because the tunnel rises up in a slope, instead of dipping downwards. She's gone right when she should have gone left. Mara shoots another glance back. The tunnel is empty. Whoever was behind her is gone. Her nerves have got the better of her – no one is tailing her after all. Mara screams to a heel-sparking stop and zaps back up to the fork. She's about to take the left-hand fork when all of a sudden there he is, right in her face.

Tony Rex.

'Mara!' He acts surprised, as if he hasn't been following her at all.

'Tony! Well, hi. Sorry, but I'm in a bit of a . . .' *Rush*, she is going to say then stops herself. Because he'll want to know why.

'What's a nice girl like you doing way out here?' Tony asks. His sleazy charm does not mask the disturbing glint in his eyes.

'Oh – just needed a long zap after a hard day's work.'

'Out here? That's a pretty dangerous zap.' He nods behind at the snarling robo-dogs.

Mara shrugs with affected carelessness. 'Why not? It's a great speed zone. I can deal with a few robos.'

And what's a nasty character like *you* doing out here, Mara asks herself. She must think of an excuse to get away, now. If he *is* a rook – and with each heart-thumping moment she is more and more sure that he is – she must throw him off her tracks and get a move on or the whole plan will fail. Any moment now New Mungo's system will be in wipeout and the nexus will plunge into darkness.

But what is she to do? What is *he* going to do? He's blocking her way, not moving. Then he does move. Mara's heartbeat thuds in her ears as, with his eyes fixed on hers, Tony Rex raises his crystal knuckle phone to his mouth.

'Yeah, I remember – you're a girl who likes a taste of *real, extreme* fear, aren't you, Mara? Well, I think I've got just the thing for you.'

With his mouth over the knuckle phone on his left hand, his right hand moves quickly to a jacket pocket. His eyes, sharp now with that indeterminate something that disturbs her so much, never leave hers. Holding his eyes, aware of his every movement, Mara slips fleet fingers into her trouser pocket. Her thoughts fly faster than light. What's in his pocket? A weapon? A gun? Who is he calling? If he's a rook and he's calling security, then it's all over for her; but she can't let that happen – not now when she's so close to escape. She *won't* let it happen.

In her pocket, her fingers make contact with the small, cold, sharpened stone blade of Wing's dagger. Carefully she turns it around in her fingers to grip the ancient bone handle. Blood pounds hard in her head, all through her body, right to her fingertips. The dagger seems to pulsate.

Tony Rex pulls a clenched hand from his jacket and opens his mouth to speak into the knuckle phone. And Mara lunges for her future. She stabs Tony Rex in the heart with the bone-handled dagger.

Stone ruptures soft flesh. Bone crunches against bone; ancient animal bone on live human bone.

Mara lets go of the dagger. She reels back against the tunnel wall and watches a world end. Tony Rex crumples and, with a cry that fills the nexus, dies slowly and brutally at her feet.

The moment is enormous, empty and ugly.

Mara stands helplessly beside the body. The awful gush of blood makes her want to pull out the dagger, plug the gaping wound and somehow bring him back to life. But she can't do anything. Her limbs are useless and she can hardly breathe. *He is dead.*

Mara looks at his clenched fingers and sees the sleek, pencil-like cylinder that he reached for. She doesn't know what it is but she's sure it's some kind of weapon.

Numb and trembling so violently that she can hardly stand, Mara follows the animal fear and instinct that tell her to get away, now, as fast as she can.

She has killed Tony Rex. And she must live with that.

The window of time has been smashed wide open and New Mungo is in seizure.

Everything that holds the city together, all the electronics, lumens, lights and security – even the backup systems – are shuddering under the onslaught of Fox's cyberflood. He has timed wipeout to hit as darkness falls to give their escape the cover of night. But Mara cannot focus on the next part of the plan; all she can think of is what she has just done to Tony Rex. Yet she must calm down and fix her mind on getting on to the Eastern sea bridge where she hopes with all her might that she will find Gorbals and Wing.

She veers out of the nexus and zooms along a single main artery, a long arm of tunnel that dips into a steep slope that seems to stretch for ever downwards. When, finally, it breaks up into building rubble, she stops. Under the dim flicker of failing lights, Mara kicks off her zapeedos and the too-tight shoes, and pulls out the scrap of paper, folded up into the tiniest parcel, from a toecap. Her fingers are trembling so much she can hardly unfold Caledon's sketch of the Eastern sea bridge extension. She smoothes the paper flat upon the ground and rubs her sore feet as she studies the sketch in the glow of her cyberwizz halo.

Well, she's definitely in the right zone. From where she is she can just see the dark circle that is the end of the tunnel. Beyond that should be the incomplete arm of the Eastern sea bridge that runs high above the ocean of Eurosea.

A distant clanking makes her press an ear to the tunnel wall. Now, the noises are amplified into industrial clangs and bangs that give her hope that she's right. But even so, it's all guesswork – *will* Gorbals be here? And Wing?

Once – *if* she finds them, she will gather together as many people as she can and tell them the city is in breakdown, that they must follow her and take this chance to rush the guards and run for their lives to the fleet of ships harboured in the legs of the city's support towers. She will issue the watertight packets containing navigation disks with their set of instructions which say that everyone must grab food supplies from the stock halls in the great towers. Meanwhile, Mara will get the Treenesters on to a ship. Then, without delay, they will sail out of the city gates and due North to the mountains of the melted ice lands.

It's all crazy. Impossible. Mara tries to remind herself that the impossible can happen – but she knows she'll need nothing short of a miracle for it all to succeed.

The lights give one last buzz and flicker then the tunnel falls into darkness. Mara gets to her feet, chucks away the cramping shoes she has come to hate, and begins to run barefoot out of the tunnel mouth on to the Eastern sea bridge.

With the lights down, and the back-up systems gone too, the city guards and their robo-dogs stumble about in confusion. Mara hears their bewildered shouts, knowing what they don't – that all their communication systems have crashed. She runs until she's out on the open bridge, high above the ocean. The cold night air feels brutal; realworld has no temperature control. Mara feels she is running through an empty universe, yelling for Gorbals and Wing as hard as she can, her cyberwizz halo held high, the only light in the blackness.

No one answers her cries. There's no sign of anyone at all. At long last she stops, drenched in cold sweat, scared she might hurtle off the unfinished end of the bridge and crash down into the ocean, far below. She delves into her backpack and finds the now-crumbly sprig of herbs. Mara shreds the dry sprig between her fingers and breathes their scent deeply. *Clear head and courage,* she tells herself over and over.

Now she moves more calmly, walking forward, holding her halo high. And with a shock she sees its glow alight upon a great huddle of dirty, exhausted faces among piles of tarpaulin and building materials. Her earlier noise and speed must have frightened them into hiding. Now, at every step, the halo glow reveals more and yet more huddles – masses upon masses of slaves.

'Gorbals! Wing!' she shouts, frantically searching every face, but there's no answer. Then at last someone moves out of one of the huddles and grabs her arm. It's a girl. She lunges a hand towards Mara's face. Mara flinches, but the girl only reaches up to trace with a finger the now-faded line of the scar on her cheek. Suddenly Mara is both laughing and crying at once, hugging the girl in relief, because it's Scarwell – the wild girl who attacked her in the cathedral. She never thought she'd be so pleased to see *her* again.

'Scarwell, where's Wing?' Mara cries. 'Do you know where Wing is? Wing!'

The girl frowns in concentration, as if she is trying to decipher Mara's words. Then her expression clears and she turns to another urchin and babbles something unintelligible. And something begins to happen. The urchins are passing some communication between them. Mara can feel it ripple through their flock, then hears some of the urchins scampering down the dark road of the sea bridge. Mara waits in the dark for what feels like an eternity. Then at last, out of the darkness, a small figure emerges. Mara holds her breath. She hardly dares hope . . . but yes – it's Wing, her own little urchin. She runs and grabs him and holds him close, crying with delight, babbling as unintelligibly as any urchin.

But Wing doesn't want to be hugged. He yanks himself free and runs back off into the dark before Mara can stop him.

'No, wait! Wing, I need you. Come here! You must help me find Gorbals!'

But Wing seems to be activating another ripple of communication; again Mara can feel the message spread. Now the urchins seem to be parting, making a clear pathway to pull a figure through – a tall, thin, gangly figure who is pushed towards her by the urchins. He's only a shadow beyond the reach of her halo beam but when he trips clumsily over a bit of rubble, Mara knows who it is.

SPLINTER

'Mara, Mara!'

Gorbals lurches into her arms. Mara hugs him tight and feels him flinch.

'Are you hurt?'

'It doesn't matter,' he assures her, but he is suffering from some pain or injury, she can tell. And he is changed: shaven-headed, thin and utterly exhausted-looking. 'I'm so glad to see you, Mara. But no,' he corrects himself. 'No, I'm not! If you're here then it means they've taken you as a slave too.'

'No, Gorbals. I'm free and soon you will be too. We're going to get the other Treenesters and all these people and children and escape on to the ships. There's no time to explain – we have to go now. Listen, everyone!' Mara raises her voice to make sure she's heard above the mass of fearful, excited voices. 'The city is in breakdown. We're going to escape and make for high land in the far north of the world. We need to get to the ships in the legs of the great towers. Everyone – spread the word and follow me! Grab anything that can be used as a weapon – bricks, tools, anything – and be ready to fight for your lives. Now let's go!'

Grabbing both Gorbals and Wing by the hand, Mara races back along the sea bridge, into the great arm of tunnel that leads to the nexus, followed by a seething mass of slaves. They have to fight through a posse of guards. Gunfire ricochets off the walls and Mara hears people scream and fall around her as they are hit, but the mass of slaves – brutal with desperation, makeshift weapons at the ready, their eyes used to the darkness of the open sea bridge – have the advantage over the shocked and confused guards.

They climb the steeply rising tunnel that connects the bridge to the city and head for the maze of the nexus. Mara must find the nearest air vents, as quickly as possible. She tried to memorize their positions on the way in, but there was light then. Now, apart from the glow of her halo, it's pitch dark.

At long last, her halo alights on a vent. With the help of Gorbals and some of the others, she kicks the metal grille until it hangs loose and can be yanked from the tunnel wall. Then, at top speed, she hands out the water-tight packages that contain the navigation disks and their pencilled instructions.

'We must escape down the spiregyres!' Mara yells. 'The sea bridge is too high to jump from and too far from the ships, and the city's electrics have crashed so the lifts won't work. Look for more air vents and jump in! Once you're down, swim for the ships in the tower legs!'

People begin to race along the tunnels in search of escape routes. Mara begins launching people down the spiregyre.

Gorbals stares into the coiling air chute in horror.

323

'No, Mara, no! I can't.'

'You must, Gorbals! It's the only way. You'll never see Broomielaw or any of the others again if you don't. Once you hit the water, swim to the Hill of Doves and I'll meet you there. Quick – go! You're almost free!'

Mara gives him a fierce hug then pushes him brutally into the chute of the spiregyre. She waits a moment then, with another fierce hug, launches Wing. Then herself. Feet first, she begins the immense helter-skelter on a cushioning blast of waste air down the great spiregyre that coils the entire length of New Mungo's vast towers.

The hurtling spin downwards is so petrifyingly violent she is sure it must kill her. Mara screams as she crashes off the sides of the chute, falling through echoes of her own terror, as her voice rebounds through the coils of the spiregyre. She is being spun and battered out of her body, out of her own self.

When at last she shoots out into thin air it's worse, a timeless moment of nothingness, of helplessly falling for ever, it seems – until it ends in a colossal black crash of such force she is sure she *is* dead, now. This vast, cold, drowning weight of darkness she has plunged into must be death. All around her are ghostly, glimmering things. *Necrotty.* The word filters into her stunned head, just as she realizes that it's not death but sea. The darkness parts and now, free and light of its dragging weight, she bursts back into the world, up into the miracle of air. She gulps huge greedy breaths of it until at last her body reclaims her self and she is Mara once more, half-drowned, drenched and reeling – but alive.

The first thing she thinks of is Fox. Has he survived this? All around her people are crashing into the water from the spiregyres, choking and struggling, thrashing and shouting. Wing will be all right, she's sure. He is as much at home in the water as on land. But Gorbals?

'Mara!' A voice splutters above the noise.

'Gorbals! Over here!'

They struggle through the mass of thrashing bodies, towards the sound of each other's shouts.

'We're alive!' he gasps. 'I thought I would die!'

'Swim hard!' cries Mara. She doesn't want to think about that terrifying spin down the spiregyre ever again. 'Swim to your island. Oh, but which way is it, which way?'

'Look, there's the arm of the broken bridge,' Gorbals splutters, as a wave hits him in the face. 'I know where we are – this way!'

The world is erupting all around them. Alarm bells are clanging, shrill and harsh, and gunfire hammers the air as tens, hundreds, thousands of crying, yelling, screaming men, women and children, the captive army of New Mungo's slaves, crack the city open and rush upon the waters of the netherworld in a mass breakout, a human explosion of trapped rage.

'What have I done?' Mara cries in panic. 'Oh, what on earth have I done?'

'Mara, you haven't done this.' Gorbals swims closer to her, bewildered at the cascade of bodies around them. 'This is immense, it's – it's . . . '

Mara is numb with the shock of what she has unleashed.

'Keep going, Mara, keep swimming. Look! Here's a raft.' Gorbals hauls and pushes her on to a metallic junk vessel and swims behind, holding on for support.

Mara wants to flop, trembling, into the junk raft but she sees how Gorbals is struggling and realizes how weak he must be from the shock of release and from his harsh term of slave labour. And he was in pain too. So she begins to use her arms as oars and now they move more steadily across the dark waters towards the Treenesters' island. Mara can still hardly believe that she has found Gorbals and Wing, that she actually rescued them, as she set out to do. Gorbals looks so unlike himself with his head shaven and his straw-like locks all gone. But he's alive.

'Can you see Wing?' she cries. It's almost impossible to see anything in the thick dark of the netherworld.

Gorbals peers through the water, his owlish night vision stronger than hers.

'Over there! It's the ratkins! Look at them go!' Gorbals exclaims.

A mass of urchins surge past, moving across the dark water in an arrow-flock, like birds or fish, as if they know exactly where they are going.

Mara can't tell if Wing is among them; she can only hope he is.

The raft hits land and they stagger on to the Hill of Doves, up to the clearing where the Treenesters have hidden themselves among the branches. A mass of huge eyes stare down in shock at the chaos that's been unleashed in their world. There's a cry and Broomielaw jumps down from a tree. She seizes Gorbals in a fierce, frightened embrace, then Mara. Her amazed eyes say what she is too overcome to put into words.

'Mara, what's happening?' cries Molendinar, landing on the grass beside her with a thump.

One by one the Treenesters drop down from the trees.

'There's no time to explain but you must all hurry and follow me to the ships in the city towers,' Mara declares.

'Ships?' gasps Broomielaw. 'You mean you've made it

happen? We are going to be free? Then this really is the stone-telling?'

'And you really are the Face in the Stone!' declares Gorbals. 'I knew it.'

'All I know,' says Mara, trying to keep a cool head, 'is that we need to move very fast, if we want to escape. Now hurry, everyone!'

'Candleriggs! Quick! Come down! Mara has saved us!' Broomielaw yells up to the greatest. Then she reaches into a tree nook and pulls out a twig lantern cage.

'See! I looked after him for the ratkin. Did you rescue him too?'

Mara looks inside the twig cage and instead of moon-moths there is the sparrow – Wing's bird-friend.

'Yes, and I just hope he's still safe. Look after his bird, Broomielaw, and we'll try to find him. Now, quick! Everyone to the rafts.'

'*They come! They come in glorious march!*' Gorbals is chanting in wild delight. '*As they dash through skill's triumphal arch, or plunge mid the dancing spray.* That long-ago poet saw all this too, Mara.'

But Mara is in a panic, piling everyone on the rafts and helping Ibrox to push them off on to the waters. What's keeping Candleriggs and Broomielaw? Baby Clayslaps is clinging round Pollock's neck, whimpering for his mother.

'Stubborn old woman!' Distraught, Broomielaw runs down the Hill of Doves. 'Mara – please go and talk to Candleriggs – she says she won't come. All these years she's waited for the stone-telling and now it's happening she won't be part of it!'

Mara rushes back uphill to the greatest.

'Candleriggs!' she cries in panic. 'You must come now! This is our only chance.'

'The stone-telling was never for me, Mara,' the old woman's voice calls down from the branches of the oak. 'It's for you and the others. That's your future. My place is here. Go now.'

Mara remembers Tain's refusal to leave his island home and wonders what she can do if the old woman really has made up her mind to stay.

'Listen to me,' Candleriggs shouts down, straining to be heard above the clangour of New Mungo's alarm bells. 'I am the last woman of a generation of Earth people who no longer exist. I have lived a life no one else will ever live. Soon I'll fall from the world like a leaf from a tree. I will be as I am until the very end of myself. But Mara,' the old woman's voice drops so that Mara can only just hear, 'just tell me one thing. Is he still alive?'

'Yes,' Mara calls up. What else should she tell?

Candleriggs is peering down through the branches, watching the thoughts flit across Mara's face.

'He never forgot you, Candleriggs. He wears a white lily right next to his heart – it's the symbol of the New World. He wants to shine its image from the moon.'

The old woman looks up through the branches of the great oak to the vast city in the sky.

'Well, then,' she says at last, and Mara will never forget the world of emotion in those two words. 'He's in his greatnest and I'm in mine. Each as stubborn as the other, neither of us forgetting the other. But I could never have lived in that tree, Mara. I could never enjoy its necrotten fruit.'

'No,' says Mara.

'Go on now. I'll stay right here. This hill has been my home my whole life and why would I leave it now?' There is a pause, then: 'Despite everything, I wish I could see him just once before our time in the world is gone.'

'You want to go back up to New Mungo?'

The idea of this gnarled, owl-eyed ancient in her tattered earthen clothing standing amid the gleaming chambers of the Nux is too outlandish to imagine. And could she really bear to meet Caledon again, after all that's happened? A sudden thought strikes Mara. Maybe Candleriggs *should* stay here in the netherworld.

'Candleriggs, look in the old university. You might find someone there who has searched a whole universe for the truth but only you can give him the answers he needs. I just hope he's got there safely.'

Mara's voice breaks with fear and Candleriggs's eyes grow even larger.

'His name is David,' continues Mara. 'My Fox. He's Caledon's grandson. You're the only one who can explain his grandfather and the story of the past to him. And maybe you can help him with the future. He's a rebel just like you. He wants to revolutionize the New World. If anyone can do it, he can. But he's all alone, Candleriggs, and I – I can't stay.'

Through her own tears, Mara sees the painful splinter that's been stuck in the old woman's heart all these years melt like ice. The meltdown fills her eyes and streams down the deep lines on her face.

The old woman reaches into her nest. Two things land with thumps on the mossy ground.

'Take these, Mara Bell!' cries Candleriggs. 'They look just your size. I've kept them clean and polished all these years, and never once worn them. Maybe I was keeping them for you.'

Astonished, Mara picks up a pair of the most beautiful

shoes she has ever seen – gleaming red leather shoes that look as good as new.

There's a clunk and a glug as something else lands on the grass.

'Take that too,' calls Candleriggs. 'Drink to me in your new world. But go now! Hurry!'

Mara picks up a tall glass bottle full of a fizzing amber liquid. She can just make out the words on the bottle's scratched metallic screw cap: *Irn-Bru*. With no time left for questions *s*he zips the bottle and the shoes in her backpack.

'We'll tell your legend, Candleriggs,' Mara promises, and she can hardly keep her voice steady. 'We'll always remember you.'

She is sobbing breathlessly as she runs back down the Hill of Doves to the last raft that is waiting to follow the others to the ships.

The urchins have ransacked the museum. With their loot they flock towards the central towers where the supply ships are harboured, unsecured now behind gaping doors, while the city erupts in chaos. The urchins are bringing with them a lost world of inventions: tools, weapons, utensils, instruments and all sorts of other objects, whatever they can carry. Swords, spears, axes, shields, fishnets, harpoons, knives, spoons, bowls, urns, flutes, horns, bugles, bassoons, drums, telescopes, compasses, gemstones, clubs, pickled brains, jewellery, engines, snowshoes, canoes, combs, baskets, animal skin mittens and hats and clothing, bits of armour, cogs, wheels, microscopes and skulls.

Wing slams on deck with the golden archway symbol from the ruin that crests the Hill of Doves. He's wearing a fur-lined, jewel-encrusted royal crown from the museum. Scarwell drags aboard the life-size model of the apeman and hugs it close.

'Treenesters!' shouts Mara, once they are safely on board one of the ships. 'Round up as many refugees as you can from the warehouses. They are collecting whatever food and water supplies they can find. But hurry! The guards and police might be here any minute. Gorbals and Broomielaw, watch out on deck for any sky people.'

Mara runs to the control cabin and looks around. In a glass case above the control panel is a handgun. She smashes the glass, pulls out the gun. Now she takes the navigation disk from its watertight package and frantically reads her own pencilled instructions. Her mind has gone blank with fear and she can't remember what she is meant to do.

Somehow, at last, she finds the slot in the panel that she needs. She feeds in the navigation disk – and hears the sirens of the impending attack of city guards and sea police she's been expecting. It will have taken them a little time to work out what is happening, then to amass and organize their forces. But now they have and there's no time to lose.

'Gorbals! Is there any sign of the others? We need to move fast!'

Mara catches sight of the megaphone button on the control panel. She switches it on.

'Ibrox! Molendinar! Pollock! Possil! Clyde! Parkhead! All Treenesters and refugees – return to the ships at once. We need to leave immediately!'

'Here they are!' cries Gorbals, peering out of the control cabin window. 'Oh no – and the sky people too!'

We'll never make it, Mara tells herself. *Will any of us get out of this alive?*

She feels the ship begin to pull out of harbour. She can hear gunfire out on deck but is terrified that the navigation disk will not take them safely out of the city gates on to the ocean, and head them due north, as Fox promised. Yet already the ship has slipped from its dark harbour in the tower. Through the control cabin window, Mara sees the open gap in the city wall where the arms of the sea have parted the disabled gates. The ship heads towards the gap.

There's a scream. *Broomielaw!* Mara grabs the gun and dashes from the control cabin. She stops dead when she sees the lurid orange sea police uniform. Pollock lies sprawled on the deck. The policeman has a gun aimed at his head. Silently, Mara raises her gun. Her trembling fingers grip the weapon. Can she aim well enough to save Pollock?

Before she can do a thing, before the policeman knows what's hit him, a flock of urchins rush out. The policeman doesn't even have a chance to switch the aim of his gun. The urchins charge and he crashes against the ship's railing. Quick as a flash the urchins grab his legs and topple him overboard.

Pollock sits up and stares in amazement at his rescuers – the ratbashers he has always despised.

The ship passes through the gate in the great wall and Mara stares out for the very last time at the city. At the far edge of the netherworld she can just make out the tall dark cone of the university steeple. Then it slips out of sight behind the bulk of New Mungo's central towers and is gone.

The moment the ship is through the city gates, Mara

rushes back into the control cabin and sets the navigation disk on pause. She switches on the ship's megaphone.

'All refugees – please listen! This is a rescue ship,' she yells. Through the cabin window she can see an instant stir among the mass of boats in the camp around the wall. 'We can take some of you. There are more ships on the way to help you!'

The words are barely out of her mouth when she hears the beginnings of a massive rush. Mara races up on deck. The sea all around the ship is already swarming with boats and bodies as the refugees from the boat camp make a frantic dash to escape. It's the most incredible sight. All the ship's ropes and ladders and lifebuoys are thrown down to help, while everyone grabs hold of whatever fishing nets and lengths of tarpaulin the refugees manage to throw up. They begin to haul up on board every person they can.

Mara's searches the chaotic scene for Rowan and Ruth, for any known face from the island, but it's useless. It's too dark, and there are too many boats and faces.

The ship begins to list and sway. The tidal wave of refugees seems endless. The ship gives a sudden precarious lurch to one side.

Mara panics. There's no more room. They are in danger of being submerged, of sinking, and then no one will escape. She races back to the megaphone in the control cabin to shout for calm.

'Stop, please! There's no more room on this ship but there are other ships on the way. Stay calm and wait till they get here or we'll sink!'

But no one listens. The refugees are too desperate. The now-perilous scramble on board continues.

Where *are* the other ships? Have they been captured?

In desperation Mara watches the city gates. The sirens of the sea police are growing louder by the second. Horrified, she sees the glare of orange lights flame upon the dark ocean. A great battalion of police waterbikes emerges through the wall and starts to fire upon the refugees in the boat camp and those in the water. Mara hesitates, her heart pounding. What can she do? What about Rowan and the others from the island? What can she do to save any of them now? But there's only one thing left to do. She resets the navigation disk. The ship powers into sudden movement. She rushes back up on deck.

The air is full of screams as the forward surge of the ship flings refugees back into the ocean. The waves boil with the foam of desperate swimmers. Mara feels sick to her soul; she can't bear to watch. But what else could she do? If she waited any longer the ship would have capsized or they would have been captured by the sea police. She slumps down on to the floor of the ship's deck, trembling from head to foot.

'Mara – look!'

Gorbals points at the great wall and a massive cheer breaks out on deck. Relief rushes through her shaking body as she sees the white forms of the other ships begin to surge out of the city. But she cannot join in the cheering. She is counting. Only some of the ships have made it through. It's better than none, Mara tells herself, but she puts her head in her arms, rocked by guilt and shock – because at that moment of panic, when it seemed that the rush of refugees would sink them all, she was consumed by the most powerful impulse to do whatever it took to save herself and those already on board, rather than stay to help the other refugees and risk everyone perishing.

Just as Caledon must have done. And how far, if pushed, would she have taken that driving impulse to survive?

'Mara, it's all right now.'

Gorbals helps her to her feet. Broomielaw hugs her, cradling her as if she is a baby. Little Clayslaps peers over his mother's shoulder with huge, scared eyes, but he's safe now, snug and secure in his papoose. Mara grips the ship's railing and looks out.

The world's ocean is calm and graceful. Scattered across it, heading north, a constellation of white ships move like a ghost fleet through the darkness. A harsh cry, an exclamation of anguish and relief, breaks from her lips as she realizes that they really are free from the sky city and its netherworld, where Fox has gone to ground.

GLORY PEEPS

Up beyond the branches of New Mungo the stars weave a vast magic. Fox has never seen anything like it. Half-drowned, he shored up among the debris of the past, and found a whole living universe right above his head. And a little bit of earth beneath his feet.

The world's wind touches his face. The eternal light of the universe shines in his eyes. All is well, after all. The universe is doing just fine, busy spinning its own dreams into infinity. It doesn't need him, doesn't need anyone at all. It doesn't matter to the universe whether a single human being exists on Earth or not.

And yet – if he were not here the universe would be one pot of dreams poorer, one immeasurable jot of human energy weaker. The universe might not need Fox but it's good all the same that he's here, a child of the world, no more or less than a tree or a star.

Now I'm skin and bone and dirt, he laughs. Now I'm real!

From a smashed window in the steeple tower of the university Fox watches his city erupt. When the very last of the white ships heads out of the city gates he feels a wrench inside that's as strong as the pull of Earth or ocean. Mara is gone. And he is left here alone, under the great black steeple that looms high into the darkness – the place where he will begin his revolution of the New World.

Down here is the truth of the past and the old world that drowned. It's here that a boy named Cal dreamed himself out of a nightmare to become the Grand Father of All the New World. And the loneliest man on Earth.

Except one, thinks Fox, as he stands all alone in the thick, empty darkness of the netherworld.

A soft, quivery light appears out of the heart of the dark. It moves across the black water towards the university tower. Nervously, Fox watches its slow approach. The fluttery light draws nearer, nearer still, until it's close enough for Fox to see that it is a lantern carried on a raft. Now, at the foot of the tower, the lantern glow reveals the one who carries it – an ancient woman, as gnarled as a tree, with the eyes of an owl and a face as moon-pale as a lily.

THE STONE-TELLING
SHALL BE

Gorbals rushes up to Mara and points towards an old man who lies in a broken heap among the shadows at the edge of the deck. He looks bent and worn from his sentence of hard slave labour.

'He says he knows you,' says Gorbals. 'You lived on the same island.'

The old man stares at her and raises his hand in greeting. Mara frowns, seeing nothing that she recognizes in the shaved head and achingly thin body. But it's hard to see in the dark. She tries to think which of the islanders it might be.

'I don't know him at all. We left all the old people on the island,' Mara murmurs. She sees Gorbals's shocked face. 'I know, it was a terrible thing and I fought against it. But now I think the old ones must have felt like Can- dleriggs – they couldn't bear to leave the place they had lived in all their lives.'

The old man now struggles to his feet and makes his way towards her with slow, agonized steps. And it's only when he draws near to the moth lanterns and their glow lights up his eyes – eyes as blue as the forget-me-not sky of a summer night on Wing – that Mara knows who it is.

'Rowan!'

She rushes over, shocked and horrified at the terrible change in him.

'Oh, Rowan, I thought you must be dead!'

'Just about, but not quite.' A frail smile creases Rowan's thin, begrimed face. He grabs hold of her. 'Mara, is this true? People are saying that you did this – that you rescued us all.'

He shakes his head in wonder.

'Not just me,' Mara says brokenly. 'Someone helped me. Someone I had to leave behind.'

And now she begins to cry as she has never cried before.

Rowan clasps her to him, his bony frame shaking with exhaustion and emotion. He holds her until she is calm enough to try to speak again.

'What about your parents?' whispers Mara. 'What about Ruth and Quinn and all the others from the island?'

'Gail's death . . .' he sighs, struggling for words. 'That killed all hope in my parents, then a wave of sickness spread round the camp – diseased drinking water this time – and they had no strength left to fight it. Once they were dead, I didn't care what happened to me. The Pickers took me up into the city to work on the sea bridge. But I saw Ruth and Quinn and some of the others before I was taken – they were so kind, they tried to help us when we fell ill. They were devastated when Mum and Dad died. I don't know what happened to them. Ruth had her baby just before I was taken. I hope they all survived.'

'They might have escaped. They might be on another ship,' says Mara, desperate to believe that they are.

'Maybe,' says Rowan, but he's full of grief, and changes the subject.

'I can't believe I'm here. Mara, what happened to you? Where did you go? How did you do all this?'

'Rowan, when I tell you, you'll never believe me. What happened is like one of those legends in the books you used to read on the island. I'll tell you everything once you've had food and rest, because it's such a long, strange tale. I'm going to tell everyone so that one day, when we find land, the story will live on in the world and the people who come after us will know how they came to be free. And maybe, somehow, our story will help them to be strong in their lives,' she says, knowing how the stories of Granny Mary and Thenew and Candleriggs helped her.

Mara's eyes burn with tears as she thinks of Fox but she blinks them back and tries to smile at her friends.

'Here you are, Treenesters – out in the world for the first time ever!' she cries. 'Well, what do you think of it?'

'I'm so happy I can't think,' Gorbals bursts out. 'I'm just *being* in the world. I can't believe all this has really happened. It's the end of the Treenesters' story but the beginning of a new one.'

He steps forward to lean on the railing and look out at the world – and trips over the ship's anchor.

Bad as she feels, Mara can't help laughing. Some things don't change. The whole world might end and Gorbals would still trip over his feet.

'Look!' Broomielaw exclaims. 'Mara, look! It's the fish with the ring.'

She points at the anchor that Gorbals has just tripped over. The metal is moulded into the shape of a fish with a split tail at the end. The large ring in its mouth holds the anchor rope.

'So it is.' Mara stares in surprise. 'But the rest didn't happen. The stone-telling didn't come together, after all. What was your rhyme?'

'The fish with the ring
The bell and the bird and the tree.
When these all come together
Then the stone-telling shall be.'

The Treenesters chant it for her. Wing, with his little sparrow friend back upon his shoulder, sits among a cluster of urchins nearby. They all cock their heads, like birds, to listen. Mara looks back at New Mungo and hopes with all her heart that Fox is safe and alive in the netherworld, that Candleriggs will find him. The sky city is no more than a faint gleam in the night sky, the furious clangour of its alarms just the gentlest peal on the sea wind.

Free at last!

Something clicks in Mara's mind, like a key turning gently in its lock. She looks at the Treenesters, enclosed within the fluttery glow of their moth lanterns, then at little bird-like Wing and his friends as they play upon the huge fish anchor. And with a huge shock she sees that maybe it *has* all come together – the fish with the ring, the bird, the tree. And she is Mara Bell.

Has the stone-telling really happened, after all?

Dizzied by the thought, Mara leans against the ship's rail. She doesn't know what to think, doesn't know if she ever will. And now she wonders if it matters, in the end. What *does* matter is that the future has been unlocked. She and Fox each hold a key to the future in their hands. But all this – the death of her family, losing Fox and

341

everything else – will have been worthless if she doesn't try as hard as she can to hold on to a sure sense of what is fair and right. Mara relives that terrible moment outside the city walls when her own fear and panic, her over-riding instinct to save herself, showed her how Caledon and the New World ended up as they did.

She turns towards the future. The Pole Star blazes in front. The bow of the ship cuts a clean white line through the dark ocean, guided by the star's torch. The ship's speed is exciting; the cold sea spray invigorating. Mara feels truly alive, full of hope and loss, pain and exhilaration. She thinks of the legend of Thenew and imagines that wretched young girl, banished from her homeland and set adrift upon the ocean in a ramshackle raft, all alone, with a child growing inside her. Yet she chanced upon land and Thenew's child, Mungo, grew up to found a whole new city – the ruins of which now lie drowned under New Mungo, the sky city that still bears his name.

Well, I'm not all alone and adrift in a ramshackle raft. I'm on a solid ship and I know where I'm going. I've got the Treenesters and Rowan and the urchins. All we need to do is find a bit of high land. It's there in the North, in the green land of the people. I'm sure it is.

And she still has Fox, in a way. Tonight she'll wait, way out on the edges of the Weave, on the Bridge to Nowhere, and hope, with all the energy she owns, that he'll be there too.

Gorbals comes to stand beside her. Mara smiles at her friend.

'I'm afraid I gave your poems away to someone who needed them,' she confesses.

'That's just what they're for,' Gorbals smiles back. He follows her intent gaze out into the darkness.

The world's wind touches her face. The night is empty and enormous. There's no ship or land in sight, nothing at all but ocean and the huge hush of the stars.

'What are you looking for, Mara?' Gorbals asks curiously.

'Miracles,' she says.